PURSUANCE
OF
JUSTICE

SID DE BEER

Sid De Beer was born in Johannesburg South Africa and is the only son of the late Sam and Joan De Beer.

He immigrated to Australia in 1993 and has been married to his wife Nadine for 47 years.

He is the father of 3 daughters Odette, Shi-Anne, and Kim, and has seven grandchildren.

He is happily retired and lives in Melbourne, Australia where his entire family resides.

The world would be a better place without dictators wanting to enrich themselves!

'Life Does Not Always Deal You The Best Hand, Adapt And Make The Best Of What You Have.'

-Sid De Beer

Dedicated to my seven grandchildren, Blake, Kegan, Shayna, Logan, Hunter, Ryder, and Sienna, who I love more than they will ever know.

I have watched you all grow up, and am proud of every one of you.

My grandchildren have been brought up to have respect and manners, the values my wife and I instilled in our three daughters.

Take the values you have been taught by your parents, and instil them in your own children one day.

I won't be around forever, however, I will always have your backs, for as long as I live.

Plan your lives, go forth, follow your dreams, and make them happen.

Acknowledgments

A special thank you to Dani Streay of Graphic, Motion, & Narrative Design from analteredaspect.com for his input and the design of the cover.

'When one door closes, another opens; but we often look so long, and so regretfully upon the closed door, that we do not see the one that has opened for us.' -Alexander Graham Bell.

Life as a CIA Agent Means That You Are In Constant Danger.

Contents

Chapter 1

Lauterbrunnen

Switzerland

Yonti stared at the stunning view of the Staubbach Waterfall in the distance, through the large bay window in the lounge. The waterfall is one of the most famous waterfalls in Switzerland and is the third highest free-falling waterfall, cascading some nine hundred and eighty-five feet from a hanging valley that ends in overhanging cliffs above Weisse Lütschine. It flows from the left flank of the Lauterbrunnen Valley in Bernese Oberland to the valley floor and the mountains offer a spectacular backdrop in the distance.

Truly beautiful he thought as he added a couple of logs to the open fireplace.

It had been snowing heavily over the past few weeks and the mountain was covered with a blanket of white powder glistening in the filtered sunlight. He watched the water cascading over the edge of the mountain in the distance heading towards the river bed far below, then snaking its way through his fifty-acre property.

The rural property that Yonti bought was three miles from the town, situated in the valley below the waterfall with various other rural small holdings scattered in the distance offering him the privacy that he had long dreamed of.

Lauterbrunnen is a small town sitting in a beautiful valley, down from the famous peaks of Switzerland including Eiger and Jungfrau. Its unique location makes it a perfect base for many outdoor activities, both challenging with easy hiking for the committed few, offering spectacular views of rural farms and small holdings scattered in the distance.

What a stunning place he thought as he placed his feet on the ottoman. So peaceful here he considered. Just then his boisterous two-year-old twin sons, Reeve and Yves burst into the room, charging towards him so he went down on his knees as they dived into his arms. He wrapped his arms around them, hugging them tightly, before hoisting them up and kissing each one on the cheek. Gives a father a lot of pleasure to hug and love his children, he thought.

He picked Reeve up, and threw him upwards before catching him and returning him to the floor, then repeated the process with Yves. The twins wrestled with him and he had to cover his private parts as they jumped onto his body. He lay on the floor, with the twins punching him repeatedly. The play fighting went on for fifteen minutes until the twins decided that they wanted to explore other things to do and amuse themselves with their toys. He smiled broadly as he watched them race out of the room towards their rumpus room.

It gave him time to reflect on his life. He had resigned from the CIA, and having married his partner Claire shortly after he resigned, they bought this stunning rural property close to Lauterbrunnen and built a five-bedroom home each with an ensuite, an open plan kitchen, dining room, lounge area, rumpus room for the kids, gymnasium, study and a games room.

He busied himself with the daily chores of checking the fencing around the property and had built various sheds to house farming implements as well as a large shed to house the three cows during the winter months. Claire had perfected the art of making cheese, which kept her busy most of the day. He tended the indoor hothouse that he had built to grow their vegetables, keeping him occupied for most of the day.

Yonti bought a Marmon-Herrington nineteen thirty-seven vintage four-wheel drive Ford farm truck and had it fully restored with a V-Eight engine, sporting a burgundy colored livery and mag wheels that seemed to make everyone drool with envy each time they saw it. They went into town weekly to do their shopping and buy supplies which often proved rather challenging as they had to make their way through thick snow along the rural roads. Fortunately, the snow chains offered enough traction, to safely navigate their way along the rural roads.

He had settled into this laid-back lifestyle, albeit that he missed the adventurous CIA assignments and often reminiscing about past escapades, reflecting on some of the daring missions and wondered what had happened to Capitaine Bastienne Petit of the French Police as well as his close friend Joseph Diamond, the two trusted partners that accompanied him on many missions.

His wife Claire, was particularly pleased that he no longer put himself in danger daily, and made him promise that he had put that life behind him. She did not want to go through watching him fight for his life in a hospital ever again.

Twice was more than enough. He had assumed the normal lifestyle of a dedicated father and husband since he resigned from the CIA, however, deep down, he missed the life he had left behind.

He zipped up his jumper and made his way onto the veranda rubbing his hands as the cold air swirled around him. Out of habit, his eyes scanned the surroundings, ensuring that everything was in order, then headed towards the shed that housed the cattle. He raked up the soiled hay, scattering fresh hay on the floor, then filled the trough with fresh water. Rather mundane, however, it was somewhat satisfying he considered.

As he made his way back to the homestead, he suddenly became aware of the whirling chopping sound of a helicopters rotor blades growling in the distance, so he quickly entered the house, walked to his safe, and removed his Glock and fitted the silencer, which he put it in the back of his pants and pocketed four clips of ammunition before making his way back onto the veranda. He called out to Claire that they had a visitor and both watched as the chopper with the distinct blue and white livery with the word, Polizei visible on the fuselage landed in an opening near the homestead. He instantly recognized the Director of the CIA, Barnaby Heathcott, as he exited the chopper.

He grimaced as the dusty snow swirled in the air agitated from the chopper's blades.

'Hello Yonti,' offered Barnaby as he made his way up the stairs to the veranda.

'Well hello Director, this is a surprise.'

'Come on in, it's freezing out here.' he said.

'Hello, Director offered Claire.' 'I hope that this is an informal visit because I am not in favor of Yonti going off on another mission.' 'He has done his time serving America, France, and the world at large,' she said emphatically staring him directly in the eye.

'I remind you, that he died on the operating table from the beating he took from those rednecks in Oregon, so no, he won't be available to do anything further for the CIA, America, France, or the world Director.' 'Besides which, he is a father now and has responsibilities to raise our twins, so I am insisting on him not getting involved in anything to do with the CIA.' 'Before you even pose a question, the answer is no, because I am not going to go through nearly losing him again.' 'Twice is more than enough, and to be clear, there may not be a third time.'

'I hope that I have made myself abundantly clear Director.'

Barnaby sat calmly and simply let Claire vent her frustration.

'Well to be truthful, I need Yonti's help, because my wife and our twin sons, Chase and Chance were kidnapped earlier today.' 'This happened as they exited the school that they attend and the kidnappers shot and killed both agents assigned to protect them, before escaping with my family.' 'I was in meetings with the Swiss and French security chiefs in Zurich when I was notified of what had happened, so I am asking for your help Yonti, because you are the best agent I have ever had the pleasure of working with,' he said, as tears welled up in his eyes.

'I suspect that ex-Senator Delarosa, now inmate number 68978, who was sentenced to twenty-five years in jail for the murder of one of his trusted cadres in the White Patriotic Front movement that he founded, may well be behind this because I testified at his trial, so clearly, his motive is revenge.' 'You may recall that he and his thugs were the ones that nearly beat you to death Yonti.'

Claire placed the palm of her hand over her mouth.

'I'm so sorry Director, I did not know.' 'I feel very foolish having said what I did.'

'Claire, I fully understand how you feel and do not blame you at all, however, I am desperate to get my family back.' 'The kidnappers have demanded the release of Delarosa and a two million US dollar ransom.'

Claire looked at Yonti, full well knowing that he would not hesitate to assist. Yonti turned and looked at Claire who merely nodded.

'I am flying back to Zurich in two hours and then directly back to Langley, so I am hoping that you will be able to accompany me Yonti.' 'I need to get my family back alive,' he said as the tears rolled down his cheeks.

Yonti stood and said, 'Give me fifteen minutes to get packed Director.'

As he left the room, he again glanced at Claire who merely nodded.

Barnaby apologized again to Claire for having to ask for Yonti's assistance.

'He is the best there is you know, so I can use his expertise right now Claire,' he said as he wiped the tears from his face.

Yonti stuffed two pairs of camouflage cargo pants, two jackets, four khaki T-shirts, socks, a toothbrush, toothpaste, and shaving gear into his toilet bag before putting them into his Reebow Military Backpack. He put his trusted Glock, and silencer as well as eight clips of ammunition into the bag. All done in a few minutes and was ready moments later. He hugged and kissed his sons and Claire goodbye. Minutes later they were airborne and on their way to Zurich airport.

'Bonjour Monsieur, long time no see,' offered the Co-Pilot as he followed Barnaby up the staircase and into the belly of the Gulfstream.

They were airborne minutes later.

'So Director what do you have so far?'

'Well, I am certain that Delarosa is involved, because as stated earlier, I testified at his trial because there is a demand for his release, which confirms my suspicion.' 'They know that I am in Zurich right now and are aware that it is rather difficult for me to coordinate a mission to free my family from here, so their timing is impeccable.' 'I have updated the FBI who are investigating, and we have all thrown additional resources at it, to try and identify who these people are.'

'What these bastards do not know, is that our Gulf Stream is equipped with all the technology required to do my day job away from my office, same as when the President travels and can run the country from Airforce One.' 'I have all our resources at the CIA currently focused on monitoring all communications from an array of suspects and we hope to pick up some chatter that would point us in the right direction.'

'So Director, one could assume that they may well be hiding somewhere in Oregon, which is their home base as they are familiar with the terrain and surroundings and backed up with like-minded rednecks.' 'I recommend that you reach out to Admiral Starwarski the commander of Seal Tem Six for assistance because I believe that wherever they have taken your family, it will be hidden and well-guarded, so I will need a backup for sure.'

Barnaby fired up satellite images of Oregon, one of the 50 US states, situated in the north-western United States. It is one of just three US states in the contiguous United States with a coastline along the Pacific Ocean.The Colombia River largely defines Oregon's border with Washington State in the north. The Snake River forms a section of its state line with Idaho in the east, and the 42nd parallel north defines the borders with California and Nevada in the south. In 1842–43, the Oregon Trail brought many new settlers to the state of Oregon. British claims to the territory were formally ceded to the US in 1846 and Oregon became the 33rd state on 14th February 1859.

Footage taken from one of the CCTV cameras at the school was displayed on the laptop as images of the abduction played out on the screen.

'Right Director, freeze it there,' said Yonti pointing to the face of one of the abductors as it came into view.

'Are you able to zoom in on this bastard's face?'

'I am almost sure that this is one of the thugs that tackled me from behind, and then beat the shit out of me after Delarosa instructed them to take me to the warehouse near the pub.' 'Fat Boy made sure that he got stuck into me because I broke his mate's knee and knocked another of his buddies out stone cold.'

Doesn't exactly hold fond memories for me thought Yonti as he gazed at the map of the state displayed on the screen, reminding him of an operation that nearly cost him his life. Right, so what would I do if I was one of them, he pondered. Take the hostages to a remote place away from prying eyes that offers a good vantage point and is well hidden, possibly not too far from Portland within the home base of the White Patriotic Front in Wood Village.

'Try to zoom in on the vehicle's number plate Director.' 'These people are not the most intelligent people on earth, so I think that they would most likely not have thought of changing their number plate.' 'It is possible that they could be holed up on a farm on the outskirts of Wood Village because this is an area that these rednecks are familiar with.'

'From the snippets of information I managed to glean from this bunch, it seemed that this fat prick is some sort of a Lieutenant in Dellarosa's racist group, so I think this is where we should start.'

'If I am not mistaken, Fat Boy has a small farm on the banks of the Wood River, so judging by his looks, I guess that the homestead would be rather derelict with farm implements and other junk scattered around the place.' 'We are due to land in a few hours so, I respectfully suggest that you speak with Admiral Starwarski and ask him to make Seal Tem Six available when we land.' 'Time is not on our side, so we will need to move quickly.'

'I think it best that this does not make it into the media from your end, and we can only hope that these rednecks don't approach the media and try to gain maximum leverage from it,' said Yonti.

Just then Barnaby's assistant called him on a secure line.

'Hello, Gizelle.'

'Hello Director, I have just received a call from one of the kidnappers demanding to speak with you.' 'I notified him that you are unavailable and that you are on your way back from Zurich, so I told him to call you at midday tomorrow.' 'The FBI and our team will monitor the incoming call tomorrow and try to establish where the call is from.'

'Thanks, Gizelle, see you in the morning,' he said ending the call.

The screeching of the tires on the tarmac announced their arrival at Bigler's Mill, the airfield near Williamsburg in York County Virginia, reserved solely for the CIA. Six out of ten for that landing Yonti thought.

They made their way down the stairs and into the waiting black SUV with tinted windows. Barnaby's detail pointed the vehicle towards Langley.

'Hello Director and hello Rafael,' said Gizelle as they entered his office, using the CIA name that he had assumed whilst working at the firm.

'Right, let's go over what we have again Yonti.'

'I am almost sure that these bastards will be holed up in Wood Village in Oregon, on a farm so let's zoom in on fat boys property again, because I believe that this stupid moron will most likely have your family holed up there,' said Rafael.

Just then Barnaby's phone rang and Gizelle announced that Admiral Starwarski was on the phone.

'Hello Jake, thanks for offering Seal Team Six's assistance, I appreciate the help.'

'The team has been briefed and is ready to be deployed on your instruction Barnaby.' 'I will have them meet your agent at Bigler's Mill tomorrow morning at zero six hundred hours.'

Gizelle buzzed Barnaby at exactly noon and notified him that the kidnapper was on the phone. All incoming communication had been set up to monitor and record any conversation with both the FBI and CIA tracing the call in the hope of establishing the location where the call was made from. Barnaby answered the call.

'Hello.'

'Is that Mr. Heathcott?'

'Yes speaking.'

'We are demanding the release of President Delarosa and two million dollars before we release your wife and children.' 'Failing that we will kill your wife first, then an hour later we will kill one of your sons and an hour later the other.' 'Do you understand?'

'Yes I understand, but I want to speak with my wife first because I want to be sure that she and the kids are still alive and after that, I will arrange for the money to be available.'

'Barnaby, these people are treating us well, so please just pay the ransom.'

The abductor snatched the phone from his wife and said, 'There you are Mr. Heathcott, they are alive so I will call you tomorrow at noon and give you instructions on where to leave the money.' 'For what it's worth, no money, no see your wife and children ever again.'

The line went dead, and Barnaby knew that there was not enough time for the CIA and FBI to get a fix on the call.

All is not lost though, he thought.

He had schooled his wife to use a secret coded message, in case something like this ever happened. The mention of the fact that the abductors were treating them well, notified him that they were holed up in the abductor's home. Right now, I need to follow my best agent's gut feeling, because he has never let me down.

'Right Yonti, I believe that they are holed up in Fat Boy's home, which we know is in Wood Village on the banks of the Wood River, so let's get a satellite to focus on this location.'

'So Director, do you want me to capture the abductors or eliminate them, sir?'

Barnaby thought for some time, before responding.

'Kill them.'

Well, eventually the boss has come around to my way of thinking, thought Yonti.

The derelict farmhouse came into view on the monitor on the wall. Debris was scattered all over the place and the grass was overgrown, typical of a run-down derelict redneck's homestead. Excellent thought

Yonti, it allows for good cover if this is the place where they have hidden Barnaby's wife and children. Will need to access the property via the river with Seal Team Six, then work our way toward the house and surprise them in the early hours of the morning.

'See the movement around the home.' 'It seems like they have guards on each corner of the house, so this is most likely the place where they are holding your family Director.' 'We will need to eliminate these guards before moving towards the homestead.' 'Best attack in the early hours of the morning as these rednecks tend to drink a lot of alcohol and will most likely be smashed or fast asleep after midnight, except for those on guard duty.'

Yonti and four members of Seal Team Six met at Bigler's Mill, the private airfield used by the CIA early the next morning and went over their plan to free the hostages. Yonti would coordinate the mission and Cree Cosay, the Seal Team Six leader would be in charge of the mission. Cree, of native Apache heritage, has an inbred understanding of survival, proven on many missions over many years, making his experience invaluable. They loaded their gear and made their way into the belly of the Gulf Stream.

The distance of two thousand three hundred and nine miles would take around five hours and were amongst the clouds minutes later. They finalized their plan to free the hostages, with Cree taking the option of canoeing down the river in rubber ducks, then approaching the homestead from the river because he believed that the abductors would not expect an attack to come from there, albeit that he could not be sure.

'So, we will use inflatable rubber ducks and paddle downstream towards the property, then make our way towards the farmhouse.' 'My team will split into four, with each Seal taking up a position on each corner of the house.' 'Yonti and I will be positioned close to the front door to the homestead, then we will eliminate the guards before entering and kill any other person we encounter.' 'We will move silently in the shadows ensuring that we are all aware that the floorboards on the veranda may well be creaky which will alert the abductors to the fact that they are about to be attacked.'

The abductor called Barnaby at midday the next day as arranged, instructing him to drop off the two million dollars at the Astoria Column, the one hundred and twenty-foot column that sits atop Coxcomb Hill the next day at noon.

He instructed Barnaby, not to have any police near the drop-off point, and if he did arrange for the cops to be in the vicinity, he would never see his family again. Barnaby was then instructed to set Delarosa free from Rikers Island Prison in Queens at the same time, transport him to the station, and allow him to catch the Babylon Branch train.

He reiterated that there was to be no police either on or anywhere near the train, or at any station along the way because he would not see his family alive again.

The Gulf Stream landed at Carvers Edge Airstrip, a small abandoned landing strip near the Silver Falls State Park sixty miles from Wood Village and the Pilot needed to guide the Gulf Stream around some potholes on the overgrown runway.

The CIA had chosen this abandoned airstrip, because of its remote location. By appearance, it was not much, essentially a strip of tar used by enthusiasts many years ago, that was now long past its use-by date. As the Gulf Stream made its way towards what originally must have been a parking area for planes, Yonti noticed the two black SUVs parked on the apron.

Yonti and The Navy Seals made their down the staircase, loaded their gear into the two waiting SUVs, and the drivers headed toward the outskirts of Wood Village. They drove into the thicket in the forest alongside the Wood River ensuring that they were well hidden, and parked. The team unpacked their gear, and immediately posted two Seals on point duty guarding the area, ensuring that no one would see them unpacking their gear. They used an Army Ultra-Lightweight Camouflage Net System, commonly known as ULCANS to disguise the two SUVs

Barnaby paced up and down in his office before eventually sitting down. He glanced at his wristwatch, noticing that it was almost twenty-three hundred hours, and focused his attention on the satellite feed, watching as Yonti and the Seals appeared to be donning their tactical gear.

Yonti looked at his watch and noted that it was twenty-three hundred hours and smiled as he slid into his gear, amazed that it was an exact fit. They inflated the Klepper Aerius 11 Model Kayaks, traditionally used by Navy Seals, Commando Units, and Special Forces. These models are foldable, meaning that they are collapsible and ideal for transportation for caching. They can be submerged and cached underwater, designed to carry a fully equipped 2-man team, tandem designs, with air-tight comportments which make them virtually unsinkable. Mission equipment and the personal kit of the operators are stored inside the kayaks. The kayaks sit low in the water, making for a very low visual signature. Other stealth characteristics include low radar, infrared, acoustic, and thermal signatures.

It was shortly after midnight when Cree gave the order to don their night vision goggles. Yonti and the Seals slid the kayaks into the water, and the jumped in. Moments later they paddled silently downstream, before stopping a mile short of the farmhouse, pulled their kayaks onto the embankment, and hid them amongst the bushes. They carefully made their way towards the farmhouse, mindful to ensure that they did not stand on a trip wire that would alert the abductors. As they got close to the farmhouse the team split into four, with each Seal silently making his way towards a corner of the house, ensuring that no noise was audible.

They watched as the four guards made their way to and fro along their assigned sections of the house, stopping to chat with each other as they met at the corners of the house. Cree and Yonti crept to within ten yards of the house using the pile of rusty farm implements as cover, noting that one bedroom window had been bordered up indicating that this was most likely the room where the abductors were holding Barnaby's family. Yonti waited patiently for a couple of minutes as the guard turned and made his way toward the opposite corner, Cree shot him in the head using an MK Twelve Mod One assault rifle fitted with a silencer. The guard fell silently to the ground. The tall grass cushioned any noise. Yonti was on his feet moments later, closing the gap as he ran towards the front door of the farmhouse. As the other guard made his way toward the corner patrolling his section of the house, one of the other Seals shot him. He also fell silently to the ground cushioned by the long grass. Yonti merely nodded at the Seal hidden in the thicket who was watching him through his GPNVG-18 night vision goggles. The other Seals eliminated the other two guards in the same manner on the opposite side of the house. Cree's headgear earpiece crackled silently to life, as the other two Seals reported that they had eliminated the other two guards, and moments later all the Seals took up positions closer to the house.

Yonti crouched and listened intently at the muffled discussion taking place in the kitchen, and peeped through a crack in the weatherboard to see two people sitting at the kitchen table drinking beer. True to form he considered. Cree's earpiece came alive again and he whispered instructions into the microphone hidden in the cuff of his tactical assault jacket.

Moments later Yonti moved towards the front door, carefully placing each foot onto the floorboards before gently placing the full weight onto his foot, ensuring that there was no creaking sound emanating from it. He turned the door handle to ensure that the door was unlocked, slowly pushed the door open, hoping that it would not make a creaking sound, and was inside a moment later followed by Cree and the other four Seals. Each Seal made their way toward the rooms checking them thoroughly. Yonti stood silently at the kitchen door, listening to the rednecks discussing the release of their beloved leader Delarosa. A moment later he put his head around the door and shot both abductors in the back of the head before quietly making his way toward the bedroom.

The Seals swept the property for any sign of other abductors and Cree heard the sound of running water coming from the bathroom, so he slowly opened the bathroom door.

He could make out a person showering through the mist in the room, opened the shower door and shot the occupant once in the head before sweeping the rest of the house in search of any other occupants.

Yonti slowly turned the door handle, only to discover that had been locked so he kicked it using a Mae Geri, a front kick he learned as a martial arts student, and was in the room an instant later. His eyes swept the darkness for any sign of an abductor before noticing Barnaby's wife and twin sons huddled up in the corner. He switched on the light and assured them they were safe just as Cree entered the room. Yonti offered his hand and lifted Barnaby's wife to her feet before instructing the twins to get up.

'You are safe now Mrs. Heathcott.' 'My name is Yonti and this is Cree, the Seal Team Six leader.' 'We have eliminated all the abductors, so time to get out of here.' 'Please follow me.'

The Seals picked up all the spent cartridges and sanitized the area as best they could before leaving, however, some boot prints remained. The police and FBI investigating the deaths of the people at the farmhouse would identify the foot prints as those of Navy Seals, and in time, the case would remain unsolved.

Chapter 2

Tampa

USA

Barnaby watched as the Gulfstream was on its final approach into Bigler's Mill.

He hugged and kissed his wife and twin sons as they deplaned, then shook the hands of Cree Cosay and the four Navy Seals before turning to face Yonti.

'I want to take this opportunity to thank you all most sincerely for saving my family.' 'I knew that this could have been a risky mission, however, I had total confidence in every one of you, that you would be able to rescue my family, so again, thank you most sincerely.'

Barnaby increased the detail assigned to protect his family to three agents.

United Airlines flight UA Fifty-Two landed on time in Zurich and Yonti was greeted by an immigration official as made his way toward customs. He was ushered through a side door and into the baggage collection area without having to clear customs or go through the rigorous security checks of the metal detector, which would undoubtedly have resulted in them discovering his Glock hidden in the rear of his pants. Amazing how much influence Barnaby has, he thought as he exited the arrivals area.

He boarded the train at Zurich station heading for Lauterbrunnen, a journey of around sixty-two miles that took around three hours, so he sat back and watched the picturesque scenery passing by. He reminded himself of another successful mission, admitting to himself, that he missed the action.

As he exited the train, he pulled his Reebow Military Backpack over his left shoulder and decided to walk home through the snow, allowing himself time to reflect on how the mission turned out. The walk took him forty-five minutes, and he silently entered the house through the rear door.

He stood in the doorway and watched his twin sons playing with their toys when suddenly Claire appeared and let out a yell. The twins ran toward him, so he bent down, and wrapped an arm around each of them, lifting, hugging, and kissing them both, before embracing his beloved wife Claire.

'Wow, what a surprise.' 'It's great to have you home safely.' 'Glad you are home because these two guys are certainly a handfull.'

'Well you seemed to have coped well, maybe I should have stayed a few days longer.'

Yonti assumed his usual daily chores, tending to the cattle and their vegetable patch in the hot house. He felt relieved to be back home with his family.

A couple of days later, Yonti's bank notified him that someone had hacked into the bank and had stolen two million dollars from several accounts, albeit that he was not affected. So it appeared that the hacker was trying to steal money in smaller amounts rather than taking huge sums of money in the hope that it may not be discovered. The hacker was setting it up for a huge hit sometime in the future.

He sat back and considered what to do. Hacking had become a worldwide problem as these anonymous people lurk in the shadows specializing in stealing confidential information or money for financial gain, so he used his expertise in computer engineering to trace the person or persons responsible.

He developed a new login security system, specifically intended to prevent hackers from being able to access any person's private banking accounts, not that any measures will ever stop hackers as they seem to be able to bypass any measures in place. He took the opportunity to introduce the new login system to the bank and they immediately adopted his system, which effectively meant that a person logging in would need to insert three sets of passwords, one alphanumeric, the other numeric alpha, as well as a unique cryptic character that the bank would forward to every customer. He sold the system to his bank for a handsome return, and the bank approached him to set up a new security protocol within their system to identify any unauthorized or unidentified intrusion into their system.

The system he set up could identify unusual activity, such as an unauthorized user or a high amount of data traffic to a particular off-site server and the intrusion detection system would alert administrators immediately. Cybercriminals have become a major threat to companies, corporations, governments, and computer users throughout the world. Many of these criminals are very bold because they believe that they can hide behind the cloak of anonymity on the Internet.

Generally, computer hackers are not untraceable and can be identified and brought to justice. No point in that, because some civil libertarian judge will merely give them a short–term sentence or a slap on the wrist and set them free, so it is best to eliminate them, thought Yonti. However, he understood that he no longer had the protection of the CIA, so he would need to do things by the book.

Sophisticated computer hackers are more cautious about having their IP addresses traced. There are a variety of Linux commands and tools that can identify the IP address of any computer that is trying to make a connection. Using a simple but effective way. A person can find the IP address of anyone trying to hack their website on your hosting logs, Google Analytics, or another analytics tool, by using the NetStat tool to identify the IP addresses of anyone trying to connect to your computer.

Having found the IP address, he could now find out where the connection was coming from, albeit he could not tell exactly where the hacker was based, it gave him a reasonable idea of what city the person was in, and what hosting provider the person was using. He used the GEOIP Tool to get a rough idea of where the hacker was located. Many hackers use proxies or dark web sites such as Tor, however, they can still be traced, but doing so is a lot more difficult.

He used various methods including the Traceart command, which is a simple tool readily available on the Internet to identify the IP address on the trace-route tool on the Princeton website to trace the hacker, and searched for a digital door left unlocked leaving an electronic footprint so that he could identify the hacker. Many government agencies including various military installations have been hacked in the past, so in reality, no matter what anti-virus software is installed, they somehow find a way around it.

He spent dozens of hours trolling through IP addresses trying to identify the person who had hacked into the bank's database, eventually discovering an IP address registered to a business aptly called Nameless.

Got you, you bastard he thought. Right, let's find this prick.

Once he had the IPv4 AND ipV6 addresses, it allowed him to look up the Geo-Location giving him some useful information. The information was narrowed down by country, state, region, and postcode including the latitude, longitude, and time zone. Albeit the latitude and longitude cover a big area, which is not exactly ideal, it helps to narrow down the search area. He discovered that the hacker was based in Tampa in the USA. Tampa tops the list when it comes to a city that has the largest number of hackers in the USA with an infection rate of five-hundred and six percent higher than the national average, so it was no surprise to find out that this was where the hacker was located.

At a G20 summit, the past President of the United States Barack Obama said, that the U.S. has the largest and the best cyber arsenal in the world. This might be true, given the sophistication of cyber-attacks allegedly carried out by the U.S. People may remember Stuxnet. The same Trojan was planted into the Iranian Nuclear Power Plant to disrupt the centrifuges. As per various estimates, the USA accounts for nearly ten percent of the world's attack traffic. It is home to many famous and infamous hackers. China is estimated to have around forty-one percent of global hackers, where around ninety-one and a half percent are males.

It is rather easy to get location info from an IP address. The internet is split up into chunks, called subnets, which are spread around the globe. Getting a location is as simple as finding which subnet an IP address falls into. Subnets are defined by CIDR notation, which is just a concise way of representing a range of IP addresses.

For example, 192.168.1.0/24 represents the range from 192.168.1.0 to 192.168.1.255. The number following the slash indicates how many bits are used for the address (in this case, the first 24 bits, which make up the first 3 bytes), and the rest are given to be allocated to devices (in this case, the final 8 bits, making up the last number in the address).

GSM tracking can either be network-based or device-based, while the former requires less or no operation from the mobile devices, the latter needs the mobile devices to install certain software and perform the calculating, and locating operation to send the data to the location server via GPRS, WiFi, 3G or 5G. Typically, a GSM network consists of mobile stations, cell towers (or base stations), and network systems. Mobile stations are mobile devices like cell phones; it has a mobile terminal and a Subscriber Identify Module (SIM). The base station has two parts, Base Transceiver Station (BTS) and Base Station Controller (BSC). A

Network system consists of a Mobile-Service Switching Center (MSC), an Operation and Maintenance Center (OMC), and a few other devices.

A handset is constantly connected to the nearest cell tower set up by the carriers. This could vary depending on the mobile maker, and some cell phones can switch to other cell towers that have better signal strength automatically, that's why they have better call quality. Each cell tower has a unique Cell ID. But it's not always the case, nowadays a base station usually has three Cell IDs and some could have up to six sectors, each covering a third of that area which is a hundred and-twenty degree sector.

The working range of a cell tower or base station is determined by a few factors, like the frequency, the transmitter's rated power, the size, and height of the antenna, as well as weather conditions.

Generally, cell towers are grouped in areas of high population density because each base station is limited by its capacity. In suburban areas, base stations/macro cells are commonly spaced one to two miles apart, and in dense urban areas, cell towers/microcells/pico cells may be as close as two hundred and eighteen yards apart or even less, so each base station covers an area of a circle with a diameter of two-hundred and eighteen yards or less. Pico cells are mostly used in offices, shopping malls, airports, etc. In some areas, there are even femtocells in houses to improve indoor signal strength.

That is why base stations are used to roughly pinpoint a handset's location.

Right, so let's try to narrow the search down to an exact location, thought Yonti.

He hacked into the service provider's database and trolled through thousands of IP addresses until he finally connected the IP address he had for the user.

He discovered that the address was listed to a person appropriately named Nameless and discovered that it was registered to an address at one twenty-eight Dockland Avenue, Davis Island, Tampa, so he Googled the address and noted that it was located in the old Norman Stockman Paint Warehouse situated in East Tampa. Right on the Docks.

I would like to go there and take this prick out, he considered. Instead, he downloaded the information to a USB stick.

OK, you dumb bastard, let's see just how smart you think you are. He searched for more information on the hacker and discovered that the person's registered name was Viggo Dardar. Sounds German he thought, so he eventually managed to access Mr. Dardar's emails by trial and error and discovered that he was born in Dusseldorf. He accessed the German Civil Registrar's Office (Standesamt) in Dusseldorf and spent dozens of hours searching for any record of Viggo Dardar. He eventually found a birth certificate registered in his name indicating that he was born twenty-five years previously and had immigrated to the USA at the age of twenty-three, so he was born in nineteen ninety-seven and immigrated to America when he was twenty-four, so a year previously.

The bastard has no money, or so it seems and is looking for an easy way to build his wealth. Yonti accessed the U.S. Citizenship and Immigration Services website and searched for the name of Viggo Darbar eventually discovering that he had applied for citizenship which could take up to two years to process. He confirmed that the address was correct on Davis Island, so clearly not a citizen of the USA yet.

Yonti waited until the early hours of the morning before hacking into his IP address and used his skill in computer engineering to gain access to Viggo's private information and discovered that he had a banking account in the Cayman Islands.The Cayman Islands is one of the world's most notorious tax shelters because it has no corporate tax, no personal income tax, and no capital gains tax. It is one of thirty countries blacklisted as a tax haven by the EU in twenty-fifteen.

Right, I wonder what bank this prick uses, considered Yonti, so he hacked into the top ten banks in search of a client by the name of Viggo Dardar and discovered that he had an account at the Cayman Wealth Investment Bank, which offered a haven for people wanting to avoid taxes in their country of citizenship.

So got this bastard's bank account and the login is in his name, now what would he use as a password, thought Yonti? Possibly reverse the name of his dark web hacking business, being Nameless so it could be sseleman or sselemaN, then he may include his date of birth in reverse as well.

Yonti tried both login names and discovered that it was the one ending with a capital N, then tried his actual date of birth which was the eighteenth of October, nineteen-ninety-seven, with no success, so he reversed his date of birth, which was seven, nine, nine, one, zero, one, eight and one. Yes, got you, you piece of shit considered Yonti.

Not that smart are you, you fucking idiot, thought Yonti.

Having accessed his account, he took note of the balance in his account, which was an amount of eight million US dollars, so clearly this bastard had hacked into various other banks or businesses and had fraudulently moved money to his Cayman Island account, so I am going to teach this prick a lesson thought Yonti. He transferred the two million dollars that he had stolen from his bank, back to the bank, then transferred six amounts of one million US dollars to various charities as an untraceable anonymous gift.

He copied all the information to a USB stick and anonymously mailed it to the FBI the next day, who immediately arrested Viggo a couple of days later.

It was almost midnight the following evening, so he poured himself a three-finger tot of his favorite drop, Johnny Walker Blue Scotch Whisky, and tossed some ice cubes into the tumbler. He sat staring at the log fire before raising the glass in a toast to himself.

The first time I have not had to kill a person guilty of committing a serious crime, he thought, however, to be truthful, I would rather have taken this bastard out because he will most certainly only get a few years in prison, then get out and continue on the path he has chosen.

The bank manager was astounded to learn that the two million dollars had somehow been returned, and wondered whether Yonti was somehow involved. The bank manager, Herr Jakob Meier, contacted Yonti and asked whether he somehow managed to retrieve the money and return it to them.

'I have no idea what you are talking about Herr Meier.' 'No not me sir.'

'Das ist wundervoll.' 'GroBartige Neuigkeiten, Herr Meier.' That is wonderful. Great news Mr. Meier.

Chapter 3

London

England

Yonti and Claire were sitting on the couch watching the news on television when the broadcast was suddenly interrupted as they switched back to the news anchor.

'We have breaking news coming to us out of London England,' said Eve McIntosh, the news anchor.

'Rasha Sudak, the Prime Minister of the United Kingdom's son has been kidnapped,' continued Eve.

The station immediately switched to their correspondent Summer Salora based in London.

'Hello Summer, what can you tell us about the kidnapping?'

'The Prime Minister's son Urdu Sudak has been kidnapped.' 'This happened as he was leaving school this afternoon, and tragically the two officers tasked with protecting him have been shot and killed,' said Summer.

'Urdu is a student at the exclusive Great Missenden Private College situated in the heart of the Chilterns Area in South East England that was once the home of the famous author Roald Dahl.' 'Missenden is thirty miles from London and is an affluent village with narrow and historic streets that provided rest and refreshment for travelers and their horses in bygone days,' continued Summer.

'The village lies on a major route between the Midlands and London overlooking the medieval Church of England and the Church of St. Peter and St. Paul.' 'The village is popular with visitors all year round.'

'From what we have managed to find out so far, is that the kidnapping occurred as Urdu was making his way out of the College accompanied by the two officers when two gunmen approached, shot, and killed the two officers.' 'They then bundled Urdu into a waiting dark-colored Ford Fiesta and sped off in the direction of Wendover which lies three miles to the southeast,' added Summer.

'Police are appealing to anyone that witnessed the kidnapping to come forward and assist the police to capture those responsible and arrest them.' 'The police are offering a million-pound reward for information leading to their arrest and are deeply concerned for Urdu's safety,' said Summer.

'All border points have been sealed and all departments have been placed on the highest Terror Threat Level nationally as they seek to prevent the kidnappers from exiting the country.'

'We are standing by to receive a briefing from Sir John Anderson, the Head of the Ministry for Home Security and we will bring it to air as soon as it happens.'

Sir John Anderson the Head of Ministry for Home Security quickly convened a meeting with the heads of the various security agencies.

Those in attendance were: -

The Foreign Secretary-Sir David Casson

The Home Office-Rt. Hon. James Clever MP

The Ministry of Defence-Rt. Hon. Andrew Murrison

Military Intelligence-Adrian Bird

Domestic Intelligence and Security-Anne Keast-Butler

Secret Intelligence Service (M16)-Ricard Moore

Security Service (MI5)-Director General Ken McCullum

Government Communication Headquarters (GCHQ)-Simon Baugh

Scotland Yard-Ms. Cressida Dick

Metropolitan Police- Sir Stephen House

National Crime Agency-Graeme Biggar

Specialist Operations Assistant-Matt Jukes

National Cyber Security Centre (NSCS)-Lindy Cameron

'Good afternoon everyone.' 'As you are aware our Prime Ministers son has been kidnapped so we need to pool our resources, find the people responsible, and bring them to justice as a matter of urgency.' 'This is the highest priority, so you need to lean on any contacts you have or any person you may consider would do this,' said Sir John in a somber tone of voice.

'We have lost two officers that were callously murdered in broad daylight in front of dozens of students and as you can see from the footage that we have obtained from the college, these murderers have masks on to hide their identity and the number plates on the car are false,' said Sir John as he pointed to the monitor on the wall.

'I want the people responsible to be arrested and charged ASAP.' 'We need to make an example of them, to discourage anybody else who may think of trying to do the same thing or something similar in the future.' 'Let's get to work people.'

The teams called their second in command and instructed them to pull out all stops to identify those responsible and bring them to justice.

A short while later Sir John fronted the media throng.

'Good afternoon ladies and gentlemen, as you all know we have a very serious situation on our hands at the moment and I have instructed all our security services to hunt down those responsible, arrest and charge them.' 'I will not be taking any questions at the end of this conference, and will schedule another conference for later this evening,' said Sir John.

'Not only have those responsible kidnapped the Prime Minister's son Urdu, but they have callously murdered two of our officers in cold blood in front of dozens of students.' 'This is a horrendous crime, something that we in Brittan never expected would happen, so we need to hunt these people down and bring them to justice ASAP.'

'I appealing to any members of the public who may have witnessed the kidnapping or had seen the dark-colored Ford Fiesta that the kidnappers used, to call the police, using this number,' said Sir John pointing to the image beamed onto the wall.

'We have grave fear for Urdu's safety and all exit points out of the country have been closed.' 'No one will be allowed to leave the country.'

Sir John ended the brief conference with the media firing questions at him as he made his way out of the room.

He headed directly to 10 Downing Street.

En route to meet with the Prime Minister, Sir John called Barnaby Heathcott, Director of the CIA.

Gizelle buzzed Barnaby notifying him that Sir John Anderson would like a word with him.

'Hello John, how are you, my friend?'

'Not good at the moment Barnaby.' 'Wish it was a courtesy call, Barnaby, however, as you know we have a huge problem over here.' 'Not only was the Prime Minister's son kidnapped, but those responsible also killed two of our police officers in cold blood.' 'I am reaching out to you, and asking if you can be of any assistance?'

'I need all the help I can get right now,' said Sir John.

'Be assured that I will do everything possible to assist you, John,' said Barnaby.

'Thanks, Barnaby, I appreciate any help that you can offer.' 'Just wondering whether you would be willing to send the same agent that arrested the two people that had planted explosives in the heavy-duty plastic barricades used to control crowds of people at large gatherings.' 'If you recall, two terrorists filled the barricades with explosives and intended to detonate it at the Trooping of the Color.' 'I can't recall his name, however, he did a sterling job by catching them, then delivered them to me personally before disappearing.' 'I could use a pair of eyes away from our people.' 'Sometimes one cannot see the trees in your forest.'

'He has retired John, however, I will put a call through to him and ask him if would be willing to assist, and I will get back to you soon,' said Barnaby as he ended the call.

Barnaby immediately called Yonti.

'Hello Yonti, this is not a courtesy call, but rather an appeal for help from Sir John Anderson in London.' 'You may remember him from the time when you and Joseph caught the two people who had planted explosives in the traffic barricades and were going to trigger an explosion at the Trooping of the Color.'

'He is reaching out and asking for a fresh set of eyes to look at things from a different angle, in case the security people in London might miss something,' said Barnaby.

'He specifically asked whether you would be able to assist.'

Claire was standing nearby when he got the call and overheard the conversation because Yonti had his mobile phone on speaker.

He looked at her and she merely shrugged her shoulders indicating that the decision to go, would be his to make.

'Well Director, what these people have done is terrible, so yes, I am willing to be a fresh set of eyes for Sir John.'

'Excellent Yonti, I will get the Swiss Chief of Police to have a helicopter pick you up in thirty minutes.' 'I think it best that you assume the usual alias of Rafael Dujon because you undoubtedly will want to keep your identity secret.' 'I will let Sir John know and will arrange for you to fly to London later this evening because this is most urgent.'

'Thanks for offering to be of assistance Yonti,' said Barnaby ending the call.

Things move quickly when the CIA organizes things, and a police helicopter picked him up thirty minutes later. They flew him to Zurich International Airport. As he made his way toward customs, a person fell in beside him and ushered him through a side door, and pointed him toward the departure gate.

This happens every time I leave Switzerland and every time I arrive in a foreign country. I feel like royalty, he thought affording himself a rare smile.

It was late afternoon and the Prime Minister's secretary received a call from one of the kidnappers demanding to speak with the Prime Minister. He was patched through just as Sir John made his way into the room.

The Prime Minister placed the call on speakerphone.

'I want you to listen very carefully.' 'We are demanding thirty million pounds for the safe return of your son.' 'You have until midday tomorrow.' 'I will call you tomorrow morning and tell you where to drop the money off.' 'You best not contact the police, and best not have them anywhere near the drop-off point because if you do, you will never see your son again.'

The Prime Minister interrupted the kidnapper.

'Today is Saturday and it's a long weekend, so the Bank of England and all other banks are closed.' 'I will not be able to get the money by tomorrow for you.' 'The bank vaults are closed and secured by time delay sequences.' 'They will only open again on Tuesday morning, so I will get you the money then.'

The line went dead because the kidnapper realized that he had been on the line too long and the police were about to get a fix on where he was making the call from.

Yonti's flight to Heathrow Airport in London took one and a half hours and landed on time. As he made his way out of the forward door of the aircraft, a man with a short-cropped military hairstyle ushered him down the staircase alongside the air bridge.

'Hello, Mr. Dujon.' 'My name is Gus McGinty and I have been instructed by Sir John to take you to the Thames Hotel to drop your bag off, then take you directly to 10 Downing Street,' 'Sir John is waiting for you there, sir,' said Gus as they jumped into the Land Rover.

Once again he did not need to clear customs. Each time he went on a mission, Director Heathcott knew that he would be carrying his beloved Glock and a pocket full of ammunition, so he pulled strings ensuring that he did not need to present himself at customs. Rafael was in awe of Barnaby Heathcott. This man has some clout, thought Rafael.

Forty minutes later Gus walked Rafael toward an old man with a hat on, seated on a bench a short distance from the throng of media people and the hordes of onlookers gathered at the barricades at the end of the street leading to 10 Downing Street.

'Monsieur Dujon, Sir John,' said Gus and excused himself.

'Hello Rafael, thank you ever so much for agreeing to come and assist me in trying to identify those responsible for this horrific crime,' said Sir John pointing to a seat on the bench next to him.

'I asked Barnaby if he could persuade you to be a fresh set of eyes for me away from our security team to cast an eye over things in case we may miss something.' 'Often one cannot see the trees in your forest as the saying goes, so I am particularly pleased that you have agreed to help me identify those responsible and bring them to justice,' said Sir John.

'We in Britain prefer to catch, charge, and then prosecute people that have committed serious crimes, rather than eliminate them.' 'A lot more civilized don't you think?'

'So, I am asking that you mingle amongst the throng of people that gather here each day.' 'Many are journalists, others are merely nosy and want to see what's happening,' continued Sir John.

'Having said that, I suspect that the kidnappers may have an informant amongst the crowd updating them on developments, which is what I specifically would like you to look out for.'

'Here are the keys to the motorbike parked over there,' he said pointing to a Honda GB 350.

'Best mode of transport when following someone.' 'Here is my business card in case you need to speak directly with me, Rafael.' 'I want to keep this confidential because our people would be highly pissed off with me if they knew that I reached out to the CIA for assistance.' 'Some big egos in our security apparatus you know.'

'Please mingle with the crowd and see if you can identify anybody suspicious amongst them, Rafael.' 'I need to get back, so once again, thank you for agreeing to assist,' said Sir John as he stood and left.

Wise old codger. Keeps his card close to his chest, just like Barnaby, thought Rafael.

It was early evening and the kidnapper called again. He was put through to the Prime Minister.

'This is a reminder to have the money ready by noon tomorrow or I will cut one of your son's fingers off and send it to you.' 'And, if you do not pay the money and still do not get the message, I will cut his hand off and send that to you as well.' 'Still not going to pay the money, you will receive his arm and if that has not convinced you to pay, I will send you a note and tell you where you can find his body.'

'As I said, it's a long weekend.' 'Today is Saturday and I am unable to get the Bank of England to open their vault and give me the money because the vault works on a time delay system and will only unlock on Tuesday, so I need you to give me time,' said Prime Minister Sudak emphatically.'

'I will give you one day's grace, have it ready tomorrow, no excuses.'

The line went dead and the police were unable to trace where the call had been made from.

The kidnapper knew that the police needed time to get a fix on the call and hung up just before they managed to trace the location of the caller.

He called back an hour later.

'I know that the police are trying to trace the call, so I will be brief.' 'I have warned you, so expect a delivery soon.'

As the kidnapper ended the call, the Prime Minister's wife begged him to pay the money.

'I don't want any harm to come to our son,' said Nivisha.

'Nivisha, I simply cannot cave into his demands because this has serious consequences, not only for our family but the entire nation.' 'If we cave in, can you imagine what will happen?' 'There will be dozens of these types of crimes popping up everywhere targeting wealthy people and don't discount the fact that people like this, will target big business as well.'

Tears streamed down her face and the Prime Minister hugged her tightly.

'We have to have confidence in Sir John's team.'

Rafael glanced at his wristwatch and noticed that it was already twenty-two hundred hours. He made his way toward the barricades erected by police to prevent the throng of people getting too close to 10 Downing Street and worked his way around the fringe. His eyes worked the crowd as he searched for any person showing suspicious behavior. The crowd had thinned out to a handful of reporters at that late hour, so Rafael made his way to the motorbike and rode back to the hotel. Will need to get back there early tomorrow, he thought.

Chapter 4

Wendover

England

The next morning, Rafael was back at zero six hundred hours and positioned himself toward the rear as the crowd swelled. Two hours later he noticed a man in a black hoodie and sunglasses making his way toward the middle of the throng. His gut told him that this person may be someone of interest, so he kept a close eye on him. An hour later the hoodie guy made a call on his mobile phone and appeared to be whispering something into the phone, then hung up. This occurred numerous times during the day and each time Rafael noticed that he made the call on the hour. The calls only lasted about a minute.

Rafael wondered whether he could be a reporter checking in each time and updating developments at 10 Downing Street, however, due to the way he was dressed, this caught his attention. Reporters don't tend to dress that way. The calls were far too brief for him to be a reporter, so he may be the person of interest that Sir John was referring to. Wonder what this guy is up to, thought Rafael.

Around midday, a courier driver handed the police sergeant a parcel addressed to the Prime Minister. The police scanned the parcel, and the sergeant opened the box. He was horrified to discover a finger in it with a blood-stained note.

The sergeant read the note, then hastily made his way into the residence and handed the parcel to Sir John Anderson. Sir John read the note and was shocked to see Urdu's finger lying in the bloodstained box.

The note read, I warned you, so if you do not have the money available tomorrow, I will send you your son's hand.

The sergeant notified Sir John that they had detained the courier driver for questioning, however, he told the police that he was instructed to collect a parcel that was left on a park bench and deliver it to 10 Downing Street. Whoever left the parcel on the bench, attached two hundred pounds in cash to the parcel as payment for the delivery.

Sir John made his way into the residence and handed the box to the Prime Minister. The Prime Minister was shocked to see his son's finger lying in the box and shielded it from his wife.

Rafael kept a close eye on the guy in the hoodie all day, and eventually at around eighteen-hundred hours he watched as he made his way toward the road, close to where he had parked the motorbike. A short while later a red Nissan X-Trail SUV stopped and picked him up.

Rafael jumped onto the motorbike and followed a mile behind. The SUV headed in the direction of Wendover, a village thirty-three miles from London that took around fifty minutes. He stayed well behind them and as they approached the town, he closed the gap. The red Nissan X-Trail turned into Jimmy's Liquor Mart on Wendover Boulevard West.

Rafael continued past the Liquor Mart and stopped one hundred yards further down the road, parked the motorbike behind two large garbage bins, and waited. A while later he saw two people make their way out of the store, each carrying a case of beer. Rafael noted that it was almost eighteen-forty-five hundred hours and was already dark. He followed the Nissan X-Trail at a distance as it continued along Wendover Boulevard heading out of town and wondered where they were headed. He purposely did not turn on the headlamp making it difficult for the driver of the Nissan X-Trail to notice that they were being tailed.

They turned into Beechwood Lane and headed past the Boddington Hill Fort located in the distance, then turned into Tedder Road. Rafael continued past the turnoff and noticed that they had turned into the driveway of the third house from the corner, so he looped around the block of what appeared to be a small farm until the houses came into view on the other side of the farmland. He parked the Honda against a clump of trees, jumped the farmer's fence, and made his way through the field toward the wooden fence at the back of the house.

He peeped over the fence, noticing that the kitchen and bedroom lights were on, so he scaled the fence and quickly made his way to the deck leading to the kitchen. A moment later the kitchen door opened so he hastily ducked behind a clump of garden bushes and watched as a person walked toward to him. The person relieved himself in one of the garden beds. Luckily he did not spot Rafael crouched behind the bushes.

The man lit a cigarette, took several puffs then nipped it, and made his way back into the kitchen. That was a close shave, thought Rafael.

The bastard nearly pissed on me. Thank heaven it's a pitch dark evening because if he saw me, he would undoubtedly have shouted a warning to his mates and it would have been game over, thought Rafael.

He made his way toward the light streaming from a split in the bedroom curtains and peeped in. He noticed a young lad sitting on the bed with a heavily bandaged hand. Right this must be the Prime Minister's son, so he made his way back to the fence, jumped over it, and made a hasty retreat toward a clump of trees on the farmer's land. He Googled the area using Google Maps and took note of the coordinates. He called Sir John, updated him on what he had discovered, and gave him the coordinates.

Sir John called Sir Patrick Stevens, commander of the SAS (Special Air Services), and gave him the coordinates that Rafael had given him, emphasizing that the informer had seen a young lad sitting on a bed with a heavily bandaged hand. He was confident that they had found Urdu.

The SAS is made up of four active saber squadrons A, B, D, and G, consisting of sixty men. Each squadron is made up of four Troops specializing in specific areas of expertise divided into Air Troop, Boat Troop, Mobility Troop, and Mountain Troop.

Sir Patrick Stevens elected to use the Mobility Troop and placed them on standby as soon as the news of the kidnapping was made public. The SAS has its base at Credenhill on the outskirts of Hereford, and the Mobility Troop was packed and ready to deploy at a moment's notice.

The soldiers jumped into two Land Rovers and headed toward Wendover a distance of one hundred and two miles that would take two and a quarter hours. Sir Patrick informed the team leader that they were to rendezvous with Rafael and he would point them to the house that the kidnappers were using. He gave the team leader the coordinates and told him not to worry because Rafael would make contact when they arrived at the location.

Rafael remained hidden in the clump of trees, and he glanced at his wristwatch, noticing that it was zero two-thirty hundred hours. An hour later he caught sight of two military vehicles as they stopped on the road and watched as five soldiers jumped the farmer's fence and headed in his direction. As they were about to pass the clump of trees where Rafael was hiding, he suddenly stood up in front of the team leader.

'Sweet Jesus in Heaven, who the fuck are you?' Demanded the team leader pointing his weapon in Rafael's direction.

'I'm Rafael, and you are who?'

'I'm Sergeant Archie McIntyre.' 'I could have shot you.' 'You gave me the fright of my life.'

Rafael gave them an overview of the situation and led the way to the fence.

The soldiers quietly scaled the fence, split into four, with each one taking up a position on the four corners of the house. Rafael and Archie headed toward the ray of light coming from a split in the bedroom curtains. They noticed a young lad curled up on the bed with a heavily bandaged hand.

'Right, this looks like Urdu,' whispered Archie.

'Amazing how lackadaisical this mob is.' 'Clearly, they never thought that we would discover their hideout so soon,' whispered Rafael.

Dumb and dumber, thought Rafael.

As they silently made their way toward the kitchen door, the outdoor light suddenly came on, so they made a hasty retreat toward the corner of the house and hid behind a clump of bushes in the garden. A minute later, a man appeared and made his way into the garden, lit a smoke, and started relieving himself.

The second time I have come close to being pissed on. Seems this prick does not like using a toilet, thought Rafael.

Rafael closed the gap like a leopard about to strike its prey and was behind him an instant later. The man heard the footsteps and as he turned to see who it was, he stared directly into Rafael's beloved Glock. Archie was alongside him a moment later and pushed his RC8 Carbine assault rifle against his nose.

Rafael placed his Glock against the man's temple and whispered, 'Don't fucking move, you piece of shit.'

Archie put his index finger onto his lips, indicating that the person should keep quiet, then taped his mouth with duct tape. Rafael placed his right leg behind him and dropped him gently onto the grass, then rolled him over onto his stomach and Archie used Flexi cuffs to handcuff his hands and secure his feet.

Rafael placed his Emerson's Specwar Custom Knife at the kidnapper's throat and whispered in his ear, 'How many people inside the house?'

'Don't lie to me, because I will slit your throat if you don't tell me the truth,' he whispered forcefully.

'Nod your head for each person.''So if there are four, nod your head four times.'

He nodded his head three times indicating that there were three people in the house and himself so a total of four.

'One down, three to go,' he whispered to Archie.

Using hand signals, Archie summoned two soldiers to pick him up and move him closer to the fence.

Rafael watched as the soldiers silently picked him up and moved him. He noticed two police paddy wagons and two ambulances as they pulled up and parked behind the two military Land Rovers in the road on the far side of the farm. No flashing lights or sirens, they merely approached the Land Rovers without their headlights on, killed their engines, and waited for instructions from Archie.

One soldier stood watch over the person that they had cuffed and Archie instructed one of his soldiers to make his way around the house toward the front using hand signals and indicated that the other should join him and Rafael.

Rafael made his way toward the kitchen door and slowly turned the handle. The door swung open and they were inside a moment later.

They noticed one person sitting at the kitchen table, so Rafael aimed his Glock in his direction. As the person turned around, he was most surprised to see two soldiers and a civilian standing in front of him, rather than his friend who had gone out to relieve himself. Rafael placed his Glock on his temple and placed his index finger on his lips indicating that the person should remain silent. One of the soldiers duct taped his mouth and bound his hands and feet with Flexi cuffs.

One soldier remained with the person in the kitchen and moments later the other soldier that had gone around the house made his way into the kitchen. He joined Rafael and Archie, as they made their way down the passage. They opened the door to the first bedroom and noticed two people fast asleep, snoring loudly in bed. Archie switched on the bedroom light, which woke both kidnappers. Startled awake, they stared down the barrels of two C8 Carbines.

Archie instructed the soldier to cuff them and duct tape their mouths.

'That's all three,' said Rafael as he made his way out of the room and headed toward the room where he had seen Urdu earlier in the evening.

As he opened the door, Urdu woke up.

'Is your name Urdu, the Prime Minister's son?' Asked Rafael.

'Yes I am,' replied Urdu shielding his eyes from the glare of light.

'No need to worry, my name's Rafael and this is Sergeant Archie,' said Rafael.

'We are here to rescue you.' 'Are you in any pain?'

'Yes my finger hurts like hell,' said Urdu.

'Hang in there for a few minutes, paramedics and an ambulance will be here shortly,' said Rafael.

Archie radioed the police and ambulance drivers parked on the other side of the farmer's field and summoned them to drive around to the front of the house. A short while later numerous police officers entered the house and placed all four kidnappers under arrest.

Rafael called Sir John and updated him on developments.

Sir John turned to face the Prime Minister and his wife.

'Excellent news Prime Minister, the CIA agent, and our SAS soldiers have rescued Urdu.' 'He is alive and well except for a missing finger and is en route to hospital right now.'

'Oh thank the Good Lord,' said the Prime Minister.

The Prime Minister turned to face his wife.

'Nivisha, luckily Urdu has only lost a finger and not his life.'

Claire switched on the television and was watching the early morning news broadcast. The news anchor switched to Summer Salora, their correspondent in London.

'Hello Summer, I believe that the Prime Minister's son has been rescued.'

'Yes, excellent news.' 'Sir John Anderson has just fronted the media and confirmed that Urdu, the Prime Minister's son has been rescued by SAS soldiers.' 'All four kidnappers have been arrested and will be charged.'

'Sir John has confirmed that an informant notified him of the location where these kidnappers were holding the Prime Minister's son, and they were taken by surprise in the early hour of this morning when SAS soldiers carried out a rescue mission.'

'Sir John stated that he was most grateful to the person who came forward and revealed the location where the kidnappers were holding Urdu.' 'The identity of the informer will not be disclosed.' 'The Prime Minister and his wife have expressed their sincere thanks to the SAS soldiers and the informant,' he said as he abruptly ended the briefing.

Claire wondered what part Yonti had played in his rescue.

Rafael looked at his wristwatch and noted that it was zero six-hundred hours as he made his way into the foyer of the Thames Hotel. A moment later Sir John tapped him on the shoulder.

'Hello Rafael Dujon.' 'I'm not going to allow you to simply disappear this time without thanking you and shaking your hand.' 'On behalf of the British Government, I would like to extend our sincere thanks for an outstanding job.' 'The Prime Minister has written you a personal letter,' said Sir John as he handed him the letter.

'I wish that you would consider coming to work for us Monsieur.' 'We could use a man of your talent.'

'Thank you, Sir John, I am happily retired, Sir.'

The following day Yonti wearily made his way up the stairs and onto the deck. Claire and the twins rushed to welcome him home.

'Thank the Good Lord you are home and safe Yonti.' 'I noticed that Sir John mentioned an informant and did not mention you by name.' 'I can understand why.'

Yonti was glad to get rid of his old CIA undercover name and happy to be back with his family. He handed Claire the unopened letter from the Prime Minister.

'You can read it, Claire.'

Chapter 5

Kandersteg

Switzerland

The display on Yonti's mobile phone lit up with an incoming call from Barnaby Heathcott on a secure line.

'Hello Director, this is a pleasant surprise.'

'Hello Yonti, I wish I could say that it is pleasant, however, as you know, we at the CIA are in the business of trying to keep America and the world safe.' 'I know that you are happily retired and that Claire does not want you to be involved with the firm any longer, however, I need your help on an issue that affects millions of people around the globe, so I am asking that you sit Claire down, and get her permission to assist.'

'We have been tracking the activities of a drug lord that America wanted to extradite to the USA from Mexico, however, he evaded capture and disappeared several years ago.' 'We recently discovered that he now resides in Switzerland, hence the reason for my call today.'

'The drug lord's name is Vincente Del La Fuente.' 'As mentioned he evaded capture in Mexico, and is now living in a town close to where you live, conducting his business activities from there,' 'He is extremely secretive, well-guarded, and surrounded by loyal henchmen, so getting close to him is almost impossible.' 'From what we have managed to uncover so far, is that he uses a Swiss Bank, namely Crédit Bank Suisse, as his haven for the fortune he has amassed, and we believe he has as much as four and a half billion US dollars stashed in his account.' 'The Swiss authorities have turned a blind eye to his activities, due to his enormous wealth which is increasing daily.'

'Apparently, he has changed his name, and has assumed a new identity.' 'He is now known as Arnborg Albano.'

'This drug lord does not care about the hundreds of thousands or even millions of people that are addicted to his drugs, and has no regret whatsoever for any that have died due to their addiction.' 'His motto is that he is supplying candy to the children.' 'He lives in Kandersteg which is a municipality in the Frutigen-Niedersimmental administrative district in the canton of Bern in Switzerland, close to where you live.' 'As you know, it is located along the valley of the River Kander, west of the Jungfrau massif, and is around fourteen miles from where you live,' said Barnaby.

'The area is noted for its spectacular mountain scenery and sylvan alpine landscapes.' 'Tourism is a very significant part of its economic life today, and it offers outdoor activities year-round, with hiking trails, mountain climbing as well as downhill and cross-country skiing.' 'Kandersteg hosted the ski jumping and Nordic combined parts of the 2018 Nordic Junior World Ski Championships.'

'He has chosen well, and his homestead is located in a valley about five miles from the center of town which is surrounded by mountains on either side.' 'From the satellite images we have of the area, it appears that he moves around freely, and has assimilated well into the community.' 'People have absolutely no idea of what he does for a living, or how many lives he has affected worldwide,' said Barnaby.

'So what we have uncovered so far, is that he moves his drugs from Mexico to the USA and other international destinations worldwide by waterproofing them, and hiding them in the storage tanks on oil tankers headed for the USA as well as other destinations such as China, Japan, Canada, Australia, Germany, and New Zealand.' 'Oil exports account for over thirty percent of the Mexican government's total revenue, which amounts to around eighteen billion US dollars annually.' 'The majority of the oil exports are to the United States, accounting for forty-eight percent of all oil produced in Mexico, with the USA importing over one hundred million barrels annually,' continued Barnaby.

'After the crude has been pumped out of the tanks, stevedores retrieve the packages and wash them down, before handing them to handlers for distribution.' 'He has threatened the stevedore's families who are under constant surveillance by his henchmen, and if any of them do not successfully dispose of the drugs to his handlers, then he has their families killed.' 'From what we understand, he has eliminated around a dozen families in the cruelest possible way, so we need to eliminate this bastard without the Swiss authorities knowing that we are involved, making it appear that a rival drug lord has stepped up and eliminated him,' continued Barnaby.

'From what we understand, he has an agreement with the Swiss Government that he will never bring any of his drugs into Switzerland in exchange for him being allowed to settle there.' 'Amazing what money can do.'

'Joaquín "El Chapo" Guzmán Loera and Pablo Escobar were violent people, however, Mister Del La Fuente, or Mr. Albano as he is now known, is even more violent than the other drug lords.' 'He also hails from Sinaloa in Mexico.'

'It seems that this is the breeding ground for these bastards, who believe that they are above the law.' 'That's the shortened version of the person we need to get rid of,' said Barnaby.

Unbeknown to anyone, Yonti had a cousin who was addicted to drugs and died from an overdose. Many years ago he made a promise to his uncle, that someday he would find the drug lord responsible and kill him. This is a worldwide problem, and yet again, if ever any of these drug lords had been caught and arrested, some civil libertarian judge would merely give them a limited sentence or would have been intimidated to release them.

Yonti sat back in his chair and admitted to himself that he missed the thrill, of playing a part to make the world a safer place. He hungered for the cut, chase, and thrill of trying to make the world a safer place which entailed killing the bad guys, so this may well be an opportunity to eliminate a person that has affected countless lives globally and possibly his cousin's life as well. He wondered whether he could hack into his bank and move all his money without ever being caught doing it. Yes, it certainly is possible, he considered.

Later that day, he sat down with Claire and told her that Barnaby had called him seeking his assistance to eliminate a Mexican drug lord now residing in Kandersteg, a town fourteen miles from where they live, and explained a promise that he made to his uncle many years ago, to find and eliminate the drug lord responsible for his cousin's death.

Claire listened intently to what Yonti was saying, before answering.

'Well, you are not the only one that has lost someone dear to you.' 'Years ago, I lost my best friend to an overdose of drugs, and I watched as she died in my arms, while we waited for an ambulance to arrive.' 'That happened when I was in my late teen years.' 'This has plagued me ever since, and I have carried the guilt of not being able to save her life.'

'Wow, you have never told me about this Claire, so we both have a reason to want revenge,' said Yonti.

'And yes, we both have a good reason to get revenge for what has happened to your friend and my cousin, so I will look into what the Director has mentioned,' continued Yonti.

Yonti called Barnaby on a secure line and asked him to forward satellite images of the drug lord's home and surrounding area, including any other useful information he had. Using code words, he mentioned that he needed some rails to complete the model railway track he was building and asked him to buy some HO gauge rails and send them to him. Barnaby understood that to be the need for a sniper's rifle, scope, and ammunition, so he made arrangements to have it delivered to him. A week later Yonti met a CIA agent in town and took possession of the parcel containing the rifle, scope, ammunition, camouflage snow, and camping gear, then made his way home.

He took the time to assemble the rifle, checking all the components. Satisfied, he disassembled it and hid it in the rafters of the shed that housed the cows during the winter months.

He studied the images and noted that the drug lord's homestead was positioned in a valley between two mountains, with what appeared to be a large building, which most likely housed a bevy of guards, so it seemed that he had chosen well. Yonti studied the mountainous terrain and noted that the top of the mountain on the west side appeared to be around a thousand yards from the homestead. Right, so from what I have seen on the images, it appears that this bastard plays in the snow with his children every day, so if I could get to the top of the mountain without being detected, I could take him out. It is always windy up there so I would need to compensate for that, which will make a shot very tricky indeed, he pondered.

Can't afford to miss, he thought.

He studied the images more closely and noted the CCTV cameras positioned around the homestead, however, none appeared to be positioned towards the side or top of the mountain. I don't want to kill him in front of his children, so I will need to explore some other options, he considered.

He also noted a creek running through the drug lord's property from the images and focused on the brief, which stated that Mr. Albano had assimilated well into the community. His two children attended the local primary school in the farming village of Kandersteg, in the heart of the Swiss Alps in Bernese Oberland, which extends along the valley of Kander. The village is popular with tourists seeking to explore the Alpine rural lifestyle, characterized by wooden chalets and homely restaurants, where visitors can taste traditional Swiss cuisine. None of the residents or tourists had any idea that one of the world's most wanted drug lords was living in their picturesque village, continuing to run his drug smuggling business from there.

He replayed the satellite images and noted that Mr. Albano went outside alone every morning at around zero six-hundred hours, and had a morning ritual, which seemed like he was doing Tai Chi, for around ten minutes before taking a dip in a hot tub and finally immersing himself in what appeared to be a tub of cold water. Yonti fast-forwarded the tape to the following day and noted that Mr. Albano appeared to do that every morning, noting that there were no guards in view during his morning ritual, so this may well present an excellent opportunity to eliminate him, without being spotted. The entire ritual seemed to last for around thirty minutes.

Bern airport is conveniently located thirty-eight miles from the village, and it appeared that Mr. Albano owned an exclusive luxury ten-room Chalet Hotel called Vista de la Montaña, which translates to, "View from the Mountain" in Spanish. This was merely a front for his illegal activities, making it appear that he was a legitimate businessman conducting a legitimate business.

Yonti walked to the sideboard and poured himself a three-finger tot of Johnny Walker Blue Scotch Whisky, then dropped some ice cubes into the tumbler. He stared at the view of the cascading waterfall in the distance, through the large bay window in his lounge, and wondered if the drug lord ever visited the hotel he owned and if so, whether that presented an opportunity to take him out there, albeit, that one would assume that he would be well-guarded.

Yonti booked a two-night stay at the hotel for the family, and Claire packed an overnight bag for the family. He chose to have his family accompany him which would reduce any suspicion because a man on his own would most likely draw unwanted attention. It would appear that the family was on vacation, and he knew that he had to be careful not to draw any attention to himself or his family.

They bundled the kids into their SUV and they drove into town. He parked the family car in a secure parking space, removed their suitcase, then walked to the Eurocar Hire business situated on the fringe of town and hired a Skoda Karoq four-wheel drive SUV under the name of Liam Brown, the identity he had used on a CIA mission some years ago. He needed to ensure that no one could trace his or his family's real identity. Yonti had retained the passport and identity documents in that name after having retired from the CIA, just in case he would ever need it in the future.

They took a leisurely drive towards Kandersteg, stopping along the way at the village of Spiez for a light lunch. The distance of nineteen miles took them thirty minutes and they booked into the hotel under the name of Mr. and Mrs. Brown.

As usual, when on a mission, Yonti cocked his Glock fitted with a silencer and put it into the back of his pants. He put four spare clips of ammunition in his pocket. Don't think there will be an opportunity to even get to see this drug lord, let alone be able to take him out, he thought. No doubt he will be surrounded by a hoard of henchmen so will need to use this trip as a reconnaissance mission.

He made his way downstairs and into the lounge, found a corner table, positioned himself with his back to the wall giving him an excellent view of the lounge and the surroundings. As he sipped his beer, he pretended to be reading a tourist brochure, while his eyes scanned the surroundings. He searched for any possible sign of the drug lord.

His gaze momentarily focused on the two huge Mexican dudes positioned on the mezzanine level outside a door that he thought may lead to an office, then noticed two other foreign-looking men sitting at a table closer to the revolving door at the entrance to the hotel. The images of the drug lord sent to him by Barnaby Heathcott were displayed on his mobile phone, so he took the time to study them more closely.

Seems Mr. Albano had security scattered all over the place, so he continued to study the brochure, occasionally pausing to take a mouthful of beer, giving him time to continue his surveillance of the premises. He noticed the various CCTV cameras strategically positioned around the reception, lounge area, and staircase.

Best be very careful, because this bastard's henchmen are most likely focused on me right now.

An hour later he made his way back to the room without having seen the drug lord. He and Claire took the kids outside and built a snowman at the rear of the complex. Yonti positioned himself facing toward the complex as he wanted to ensure that he got a clear view of the drug lord if he happened to exit the rear of the building. The family had a snow fight, typical of a family frolicking and having fun in the snow. Yonti took some photographs of the family on his mobile phone. A moment later the rear door of the complex opened, and the drug lord accompanied by another person emerged, surrounded by four heavies, as they made their way towards a waiting SUV. The two were in deep conversation as they walked towards the parked vehicle and hardly looked in his direction.

Yonti carefully enlarged the image on his mobile phone and whilst it appeared that he was taking photographs of the family, he was focused on the drug lord and the person accompanying him. He was careful not to look in their direction ensuring that he did not draw any suspicion to what he was doing. The family continued to frolic in the snow and he heard the diver of the SUV fire up the engine and depart from the parking lot behind him. He did not turn and look in their direction.

Where on earth do I know this other guy from thought Yonti, as he reviewed the image of the drug lord on his phone and compared them to the photographs sent to him by Barnaby.

He focused on the other person. I have seen this guy somewhere before and he tried as best he could to remember where he had seen him. The image of the drug lord confirmed that he was looking at the same person that Barnaby had sent him.

Right, I have seen him in person he thought, so how the hell am I going to get rid of this bastard he considered?

Back home two days later, he reviewed the satellite images sent to him by Barnaby and focused on the mountain range surrounding the drug lord's homestead. Will be very tricky to try and take a sniper's shot from there because of wind speed and constant turbulence, so how the hell am I going to take this bastard out, he considered.

Yonti was consumed with trying to recall who the other person in the photograph was. I know and have seen pictures of him several times, but who the hell is he, thought Yonti. May need to get the CIA to identify him, and why on earth he's meeting with Mr. Albano.

Yonti sent a copy of the photograph to Barnaby on a secure SMS and asked him to confirm that the image was that of the drug lord and whether he was able to identify the other person in the photograph.

He immediately received a call from the Director.

'Hello Yonti, well that is interesting because we have been investigating the drug lord for some time, as well as his companion on another matter.' 'We have had eyes on this other guy for some time, and we have been watching him for many months.' 'I can confirm that the drug lord is Vincente Del La Fuente, or as he is known in Switzerland, Arnborg Albano.'

'As mentioned, he changed his name before he applied for permanent residence in Switzerland.' 'The other person in the photograph is Eduardo Batista, who was born in Batananó, a village thirty-five miles from Havana in Cuba, and immigrated to Miami in Florida twenty-five years ago.'

'Over one and a half million ex-Cubans live in Florida,' continued Barnaby.

'Eduardo Batista is the Deputy Director, holding the position of Chief Operating Officer of the Bureau of Alcohol, Tobacco, Firearms, and Explosives, commonly referred to as ATF, so he is well positioned to control the movement of firearms.' 'The Hispanic and Latino vote accounts for around twenty-six percent of the vote in Florida, so that's how he was voted into office,' continued Barnaby.

'The Bureau of Alcohol, Tobacco, Firearms and Explosives (BATFE), is a domestic law enforcement agency within the United States Department of Justice.' 'Its responsibilities include the investigation and prevention of federal offenses involving the unlawful use, manufacture, and possession of firearms including explosives.' 'They also investigate acts of arson and bombings, as well as illegal trafficking, tax evasion of alcohol and tobacco products.'

'The ATF also regulates via licensing the sale, possession, and transportation of firearms, ammunition, and explosives in interstate commerce.' 'It operates a unique fire research laboratory in Beltsville, Maryland, where full-scale mock-ups of criminal arson can be reconstructed, and employ around five-thousand two-hundred and eighty-five people with an annual budget of almost one and a half billion US dollars,' said Barnaby.

'The CIA has long suspected that Mr. Batista has been involved in illegal activities, and we suspect that he has been supplying the Mexican Drug Lords with arms.' 'It has come to light recently that a cache of arms went missing from a stockpile of confiscated weapons housed in a warehouse in Arizona, waiting to be destroyed' 'Once a year the confiscated guns are melted down, so one can only hope that the authorities kept records of the number of guns they have destroyed or that were scheduled to be destroyed.' 'We never suspected him of knowing Mr. Albano, so interesting that he has met with him.'

'The FBI is currently investigating the matter and is now in the process of doing an inventory count so that they can establish exactly how many weapons have gone missing.' 'This could be why he met with Mr. Albano.'

'Thanks for the good work Yonti.' 'I will call you as soon as I know something,' said Barnaby ending the call.

So, that's where I have seen photographs of Mr. Batista, thought Yonti. He sat back and considered how he could eliminate this drug lord, finally settling on a sniper shot from the icy creek running through his property. He studied the terrain carefully noting that the creek ran through a gully that had an embankment on the homestead side. This, offered excellent cover, allowing him to work his way closer to the homestead, and take him out without being noticed. The creek was around two hundred yards from the homestead, however, he would need to be able to make a quick exit, as there would most likely only be minutes before the drug lord's henchmen discovered Mr. Albano's body and launched a massive manhunt, so he would need to high tail it out of there very quickly once he had eliminated him.

Two days later an agent delivered a second parcel to his home with a sticker detailing "Hobby Goods".

Yonti unpacked the parcel and laid the contents out on the floor in the shed. He stared at the Remington 700XCR (Xtreme Conditions Rifle) for some time. The long-range tactical bolt action rifle is made in the USA using .300 Winchester Magnum rounds of ammunition with a three-plus-one capacity. The rifle is rated as the top sniper's rifle in the USA with legendary accuracy and unfailing performance. Very impressive, he thought.

He removed the rifle from the carry case, assembled it, checked all the components, before attaching the scope and silencer, then cocked the weapon several times to ensure that everything was in working order.

Satisfied, he placed several rounds in his pocket and made his way outdoors toward the clump of trees on the fringe of his property.

He aimed at a branch of a tree which he estimated to be around two hundred yards away. That would be around the same distance that I need to take the shot at the drug lord, he thought.

The first shot was a little to the left, so he sighted the rifle and made the necessary adjustments before reloading and taking another shot. He continued with the routine until he was satisfied that he had sighted the rifle correctly, then made his way back to the shed, disassembled the weapon, and placed it into the white sling case. He unpacked the rest of the contents, which contained a box of ammunition, a white camouflage combat suit, white waterproof waders similar to those used by fly fishermen, and a white sleeping bag. It all fitted neatly into the backpack. Seems like it's all here, he considered.

The following day, Yonti drove to Kandersteg and parked his car in a secure spot on the fringe of the town. He walked to the Eurocar rental company and hired a Skoda Kodiaq four-wheel drive SUV in the name of Jon Jones, an alias that he had used on another mission for the CIA. He had retained the passport as well as the identity documents, just in case he ever needed it in the future. It was late afternoon when he arrived back home, and parked the vehicle at the back of the shed, ensuring that Claire could not see it.

He knew when the time came, he would have around twenty minutes to take the shot, complete the mission, and get to safety before a manhunt was launched to capture the person responsible, so he decided to carry out the mission the next day, a Sunday morning. Traditionally a day of prayer and relaxation around the world, where people tend to be far more at ease.

He put the twins to bed, then kissed his wife goodnight as she decided to retire early, and made his way to the study. He glanced at his wristwatch and noted that it was almost twenty hundred hours, so he fired up his laptop and signed into the Internet using one of the hundreds of accounts that he had set up whilst working for the CIA and hacked into the Crédit Bank Suisse database. He knew that it was still early in the evening and a risk to access the drug lord's account, however, he hoped that that the drug lord would be snuggled up in bed at that time. A calculated risk he considered.

Right, got into Mr. Albano's account, however, what on earth would his password be, he thought.

He used his expertise in computer engineering to troll through the bank's database, finally managing to identify the bank IT Manager's details and spent a couple of hours trolling through their database. Finally managing to identify Mr. Albano's account, listed under the name of Intocable, which in Spanish, translates to Untouchable. Arrogant prick thought Yonti.

He managed to bypass the DLP, (Data Loss Prevention) system that the bank had set up, which is used to mitigate insider threats, safeguarding customers' data, like names, credit card details, and account numbers keeping their information secure. The bank also used a biometric authentication technique to verify their customers' identity, including behavioral biometrics, when they interact with systems like IVR, (Interactive Voice Recognition), allowing their computer and intelligent devices to interact with humans. He knew that the bank would send an SMS with a verification code to Mr. Albano's mobile number. So a few minutes earlier, he redirected the contact number listed in Mr. Albano's account to one of the mobile phones he had hidden whilst working for the CIA. That allowed him to receive the verification code and once he had it, he would transfer all the funds in the account to a clandestine CIA account, held in the Cayman Islands. Thereafter he would cancel the mobile number, and revert it to Mr. Albano's contact number, so anybody checking would not discover what had been done.

So how do I get around the Biometric Authorization point of sale (POS) Technology that banks use, he thought.

Banks use physical characteristics to identify the user and authorize a deduction from a person's bank account. They require a person to identify themselves by pressing their finger against a smooth surface. The finger ridges and valleys are scanned and a series of distinct points, where the valleys and ridges meet, are called minutiae. These minutiae are points that a fingerprint recognition system uses for comparison.

So he accessed the bank's Biometric templates, which are binary files encompassing the unique traits of an individual's biometric data that make it unreadable without the correct algorithm, and he used the Apple Secure Enclave which is commonly used on smartphones, to download a copy of Mr. Albano's fingerprint. He donned a pair of skin-colored gloves, then made a copy of Mr. Albano's fingerprint, and saved it on a sticky adhesive sheet, before deleting it. He then peeled back the sticky layer of plastic on the sheet and pressed the image onto the acetate sheet, ensuring that a clear copy of the fingerprint was saved, similar to what police use to lift fingerprints from a crime scene. Using a three-D printer, he scanned the fingerprint to collect the data and used it to create a three-dimensional data image of its shape and color. It captured the depth, perception, and valleys of the fingerprint, which he would use to construct a digital three-D model.

The saved copy of the fingerprint would be used to authorize a withdrawal from the account.

Using ChatGPT Artificial Intelligence technology, also known as VALL-E to clone Mr. Albano's voice, and he hoped that the drug lord would be sound asleep at that hour, which was heading toward midnight.

Yonti sat back and thought, that these financial institutions need to lift their game and install world-leading-edge cyber security. It seems very odd that they are complacent and have not stayed abreast of cybercrime.

He logged into Mr. Albano's account, took the image that he had made on the three-D printed and pressed it against the screen allowing him access, then checked the bank balance in the account, which was a staggering CHF three billion nine hundred and eighty-two Swiss Francs which equates to around four and a half billion US dollars, and waited for a call from the bank to verify that they were communicating with Mr. Albano. Moments later, the mobile lit up with an incoming call from the bank, wanting to verify that they were communicating with the correct person, so he played back the recording he had made of Mr. Albano's voice which satisfied the bank.

He transferred all the funds in the account to the CIA's clandestine account held in the Cayman Islands and waited a few minutes before checking that the balance was zero. As soon as he had confirmation that the funds had been transferred, he deleted his mobile number in the bank's system and reverted it to the drug lord's number, ensuring that it could not be traced back to him.

After the transfer had taken place, the money was redistributed to twenty CIA bank accounts scattered across the globe, making it impossible to trace.

Satisfied that he had successfully transferred the funds, he packed his gear into the SUV that he had hired the previous day and pointed it in the direction of the drug lord's home. The drive took forty minutes, and as he turned onto a dirt road near the homestead, he glanced at his watch, noting that it was zero four hundred hours. Just enough time to get set up before the drug lord started his morning ritual. Time to send this bastard to hell, he thought.

As he got closer to the drug lord's home, he dimmed the headlight beam and changed it to the parking lights mode, just in case a beam of light would alert anybody who happened to be on guard duty. He checked the map that he had downloaded from a file sent to him by Barnaby to ensure that he was close to the homestead, then found an ideal spot to park the vehicle amongst the bushes and killed the engine.He removed his gear from the rear compartment of the SUV, before picking up the rifle carry case, and made his way on foot toward the drug lord's homestead. A walk of around a mile.

The dial on his wristwatch indicated that he had been walking through the thick snow for around thirty minutes, before stopping approximately two hundred meters from the homestead on the hillside opposite it. He made his way through the creek and up the embankment on the other side, then leopard crawled toward a clump of bushes and positioned himself ensuring that he had an excellent view of the homestead. Using the night vision binoculars, he checked for any activity in the area and satisfied that the coast was clear, unzipped the rifle carry bag, and extracted the sniper rifle, then fitted the scope, tripod and silencer. He measured the distance on the Integrated Ultralight I-CUGR Laser range finder manufactured by Safran Optics 1 Inc. as well as checking the wind direction and speed, before making the necessary adjustments.

Satisfied, he positioned the rifle and lay waiting for the right opportunity to take the shot. As the early dawn started to illuminate the horizon, the spotlight on the deck suddenly lit up, and he watched as the drug lord made his way down the stairs heading towards what appeared to be a hot tub with a cup of coffee in hand. His mind wandered back to the cousin that he lost to an overdose of drugs, reminding himself of the promise that he had made to his uncle, which was to track down the drug lord and kill him.

Not sure if this is the guy who was responsible for the drugs that his cousin or Claire's best friend had taken, however, no matter, I will consider him the responsible person. He shivered in the early morning chill, ensuring that he lay still because he did not want the drug lord to detect any movement.

Moments later the spotlight illuminated movement as the drug lord made his way toward a hot tub and removed the cover. He sipped his coffee and turned to face the coming dawn, then removed his gown. Yonti watched through the scope as the drug lord stood naked then started his five minute morning ritual of Tai Chi. Clearly the drug lord did not want his henchmen to see him naked. Satisfied that no other person was visible, Yonti activated the safety switch, waited momentarily until the drug lord turned towards his direction, and then gently squeezed the trigger.

He watched as the drug lord's head burst open like a melon, and wasted no time as he reverse leopard crawled back down the embankment, and once he was able to stand undetected, he was quick to his feet and hurriedly made his way back to where he had parked the SUV.

He was aware that the tracks in the snow would guide Mr. Albano's henchmen to follow him, and that he had no more than ten minutes to get back onto the road to Kandersteg before they launched an aerial search possibly using a drone or a helicopter. It was snowing heavily, and there would be insufficient snow dumped over a short period to cover his tracks.

He hightailed it through the snow toward the SUV and estimated that it took almost ten minutes to reach the vehicle. He quickly jumped in, fired up the engine and headed toward the main road. As he approached the intersection to the main road, he checked to ensure that there were no cars in sight and hurriedly turned toward the town. The SUV made its way around a curve in the road, and he thought that he had caught a glimpse of a drone in the distance.

He felt it best to continue towards Spiez, a town on the shores of Lake Thun in the Bernese Oberland Region of the Swiss Canton of Bern, and lie low for several days until he felt that it safe to return to Kandersteg and return the SUV to Eurocar.

He stopped at the local supermarket close to the town of Spiez and picked up some supplies before continuing toward Niederhorn, which is six-thousand-two-hundred and thirty-three feet high in the southernmost peak of the Güggisgrats. It rises prominently above Lake Thun and from here one can enjoy a picturesque view of the lake and the Bernese Alps in the south and the elongated Justistal. The Justistal is a hidden gem nestled between the majestic Niederhorn with a majestic towering peak that serves as the entrance to this secluded valley and Sigriswiler Rothorn in the heart of the Swiss Alps.

He drove up a steep hill, before veering off the track, as he reached the top and headed towards the fringe of a wooded area. Truly breathtaking view he thought as he parked the SUV close to the edge. An ideal place to hide for a few days. Need to camp here for a few days and let the heat settle, because there is no doubt that the police will be conducting random checks on the outskirts of Kandersteg. It was zero-eight hundred hours, so he parked the SUV and unpacked his camping gear.

He had instructed Claire not to call him because he believed that the police would possibly be monitoring all calls to and from the area, and told her that he may be away for several days. Right, all done he thought, and albeit that it was early morning, he poured himself a three-finger tot of Johnny Walker Blue Label whisky, and held the glass up to the heavens.

'To you, my cousin, and to Claire's best friend.' 'May you both rest in Peace?'

Three days later he returned the Skoda to the hire company and made his way back home to his beloved wife and twin sons. He placed a call to Barnaby Heathcott on a secure line.

'Daddy has left and as I understand it, he is 'Down Under.' 'Dad left you something in the will, so best you check it.'

Barnaby understood the use of the Australian phrase "Down Under," meant that he was deceased and in Hell. He also understood that something had been left in the will, would mean that a sum of money had been transferred into the clandestine CIA account in the Cayman Islands.

'Thanks for letting me know Yonti.' 'I am sure that we will all miss Dad.'

He popped the cork of a bottle of Dom Pérignon Champagne and turned to face Claire.

'À la vôtre, Cheers Mon Pidgeon.' 'To your best friend and my cousin.' 'May they rest in peace knowing that the person responsible for their death has passed into the gates of Hell?'

Chapter 6

Portland

Oregon Usa

The display on Claire's mobile lit up, announcing an incoming call.
'Hello.'

'Hello Claire, it's your cousin Dushenka.'

'Oh my goodness, what a surprise' 'Let's see, it must be almost ten years since I last spoke with you.' 'How are you?'

'Wish I could say fine, but I'm not fine at all.'

'Why, what's happened?'

'Well, you may not know that I got married thirteen years ago and have two children, a boy named Pepe, and a girl that we named Kiki.' 'Pepe is ten and Kiki is twelve, however, she is very well developed and looks like she could be fifteen.'

'Yesterday Kiki did not come home from school.' 'We found a note under our front door when we got home from work which read, do not contact the police or FBI.' 'If you do, you will suffer the consequences.' 'Whatever that means.'

'We have searched everywhere and contacted everyone she knows and nobody has seen her.' 'Thus far, we have not been able to find her and according to her friends, she stayed after school to do her homework.' 'I fear that she may have been abducted and we don't know who to turn to for help, hence the reason for my call.'

'As I understand it, you got married, and from what I have been told, your husband works for the CIA, which is the reason I am reaching out to you for assistance.' 'Time is of the essence now, as it is early evening here and we have grave fears for our daughter's safety.'

'We are at a loss, as to what has happened, because she has simply disappeared.' 'My husband Carlos and I, fear that she may have been abducted into sex slavery by human traffickers.'

'We have contacted all the various organizations that deal in human trafficking including, The National Centre for Sexual Exploitation, Shared Hope International, Exodus Cry, RIGHTS4GIRLS, Demand Abolition, and Ecpat International for any assistance they can render, and as of right now, we have heard nothing.' 'I know that it has only been several hours, but my intuition tells me that there is something very wrong.'

'So Claire, I am appealing to you to please ask your husband to try and help us, because we don't know where else to go or who else to turn to for assistance.' 'Please Claire, we are desperate.'

'Oh my goodness Dushenka, that's horrible.' 'Yonti no longer works for the CIA, however, I will ask him if he can help, and I will get back to you soon.' 'Send me everything you have on Kiki, recent photographs, the school she attends, friends, hobbies, activities she does, sports, and any other relevant information of interest.'

An hour later Claire's mobile phone lit up with an SMS from Dushenka detailing everything that she had asked for.

Yonti glanced towards the west and watched as the sun kissed the horizon. Going to be dark soon he thought, so he headed towards the shed and packed his tools away. Being a hard day out in the field, however, he felt satisfied that he had accomplished all the tasks that he set himself for the day. Darkness was slowly approaching as he wearily made his way up the stairs towards the house. Starving he reminded himself.

'Hello Mon Pétale,' he said as he made his way onto the deck.

Looking at Claire, he noticed some tears welled up in her eyes. 'What's wrong Claire?'

'Come in Yonti and I will tell you.'

They sat down in the lounge and Claire turned to face him.

'Well, it's my cousin Dushenka.' 'She called me earlier and begged me to ask you for assistance.'

'Her daughter, Kiki has gone missing earlier today, and they fear that she may have been abducted.' 'When they got home from work, they saw a note that had been put under the door which read, Do Not Call the Police or the FBI, because if you do, it will result in fatal consequences.' 'She called me and pleaded with me to ask you to assist.' 'She believes that you work for the CIA, hence the reason she reached out to us for help.'

'I told her that you are no longer at the CIA, however, she feels you may still have connections there that can assist.'

'She does not know who to turn to for help Yonti.'

'They have called all the daughter's friends and they were told that Kiki stayed after school to do her homework and nobody has seen her since the school broke up for the day.'

Yonti walked to the kitchen and poured a glass of chardonnay for Claire, then tossed some ice cubes into a tumbler, and poured himself his usual three-finger tot of Johnny Walker Blue Scotch Whisky, before sitting down in the lounge, considering what he had just been told.

Well, that's tragic, he thought.

I cannot involve the CIA nor can I speak with the police or FBI, so I will need to do this on my own. If I eliminate one or a couple of the people responsible, I will be charged with murder, so I best try to solve this on my own, without anybody knowing.

Claire activated her mobile phone and opened the page sent to her by Dushenka, then forwarded it to Yonti. He scrolled through the pictures on the screen, then forwarded it to his email address and printed everything that Dushenka had sent. Wow, she is an attractive young girl, he thought.

He read through the notes in the attachment and noted the name of the school that she attends. An hour later Claire's mobile lit up with an incoming SMS from Dushenka asking whether she had received all the information she had sent.

Many atrocities are often perpetrated by a family member, a close friend, or a trusted person, so Yonti thought that he should look at Kiki's teachers and principal as the first possible option. He read the SMS sent to Claire for a second time, considering who the most likely person could be regarding Kiki's disappearance. So, this young girl simply disappears after having stayed after school. If she has been kidnapped, I need to find the person or persons responsible and kill them, he considered.

Can't stand bastards like these. The world needs to be rid of them.

She was not at a friend's place, because the parents have checked, and it does not seem like she has run away from home either. All indications are that they have a very happy household, so a well-developed twelve-year-old girl who looks like she could be fifteen, would undoubtedly be a target for a paedophile. Why then, would a note be left under their door, he considered.

No ransom note either, he thought.

Some sick bastard is sending the parents a warning not to call law enforcement authorities. Why someone would do that, I have no idea, he wondered.

He reminded himself, that more often than not, when there has been a case of rape or physical abuse, it is either a parent, a family member, a close friend, or a trusted person known to the family, so this will be the starting point he decided.

Can't discount a church elder, pedophile priest, or school teacher either. Think I will start at the school, so he Googled the school that she attended and scrolled through the website. He clicked on the Management Team noting that there were fifteen female teachers, and having carefully looked at each of them, he discounted all of them as unlikely suspects and then focused on the male teachers. A total of twenty, so he studied the images of everyone carefully and finally took the time to study the image of the Principal. Mr. Kent Santiago. Something about this gentleman caught his attention. A gut feeling. The type of feeling you get when your inner sense gets that uncomfortable feeling, almost a warning that there is something strange about the person's looks.

The principal seemed to have an arrogant, almost smug look about him. He noted that the family lived in Portland Oregon and that Kiki attended the Oregon Private School located around five miles from the family home. As he scrolled through the notes, he took note of the names of the teachers as well as the principal.

He had very bad memories of Oregon, where he almost lost his life in an operation, however, he compartmentalized that in his memory, and concentrated on the task at hand.

Yonti trolled through the Internet searching for any information on Mr. Santiago, however, to no avail. He then accessed the Oregon Free Public Criminal Records and searched for any indication that Mr. Santiago was ever charged with an offense. He noticed that there was a record of Mr. Santiago having been charged with a minor offense of child fondling, however, due to the sketchy testimony by the young girl that accused him of the offense he was alleged to have committed, the case was dismissed.

I hate bastards that prey on innocent young children. Fuck them, I need to find whoever is responsible and eliminate him or her, he thought.

Right, so where there's smoke, there is fire. Need to check this person thoroughly. Time is of the essence right now, so he trolled the Internet, Facebook, and Instagram for anything on Mr. Santiago and discovered that he was a preacher in the Forgiveness Church based in Portland, the capital of Oregon.

Amazing how people hang their washing out on social media for everyone to read. People can learn so much about a person on Facebook and Instagram, as they tend to openly disclose many aspects of their private lives.

Yonti Googled the Forgiveness Church and discovered that they had set up a church in a warehouse in the industrial estate of Rivergate, adjacent to the Port of Portland. It appeared that they conduct two services on Sundays, one at zero ten hundred hours and the other at eighteen hundred hours.

He also noticed that the church had a retreat complex at the foot of Forest Park, which is a public municipal park in the Tualatin Mountains west of downtown Portland, Oregon, United States. The mountains stretch for more than 8 miles on a hillside overlooking the Willamette River. It is one of the country's largest urban forest reserves, so he used Google Maps to ascertain its exact location, noting that the complex was situated alongside a wooded area.

The retreat appeared to be self-sustaining with what appeared to be a large vegetable garden, a couple of cows, and a chicken coop. It also had a structure that looked like a house or dormitory of some sort, so clearly, it was constructed to accommodate people. Very interesting he thought.

The line between delusion and what the rest of us believe may be blurrier than we think, he thought.

Yonti read the church's Mission Statement and was intrigued to discover its openness regarding its charter. It read Magister Sororum Obediens, Latin for "Obedient Master of the Sisters." "Complicit and Obedience" are the pillars on which the church was founded, it stated.

Further investigation revealed that Mr. Santiago appeared to be, not only the priest but also a cult leader, who undoubtedly would most likely dominate various cult members, isolating them from the rest of society. Some individuals who join cults remain lifelong members. Others break free and share how it felt to be brainwashed by a charismatic leader.

Yonti stared at the information sent to Claire for some time, reminding himself that he may be barking up the wrong tree, so he concentrated his focus on the principal, who one would assume, would be viewed as a trusted person. I hate bastards that prey on innocent young children. I need to find those responsible and eliminate them, he thought.

He reminded himself of the need to proceed with caution because he did not have the backing of the CIA, and if he eliminated someone, and got caught, he would be arrested and put on trial and spend the rest of his life in prison.

Protestants accounted for thirty percent of all denominations in Oregon, with the Church of Latter Day Saints accounting for around five percent, Buddhists around two percent, and other unaffiliated churches around twenty-seven percent. A poll conducted in two-thousand and nine found that sixty-nine percent of Oregonians identified with a Christian Religion.

So, this could be a lead, however, I may be way off track, so this deserves further scrutiny. His gut told him to follow the lead. One's intuition is often correct, he reminded himself.

On the other hand, he realized that he could be wrong and needed to keep an open mind. He studied the photograph of the principal closely and was convinced that Mr. Santiago could be a suspect and that his earlier assessment of him may well be correct.

Yonti booked a business class seat on a Swiss Air flight from Zurich to New York departing the following evening with a connecting flight to Oregon, so he packed his bags, bid Claire and the twins farewell, and caught the train from Kandersteg to Zurich the following morning. He needed to get as much shut-eye as possible on the flight because he needed to hit the road running when he landed.

The sudden thud and screeching of the tires hitting the runway woke him from a deep sleep. Six out of ten for that landing he thought as he made his way through customs and headed towards the domestic terminal. He boarded the flight to Portland. The flight time was five hours and thirty minutes and landed on time. He used one of the many passports he had used during his years at the CIA when he hired a SUV and thirty minutes later, he pointed the hired Jeep Grand Cherokee in the direction of the city center, eventually finding a parking spot near the Loyalist Bank of Oregon.

A few minutes later he was shown to the safety deposit box that he had hired years previously when he was an active CIA agent. He had registered safety boxes at various banks in New York, Zurich, Paris and Oregon, and had stashed a Glock, twenty clips of ammunition, and silencers in each box, as well as passports in various names as a precaution for any future possible need. Never know what the future holds, he thought at the time.

He paid the rental fees for ten years in advance and wanted nobody, including the CIA to ever know about the hidden weapons, just in case he ever needed them in the future, like now. The weapons had been confiscated from various criminals during CIA operations and were never registered, so the CIA did not know of them. He hid them for possible use in the future, and they could never be traced back to him.

Later he pointed the Jeep Grand Cherokee in the direction of the Portland Exquisite Inn Hotel, a modest three-star hotel, ideal for a tourist traveling through the state and booked in.

He unpacked his belongings, jumped into the Jeep, punched in the address of the Forgiveness Church into the GPS, and headed towards the industrial estate of Rivergate. As he drove slowly through the estate, he noted the security cameras positioned around the complex, then pointed the Jeep in the direction of the Oregon Private School that Kiki attends.

Everything looked normal, he thought as he slowly passed by.

Right now, I need to find the retreat he reminded himself, so he punched the address into the GPS and discovered that it was six-and-a-half miles from Portland. He was starting to feel a little fatigued, due to the number our hours he had been awake, however, he needed to clear his head and push on.

Time was of the essence right now, so he shook his head hoping that it would clear his mind, reminding himself to remain focused. The drive to the retreat along the Willamette River took thirteen minutes, before passing the St. John's Bridge, he then veered towards Forest Park.

He eventually noticed the retreat in the distance, so he turned off the road, headed towards a wooded area at the foot of the mountain, and parked in a bushy area that offered an excellent view of the complex.

Using his binoculars, he scanned the area and noted the security fence surrounding the complex as well as the CCTV cameras scattered around the fringes of the complex. He noticed four young girls tending the gardens, one appeared to be milking the cows, so he focused on a person sitting on a log, seeming to be overseeing the young girls working in the fields. Seems rather odd that they have a person on guard duty watching over the young girls, concluding that they are most likely there against their will.

They appeared to be finishing the day's activities as the sun started dipping behind the mountain. Right, he needed to get a closer look at this joint, so he donned a pair of plastic gloves and put a roll of duct tape in his pocket. He got out of the SUV, placed his body against the door and closed it, rather than close it in the normal way which would have resulted in a loud thump, a noise that would alert anybody within earshot, especially the person that appeared to be on guard duty. As he made his way toward the retreat, he ensured that he remained well hidden in the thicket.

The person walking amongst the girls tending the fields caught his attention, which reminded him of a master overseeing his slaves, similar to the days of slavery during the seventeenth and eighteenth centuries in the USA. He noticed what appeared to be a dormitory, clearly designed to house people, and took note of a large shed close to the building. May need to use this shed as cover to get close to the place without being noticed. Amazing how relaxed everyone appeared, which made him think that he may be barking up the wrong tree, however, he was troubled by the need to have a guard overseeing the young girls working in the field. No sign of Kiki he thought, as he scanned the area through his binoculars. Right, if she is here, she may be locked up somewhere, so I need to keep an open mind. Moments later, the guard and the girls made their way towards the complex.

The front entrance side of the complex appeared to have multiple CCTV cameras set up on the corners, so clearly whoever set it up, would have viewed this as the most important area to keep under surveillance ensuring privacy and to keep intruders out. Wonder if they have done the same at the rear of the complex he considered, so he made his way around the complex through the dense bush ensuring that he remained well hidden, eventually reaching the rear end. Darkness was fast approaching, so he scanned the area through his binoculars and noted that there only appeared to be one CCTV camera pointing towards the west. Dumb bastards, he thought as he scouted the area for a possible entry into the complex and noticed a tree alongside the fence which he decided to use to get into the complex. Will need to scale the fence, so hopefully it is not an electrified fence, he thought.

Feeling totally fatigued and rather exhausted, he mentally revisited what he had read about Kiki's disappearance. He glanced at his watch noting that it was almost eighteen hundred hours with darkness fast approaching, he reminded himself that it was Friday night. Everything that he had read about the principal convinced him that there was something very strange about this person. Seems I have already judged Mr. Santiago as guilty, which may well be unfair, however, his intuition had never let him down, so he trusted his gut feeling.

Suddenly a beam of light from an approaching vehicle caught his attention, so he ducked into the undergrowth, ensuring that he remained hidden behind the large tree, and focused the binoculars on the vehicle as it made its way around the complex towards the front entrance. He caught a glimpse of the male driver as it passed close by. Could be Mr. Santiago he thought, reminding himself of Kiki's plight. He remained hidden for some time and waited until he felt it was safe to proceed.

Time to take a closer look, so he inserted a loaded magazine into the Glock, screwed on the silencer, cocked it, and activated the safety switch, before putting it into the rear of his pants. He ran his hand over his pants pocket to ensure that he had the four clips of ammunition in it, before scaling the fence and making his way towards the east side of the complex, ensuring that the CCTV camera facing west did not pick up any movement. He carefully approached a beam of light shining through a window and peeped in.

The four young girls were lined up at the kitchen hatch for their evening meal, holding French Metal Army Meal Trays, typical of those used in prison and military messes internationally. Right, so one male in the kitchen and no others visible. Where is the guard he saw earlier in the field, he wondered.

He slowly made his way along the outside wall toward another well-lit room, carefully peeped in, ensuring that he was not detected, and noticed a person seated around a table in what appeared to be an office. Must be the guard he saw in the field, so two males thus far, as well as the person that had driven into the complex earlier, so a total of three.

Moments later, another person entered the office and seated himself at the head of the table, which he assumed could be Mr. Santiago. Right, so four people in total. He watched as one of them appeared to be reporting on activities at the complex.

He listened to the muffled voices and tried to make out what was being said. Rather difficult, however, he heard the person, who he assumed was Mr. Santiago, refer to the young girl in solitary confinement, which he understood could be Kiki.

Right, time to get into this joint, so he made his way towards the side door that he had seen earlier, carefully tried the door handle, and was pleased to discover that it was unlocked, so he entered and slowly walked towards the office where he had seen the people seated around the table. He listened to the conversation for a few minutes, barely making out what was being said.

'I think it's time to break in our new arrival, stated the man at the head of the table.' 'I will take care of it after dinner,' he said.

The sound of a chair scraping on the floor alerted Yonti that the person had stood up, and was about to exit the office so he hurried to seek a suitable hiding place.

He found a cupboard door further down the passage and was pleased to discover that it was a broom cupboard. Probably an ideal place to hide, so he quickly entered and closed the door. He heard muffled voices as they passed by minutes later and waited until there was complete silence before venturing back into the passage. As he walked down the passage, he opened various doors and looked in. All appeared to be storage cupboards containing various items before he finally discovered a door with a staircase leading to a basement. He quietly entered and gently closed the door behind him, then made his way down the stairs, noticing what appeared to be two cells.

The first cell was empty, however, the second cell appeared to have someone curled up on a bed. Hard to tell in the dim light, so he made his way back to the door at the bottom of the stairs and positioned himself on the inside, ensuring that whoever opened it, would not be able to see him. As he stood with his back to the wall, he felt the hunger pains in his stomach and reminded himself that he had not eaten since the meal he had on the flight.

Feeling a little light-headed and drowsy from the lack of sleep, he shook his head again to keep himself awake, removed the Glock from the rear of his pants, doubled checked that it was cocked and loaded and that he had activated the safety switch ensuring that it was ready to be fired. He stood there for what seemed an eternity, when suddenly the passage door swung open, putting him on high alert, and he heard a person's footsteps echoing as he made his way down the stairs. Suddenly the basement door swung open, and the person entering did not bother to close the door, moving nonchalantly towards the second cell at the far end of the basement in the darkened light. He stared at the back of the person's head, concluding that the person was a male and that it could be Mr. Santiago.

Yonti moved silently down the passage, following close behind the person, ensuring that he positioned himself against the wall on the right-hand side, behind him as he unlocked the cell door.

'Right, if you behave yourself, I will ensure that you get fed,' said the stranger in a raised voice to the petrified young girl lying on the bed as he started to undress.

'I am going to break you in,' he said callously.

The young girl lying on the bed had her legs folded in a defensive position and looked terrified. Moments later she caught a glimpse of a movement behind the person undressing as Yonti as he moved to position himself behind him. The person spun around to see what the young girl was looking at and noticed that someone had followed him into the cell. As he swung around, he stared directly into the barrel of Yonti's Glock.

'Don't move,' whispered Yonti in a calm voice.

'Hello, I take it that you are Mr. Santiago.' 'On your knees,' instructed Yonti.

Santiago was astounded to discover that someone had followed him into the basement without him even being aware that someone else was in the basement. He did as instructed, and Yonti kicked him with a Mae-geri, in the middle of his back, a kick he had learned as a Karate student years previously which propelled him towards the bed, resulting him in crashing head first into the side of the bed. He looked at Santiago lying unconscious next to the bed, hoping that the noise did not attract any unwanted attention.

'Are you Kiki?'

'Yes, I am.' 'Is this man your principal?'

'Yes.'

'Ok, no need to be scared.' 'Your parents sent me to rescue you, so you need to follow my instructions to the letter and do exactly what I tell you.' 'Do you understand?'

'Yes sir.'

'My name is Jon, and I need to get you out of here.'

He chose to use an alias he had used as a CIA agent on many missions, ensuring that there would be no way of authorities ever being able to track him.

'So, your principal kidnapped you, and brought you here against your will.' 'And, he has locked you up in this cell since you got here.' 'Is that correct?'

'Yes.'

'Tell me what happened?'

'I was walking home from school and Mr. Santiago offered me a lift.' 'He was heading towards my home, so I got into the car.' 'He made a U-Turn and told me that he forgot something at school and that he needed to pick it up, and would then take me home.' 'When we reached the school, he put a cloth over my mouth and when I regained consciousness, he had gagged and cuffed me.' 'I woke up in the boot of the car, which was when I realized that I had been kidnapped by someone I trusted.'

'Are the other girls also being held against their will?'

'I don't know because I have not spoken to them at all.' 'I have been locked up down here for a couple of days.'

'Right Kiki, I want you to go to the door at the top of the stairs and wait for me.' 'Do not open the door at all.' 'Simply wait for me,' he instructed.

He wanted to ensure that Kiki did not witness what he was about to do, and waited until she was out of sight, then pointed the pistol at Santiago's head just as he started regaining consciousness.

'Are you Santiago, the school principal?' 'Yes I am, and who the hell are you?' He demanded.

'Oh, I am no one special, merely the Emancipator.'

'Why did you kidnap Kiki?' He said forcefully.

'Who, says she has been kidnapped?'

'Kiki told me, you bastard.' 'Judging by the fact that you were standing here almost naked and about to rape Kiki, you have kidnapped her and enslaved her for your sexual pleasure, just like you have done to the other girls upstairs, you piece of fucking shit.'

The only sound audible, was a faint popping noise as he pulled the trigger. He bent down to pick up the empty cartridge, then turned and made his way out of the cell.

He wanted to ensure that Kiki did not witness him killing Santiago.

'Right Kiki, follow me he instructed as he reached the top of the stairs.'

He gently opened the door and peered into the passage ensuring that the coast was clear, then taking Kiki by the hand, he moved towards the broom cupboard further down the passage, opened the door, and instructed Kiki to get in and stay there until he returned. He made his way towards the dormitory and opened the door. The four girls were all seated on one of the beds huddled together and seemed frightened and surprised to see a stranger entering.

'Hello, my name is Jon.' 'Can you confirm that you girls are here against your will?'

One of the girls who appeared to be the eldest, responded.

'Yes sir, we are being held against our will.'

'OK, no need to be scared, because I am here to rescue a girl named Kiki, who has been in a cell in the basement, so have any of you been abused?'

Instantly all nodded and confirmed that they had been sexually abused by all the men at the complex. The eldest was the first to speak again.

'The Duke is the one that is always the first to rape any new girl entering the complex, and then all of the others take their turn.'

'So have your parents not tried to find you?' He questioned.

'We all have no parents and lived on the street, then the Duke picked each one of us up, and offered us shelter as well as clothing and food.' 'We thought that it was out of the kindness of his heart, only to discover that we had all been kidnapped,' she said with tears rolling down her cheeks.

'Can you all confirm that this is what has happened to all of you?'

All nodded and it was evident that the Duke was Santiago.

'OK, I am going to take you four girls as well as Kiki, the girl that was locked up in the cell downstairs away from here, and find you all a safe place to stay, so I want you all to remain calm and sit quietly until I return.' 'Do you all understand?'

'Yes sir.'

He made his way to the kitchen, gently opened the door, and saw that the person was busy washing dishes and was unaware that he had entered, so he quickly closed the gap. He placed the Glock against his head and pulled the trigger, reminding himself to pick up the cartridge. Blood splattered all over the wall.

The girls confirmed that there were normally three men in the complex, however, over weekends, the Duke was also present, so a total of four.

Yonti was confident that he had not killed an innocent person.

Fucking bastard, you deserve to die, he thought, as he made his way back to the office and opened the door. The two people sitting at the desk were astounded to learn that a stranger had entered the complex and as they tried to stand, Yonti shot both of them in the forehead.

Right, all four Kaput, so time to get all the girls out of here, he considered as he made his way back to the dormitory. He instructed the girls to collect all their belongings and wait until he returned.

'Right Kiki, it's time to leave,' he said as he opened the cupboard door in the passage.

'Follow me,' he instructed.

They made their way to the dormitory and he instructed the girls to follow him. As they made their way towards the Jeep, he started to doubt himself. Maybe, I could have merely called the police and had these bastards arrested.

Then again, as is usually the case, some civil libertarian judge would merely give these bastards a short-term sentence, or a slap on the wrist. Need to rid the world of people like these.

He Googled a children's Shelter in Oregon and discovered "The Haven", a shelter for homeless Women and Children in Portland. An ideal place to hand over the children into community care, so he pointed the Jeep in that direction and pulled up outside the complex twenty minutes later.

He turned to face the girls.

'Right you young ladies, you are safe and free now.' 'I want you to knock on the door, tell them you are homeless, and ask for help.' 'At some point, I am sure that the police will be contacted, so I want you all to promise that you will not mention me at all, merely focus on the trauma that you have experienced.' 'Merely think of me as your savior and friend.' 'Tell the police that you have been living on the street, because I don't want them to ever find me, nor the place where you had been held prisoner.'

'Good luck girls.'

He watched as they made their way to the front door. A couple of minutes later an elderly lady opened the door and welcomed them in.

'Right Kiki, I need to get you home, so let's get moving.' 'Your parents will be very happy to see you.'

He pulled up at Kiki's home, gave her a high five, and watched as her mother opened the door and burst into tears, hugging her. Kiki turned, waved, and blew him a kiss as he drove off.

Two days later, he warily made his way up the stairs and onto the deck and was greeted by Claire. She hugged and kissed him passionately. Moments later the twins ran into his arms hugging him.

'Thank you Yonti, for what you have done.' 'Dushenka called me and asked me to thank you from the bottom of her heart.' 'Kiki has also passed on her thanks, and told her parents that you saved her life.' 'The good news is, that they have had her medically checked, and it is conclusive that she was not raped.'

Yonti slumped onto the sofa and was sound asleep minutes later.

Chapter 7

Paris

France

Yonti made his way onto the deck and turned to look at the green fields basking in the midday sun on yet another beautiful summer day in Lauterbrunnen. Albeit that the temperature was a modest sixteen degrees centigrade, it felt a lot warmer, when the display on his mobile phone suddenly lit up, announcing an incoming call from the French Police. The caller instructed Yonti to stand by for a call from Chef d'Escadron Petit.

The rank of Chef d'Escadron is the equivalent of a military rank of Major in the French Police, in charge of a local police unit. Moments later the call was patched through.

'Bonjour Monsieur Rafael.'

'Bonjour Chef d'Escadron Petit, and congratulations on your promotion.' 'Long time, no speak Chef.'

Yonti realized that his old friend was using the undercover name of Rafael that he had used during his time at the CIA. He was known to everyone in the firm by that name and those that he had befriended only knew him by that undercover name.

'Well Rafael, I am afraid that this is not a courtesy call.' 'I have some disturbing news.'

Yonti froze for an instant and braced himself for bad news, a feeling of dread and despair overcame him, as he immediately realized that his family may well have been caught up in the riots that engulfed Paris. His beloved wife Claire and the twins had gone to Paris to catch up with her parents and to spend some quality time together.

He listened intently to what Chef Petit had to say.

'As you know, the riots in Paris flared up suddenly and started after the shooting of the seventeen-year-old boy namely, Nahek Merzouk.' 'He is of Moroccan and Algerian descent.' 'He was shot by the police at a routine traffic stop in Nanterre, a suburb of Paris.' 'The riots are widespread across towns like Paris, Lille, Toulouse, Marseille, Pau and Lyons.'

'From what I have managed to find out, your family were caught up in the riots as they suddenly spread.' 'Apparently, they were trying to make their way back to their hotel and were separated.' 'The police use several face recognition software tools predominately to identify bad guys, and I identified Claire through a few of the interfaces that we use, such as the CompreFace and the Firstface recognition software.'

'Our intelligence and CCTV footage have confirmed that your wife got separated from your two sons in the chaos, as she tried to shield two elderly people accompanying her from the violence.' 'It appears that your two young boys accompanying her have just vanished, so we are deeply concerned that they may have been taken hostage by a group of radical youths.' 'We have been monitoring these radical youths for some time, and of concern, is that they kidnap young males and train them to become radical.'

'So, you have no idea where the boys are at this time?' 'Is that correct Chef?'

'Oui Rafael, that is correct.' 'I have arranged for a helicopter to pick you up within the next three hours and fly you directly to my headquarters here in Paris where I will meet you.' 'The Swiss authorities have given me clearance to enter into their airspace, so get ready.'

Yonti immediately called Claire, however, there was no reply, so he tried both his son's mobile numbers and there was no response from them either, then he tried both Claire's parent's numbers, and still no response.

Yonti called his neighbor, Herr Torkel Kaufmann, and mentioned that his wife and twin sons had been caught up in the riots in Paris and that the boys had been separated from their mother and were missing, thus he needed to urgently go to Paris. He asked Torkel to tend and milk his two cows and keep the milk for himself until he returned. Shortly after his call to Torkel, his mobile phone rang with an incoming call from a landline.

'Yonti, the twins are missing,' shouted Claire hysterically, above the deafening noise of the rioters.

'Yes, I know Claire, my old friend Bastienne Petit has just called me and told me.' 'I have been trying to call you, as well as the boys and your parents and there has been no answer.'

Claire was crying uncontrollably and he could hardly make out what she was saying.

'Claire, listen to me, are you and your parents OK?'

'Yes we are however, my father was hit by a Molotov cocktail that someone had thrown in our direction and has burns to his body.' 'He has been taken to hospital by ambulance.'

'My mother has also been injured due to someone throwing an object in our direction and has also been taken to hospital as well.' 'I have no idea of their condition because I am searching for the twins.' 'I have to find my boys, she shouted,' hysterically.

'Claire, try to make your way safely back to the hotel because I am leaving for Paris shortly.' 'Bastienne identified you through the face recognition software they use, and told me that the boys were separated from you, as you tried to shield your parents from the rioters.' 'He has arranged for a helicopter to pick me up in the next couple of hours and fly me to Paris, so I will see you later.' 'I want you to be careful and I will search for the boys as soon as I get there.'

The line went dead. Yonti tried to redial the number, however, it did not ring.

For fucks sake, he shouted in frustration.

He made his way into the bedroom and opened the safe, removed his beloved Glock, silencer, a box of ammunition, and an Emerson's Specwar Custom Knife, then packed it all, including his tactical gear as well as a change of clothing into his USA military canvas duffle backpack. He reminded himself to pack the Kufi hat and Hijab just in case he may need it, then locked the door and made his way onto the front porch, sat and waited.

A while later he dialled Barnaby Heathcott on a secure line.

'Hello Director.' 'I am calling because I need your help, sir.' 'As you know there are riots in numerous cities across France.' 'Claire and my twin sons went to Paris to meet up with her parents to spend some time together.' 'They have been caught up in the rioting and the twins were separated from Claire, so as of now, I have no idea where they are,' he said.

'My good friend Bastienne Petit of the French police, called me a short while ago and notified me that he identified Claire on the face recognition software that they use, and watched how she and the twins got separated in the riot, so I am reaching out to you Director to please try to hone in to what is happening in Paris.' 'I need your help to find my sons.'

'Yes, Yonti, I am aware of what's happening in Paris, because I got a call from Chef d'Escadron Petit a short while ago requesting our assistance.' 'I have a team of people currently reviewing all the satellite footage we have of Paris, and in particular, the area that they were in when the riot broke out.' 'We will do our best to try and trace your boys, and I hope that I can give you some guidance shortly.'

'I will call you as soon as I have something concrete Yonti.'

Thank you, Director.' 'I appreciate all the help I can get right now.'

Barnaby sat back in his chair and reminded himself that he owed Yonti a favor because he had saved his wife and sons who had been kidnapped by radicals in Oregon, so he needed to repay his debt and help him find his twin sons.

The chopper arrived a few hours later, and Yonti introduced himself to the pilot as he jumped into the front seat.

'Bonjour Monsieur, my name is Rafael.'

He purposely used the undercover name he had always used as a CIA agent because that is the name that Bastienne had known him by during the time he worked for the firm.

'Bonjour Monsieur Rafael, my name is Étienne Defour.' 'Chef d'Escadron Petit has instructed me to fly you directly to his headquarters, however, we will need to stop in Zurich to get some fuel.'

Four hours later the helicopter landed on a landing pad on the roof of a building, which Yonti believed was the headquarters where Chef Petit's police unit was based. He grabbed his gear from the rear seat and bid the pilot farewell, then made his way towards a waiting police officer.

'Bonjour Monsieur Rafael, follow me please,' said the officer.

A short while later, he found himself in the operations room surrounded by a bevy of television sets and police dressed in battle fatigues. Chef Petit tapped him lightly on the shoulder and summoned him to follow him to his office.

'Bonjour Rafael, sorry we are not meeting under better circumstances.'

Bastienne fired up his laptop.

'Right this is what we have from our surveillance cameras as well as the images sent to us by the CIA, which shows your sons being pushed away from your wife.' 'Your wife did not immediately notice it, as she was tending to the two elderly people who had been injured in the riot.' 'It appears that they were trying to make their way back to their hotel when they were caught up in the riot.'

He played the footage of the incident, relaying it onto a monitor on the wall, which clearly showed the twins being shoved away from their mother towards a crowd of militant youths on the fringe of the riot.

They quickly surrounded the boys and appeared to be manhandled them down a side street toward a waiting vehicle. Bastienne then zoomed in on footage of the vehicle as it made a hasty retreat towards Saint-Denis, a suburb seventeen miles on the outskirts of Paris.

He switched to the satellite footage that he received from the CIA and followed the Citroen on the monitor.

At ground level, the suburb or 'banlieue' of Saint-Denis, France's new and extraordinary state of emergency laws, were enacted after the Islamist carnage, as the local population was confronted with a very different reality.

Saint-Denis received international attention days after the previous two Paris attacks when accused mastermind Abdelhamid Abaaoud and two accomplices died in a bloody shootout with police at an apartment in the suburb. Violence and dissents have long defined the banlieues that form the outer ring of north-eastern Paris. Derogatively known as slums, they are dominated by mostly Muslim migrants.

The area is rife with crime and drugs, separated geographically and culturally from the cosmopolitan center. The housing projects of Saint-Denis are regarded by some as incubators for radical Islam. At the bustling center of Saint-Denis, men in Jellabiyas and skullcaps congregate on corners. Women wear a variety of hijabs or none. Halal butcheries butt up against African barbers and Islamic bookstores.

Street vendors sell nuts and kebabs from mobile stalls. The soul-searching, following the attacks has seen a flood of journalists pour into the suburb, seeking answers, as to why France has been the target of Islamist radicals twice in a year. The attention has riled residents who say they are under siege by the media, and accuse the fourth estate of being determined to link Muslims with terrorism. Islamic Cultural Centre president, Zouheir Ababou is indignant over what he calls, "provocative media" which he claims has no evidence that jihadis come from the banlieues.

'Right, this is where these bastards have taken the boys and where they are at the moment,' said Bastienne as he pointed to the monitor.

'This is a scary and dangerous place, so we will need to be very careful Rafael.' 'From what we can see, it appearsthat these people have taken your boys to a derelict homemade tin structure located alongside a bridge that trams travel over, which is also next to the rail line near the La Plaine Stade de Frace-Saint Denis-Aubervilliers, a station on the B line of the Réseau Express Rêgional rapid transit line.'

Ironically the Stade de France, the national stadium of France is located nearby in Saint-Denis and is used by football and rugby sporting teams for international competitions.

'It appears that they have taken your sons to a shack right alongside the bridge, so we will need to abseil a few meters down the side of the bridge using the railing to secure the rope and land right next to the shack, then free the boys.' 'No time to waste my friend because they will most likely relocate the boy's tomorrow morning to another location, so let's get moving.'

Bastienne had chosen six of his most trusted officers. Men who had been on many missions with him in the past and shared the same vision and values as he did.

The driver parked the 4 x 4 all-terrain Panhard VBL, Light Armoured Vehicle on a side road away from prying eyes near the bridge. They unpacked their gear, and Bastienne positioned two special tactical unit operatives on the road at each end of the bridge and instructed the other two to follow him. He told his men to remain hidden from any passing foot or vehicle traffic. Luckily there was no traffic at that hour.

Rafael glanced at his wristwatch, noting that it was zero three hundred hours, so a good time to conduct an operation. Bastienne instructed the other two officers to be ready for action. They turned on their night-vision goggles, tied ropes onto the railing of the bridge, and silently fast-roped down, landing near the shack. Moments later Bastienne, Rafael, and the two operatives silently made their way toward the tin shanty that they had identified on the satellite footage.

They moved quietly in the darkness, like leopards stalking their prey, and stopped outside what appeared to be a door, and listened for any movement inside the shack, before opening the door. As soon as they entered, their night-vision goggled allowed them to be able to see in the dark. They chose not to use their Princeton Tactical Headlamps because the bright two-hundred-lumen LED lights would illuminate the room, and the sudden brightness of light would alert other people in the shanty town that there was some sort of a problem. The occupants were taken by surprise and the Special Force officers quickly secured the room and whispered instructions to the two occupants to lie face down on the floor. Rafael quickly identified the twins lying in the corner with their hands and feet bound by ropes.

The boys were petrified. All they could see were dark shadows moving silently around the room.

'It's your dad, boys,' he whispered as he cut them loose.

He then removed the duct tape stuck around their mouths, hugged and kissed them, and instructed the boys to be quiet and follow the two Special Force officers. He watched as the two officers led the boys out of the shack and headed toward the armored vehicle.

As soon as they were out of sight, Bastienne scattered a few plastic zip-lock bags filled with cocaine around the room, making it seem like the shack belonged to a drug dealer.

He had cleansed the bags of any fingerprints earlier ensuring that it could not be traced back to himself or anyone else, and watched as Rafael shot the two occupants in the back of the head. The only sound audible was a faint popping sound coming from the silencer.

'Like your work.' 'Just like old times Monsieur Rafael.' 'You really should come and work for us my friend.'

'Oui Chef, I have to admit, I miss the action.'

They quickly made their way back to the Armoured Vehicle and the driver pointed it in the direction of police headquarters. Bastienne instructed the driver to drop Rafael and the boys off at the hotel.

He placed his arms around his sons, hugged and kissed them again.

'Your mother has been worried sick about you guys.'

Rafael bid Basitenne and the Special Force officer's farewell as the driver pulled up at the Royal Paris Hotel situated near the Louvre, and quickly made his way into the reception area. He summoned the night manager and notified him that he was bringing his children back to the hotel and that he needed to search for his missing wife who got caught up in the riot. The night manager recognized the twins and was happy to give him a key to the room, wishing him well in the search for his wife. He promised to keep an eye on the camera footage in the corridor leading to their room.

'I want you guys to stay in the room and not open the door for anyone.' 'I am going to find your mother, so please just stay here and wait.'

He removed the Kufi hat and Hijab that he had packed from his duffle backpack because he believed that the riot was most likely orchestrated by some radical Muslim elements. He needed it to ensure that he assimilated well into the crowd, then made his way downstairs and headed towards the area where the riots were taking place.

He arrived on the fringe of the riot thirty minutes later and scanned the carnage caused by the rioters. They had randomly chosen parked cars, set them on fire, and threw Molotov cocktails through broken shop windows setting buildings on fire. He watched as the police charged down the street, batons and guns at the ready as they confronted the crowd, so he took refuge in a doorway and waited until they were well down the road. Civil disorder was evident everywhere and the street looked like a war zone. It seemed that the entire city had gone up in flames, so he walked some distance behind the police line, ensuring that he remained safe albeit that he was constantly dodging objects thrown by rioters at the police.

He followed the police as they rounded a corner on Rue Royale chasing the rioters down the street when he caught a glimpse of a lady huddled up in a doorway taking shelter from the violence through the haze of smoke and realized that he had found his beloved wife. He recognized the dress she was wearing, quickly ran over the road, and was alongside her moments later. He helped her to her feet, noticing the blood trickling from a wound on the side of her head, so he used the Hijab to wipe the blood from her face and embraced her tightly.

She was crying uncontrollably and buried her face against his chest.

'Yonti, I have to find the boys,' she shouted as the tears streamed down her cheeks.

He gently pushed her away from his body and stared at her blood-stained face, then cupped the palms of his hands and placed them on her cheeks.

'You need to find the boys Yonti,' she shouted.

'Claire, I have found them, and they are safe.'

'Oh thank the Good Lord.'

They made their way back to the hotel, careful to avoid the ongoing violence. An ambulance crew stopped them and rendered first aid. They cleaned the wound and put a bandage around her head, making her look like a wounded soldier.

As he opened the door, the twins ran into her arms. She hugged and kissed them passionately, then looked at Yonti.

'How did you know where to find me?'

'Truthfully, I had no idea of where to look, and followed the line of police as they chased after the rioters when I luckily noticed you huddled up lying in the doorway,' 'I recognized the dress you were wearing, so it was a very lucky break.'

'Yonti, I was beaten and kicked by a thug.' 'He hit me on the head with what appeared to be a piece of wood and luckily he stopped when he noticed the police gathering at the end of the street, so I was extremely lucky he did not rape me.'

'Could you recognize him if you saw him, Claire?'

'Yes, however, he had covered his head with a scarf, but I caught a glimpse of a scar he had on his right cheek and he had a bright yellow hoodie on with the words, "Allah est grand" printed on the front and word "Châtiment" on the back.' 'As you know this means "Allah is Great" and "Retribution," so I hope that Bastienne can identify this thug.'

'OK, I am going to get Bastienne to try and identify this bastard, and I promise that when I find him, I will punish him.' 'As I understand it your parents are in hospital so I suggest that you best call them and see how they are.'

Yonti called Bastienne on his mobile phone.

'Bonjour Chef, I managed to find Claire, so all is well'. 'I know that you have your hands full, however, I am hoping that you have footage of the riot in Rue Royale.' 'Claire has identified the thug that beat her up.' 'This bastard had a bright yellow hoodie on with the words Allah est grand on the front and Châtiment printed on the back of it.'

'I need to find this bastard because Claire said that if were not for the police about to charge down the street, he would have raped her, so I need even the score.'

'Thank goodness Claire is fine.' 'OK, laisse-moi faire.' OK, leave it to me.

Bastienne sent an armored vehicle to pick Yonti up. The driver made several detours to avoid rioters, eventually pulling up at his headquarters. Claire's parents were released from the hospital and were reunited with her and the twins at the hotel, shortly after Yonti had left the hotel.

'Bonjour Rafael,' he said using the name he knew him by, extending his hand in a greeting.

'That was a lucky break Chef, and thank the almighty Claire was not badly injured.'

Bastienne ushered him into his office, fired up his laptop, and beamed the footage onto the monitor on the wall.

'This is the footage of Rue Royale, and if you look closely, you will see the bastard in the yellow hoodie, manhandling Claire, then he seems to hit her with a piece of wood.' 'Look closely Rafael and you will see him drag Claire into the doorway of a shop and it seems like this piece of shit was about to rape her, then he suddenly turns, sees the police contingent, heading his way, and makes a hasty getaway down the street.'

'The police had assembled at the corner, and were waiting for reinforcements, before confronting the rioters, so he either got scared because he would have been caught or on instinct, decided to re-join the rioters at the end of the street.'

Rafael asked Bastienne to rewind the footage and hone in on the bastard's face. Please freeze it there, he said as his face came into view. The scar on his right cheek face was visible. Right got you. Now I am going to hunt you down and kill you, you fucking piece of shit, he thought.

He rang Claire and told her to remain in the hotel and wait for his call, which may take a few days. As he looked at the footage of the riot, he ran his hand down the back of his pants, feeling his beloved Glock fitted with the silencer, then checked to ensure that he had four clips of ammunition in his pocket. Doing this always gave him comfort.

'Right Chef, I need a favor, please.' 'I know that you have a huge problem on your hands right now and need to focus on all the hot spots, however, if possible can you ask one of your officers to keep track of him and follow his every move.' 'I need to find this prick and punish him.'

'Oui Monsieur, already done, because it appears that he is one of the main instigators, so I also want to meet him.'

Bastienne set up a laptop in his office and allowed Rafael full access to all the live CCTV footage that the police were monitoring of the riots. He remained at Bastienne's headquarters for the remainder of the day and followed every move that the guy in the yellow hoodie made on the CCTV footage.

The police eventually got control of the situation a few days later, as the rioters dispersed and law and order was restored. The council started clearing up the debris and streets.He remained at Bastienne's headquarters and followed every move that the guy in the yellow hoodie made on the CCTV footage that the police had.

He tried as best he could to follow the yellow hooded man as he trolled through hours of footage of the riot, and noticed that he seemed to grab some sleep whenever possible in various doorways each evening, then resumed the violent confrontation with police every so often. He had somehow managed to avoid being one of the hundreds of protestors that police had arrested during the riots, so clearly he was gutter smart. It was impossible to track his every move as there was limited footage of where he was at any given time, however as the riots drew to an end, it seemed like he was headed towardCour des miracles ("court of miracles"), a French term used when referring to the slum districts of Paris. It appeared that he may live in a migrant camp in the La Chapelle area of Paris, where it has been reported that around four hundred people live in tents in squalid conditions.

'Right Chef, thank you for allowing me to stay and monitor this bastard. It's time for me to find this prick and even the score.'

Right, this is where I will start looking, thought Yonti. He drove toward La Chapelle ensuring that he avoided any police checkpoints along the way and parked in a parking lot neat some restaurants, then wandered around the neighborhood searching for the guy with the yellow hoodie.

He could possibly still be wearing it because the migrants living in squatter camps do not have money to buy clothing, so he may well be wearing his favorite piece of clothing. He spent all day searching for the bastard and called it a day around twenty-one hundred hours.

He was back early the next morning and drove to the fringe of the town and parked. He wandered around the neighborhood, walking up and down the streets and alleyways, however to no avail.

He eventually made his way up a flight of stairs and onto the rooftop of a low-rise building overlooking the camp. He positioned himself at the edge of the building overlooking the town, waited, and watched for several hours, eventually considering that this bastard may not even be there.

It was almost eighteen hundred hours and he felt drowsy from a lack of sleep when he suddenly caught a glimpse of a person in a yellow hoodie making his way out of the camp toward the center of the town. He quickly made his way downstairs and followed the person at a distance as he made his way toward a couple of restaurants, and watched as headed down a laneway, rummaging through garbage bins searching for scraps of food.

Yonti waited at the entrance to the alleyway and a short while later the man headed in his direction. He stopped to ask for some money to buy food and Yonti noticed the scar on his right cheek. Got the right person, he thought.

'Are you hungry Monsieur'?

'Oui, I am starving.' 'No job, no money, no food, no clothing, and nowhere to stay.' 'Please help me.'

'OK, Follow me.'

Yonti knew that he had to coax him away from the neighborhood and get him to a place where he could even the score without anybody noticing.

'So where were you born Monsieur, and what is your name'?

'I'm from Morocco, and my name is Hazim Ghulam.' 'I have been here for two years living in the camp over there,' he said pointing in the direction of the squatter camp in the distance.

'Well, I may be able to offer you a job to clean up an old warehouse that I have just bought.' 'Let's take a drive and I will show you.'

They jumped into the car that Yonti had hired and he stopped along the way at a bakery. He got him something to eat, then drove towards a derelict warehouse on the outskirts of Paris. He purposely made small talk along the way to put the man at ease and drove to the same warehouse that he and Bastienne had used in the past. This was where they shot and killed a terrorist who had planned to kill the Israeli Ambassador.

Yonti knew that he had to be careful not to raise any suspicion and chatted about Morocco as well as the hard time that Hazim had trying to find a job, ensuring that the man felt comfortable. Hazim was not taking any notice of where they were headed. Thirty minutes later he turned into the open doors of the warehouse and parked well inside, ensuring that they were not visible to any prying eyes.

'Right this is the place.' 'As you can see it needs a thorough clean up,' he said as they exited the car.

Hazim looked at the mess in the warehouse, and as he turned to look at Yonti, he stared directly down the barrel of the Glock.

'Right, you don't know me, however, I know you.' 'You are one of the bastards that rioted in the city and beat up my wife in a doorway with a piece of wood, then just as you were about to rape her, you noticed the police congregating at the corner getting ready to charge, when you changed your mind.'

'No not me he shouted.'

'Yes you, here's the proof,' he said as he played the footage on his mobile phone.

'So, you beat up my wife, and your mates kidnapped my twin sons, so now you will face my civil justice, you piece of shit.'

He pleaded his innocence and begged not to be shot.

'Get down on your knees and put your hands behind your head.' 'You see, I am the prosecutor, judge, and jury, and I Yonti Barr, sentence you to death.'

He aimed the barrel at his forehead and pulled the trigger. The world is a better place without scum like you, he thought.

Thirty minutes later he made his way down the passage in the hotel and opened the door.

Claire jumped up from the bed and ran into his arms. He hugged and kissed her then picked up both twins up and hugged them.

'Thank God you are back Yonti.'

'Well Claire, I found the bastard that attacked you and have taken care of it.'

She understood that to mean that he had eliminated him, and did not question him about it.

'How's your parents?'

'Good thanks, they left to go to the French countryside and visit Gordes (Provence), La Roque-Gageac (Périgord), Riquewihr (Alsace), Yvoire (Haute-Savoie).' 'I hope that I pronounced that correctly.' 'I hope to spend the last few days I have with them in peace.'

Yonti had purposely avoided meeting with her parents because her father was most disappointed when she told him that she was going to marry him. A lifelong Protestant, that attended church every Sunday, he did not like Yonti at all, because he believed that CIA agents like him, eliminate people at will, and commit cardinal sins daily. He believed that people like Yonti should be punished for the sins that they had committed, and in his opinion, he believed that Yonti had killed people. Albeit that Claire had a good understanding of what he did as a CIA agent, she compartmentalized what she knew about him and chose not to think of, nor judge him, when he was called upon to get rid of the bad guys. She knew, but pushed any thoughts out of her mind and she tried as best she could, to convince her father that he acts within the law, however, he did not believe her.

 'I need to get back home Claire, so say hello to your mom for me.' 'I asked Torkel Kaufmann to look after the cows until I return, so I will need to get back ASAP.'

Chapter 8

Zurich

Switzerland

Yonti's bank manager invited him to meet with him at the bank's headquarters in Zurich to discuss some investment options, so he drove the seventy-two miles, which took around two hours. He stopped along the way at the small town of Zofingen, at the western tip of Aargau canton, once the seat of the Frohburgs, famed for its beautifully intact Old Town with gardens along the former surrounding walls, and the Heiternplatz square at the top of Zofingen's "own" hill. It is the venue for the annual Heitere Open Air festival and the old town of Zofingen is well-preserved with twenty-two active fountains. The most famous of these is the Niklaus Thut Fountain, which was created in 1894.

Having met with the bank manager and discussed various investment opportunities, he drove to The Grand Hotel, a stately building dating back to 1899 that offered sweeping views of the Alps and Lake Zurich, and made his way into the foyer. This reminded him of a mission he conducted as a CIA agent, using the alias of Aaron Armando, when he met with Victor Portnorsky, the Russian President Pushkin's personal security chief, and took possession of a USB stick of video footage of a meeting between Pushkin and the Chinese Leader, Xiu Jaoping at a cocktail party hosted by The Three Sixty Degrees Group. Brings back fond memories of a successful mission he considered, as he looked at the air vent where he had hidden the mini camera that recorded the conversation. He wondered whether the camera was still in there.

Yonti made his way into the lounge and found a seat against the back wall with an excellent view of the room. His eyes scanned the room as he normally did, and focused on the four people seated in the corner close to where he was seated. The room was filled with people chatting and he noticed two gentlemen seated close to the table of four, however, he considered that they were obviously alone and merely killing time. Moments later he caught a glance at what appeared to be a wad of notes neatly stacked inside an attaché case, just as one of the men turned it around to face the two people seated opposite him. This must be payment for services rendered, possible payment for drugs, weapons, or some other illegal activity, he thought.

He pretended to be texting a message to someone, however, he was recording what he had just seen on his mobile phone, and zoomed in on the people seated at the table, then sat back in his chair and wondered what they could be up to. Conscious not to stare in their direction, he made it appear as if he was reading something on his mobile phone, all the while he was recording what he had seen.

They were bent over, having a serious conversation, and speaking in hushed tones that appeared to get a little heated at times.

He replayed the video on his mobile phone, wondering what that could have been about, then zoomed in on the images of the men and tried to get a better look at their faces. Not sure who they were and what this could be about, he thought as he viewed the footage of the people seated around the table more closely. Two of the people appeared to be of Korean descent and the other two were of Middle Eastern appearance.

He picked up the local newspaper and pretended to be reading it when a man suddenly appeared and seated himself opposite him.

'Bonjour Monsieur Rafael Dujon.' 'Hope you remember me?'

Yonti immediately got suspicious when he heard the name Rafael mentioned because he instinctively knew that it would relate to the CIA.

'Oui, I remember you.' 'You are Herr Hans Vogel, the head of the Swiss Police.' 'Also seen you on TV numerous times.' 'We met briefly once before at the Zermatt Lodge Hotel when you needed me to do a favor for you, and get rid of two Neo Nazis.'

'Yes, that is correct.' 'I never had the opportunity to thank you, so thank you for getting rid of our problem.' 'I do appreciate it, as well as the quick and efficient manner in which you took care of it.'

'So how did you know where to find me?'

'Your ex-boss, Herr Heathcott told me where to find you.'

'Oh, is that so.'

Yonti wondered how the CIA was able to follow his every move, and how on earth they would know exactly where he was at any given time of the day. This made him feel most uncomfortable. Surely, they should be focused on far more important issues, rather than keeping tabs on him.

Crime in Switzerland is mainly restricted to petty crime such as theft of motor vehicles and bicycles.

There have been numerous cases of more severe types of crime, such as rape which has increased by around fifty-three percent over the previous year, and criminal pornography offenses which have increased by fifty-six percent. Amazingly drug-related offences decreased by seven percent.

'I have another problem, and hope that you will be willing to assist.'

'The CIA has been tracking two of the four people seated at the table in the corner and have asked for our assistance.' 'Two of them are North Korean, and whilst they are unsure who the other two are, they believe that they may be some Islamic fundamentalist's intent on getting a dirty bomb to destroy Israel.'

'The CIA has asked us to get involved because they intercepted a communication on the wire from the North Koreans, which was sent to the two Islamic Fundamentalists seated at the table, suggesting that they meet here in Zurich, in the hope that it would not raise any suspicion.' 'Your ex-boss notified me that the two Koreans are Won-Shik D-hyun and the other is Hak-Kun Min-ji. The names of the other two are unknown to the CIA.'

'What we have discovered is, that the two people of two Middle-Eastern appearances are, Bahiri Yasdani and Pridoni Yasdani.' 'Both are Iranian and are brothers.' 'They are most likely meeting here in Zurich, not only because they think it will not raise any suspicion, but because they have opened a bank account at Crédit Bank Suisse, and intend possibly depositing large sums of money that can be hidden from authorities.'

'Barnaby suggested that I contact you for assistance, because we in Switzerland are not used to dealing with dangerous people like these, and because they are meeting, in our country.' 'He called me a little earlier and told me where to find you.'

'So, he knew exactly where you could find me?'

'Sure did.'

Yonti was so engrossed in the conversation with the head of the Swiss Police, and focused on the four people seated around the corner table, that he did not notice a man enter and take a seat close to where the four were seated.

'So Herr Vogel what are you asking me to do?'

He placed a folder on the table.

'This is what Director Heathcott sent me,' he said, as he handed a folder to Yonti.

'Barnaby mentioned that you were the best agent he ever had, and if anyone can find out what these people are up to, it would be you.' 'It's all in there, including my contact number.' 'Please consider getting involved Monsieur Rafael, and feel free to call me at any time.'

With that, Herr Vogel stood, took his hand, and bid him farewell.

He sat back and wondered why Barnaby kept on getting him involved. Surely, he has other capable agents that can do the job. Doesn't Barnaby realize that I am retired, and whilst I do miss the thrill of the cut and chase as well as getting rid of the bad guys, I'm not interested.

He read the dossier on the North Koreans and was disturbed by what he had just read, closed the folder, and sat back contemplating whether he should get involved. As he looked around the room, he was surprised to see his old friend Joseph Diamond seated at the table next to the Koreans and the two Iranians. Joseph merely bowed and tilted his head slightly as he made eye contact with Yonti.

Yonti instinctively knew that his friend from Mossad, whom had not seen for some time, was most likely recording the conversation taking place at the table next to him, which confirmed the seriousness of what he had just read in the dossier. A while later the four stood, shook hands and Yonti noticed that one of the Iranians had passed the attaché case onto one of the North Koreans. As the four made their way out of the lounge, Yonti noticed that the two gentlemen seated at separate tables near the window, also stood and seemed to be following the four that were heading toward the exit. Seems like my friend from Mossad has two agents following them, he thought.

Joseph Diamond made his way over to his table.

'Hello Rafael,' he said, using the name that he knew him by. 'Let's see, it has been some time since I last saw you, my friend.' 'So what brings you here?'

'Well I should ask you the same, however, it's clear to me that you seated yourself close to the Koreans and the Iranians, and that you were probably recording their conversation.' 'Then as they left, you had two agents follow and tail them.' 'How am I doing so far?'

'Still as sharp as a tack I see.' 'I noticed that you met with Herr Vogel, Chief of the Swiss Police as well, so how am I doing?'

'Yep pretty good for an old fellow.' 'Seems like we have a problem, my friend.'

'Yep, we certainly have a problem,' said Joseph.

'So I assume that Herr Vogel brought you up to date on the danger facing Israel, France, the UK, Saudi Arabia, and the USA?'

'Yes, he did.'

'We in Mossad have been tracking brothers Bahiri and Pridoni Yasdani, the two Iranians for a long time, and the CIA has kept us in the loop with everything they have on the two Koreans.' 'We know exactly who they are and what they intend to do.' 'We have also been tracking the North Koreans namely, Monsieur Won-Shik D-hyun and Hak-Kun Min-ji, for some time as well.' 'They are firmly in our sights.'

'The two Iranians hail from Tehran and may well be involved with The Government of the Islamic Republic of Iran known simply as Nezām, who intends to use the mini-nukes that they are going to source from North Koreans, in the countries mentioned earlier.' 'These mini-nukes are understood to be around a foot long and about eight inches in width, so easily hidden, hence their meeting with the North Koreans.'

'As you know Iran is an Islamic theocracy, with a Supreme Leader who sets the tone and direction of domestic and foreign policies.' 'He exerts political control over a system dominated by clerics, who shadow every major function of the state.' 'The Supreme Leader is also the commander in chief of the armed forces and commander of the Islamic Revolutionary Guard Corps, and he alone can declare war or peace.'

'The former Iranian President Mahmoud Ahmadinejad, called for Israel's destruction in 2005, when paraphrasing a line from the founding father of the Islamic Republic, Ayatollah Ruhollah Khomeini.' 'Quite literally, Ahmadinejad said, "The occupying regime of Jerusalem must disappear from the page of time," which has been interpreted as calling for Israel to be wiped off the map.'

'They intend using their nukes in the countries that have supported America militarily, and they also intend destroying the Saudi Arabian oil depots in Jeddah & the Ghawar Oil Field which are located approximately sixty-two miles from Dhahran and about one hundred and twenty-two miles east of Riyadh in the Al Hasa Province.' 'Ghawar is the world's biggest conventional onshore oil field, both in reserves and daily output, producing Arabian Light Crude, contributing to more than half of Saudi Arabia's cumulative crude production as well as the biggest source of associated gas.'

'Their intention in destroying the oil depot in Jeddah and Ghawar is to cause a major oil shortage worldwide, which will cause mass panic in the western world and put the entire world on notice that they can strike, when, where, and if ever they choose.'

'So Rafael, as you can see, if we don't neutralize this threat, Israel and the world at large will be that deep in the shit, we may not be able to recover for decades.' 'I'm sure, that the folder that Herr Vogel handed you, may well have explained some of the issues that the world is facing, however, we in Mossad have discovered far more of the problem, which I have just disclosed to you.'

'I hope that you will consider helping us solve this problem, my friend.' 'I could use someone like you,' said Joseph.

He raised his eyebrows and tilted his head without answering. Deep in thought, his gaze fixed on a chair, as he sat staring at nothing in particular, his mind caught between getting involved, doing what he loved and what he was trained to do, or remaining in a state of numbness, tending to the farm as well as doing his daily chores. Claire won't be happy at all if I decide to get involved with the CIA again and I will need to think carefully before I commit, albeit that I miss the cut and chase. One part of me is enjoying the laid-back lifestyle of not needing to kill the bad guys, he thought.

'Hey Rafael, are you still with me.'

'Yes, I will consider it, however, I need to consult with my wife and twin sons before I give you an answer, so I will let you know soon.'

'Oh, by the way, how's married life?' Asked Joseph.

'Good thanks.' 'I married Claire and settled in Kandersteg, a small town in Switzerland.'

'Yes I know, your ex-boss told me.'

For fucks sake, what else does Barnaby know about me? Does he know how many times a week I make love to my wife, or how many times a week I take a shit, he thought.

Just then Joseph's mobile rang.

'What do you have for me, Habibi?' Asked Joseph, using an Arabic phrase.

'I see, so they are there right now.' 'Right stay put and keep an eye on them.' 'I will see you soon.'

Rising he said, 'Are you in Rafael, because these two Iranians are at a gay bar called "Seventh Heaven on Earth" located on Spitalgasse in the city?'

Instinctively, he followed Joseph as he exited the Hotel, and ran his hand over the back of his pants ensuring that his beloved Glock was exactly where it should be, then checked his pocket, making sure that the four clips of ammunition were also still there. He always did that out of habit. It somehow gave him comfort. They jumped into the car that Joseph had hired and twenty minutes later, both held hands as they entered the bar. They needed to assimilate into the environment and appear to be two gay guys in love.

'Could have found someone better looking than you,' he said, looking at Joseph as they made their way toward the end of the bar.

'Fuck me, your mother must have run a mile when you popped out,' whispered Rafael as they ordered a round of drinks.

Joseph scanned the crowded bar as they entered, noticing his agents seated on either side of the two Iranians, who appeared to have made the acquaintance of two transvestites. They ordered a bottle of Dom Pérignon champagne and toasted each other. Both watched as the two Iranians fondled the two transvestites and a while later, one of them, who Joseph identified as Pridoni Yasdani, summoned the manager to arrange for a room for himself and his friend. The two Mossad agents seated alongside the Iranians overheard the manager say that they could use room twenty on the first floor. He also mentioned that they could rent the room twenty one next door if they wanted, which has an inter-leading door, just in case they wish to spice things up a little.

Pridoni told the manager that they all preferred to be in one bed, and that would be spicy enough.

Joseph leaned over and whispered, 'Well my darling, isn't it amazing, when these Muslims are away from prying eyes, they consume alcohol like no tomorrow, and who knows, maybe even eat pork.'

'Clearly, these brothers are cut from the same cloth and like transvestites.' 'Nothing like keeping it in the family, as they say,' continued Joseph.

Joseph summoned the manager and asked for a room on the first floor, possibly room twenty-one, as he had used it previously and felt that it was his lucky number. The manager confirmed that the room was available and that they could make their way upstairs whenever they were ready. The two Mossad agents seated on either side of the Iranians heard the manager refer to an inter-leading door. How convenient he thought, because that will make things a lot easier.

Both held hands as they made their way upstairs and moments later both Mossad agents followed and positioned themselves at either end of the corridor on the first floor. Joseph unlocked the door to the apartment and entered. As he entered, he was happy to see that the room did have an inter-leading door to apartment twenty which was next door and would be most beneficial.

He waited for some time, listening to the noise and muffled voices coming from the room next door, before picking the lock of the inter-leading door, and gently pushing the door open. The four were frolicking on the bed and had not noticed Rafael and Joseph standing quietly in the doorway watching them in the act of pleasing each other. Rafael was conscious that he had to move swiftly to avoid any of them screaming, so he quickly made his way to the edge of the bed, pointed the Glock at the Pridoni's head, and pulled the trigger. Moments later Joseph shot Bahiri in the same manner. The only sound audible was a gentle popping sound coming from the silencers.

The two transvestites were splattered with blood and merely lay staring wide-eyed at Rafael and Joseph, too scared to move. They hoped that they would be spared, which proved, not to be the case. Rafael shot both in quick succession. Can't leave any evidence, he considered, so they picked up the empty shell cartridges, then they made their way down the passage toward the fire escape and exited the complex.

Sorry we had to kill those two innocent people, however, in this business, you simply cannot leave a trail for someone to follow, thought Joseph.

As Joseph pointed the car in the direction of the city, he turned to face his good friend.

'Well done honey that was easy as.' 'Good to get rid of these two pieces of shit, however as we know, we eliminate one problem and another rears its head, so we are a long way from finished my friend,' said Joseph.

Both Mossad agents were bent over in fits of laughter.

'This is just the beginning my friend.' 'We have a lot of work ahead of us because we need to get rid of the Koreans as well.' 'I hope that this will entice you to join us in the hunt for these two.' 'We in Mossad now need to find these North Koreans and pay them a friendly visit,' added Joseph.

'Thanks for assisting darling,' said Joseph.

'Pleasure honey.' 'All in a day's work, sweetheart,' said Rafael, blowing him a kiss.

Both Mossad agents were bent over laughing.

Chapter 9

Basel

Switzerland

Claire's mobile phone rang with an incoming call from Brielle Barr, Yonti's mother.

'Bonjour Brielle, what a pleasant surprise.'

'Bonjour Claire, I hope that you, Yonti, and the twins are well?'

'Oui Merci, thanks we are all well.'

'Marcel and I want to come and visit you, however, we want it to be a surprise for Yonti.' 'We have not seen you guys for a few years and as the saying goes, Mohammed won't come to the mountain, so the mountain will come to Mohammed.'

'That would be wonderful, when do you intend to come?'

'Well, if it's OK with you, we will fly to Zurich a week from today, then catch the train to Kandersteg and hopefully you can pick us up at the station.'

'Brilliant Brielle.' 'I will keep it a secret, and you and Marcel can give him a huge surprise.' 'SMS me with all the details and let's keep it between us.'

A week later Claire told Yonti that she was taking the twins to the optometrist to have their eyes tested. She buckled the kids up in the back seat of the SUV and drove to the station.

'Now boys, I have a big surprise for you.'

'What is it, mom?'

'Are we going somewhere?'

'No guys, just wait and see,'

Thirty minutes later the train pulled into Kandersteg station. Marcel and Brielle disembarked. As they made their way toward Claire and the twins, she instructed the boys to close their eyes and not to peep.

'OK, guys, you can open your eyes now.'

The twins were surprised to see their grandparents heading toward them and ran to hug them.

'Bonjour les beaux gars.' 'Regarde comme tu as grandi.' Hello handsome guys. Look how grown up you are.

The twins held their grandparent's hands and led them toward the SUV.

Thirty minutes later, Claire turned into their driveway and scanned the field to see if she could see Yonti. The coast seemed clear, so they quickly made their way into the house. Marcel and Brielle unpacked and made themselves comfortable in the lounge. Later that afternoon Yonti made his way into the house and was surprised to see his parents seated near the log fire.

'Oh, wow, what a surprise.'

His mother hugged and kissed him. His father shook his hand.

'So Yonti, you have not come to see us for a few years, so we thought that we would come and see you and the family.'

'Sorry Mom, I've been very busy here on the farm.' 'How's Pierre doing?'

'He's fine Yonti.' 'Your father and I are retired now, so your brother is running the place.' 'We have employed a full-time chef, however, I come in once a week these days, because many of our guests insist that I make them my specialty, the Seafood Mornay, which tends to keep me occupied for a day.' 'Your father potters around the place doing odd jobs, keeping himself busy.'

Marcel knew that Yonti never wanted to be involved in the family business, and had long accepted that someday he would be gone, so he trained his younger son, Pierre to be the heir to the family business. He had never been able to find out exactly what Yonti did for a living, however, on the odd occasion, he was fed snippets of information, which made him believe that his son was involved in some sort of police work, albeit that it was never confirmed.

Brielle, a gourmet chef in her own right, took control of the kitchen giving Claire a much-needed break, and Marcel pottered around, tending to the garden.

'Wow, how time flies.' 'You guys leave tomorrow.' 'It's been great having you visit us, and I promise, that the family will make the effort to come and visit you soon,' said Yonti.

Yonti drove his parents to the station and waved goodbye as the train departed. A feint tear welled up in his eye, as he considered that he had not made an effort to visit his parents over the past couple of years. Deep down, he felt a little resentment towards his brother, because his father had favored his younger brother, however, he came to realize that he was right, because he knew that Yonti's interest lay elsewhere. Can't blame Dad for favoring his younger brother from a young age. In reality, he had no reason to feel that way, because, he had long made up his mind that he did not want to eventually run the family business. His interest lay elsewhere, so he accepted that.

Back to work, he thought as he jumped into the SUV and headed home. Lots of work to be done.

His parents extended their holiday to include a trip to Jungfraujoch Mountain. It lies at an elevation of eleven thousand, three hundred and sixty-two feet above sea level, directly overlooked by the rocky prominence of the Sphinx. The Jungfraujoch is a glacier saddle, on the upper snow of the Aletsch Glacier, and part of the Jungfrau-Aletsch area, situated on the boundary between the cantons of Bern and Valais, halfway between Interlaken and Fiesch.

They made their way to Lucerne and caught the Mount Pilatus Cog Wheel Train and Cable car which is the world's steepest cog railway that starts its climb at Alpnachstad, tackling a maximum gradient of forty-eight percent, passing forests, meadows, and rock faces. On the north side, is a gondola cableway and an aerial cableway connect Kriens to Pilatus Kulm, taking a mere three and a half minutes to reach Pilatus from the intermediate station, Fräkmüntegg. Thanks to spacious seating, a cockpit-like structure, and large windows, the cableway offers a unique view of Lucerne and its lake.

Marcel turned to his wife, 'I can see why Yonti chose to live in Switzerland.' 'It's truly a beautiful place.'

A week later Yonti's mobile rang announcing an incoming call from his brother Pierre. He answered it on hands-free because he was busy milking one of the cows.

'Hello Pierre, long time no speak.'

'Don't fucking hello me.' 'It's all your fault.'

'What the hell are you talking about, Pierre?'

'If you got off your backside and visited us, this would not have happened,' he shouted down the line.

'What on earth are you talking about Pierre?'

'Have you not heard, our parents are both dead?'

'What?' 'How did that happen?'

'Have you not watched the news?'

'No, I am busy milking my cows.' 'So what has happened?'

'The plane that they were on, blew up.' 'Apparently, someone planted a bomb in it.' 'It appears that a bomb was planted on board the Air France flight AF1415 headed from Zurich to Paris, with one hundred and twenty people and a crew of six on board.' 'This is the plane that our parents were on and it appears that there were no survivors.'

Yonti had accidentally disconnected the call as he picked up his mobile phone, then placed his head on the cow's leg to steady himself. He felt dizzy and needed a moment to digest what he had just heard. A moment later Claire ran into the shed and saw his head leaning against the cow, and she instinctively knew that he had just received the news.

'Oh, dear Lord, let's pray that your parents were not on that plane Yonti.'

She embraced him and pulled his head to her bosom. Tears welled up in his eyes. She had never seen her handsome athletic man, shed a tear in all the years she had known him.

He tried to call his brother, however, he did not answer, and the call was diverted to voice mail. No good leaving a message, because he blames me for what has happened. They made their back to the house and watched the breaking news story.

'An Air France flight from Zurich to Paris has blown up in a mid-air disaster, and it is believed that there are no survivors.' 'The disaster is similar to what happened to the Pan Am Air Flight 103, that exploded over Lockerbie in Scotland, on the twenty-first of December nineteen eighty-eight, where all two hundred and fifty-nine people on board, and nine people on the ground lost their lives,' continued the reporter.

'Emergency crews are on the scene, and police have cordoned off the area.' 'The plane blew up as it flew over the mountains surrounding the city of Basel, adding to the difficulty that rescue crews are confronted with.' 'Debris is scattered over a wide area, and police have asked the public to refrain from visiting the area.'

In a statement, the Chief of Swiss police said, 'crash scene investigators are at the scene, and are searching for any survivors, as well as clues and the black box which they hope will shed light on what has happened.' 'Eyewitnesses said, that the plane simply blew up in the sky.' 'They heard a loud bang in the air and saw the plane disintegrate mid-air,' said the reporter.

Yonti sat silently and watched the footage without saying anything. Claire looked at him and instinctively knew that he would leave soon, and hunt for those responsible. She shivered at the thought of him once again putting himself in danger's way, and folded her arms around her chest, clutching her shoulders with her hands.

'It has been revealed that the Deputy Director of the CIA namely, David Davidson, the Deputy Direction générale de la Sécurité extérieure, (DGSE), Henri La Cour, and the Deputy Director of Mossad, Dahl Jedit were on board the flight.' 'It has been established that the three attended a security briefing in Zurich with various other heads of security in their respective countries,' continued the reporter.

'Clearly, whoever is responsible for this, must have somehow found out that these deputy security chiefs were on board, and must have had inside information.' 'The police are currently following every possible lead,' stated the reporter.

Claire watched as Yonti made his way onto the deck. His upright posture indicated his determination to hunt whoever was responsible and kill them. He stared at the beautiful countryside, and the stunning view of the Staubbach Waterfall cascading down the cliff face in the distance, wondering why there is so much hatred in the world. Claire knew, not to interrupt his thoughts, so she merely sat and watched.

CIA Director Barnaby Heathcott, turned to the footnote in the memo submitted by Jose Hernandez, Yonti Barr's handler at Camp Perry, after he had completed his basic training. The Hulk, as he is fondly known in the firm, due to his huge physique, had submitted an assessment of his student after he had completed his training years previously. The footnote read that Yonti Barr is an exceptionally talented, highly intelligent, analytical, athletic, cunning, smart, and aggressive person. I believe that you have uncovered a unique individual, driven by an unwavering desire, to rid the world of people that have committed serious crimes. He harbors no sympathy for those responsible for heinous crimes and will hunt them down and eliminate them.

Barnaby closed the file, sat back, and considered what Yonti might do. His parents had perished on the flight, so he knew instinctively that Yonti would get involved in the hunt for those responsible.

The CIA uncovered intelligence that placed Iran squarely in the frame, which was confirmed by Mossad. The CIA had intercepted a communication on the wire from a person by the name of Jalil Zaman, when he called an associate, Kurosh Ghasemi celebrating the killing of the deputy the security chiefs of America, Israel, and France. They believed that these people were responsible for the killing of tens of thousands of their countrymen.

It was reported on Aljazeera, that it is widely believed that Iran had taken revenge because of America, Israel, and France's support of the Mojahedin-e Khalq (MEK), a group that openly calls for overthrowing the current Iranian establishment. Israel and America have openly declared that they are committed to preventing Iran from acquiring nuclear weapons. Maryam Rajavi is the leader of MEK, the People's Mojahedin of Iran-PMOI/MEK, and has accused the Iranian government of terrorism and belligerence.

The Iranian government had demanded the release of Assadollah Assadi, 49, who worked at the Iranian embassy in Vienna and was given a 20-year jail term by a court in Antwerp in Belgium, for a plot to bomb a big French rally held by the exiled opposition group. To date, he remains in a jail cell and the Iranians warned, that they would seek retribution. It is believed that the downing of the Air France Airbus is directly attributed to that. Assadollah was arrested after a joint operation by German, French, and Belgian police and was the first time an Iranian official had faced such charges in the EU since the 1979 revolution.

Yonti called Barnaby on a secure line.

'Bonjour Director.'

'Bonjour Rafael.'

Barnaby chose to use his undercover name, albeit that he was calling on a secure line, however, needed to be sure that he did not use his family name. Barnaby was certain that he would ring, and would certainly want to hunt those responsible for killing his parents, as well as, all those on board that lost their lives, and kill them. The CIA's Gulfstream remained in Paris, awaiting orders.

Barnaby knew that Yonti Barr and death are inextricably linked.

'I am deeply sorry for the loss of your parents Rafael, and I can assure you that we are doing everything we can to identify where the bastards responsible are right now.'

'Thank you, director.' 'I need to find whoever is responsible and bring them to justice, so I am reaching out to you to please let me know where I can find them.'

'OK, Rafael, I suggest that you make your way to Paris, so jump on board the Gulfstream. It's currently at Paris Le Bourget Airport, and was waiting to transport my late Deputy back to the US, when this tragedy occurred, so you can hitch a ride on it and fly back to the States, then come and see me.' 'I will instruct the pilots to expect you.'

Claire watched as Yonti packed his gear, removed his beloved Glock and twenty clips of ammunition from the safe, then stood, hugged, and kissed his beloved wife, before going down on his knees and embracing his twin sons. She knew that there was nothing that she could say or do, and hoped that he would return safely.

'I want you guys to look after Mom until I get back.' 'I love you guys more than you will ever know,' he said as he hugged them.

'Au Revoir Mon Pigeon, you know that I need to do this,' 'Remember that I love you too, beautiful.' 'I will probably go into Iran to even the score.' 'As you know it is a very dangerous place, so if I don't make it back, always remember that I love you,' he said as he hugged her one more time.

A feeling of despair overcame Claire because he had never openly admitted that a mission was fraught with danger, nor that he may not make it back, albeit that every mission he conducted was dangerous. His tone of voice, troubled her deeply, and she knew that each time he went on a mission, he put himself in danger, however, this mission, aimed at hunting those responsible worried her.

She stood at the door and watched as the taxi disappeared in the distance, tears streaming down her cheeks. The palm of her hand covered her mouth because she knew that she couldn't bear to see him lying injured on a hospital bed again. Been there, done that. I just cannot do that again, she thought.

I have to set him free because he and the CIA are inextricably linked and there is nothing that I can do to change that, she considered.

He caught the train to Zurich and as he disembarked, an agent fell in beside him, pointing him in the direction of a parked SUV. The agent told him that Director Heathcott had instructed him to drive him to Zurich airport.

Amazing, how they know who and where I am each time. The CIA seemed to know his every move and was capable of manipulating things in their favor.

As he made his way up the stairs and into the belly of the jet, he was greeted by the Co-Pilot.

'Bonjour Monsieur Rafael.' 'Long time no see.'

'Thanks for keeping my plane in good shape,' he quipped as he made his way to his usual seat on the port side.

'The meal is in the warmer Monsieur, and ready whenever you feel like eating.'

'Merci Beaucoup.'

He watched as they climbed toward the heavens on a clear sunny day, and hoped that this would be an omen for what was to come as the Swiss countryside disappeared below.

They landed at Bigler's Mill eight and a half hours later. Eight out of ten for that landing. He reminded himself, that once again, he had not seen the pilot, then noticed agent's d'Avray and Van Der Jong, leaning against the dark-colored SUV waiting for him. They were always tasked with transporting him to the CIA headquarters in Virginia when he worked for the CIA.

'Well, well, not you two again,' he said as he deplaned.

'Nothing has changed.' 'Still in the same cushy job, I see.' 'How the hell can I qualify for a job like yours, boys?'

'Bonjour Monsieur, good to see you too,' offered agent d'Avray.

They drove to the CIA headquarters in silence. Yonti stared at the passing countryside as he had done so many times in the past, and wondered what awaited him.

Barnaby invited him to a meeting at the CIA's headquarters in Virginia and was ushered into the conference room by Gizelle.

Chaviv Yudin, Director of Mossad and Étienne Beaulieu, the Direction générale de la Sécurité extérieure, (DGSE) France were in attendance.

'Gentlemen meet Rafael Dujon, the best agent I have ever had,' said Barnaby as he did the customary introductions.

Chaviv and Étienne had never met Rafael, however, they were fully aware of his reputation as a person who preferred to eliminate the bad guys, rather than take them into custody.

Rafael assumed his seat and looked at the two Directors seated around the table.

'Thank you for meeting with me at short notice gentlemen.' 'We are all deeply sorry for the loss of our Deputy Directors as well as those who lost their lives on the flight, and we now need to hunt for the perpetrators of this tragedy and bring them to justice,' said Barnaby.

'I am also deeply sorry that you lost your parents on that flight Rafael,' added Barnaby.

All in the room shared the same view, which was to eliminate them rather than take them into custody, however, they knew that they dared not say that out aloud.

'So what we know, is that there are two people who we believe were responsible for the bombing, and both are Iranians.' 'From what we have uncovered so far, is that we believe that they are currently in Urmia or Orumiyeh, as it is known in Persia.'

'It is the largest city in West Azerbaijan Province lying at an altitude of four thousand, three hundred and sixty feet above sea level, located along the Shahar River which runs into Lake Urmia, one of the largest salt lakes in the world.' 'Turkey lies to the west, and the city has a population of over half a million people.' 'We understand that they are residing there,' said Barnaby.

'We have uncovered that these two, are retired members of the Islamic Revolutionary Guard Corps, also called Sepah or Pasdaran, a multi-service primary branch of the Iranian Armed Forces.' 'So, one will need to treat them as extremely hostile,' continued Barnaby.

'I am suggesting a joint operation comprising three agents, as discussed. The agents are Rafael, a Mossad agent, by the name of Joseph Diamond, and the other is a French Police Officer, namely Chef Bastienne Petit, as per the brief I sent you.' 'These guys have worked together in the past, and have proven to be highly skilled, efficient, and clinical at what they do, hence my request to you, to allow your agents to be part of the operation I am proposing.'

'I suggest that we have the three enter Iran separately, one posing as a United Nations Scientist wanting to investigate what the effects of an endorheic salt lake, such as Lake Urmia has on the community.' 'We can concoct something along the lines of bacteria forming in the internal drainage basin and the effect it has on the population.' 'As we know, endorheic lakes retain water, and have no outflow to other external bodies of water, thus water is permanently retained in a closed basin that only equilibrates through evaporation.'

'The second can enter as an inspector from the World Health Organization wanting to evaluate the child mortality rate in Iran, and what the WHO can do to reduce this problem.' 'Iran has a very high mortality rate for children under the age of five.' 'Premature birth, pneumonia, pelvic congestion, and diarrhea are the main causes of infant mortality, over there,' continued Barnaby.

'And, the last person could enter, posing as a Hydrologic Technician or a Water Scientist, in layman's terms.'

'According to reports, fifteen percent of the rural population do not have access to quality drinkable water in Iran, so this could be a good cover.' 'He could be sponsored by a wealthy Philanthropist for example, and enter via the U.K,' added Barnaby.

'We will arrange the necessary cover and backup for these agents, so I don't foresee any issues in that regard.'

'I have to compliment you Barnaby, you have certainly done your homework, so this sounds feasible and solid to me,' said Chaviv.

Étienne agreed that the plan was good.

Chaviv sat back, knowing exactly who Rafael was, and that he had a reputation of being clinical and deadly, so a good choice for an operation like this. He also knew that Rafael elected to eliminate terrorists, rather than take them prisoner, because he believed that the justice system in the Western world was way too lenient. He shared the Frenchman's philosophy of eliminating bad guys.

He had heard Rafael Dujon's name mentioned in numerous debriefings in the past and knew that the CIA had changed Yonti Barr's name to Rafael Dujon when he joined the years previously, albeit, that he was not going to admit it to Barnaby. Mossad are shrouded in secrecy and tend to keep all that they know and do, well hidden. He was aware of several missions that his Mossad agent, Joseph Diamond, Rafael Dujon, and Chef Petit had conducted in the past and that they were a formidable trio. He also knew that Yonti lost his parents in the plane that blew up, so revenge was firmly on his radar.

'I am suggesting that Mossad is involved, because, you are far better placed and experienced when it comes to matters in the Middle East,' added Barnaby.

'As mentioned, these two are residents of Orumiyeh in Iran.' 'It is the Capital city of West Azarbayjan Province in Northwest Iran.' 'I think it would be best to have the agents make their way to Turkey separately, and head toward a town called Van which is a city in eastern Turkey that lies on the eastern shore of Lake Van.'

'They can cross into Iran at Kapikoy Checkpoint which is an hour and a half by car east of Lake Van on the D300.' 'The Turkish roads are rough, however, they are far worse in Iran, which is probably why Kapikoy sees little traffic, so probably an ideal place to cross into Iran.'

'Our agents can start their work in Van then move to Iran and continue their work under the guise I suggested, before rendezvousing at Orumiyeh and eliminating these two murderers.' 'I will ensure that they get the correct cover posing as Scientists from the United Nations and the WHO.' 'We will need for you to arrange to get your agent into Iran undetected Chaviv, and I am sure that you know exactly how to do that, my friend.'

Forty minutes later, Gizelle, ushered Joseph Diamond into the conference room.

Barnaby introduced him to Étienne, the only one he did not know him.

'Sweet Lord in heaven, we can't keep on meeting like this Joseph,' quipped Rafael making a light-hearted comment.

'It will cause tongues to wag, my friend.' 'Hello old boy, how are you?' Said Rafael taking his hand.

'Shalom, to you too my friend,' replied Joseph.

Chaviv and Étienne seemed rather amused at the banter between them.

'I take it that you both agree,' said Barnaby, looking at Chaviv and Étienne.

The meeting ended with an agreement to proceed and to implement Barnaby's plan.

Barnaby asked Rafael to remain on for a few minutes.

'I need you to give me your Glock, or as you call it, your equalizer, because you will not be able to smuggle it into Iran, so I will keep it in my safe until you return.' 'You will be provided with a weapon after you have entered Iran.' 'No need to worry, an agent will find you and provide you with what you need.'

Rafael and Joseph left and made their way into the Virginia Comfort Hotel in Fairfax County, and found a seat at the bar.

'I reached out to Director Heathcott to help me find whoever was responsible for the downing of the Air France Flight AF1415 headed from Zurich to Paris, because, as you know my parents were on board, and I need to settle the score.'

'I am deeply sorry to hear that your parents were on that flight Rafael, however, I'm pleased that they have paired us together again, and I will gladly be there for you my friend?' Said Joseph.

Moments later, Chef Petit found his way to where they were seated at the bar, offering his hand in a greeting.

'Well, if it's not the three musketeers, all in one room.' 'Bonjour to both of you,' offered Chef Petit.

'Pray tell, what are you doing here?' Asked Joseph.

'Well the Direction générale de la Sécurité extérieure, (DGSE) France, namely, Étienne Beaulieu, instructed me to be here, so I assume it must have something to do with the Air France plane tragedy.'

'The last time I saw you, you were a captain, now you are a Chef.' 'Congratulations on your promotion,' said Joseph.

'Merci Beaucoup.' 'Right, the question is, how to even the score with these people, who we believe are responsible for this heinous crime?' added Bastienne.

'All taken care of Monsieur Petit.' 'I will fill you in on the details later.' 'Let's order some drinks, shall we,' said Rafael.

'Á Votre Santé gentlemen', added Rafael as they clinked glasses.

'L'Chaim,' replied Joseph.

'This is a very dangerous mission, my friends, so we will need to be extremely careful,' said Rafael.

'As I understand it, yesterday the CIA intercepted a call, indicating that there are two people responsible for the bombing of the Air France Airbus and both are currently back in Iran, however, that needs to be verified.' 'All available agents have been tasked with trying to establish exactly where Jalil Zaman and Kurosh Ghasemi, the two Iranians that the CIA believes are responsible for this heinous crime are at present, however, they believe that they are in Orumiyeh or Urmia as it's known in Iran, which is in northwestern Iran on the shores of Lake Urmia.'

'Our countries have all lost our Deputy Directors of Intelligence in that plane crash, so our governments want revenge.' 'Sadly you lost your parents Monsieur Rafael.' 'My deepest sympathy.' 'All the more reason to find and kill these bastards,' said Bastienne.

'Directors Yudin, Beaulieu, and Heathcott will fully understand if you opt out guys because this will be an extremely dangerous mission,' said Rafael.

'We cannot allow this to go unpunished,' added Joseph.

Mossad had been monitoring Bahador Mohammad's mobile phone because they had long believed that this past Iranian President had associated himself with a radical Islamist group, dead set on revenge. They intercepted a call that he made to Jalil Zaman, and chose not to share the information with the CIA or the French.

They believed it was best, to keep their cards close to their chest, the same as America did, when they identified Osama Bin Laden, the leader of al Qaeda in Abbottabad, Pakistan as the person responsible for downing the two World Trade Centres on the first of May two thousand and eleven.

Chapter 10

Orumiyeh

Iran

Agent d'Avray and Van Der Jong greeted Rafael as he deplaned and loaded his gear into the cargo compartment of the SUV.

'We meet again, Monsieur Rafael.' 'Long time, no see,' said agent d'Avray.

'Oui, here we go again gentlemen.' 'You guys have still not told me how I can get a cushy job like yours.'

'So Monsieur, it looks like you are back at the firm?'

'Non pas du tout, juste de passage.' No not at all, just passing through.

The drive to Washington Dulles International Airport, a distance of two hundred and fifteen miles, took three and three-quarters of an hour, and Rafael bid the agents farewell as he picked up his baggage, then turned and made his way toward international departures. He found his way to the Turkish Airlines International check-in counter and booked in for the eleven-hour flight to Istanbul.

Never flown on Turkish Airlines, nor have I ever been to Istanbul, so this will be a new experience. Seven out of ten for that landing, he thought.

The immigration official eyed him suspiciously as he presented his passport, then scanned the image of his photograph, before flicking through the pages noting, dozens of entry and exit stamps from various countries.

'Birçok ülkeyi ziyaret ettiğinizi fark ettim, Bey Benoît Leblanc.' I notice that you have visited many countries, Mr.Benoît Leblanc.

'What is the purpose of your visit to Turkey?'

'I am a Hydraulic Technician or Water Scientist working for the United Nations, and have been sent to Iran to investigate the effects of an endorheic salt lake on its population, and am merely traveling through Turkey on my way to Lake Urmia in Iran.' 'I will investigate what long-term effect an endorheic salt lake such as Lake Urmia, has on the community.' 'Please review my visa, and you will see that I have special permission to pass through Turkey on my way to Orumiyeh to conduct humanitarian work there that will benefit their population.'

'What kind of lake is that?'

'An endorheic lake is also called a sink lake, or terminal lake which is a collection of water within an endorheic basin, or sink, with no evident outlet.' 'Endorheic lakes are generally saline, as a result of being unable to get rid of solutes left in the lake by evaporation.' 'These lakes can be used as indicators of anthropogenic change, such as irrigation, or climate change, in the areas surrounding them. Lakes with subsurface drainage are considered cryptorheic,' said Benoît.

He pushed his glasses up on his nose and continued, 'the collected water of the lake, instead of discharging it, can only be lost due to either evapotranspiration or percolation, through water sinking underground to become groundwater in an aquifer.'

'How long will you be staying in Istanbul?'

'I'm just passing through Istanbul on my way to Van, and will catch the connecting flight in an hour.'

'I see,' said the immigration official.

The customs official seemed rather baffled by what he had been told and stamped his passport, allowing him to proceed to the baggage carousel. He collected his bags, then made his way to customs and was subject to a rigorous baggage search. He was once again asked what the purpose of his visit to Turkey was, and had to repeat what he had just said to the immigration official before finally being allowed to proceed.

Exactly what I expected, from Turkish immigration, he considered. Amazing how the CIA can concoct a story, of him being a Hydraulic Technician, and furnish him with a false passport, complete with dozens of entry and exit stamps from various countries around the globe, making it appear that he is legit. He was given a credit card in his undercover name as well as a new mobile phone. Love the plain lens nerdy glasses as well, he thought as he once again pushed the glasses up his nose.

Thank goodness they put me through a crash course on Hydraulic Water Management, so I think I passed this first part with flying colors, he thought.

Albeit, that what I said was true, bullshit can often baffle brains at times, he considered.

He made his way to domestic departures and boarded the two-and-a-half-hour Pegasus Airlines flight PC2500 from SAW Istanbul Sabiha Goksen Airport to Van Airport, and was pleased that the flight arrived on time. As he departed the arrivals hall, a tall man, with a beard fell in beside him. He was dressed in traditional Turkish clothing with a Sarband headdress and a long white robe.

'Follow me he whispered,' as they made their way toward the carpark.

The new Audi Q Seven Quattro all-wheel drive SUV, sporting a two hundred and ten Kw, V6 TDI engine, was parked in a reserved parking spot.

'This is your vehicle, compliments of Director Heathcott.' 'It has a GPS and you will find a bevy of maps in the glove compartment.' 'After you have finished your mission, simply leave it wherever you choose.'

'The coordinates for Orumiyeh are detailed in the memo, which is included in the overview of what you need to do from Director Heathcott.' 'This is also in the glove compartment and he asked that you read it, memorize it, digest it, and then destroy it.'

'You have been booked into the Van International Hotel under the name of Benoît Leblanc, same as your passport, so I suggest that you get used to using that name from now on.' 'Here is your booking reservation confirmation, for the one-night stay at the hotel in the city tonight,' he said as he handed him the plastic wallet.

'I have highlighted the route to your hotel on the map from here, so simply follow it,' he said handing him the map.

'Tomorrow you can start your journey to the border, which is a distance of one hundred-and-ninety miles that will take around four hours.' 'Simply punch Kapikoy Checkpoint into the GPS and follow the instructions.' 'After you have crossed, make your way to Orumiyeh using the GPS again, and book into The City Park International Hotel.' 'The reservation is in the name of Benoît Leblanc.'

'You may need the maps, to navigate your way through Iran, just in case something goes wrong with the GPS as well as directions to Orumiyeh, and you will find all the camping gear that you may need in the cargo compartment.'

Certainly impressive he thought.

'Once inside Iran, you will be met by an Iranian man by the name of Mousa Yousefi.' 'No need to worry, he will find you, and he will identify himself with the phrase, "a dog always recognizes its owner," that will indicate that you can trust him.'

'Tomorrow morning, after you have crossed into Iran, you can drive from Kapikoy Checkpoint border crossing to Orumiyeh which will take around an hour and a half.' 'The road is in a shocking condition, so I recommend that you drive slowly.'

Benoît jumped into the Audi, punched the address for the Van International Hotel into the GPS, and headed in that direction. He booked in and chose to order a meal delivered to his room and remain indoors for the evening.

The next morning he was up early and booked out of the hotel, then loaded his gear into the Audi. He punched the address for Kapikoy Checkpoint into the GPS, then made his way out of the hotel parking, turned onto the road, and headed east. The friendly Iranian customs official noted his special visa clearance and conducted a brief baggage check, then allowed him to proceed. He punched in the GPS coordinates for The City Park International Hotel and proceeded cautiously down the bumpy road toward Orumiyeh. The road was in extremely poor condition, so he drove slowly because it was commonly known that road deaths are the third cause of death in the country and he certainly did not want to become an addition to that statistic.

That was certainly an experience he thought as he pulled up at The City Park International Hotel, a modest three-star hotel and booked in. He dropped his gear in the room, before making his way downstairs, and decided to take a walk down the street in search of a place to eat. He made his way into The Ottoman Café, located at İkinisan Caddesi, found a corner table, seated himself against the wall with a view of the whole restaurant, and ordered a pizza, as well as a cup of tea, all the while his eyes worked the room, eyeing all those seated, searching anyone showing undue interest in him as a foreigner. It seemed like, there was no one tailing him or anyone wanting to know why I was there, so he sat back and enjoyed his meal.

Later he checked his gear, ensuring that everything that he may need was packed into the backpack, and read the memo given to him thoroughly, noting that Barnaby had instructed him to visit the Segonbad Ancient Historical Ruins, where a person would meet him and give him further instructions. He was up early the next morning, loaded his gear into the Audi, then punched the coordinates into the GPS and pointed the Audi in the direction of the Ruins. He parked in the designated parking area, then walked around the historical structure, known as the Three Gonbads admiring its architecture, and noted the three inscriptions in the Kufic script placed on the entrance door. Segonbad is a remnant of the Seljuk period. A while later, an elderly man approached him and said, 'a dog always recognizes its owner.'

'Hello Benoît, my name is Mousa Yousefi, so keep walking, and I will pretend to be your guide.'

'Director Heathcott instructed me to give this to you,' he said as he handed him a handwritten note.

'Put it in your pocket, read it in private, memorize it, then destroy it.' 'My contact number is written on the note, in case you ever need assistance.' 'When you return to your vehicle, you need to look behind the front driver's side wheel.' 'I have placed a gun, some ammunition, and a knife in a bag for you.'

'After you have completed your mission, get rid of everything.'

Mousa bid Benoît farewell, promptly turned, and left.

An hour later Benoît made his way back to the hotel. He unfolded the note and read it in the privacy of his room. It detailed exactly where he could find the two perpetrators of the bombing of the Air France flight. The note read, that it has been established that Jalil and Kurosh own a Spa Resort on the shores of Lake Urmia, where people came to bathe in the salt water. Bathing in mineral-rich water is called balneotherapy, which has a high concentration of minerals and it has been reported to cure arthritis, psoriasis as well as hay fever. They have set up shower facilities so that people can wash the salt off their skin after they have bathed in the salt lake. The name of the Spa Resort that they own is Orumiyeh Muntajae Sihiyun which translates to Orumiyeh Health Spa Resort.

Having read the note, he burnt it and flushed it down the toilet. Right, now I have the location where these two bastards are, so I will start my water testing procedure in the same location.

Best get used to using this undercover name, thought Benoît.

The following day he drove to the Spa Resort and presented himself at the reception desk. He asked to see the owner and a short while later two men introduced themselves as Jalil Zaman and Kurosh Ghasemi, the owners of the Spa Resort.

Ah, so these are the two that killed my parents and all those on the Air France flight. You have no idea how happy I am to meet you both, he thought.

'Hello, my name is Benoît Leblanc.' 'I am a Hydraulic Technician or Water Scientist, working for the United Nations and I have been sent here to investigate the effects of this endorheic Urmia Salt Lake has on the local population,' he said producing his passport.

'The United Nations has been granted special permission by the Iranian Government to conduct a series of tests in the lake.' 'The reason I am introducing myself is that I am respectfully asking whether you will grant me permission to use your shower facilities after I have conducted tests because as you know, a person needs to wash the salt off of the skin to avoid irritation.'

Both viewed him suspiciously because of his French accent. After all, it was a French Airbus that they blew up.

'You have a French accent, so I take it that you are from France?'

'I have a French accent because I was born to French parents, however, I have lived in Papeete on Tahiti's north-western coast, which is also the capital of French Polynesia all my life, and more recently moved to Mauritius where I have lived most of my life.'

This seemed to satisfy them somewhat.

'OK, if the United Nations sent you, we will be happy to allow you to use our shower facilities whenever you please.' 'By the way, what do you believe the effect of salt has on the population?' Asked Jalil.

'Well, it has a high concentration of minerals in it that can cause skin irritation for example.' 'If people do not wash the salt off after having taken a dip, it is believed, that it can have severe negative consequences for the health of an affected population.'

'The United Nations investigated the spatiotemporal correlation of the lake drought and the state of health of the local population a few years ago here in Orumiyeh, and we now want to do follow-up testing to establish if any action will be recommended.' 'In the previous study, we applied a GIScience multiple decision analysis to identify areas affected by salt-dust particles and related these to the health status of the population.' 'The last study concluded, that the lake drought had significantly contributed to increasing cases of hypertension in the local population.'

He looked at the two, who seemed baffled by what he had just said. Yep, albeit that what I have just said is true, bullshit can baffle brains, however, these two don't seem to have much of that. Convinced, the two offered me the use of all their facilities at the resort and invited him to join them for a dinner in two days-time, because they needed to understand what, if any effect, it may have on their resort.

Don't want to socialize with these two killers, however, I seem to have convinced them that I am legit, so joining them for dinner will allow me to work out how to get rid of them. As he turned to make his way to the Audi and unpack his testing equipment, he caught a glimpse of his friend Joseph Diamond. His eyes worked the surroundings, satisfied that there was no apparent danger, he looked at him sunning himself on a deck chair.

He made eye contact with him, however, ensured that he did not acknowledge him, merely tilted his head slightly and offered a slight smile, then turned and made his way out of the complex. He knew that he would be here somewhere, and wondered where Chef Petit could be.

He made his way toward the edge of the lake, unpacked his gear, and was conscious that the owners were watching.Half an hour later he donned his long-leg utility gumboots and wadded into the water, collecting samples of water from various sections of the lake, then returned to the table and laid them out for testing. He conducted a salinity test, taking specific gravity and temperature measurements, then compared them to standardized values taken in the past.

Gravity is measured in the field by testing a water sample with a device similar to a battery or antifreeze tester and analyzing it using the Hyperion water quality index, and hazard quotient.

Rather convincing, he thought, as he went about his work.

A short while later, he became aware of the noise of an approaching military transport truck and watched as they pulled up at the front entrance to the Spa Resort. Six troops dressed in military uniforms lined up. The officer in charge instructed the troops to change into their bathers and watched as they charged into the salty lake a short while later.

Benoît wondered whether this was part of their supposed elite force, and watched with interest at their interaction with each other, noting the aloofness and arrogance of the officer in charge. The officer meandered over to where Benoît was busy taking water samples and introduced himself.

'I am Major Farukh Zoheri, of the Iranian Revolutionary Guard Corps, so what is the purpose of you being here?'

Benoît presented his passport and opened it to the page displaying the special Visa granted to him as a United Nations employee, tasked with testing the effects of salination in the water on the population that resides near Lake Urmia. This seemed to satisfy the major.

'You speak English very well Major.' 'You even have a slight American accent.'

'Yes that's correct, I studied in America for four years.' 'You see, it was important for me to get to know Iran's arch- enemy, and understand their imperialism.' 'I then returned to Iran and joined the Revolutionary Guard.'

The Major turned and headed off in the direction of the resort. Benoît noticed that he stopped to chat with the two owners.

This bastard could be a massive problem. Need to keep a close eye on him for sure, considered Benoît.

He watched with interest as the Major and the two murders interacted, joking amongst themselves. Seems they know each other, pretty well, so I best be careful. Thirty minutes later, the troops made their way toward the shower, having frolicked in the saltwater for half an hour. Later the troops got back into the trucks, and they made their way out of the complex heading in a westerly direction toward the Turkish border. That's my planned escape route, because it's the shortest route, so this could be a problem, thought Benoît.

He watched the two murderers take an early morning walk every day at zero seven hundred hours, heading in the direction of the wooded area surrounding the lake on the east side and noted that they tended to return two hours later, so by his calculation it appeared that they would have walked for around seven miles.

Right, this this where I am going the kill these two bastards, thought Benoît.

The following evening he arrived for dinner at eighteen hundred hours and was pleased to see that his friend Joseph Diamond had also been invited. Pretending not to know Joseph, he introduced himself as he took his seat at the table.

Jalil was the first to speak, 'So what brings you to Urmia Mr. Dawson?'

Joseph was using the undercover name of John Dawson and was traveling on a British passport organized by the CIA.

'Well I work for the World Health Organization, and they have sent me to Iran to investigate child mortality, and what the WHO can do to reduce this problem.' 'I have studied the effects in numerous remote villages and am taking a short break before I head toward Tabriz, where I will conduct my investigation'

Continuing he said, 'since the WHO got involved in two thousand and ten, the under five-year-old child mortality rate has drastically reduced by seventy percent which means that Iran is one of the best performers in the Middle East and the North African region.' 'We used empirical data sources and strict eligibility criteria to compile our report, to overcome the crucial problem of low-quality databases, and the high percentage of missing data in previous surveys.'

'In nineteen hundred, the child mortality rate in Iran was approximately five hundred and six deaths for every thousand live births, meaning that approximately half of all babies born at this time would not make it past their fifth birthday.' 'Child mortality would fall gradually for the first four decades of the twentieth century, falling to four hundred and sixty-four deaths by nineteen forty, following the implementation of mass vaccinations in the country by the Iranian government and rapid modernization of the country's healthcare, facilitated by the economic boost granted by Iran's oil industry.'

'As improved healthcare saw a large reduction in most cases of child mortality, the rate continued to fall throughout the twentieth century and into the twenty-first century.' 'As a result, in the year twenty-twenty it was estimated that almost ninety-nine percent of all babies born in Iran would live past their fifth birthday.'

Very convincing thought Benoît, as he glanced at these two murderers seated opposite him, who were impressed by his overview of what he does for the WHO, and it seemed that these two were baffled by bullshit again. Bullshit can baffle brains, not that these had an abundance of that he thought.

He was up before dawn the next morning and made his way into the wooded area, following a well-trodden track that these two murders seemed to take each day on their morning walk.

As he walked along the sandy path he took note of the footprints, confirming the direction that these two normally take, before rounding a corner and reaching a clearing in the thicket. He positioned himself on a log and waited. The muffled sound of someone walking in his direction altered him. A short while later his friend Joseph rounded the corner and came into view, and was startled to see him sitting on the log.

'Well, well we meet again Joseph, or shall I say Mr. Dawson.' 'I have to say, your explanation last night of what you do for the WHO, was most convincing indeed old chap.'

'Well, great minds think alike my friend.' 'I noticed you walking in the direction of the woodlands, and knew that you were preparing to rid the world of these two murderers, so I thought that I would come along for the ride.'

He glanced at his wristwatch and noted that it was almost zero seven hundred hours, which is around the time that these two normally start their early morning walk. He put on a pair of tight-fitting rubber gloves, removed the magazine, wiped all the cartridges clean of any fingerprints, and then did the same to the outside of the weapon, ensuring that it could not be traced back to him. They sat in silence waiting for two to appear, so he took the time to check that the weapon was cocked with a round in the chamber and checked that the silencer was attached properly. He activated the safety switch, ensuring that it was ready to be fired. Impressed how the CIA can move undetected in hostile countries, and have weapons readily available. Amazing, he thought.

'I'm all packed and ready to leave Joseph.' 'Hope that you too are ready to move as soon as we put these two to sleep,'

'Been ready since I arrived three days ago, my friend.'

Twenty minutes later they heard the mumblings of a conversation in the distance, then caught a glimpse of movement through the thicket of dense bush, and waited until these two were almost upon them. Joseph hid in the thicket where the pathway curved and waited as they headed in their direction, ensuring that he covered an escape route that these two may try to use as they fled.

As the two rounded the bend, they stopped in their tracks and seemed surprised to see Benoît seated on a log with a gun in his hand. They quickly realized the threat and turned to make a hasty retreat, and as they turned, they stared down the barrel of the semi-automatic Uzi Pro Pistol, held by Joseph. The Uzi is a standard Israeli military issue, also used by Mossad agents.

'Ah, gentlemen, as you can see, you two have a massive problem, and your early instincts of viewing us with suspicion was correct, however as the saying goes, bullshit baffles brains.' 'So both of you, get down on your knees, with your hands behind your head.'

Joseph watched as his friend walked closer to the two murderers.

'So let me explain it to both of you.' 'You two bastards planted a bomb on the Air France Airbus Flight AF1415 and detonated it as it flew from Zurich to Paris, over the Swiss city of Basel, killing all one hundred and twenty people and a crew of six on board.'

'What you do know, is that the Deputy Director of the CIA namely, David Davidson, the Deputy Direction générale de la Sécurité extérieure, (DGSE), The General Directorate for External Security in France, Henri La Cour, and the Deputy Director of Mossad, Dahl Jedit were on board the flight.' 'Clearly, you aimed to kill these people, so you have succeeded, however, what you do not know, is that my parents were also on board that flight.'

'So Mr. Zaman and Mr. Ghasemi, it's time for you two to enter Muslim Hell.' 'No virgins waiting for you there.'

'This is at the pleasure of my friend over there, who is a Mossad agent as well as myself, a retired CIA agent.'

Both were taken by surprise and stared wide-eyed in his direction. They instinctively knew what awaited them and considered making a run for it.

'No doubt, you would have been instructed to carry out the bombing of the Air France Airbus with the blessing of the Supreme Leader of Iran as well as the Iranian Government, and they would have chalked it down to retribution for the jailing of Assadollah Assadi, who was given a twenty-year jail term by the court in Antwerp in Belgium.

'How am I doing so far?'

The two were mumbling something inaudible in Arabic.

'So, my friend and I are the Prosecution, Judge, and Jury and we are sentencing you both to death.'

'And no, don't even think of trying to make a run for it, because you will be dead before you even make it to your feet,' said Benoît.

A real pity, he thought. I would have liked to have punished these two bastards for what they have done, cut their balls off and made them eat it, then cut their hands off as well as their feet, however, circumstances do not allow me to do that, because we need to hightail it out of here.

They forced both to their feet and headed into the dense bush. Each of them selected one of the murderers, aimed at their heads, and pulled the trigger. The silent popping noise was only audible at close range.

The two slumped backward, so they quickly dragged their bodies deeper into the bushes and covered them with branches. They then used branches to sweep over the sand, ensuring that they covered any blood stains, and used the branches to rake over any footprints that they may have left in the sand, then quickly headed back toward the Resort and split as they approached.

'Be quick my friend.' 'I will meet you on the dirt road because we need to get the hell out of here.'

'No need to worry, I will be ready and waiting for you near the dirt road.'

Ten minutes later, Rafael stopped to pick Joseph up and pointed the Audi in the direction of the Turkish border.

'I think it best that we do not travel together Joseph, so I will drop you off near the village of Razi and it would be best if you caught a taxi to Kapikoy Checkpoint.'

'Just in case we need to back each other up because you never know what we may encounter along the way.' 'Not sure whether you noticed the Major and his Revolutionary Guards were headed in that direction.' 'Let's hope like hell that we don't bump into them again.' 'This could be a huge problem, my friend.'

Rafael stopped at a remote site along the way. Both dismantled their weapons and threw the parts into the river, ensuring that they selected the deepest part of the river.

'Small justice for what these two bastards have done my friend.' 'I wish that I could have punished them more severely, however, we need to high tail it out of here.'

Chapter 11

Mount Sahand

Iran

Rafael parked on the fringe of Razi village and watched as Joseph made his way toward a taxi. After what appeared to be a negotiation regarding the fare, he jumped into the taxi, and a while later the taxi headed toward Kapikoy Checkpoint at the Turkish border, a distance of around six-and-a-half miles.

He followed some distance behind and as they rounded a corner near the border, they were suddenly stopped at a military security checkpoint. As he pulled up behind the taxi, he saw Joseph being manhandled by the Major and his troops as he exited the taxi. Moments later he was afforded the same treatment. They were shoved into a tent that had been erected alongside the dirt road, and guards with guns stood menacingly around the two.

'You again.' 'I am Major Farukh Zoheri.' 'I believe that we met at Orumiyeh Muntajae Sihiyun Spa Resort, and if my memory serves me correctly, you are the person who works for the United Nations.' 'Is that correct?'

'Yes major, that is correct.'

'Remind me, of your name again.'

'It's Benoît Leblanc.'

'Yes, I remember now.' 'So have you finished your work here in Iran?'

'I have.'

He turned to face Joseph, and asked, 'And you are who?'

'I am John Dawson major, and I work for the World Health Organization.'

'And what was the purpose of you being in Iran?'

'I was sent here to investigate child mortality in the country, and what the WHO can do to reduce this problem.' 'I am studying the effects in numerous remote villages in Iran and took a short break before heading to Tabriz, however, I have been recalled and instructed to return to Geneva in Switzerland immediately.'

Just then the military radio came to life and what they could make out, the caller's voice appeared extremely stressed.

The major turned his attention to the two standing in front of him.

'You were both at the Spa Resort and when exactly did you leave?'

'We left three hours ago Major,' replied Benoît.

'I see, and did you see the owners before you left?'

'No, however, as we departed, I did see them taking their morning walk,' said Benoît.

'Did you give Mr. Dawson a lift?'

'Yes, I did, however, I dropped him off at Razi, because he had to send a report back to his boss at the World Health Organization.'

'So explain to me, how come you both have arrived here at the same time Mr. Leblanc?' Asked the Major forcefully.

'I have no idea, merely coincidental.' 'I had no idea that Mr. Dawson was even in the taxi until I saw your guards escort him into the tent.'

The Major paced up and down. He took a seat at the table and seemed distressed about something.

'Well, I have just received a report on the radio that both of the owners have been killed, so I am wondering whether you two were involved.'

'Good heavens no, that's terrible.' 'Who on earth would want to do that?' replied Benoît.

'Well that's what I am going to find out, so I am placing both of you under arrest.'

Despite their protest of innocence, the guards bound their hands and feet and then escorted them to an adjacent tent. The Major placed two guards on duty to protect them. They were searched and one of the soldiers removed all their belongings, then searched the SUV, placing all of Benoît's water testing equipment on the table for the Major to inspect.

Later that evening, they were bundled into the military truck and were driven back to the Spa Resort.

Benoît leaned over to Joseph, hoping that the guards did not understand Yiddish, and whispered, 'This is going to be a schlep and I think that this putz is going to put us through the ringer.'

'Did not know that you speak Yiddish, my friend.' 'And yes, I agree that this schlep will be a journey with difficulty and this putz jerk is going to punish us.'

Seemed all pleasant for now, he considered, however, as soon as the Major sees the bodies of his friends, everything will undoubtedly change, thought Benoît.

As they pulled up at the entrance to the Spa Resort, staff members rushed to meet the truck and all were shouting at the same time. The Major got out of the truck and accompanied them to where they had discovered the bodies. He inspected the area carefully, then turned and made his way back. He instructed the guards to erect a tent and place Benoît Leblanc and John Dawson under guard inside the tent. Both continued to protest their innocence which fell on deaf ears. The Major seemed convinced that these two were responsible for the death of the two owners.

A short while later he entered the tent and the mood changed.

'So let's see if I have this correct.' 'You two are not who you say you are.' 'I think that you are imperialist spies sent to Iran to kill two of my comrades in arms because they took revenge on your governments for jailing another comrade of ours.' 'I believe that you are French Mr. Leblanc, and that you are a Jew, Mr. Dawson.'

'How am I doing so far gentlemen?'

'No Major that is not correct.' 'Look at my passport and you will see that I am British and not an Israeli'.

'And I was born of French parents in Papeete, on Tahiti's northwestern coast, which is also the capital of French Polynesia, and spent all my life there before moving to Mauritius, then moved to America where I joined the United Nations as a Water Hydraulic Technician, or more appropriately a Water Scientist.' 'I have been sent here to investigate how we can assist Iran in purifying its rural water supply, and this is how you treat me and Mr. Dawson?'

'Papeete is a French colony, and that is where my French accent comes from.' 'Look at my passport and you will see.' 'My superiors will be outraged at the treatment we are receiving from you in particular Major, and I can assure you that they will undoubtedly raise this issue with your Supreme Commander,' said Benoît forcefully.

'I don't give a damn what passports you carry, because whoever it is that you work for, would have issued you with false passports.' 'So you are under arrest for the murder of my two former colleagues, and I will conduct a trial here and now.' 'As a Major in the Revolutionary Army, I am allowed to conduct my investigation and hand out an appropriate sentence.'

Both protested their innocence. The Major walked around the table and started proceedings. He hit Benoît on the head with a baton, knocking him to the ground, then turned and did the same thing to John. Both lay there semi-conscious. The guards pulled them to their feet and watched as the Major punched each person repeatedly. An hour later Benoît and John, lay battered and bruised on the sandy floor with blood streaming down their cheeks.

Benoît peered at the Major through swollen eye sockets, spat out blood and some broken teeth. I will kill you when I get the chance, he thought.

Benoît's eye sockets were badly swollen and almost closed, however, he managed to see John, lying unconscious in the sand and watched as the out-of-breath Major, made his way out of the tent. Fucking piece of shit. Best you kill me because if you don't and I get a hold of you in the future, you will regret not killing me.

His body pained from the relentless beating. He lay there and he glanced at his friend lying listlessly in the sand. Sweet Jesus, I hope that the Major has not killed him. An hour later the Major returned to the tent and ordered the guards to pick them up and put them on a chair, then continued the interrogation.

'So you two have come here under the pretense of being some sort of humanitarians offering to do some good for Iran and instead of doing that, you have killed two of our comrades because they blew up a plane.'

Ah, so there you have it, thought Benoît. Confirmation of their involvement. How fucking dumb of the Major to openly say that. A small consolation he thought, as his body ached. I need to survive this and live to kill this bastard as revenge for them killing my parents as well as all the others on that ill-fated flight.

Both survived the beating and the next morning the Major continued the interrogation, demanding confirmation of their involvement in killing the two owners of the Spa Resort. He continued to beat both of them relentlessly until both fell into a state of unconsciousness. They eventually woke up as the truck rattled along a bumpy sand road. Benoît's face grimaced with pain. His entire body ached and he noticed the sun rising in the East which meant that they were headed inland in a westerly direction, possibly in the direction of Tabriz. This would make any attempt to escape a lot more difficult, considered Benoît. He glanced at his friend lying on the floor through the slits in his swollen eyes and noticed that he appeared to be alive and breathing shallowly.

The truck eventually ground to a stop at a remote site near Tabriz alongside the Talkheh River, situated three hundred and eighty-five miles from Tehran.

Of concern was that the Major was heading towards Tehran and would put them on trial in a public square before executing them, so Benoît knew that time was fast running out, and that they had to escape long before that happened. From what he could recall, when he studied a map of Iran before he left Turkey, Tabriz is the second largest city in Iran, situated in a valley to the north of the long ridge of Mount Sahand. May be a blessing, because the rugged mountainous region may offer an opportunity to escape.

Lying on the floor of the truck he glanced at his friend who appeared to be breathing normally and wondered if they did manage to escape, whether his friend would be able to make it out of Iran. He shivered through the cool morning temperature and waited to learn what the Major had in store for them. He caught a glimpse of the snow-covered peak of the mountain in the distance as the guards dragged them out of the truck and pulled them into a tent that they had erected.

As usual, he was always exploring any possible opportunity to escape, however, he realized that his friend would not be able to make it up the mountain, so he needed to expand his thoughts in another direction. Just need an opportunity to eliminate these bastards he considered.

The day dragged on without incident and the fading sun indicated the coming evening. He watched as the guards all gathered around a portable radio and were merrily interacting with each other. They appeared to be drinking some sort of liquor which of course is taboo in Iran, however, away from prying eyes, nobody would ever know, and they seemed to be getting a little tipsy. He noticed that the Major was not amongst the group seated around a log fire, and wondered where he could be.

It appeared that the group was listening to a broadcast of what seemed to be a football match and cheered each time the announcer excitedly raised his voice.

'It's Iran versus England in a Soccer World Cup match,' said John with great difficulty through his swollen lips.

'Sweet God in Heaven, it's good to see you are still in the land of the living my friend.' 'How do you know that it is a soccer match?'

'Because I understand Arabic.' 'We need to get the fuck out of here my friend,' said Benoît.

'Yes, I know.'

He watched as the guards boisterously celebrated a goal in Iran's favor with the group merrily hugging each other and dancing around the fire. He managed to wriggle his hands-free, then crept out of the tent, noticing that the guards had positioned their rifles in a circle with the barrels facing skywards. Right, got to crawl up to these rifles and grab one he thought, so he leopard crawled toward the rifles, and removed one carefully, ensuring that the others did not fall to the ground. He glanced at the guards and was happy to see that none were aware of his presence so he removed the magazine, checked that it was fully loaded, then gently half-cocked the rifle to ensure that there was a round in the chamber. All looked good, so he replaced the magazine, activated the safety switch, stood, and walked with great difficulty toward the group. None of them noticed him until he was almost amongst them.

'Right, you fucking bunch of bastards, time for all of you to face justice.'

The guards were caught off guard and turned to face him, attempting to rise. He aimed at the one closest to him and squeezed the trigger, then trained the barrel on each of the other guards and shot them. The sound of the shots alerted the Major who had been bathing himself in a basin of water. He ran naked toward the truck, rounding the rear end, just as a bullet ricocheted off the rear fender, so he jumped into the cab and raced off in a cloud of dust. A hail of bullets followed, however, luckily for him, he was not hit. Benoît watched as the truck disappeared in a cloud of dust.

No more bullets, so this prick can count himself very lucky because my vision has been impaired by the beatings I took. He picked up the Majors clothes, then made his way back to his friend and untied his hands. This uniform may come in handy, he thought.

'Are you able to walk Joseph?' he asked using his real name.

'We need to move and get out of here before the Major returns with the whole Iranian army.'

'Yes you are right Rafael,' said Joseph reverting to the name he knew him by.

He removed three magazines from the rifles, shouldered one rifle, and then walked with Joseph leaning heavily on his shoulder toward the mountain in the distance.

'It's dark, which is an advantage, however, I think we may only have a couple of hours before the helicopters arrive with searchlights, so let's try and put as much distance behind us and this place as possible, Joe, or is it, Mr. Dawson?'

Barnaby had been monitoring the events taking place, and was in constant communication with Chaviv Yudin, Director of Mossad and Étienne Beaulieu, the Direction générale de la Sécurité extérieure, (DGSE) France. All were up to date with the predicament that these two were facing.

'We have one other option gentlemen.' 'Two of our agents based in Iran as well as Bastienne Petit have been following the group and are relatively close to where they are at the moment.' 'I am monitoring their movements at the moment and as of now, it appears that the Major has not communicated with the Revolutionary Guards Head Quarters, so hopefully we have a bit of time on our side.'

Mousa Yousefi, and Wuhaib Tayyebi, two CIA operatives accompanied by Chef Petit, headed toward the coordinates given to them along a rugged mountain road and stopped at a point they considered would be most likely place where Joseph and Rafael would cross the road. Using night vision binoculars, Chef Petit scanned the horizon, eventually seeing the two staggering along a footpath in the hills. They waited patiently for the two to reach where they had stopped.

'It seems like these guys are heading toward Mount Sahand, trying to find somewhere to hide.' 'Clearly, my friends must believe that the Army will launch a massive manhunt, so they are most likely seeking an unlikely place to take cover.' 'As we know, Mount Sahand is the highest mountain in the East Azarbaijan province with a massive, heavily eroded stratovolcano that has a ceiling of twelve thousand one hundred and sixty-two feet.'

'Who knows why they would be headed there.' 'Maybe they think that they could hide in some crevasse or other.' 'Wonder if they know that this is a dormant volcano that has been sporadically active from twelve million years ago, up to almost zero, point one for years.' 'Please God, it stays asleep,' said Bastienne.

An hour later, the two staggered onto the dirt road and were alerted by movements in the dark.

'Somebody's here Rafael,' said Joseph using the name he knew him by.

Rafael was quick to unshoulder the rifle and a moment later, he heard a familiar voice in the dark.

'Don't shoot, Monsieur Rafael, it's me, Bastienne Petit,' he said.

'Basteinne and the two CIA operatives had been monitoring their progress through night vision and thermal imaging goggles.

'Where the fuck have you come from?' Asked Rafael.

'Your boss sent me because he thought that you two may get lost in the wilderness and asked me to find you guys.'

'Geez, I am happy to see you, my friend.'

'Good Lord, what happened to you guys?' said Bastienne as he shone the torch onto their faces.

He was horrified to see how badly the two had been beaten.

'Who are these two?' Asked Rafael.

'This is Mousa Yousefi and Wuhaib Tayyebi, two CIA two operatives that your boss Mr. Barnaby asked to join me to rescue you guys,' said Bastienne.

Rafael turned to face Mousa.

'I think we met before if I'm not mistaken,' he said, straining to get a clear image of him through his swollen eyes.

'Yes we have, replied Mousa.'

He looked at all three and said, 'Thanks guys, much appreciated.'

'We need to hightail it out of here before the whole Iranian army arrives,' reiterated Rafael.

As they made their way toward the parked SUV, the whooping and whirling sound of the blades of a helicopter became audible in the distance, and a short while later they caught a glimpse of a searchlight mounted on a helicopter scouring the countryside. It became evident that a second helicopter was also searching the countryside some distance behind.

'We have company.' 'Reinforcements have arrived guys, and it will only be a matter of time before they shine a light on us,' said Rafael.

Mousa and Wuhaib quickly made their way to the SUV and extracted two portable Manpad FIM-43 Red Eye Infrared Heat Seeking Missiles, loaded them, and made their way in separate directions ensuring that should one be taken out, the other would still be operative. Chef Petit was quick to grab some extra missiles and take them to the two operatives that had positioned themselves two hundred yards apart.

'No doubt, the helicopters will be using thermal imaging cameras to try to find us,' said Rafael.

The helicopters headed in their direction and they watched as the beams from their searchlights played across the rugged terrain. It wasn't long before the beam of light from the lead helicopter shone on the SUV. The vehicle was raked with rounds fired from the chopper's machine guns as it passed. Luckily only a few rounds found their mark, causing minimal damage.

Rafael, Joseph, and Chef Petit had scattered in various directions and sought cover as best they could. Rafael activated the safety switch on the rifle, steadied himself, and took aim at the windshield of the lead helicopter as it swooped toward them.

He pulled the trigger and was not sure whether it was going to do much good, however, I will give it my best shot and try to kill the pilot if possible, he thought.

Impossible to assess whether he hit the chopper through his swollen eyes because his vision had been impaired.

The sky lit up as the helicopter pilot continued to fire blindly in their direction.

There was a hiss from the Heat Seeking Missile fired by Wuhaib as it propelled itself toward the chopper and the trail of smoke was barely visible in the night sky. It fixed onto the chopper at close range and a moment later there was a massive explosion that lit up the sky like fireworks going off at a Guy Fawkes display. They watched as the helicopter tumbled to earth.

The second helicopter took evasive action, swiveling and swerving from side to side trying to avoid any other missiles that may be launched. It was flying perilously close to the ground and banked as the pilot tried to execute a one-hundred-and-eighty- degree turn and head back in that direction. Mousa aimed at the exhaust and squeezed the trigger. They watched as the missile's trail of smoke honed in on its target in the dark. It hit the helicopter's fuselage forcing it to the ground in a ball of fire, exploding on impact.

'Be a miracle if anybody survived that, however, one can never be sure because we don't have time to check it out.' 'Let's get the fuck out of here guys,' said Rafael forcefully.

'Please Dear Lord, let the SUV not be damaged and able to get us out of here.' 'I promise that I will come to church on your birthday every year to reward you for saving our lives,' whispered Rafael.

Wuhaib fired up the motor and they raced off in the direction of the Turkish border. Thankfully the only damage to the SUV was a shattered read window and numerous bullet holes in the cargo door. They needed to put as much distance between where they had shot the helicopters down and the border at Kapikoy Checkpoint, a distance of one hundred-and-twelve miles that would take around three-and-a-half hours.

Wonder if the Major was on board the second helicopter and if so, I don't believe that he would have survived, thought Rafael.

Wish I had time to go and check because I desperately want to punish that bastard. If he was on board the first helicopter, he could have survived, however, if he was in the second helicopter, he would most certainly have died in that ball of fire. Who knows? Considered Rafael.

Rafael looked at Joseph, 'did you notice that those two choppers were American Apache's.' 'They must have acquired them from the Taliban when the Yanks left Afghanistan.'

'We know that Iran and the Taliban are not friends, however, they are strategically aligned on key issues and share the same ideology,' said Rafael through swollen lips.

'Yes, we Israeli's know that only too well Rafael.' 'Going to be a huge problem if these two hold hands and fall in love, because the Iranians will make the Taliban do their dirty work for them.'

'Can you slow this thing down a little, Wuhaib?' 'We do want to make it to the border my friend,' said Rafael forcefully as they bounced along the road.

Three hours later, they could see a few lights in the distance as they got closer to the Kapikoy Checkpoint. Wuhaib turned onto a dirt track that ran parallel to the border with Turkey and drove a further ten miles along the fence line. He stopped at a remote site and killed the motor. Mousa was quickly out of the vehicle and checked to ensure that the coast was clear.

'Right guys, this is where you need to cross the border,' said Mousa.

'The border is about a mile away, and once over the border make your way northwest for about two miles heading directly toward the brightest star, namely Venus which will be fading fast as dawn approaches.' 'You will reach the foot of a small mountain range in around an hour which is around four miles inland from the border, and once there, you need to lie low.' 'A handler by the name of Hasan Uzan will pick you up at sunrise and get you guys to safety.'

'Use the phrase, "wish it would rain."'

To what Hasan will reply, 'Yes we need it.' 'That way you will be sure that you are in safe hands.'

The magenta coloring in the sky announced the coming dawn as Rafael, Joseph, and Bastienne neared the foot of the mountain range. They sought a suitable hiding spot and lay low.

'Bon sang, vous êtes vraiment dans le pétrin,' said Bastienne as he got a better look at Rafael and Joseph in the morning light. Damn, you guys are messed up.

'Oui, we are.' 'Very lucky to have escaped, and that you and the two agents were there to help us.' 'Very lucky indeed my friend.'

'We need to get you guys to hospital and get you checked, because, the way I see it, you may have some serious internal injuries,' said Bastienne.

Rafael felt the morning sun warm his face as they headed east, and an hour later they could hear a faint clunking noise of a vehicle as it rattled over the bumpy road in the distance, kicking up a trail of dust in its wake. They watched as the battered-out old Dolmus Minibus ground to a halt, close to where they were hidden.

The driver jumped out of the vehicle and stretched himself, then relieved himself. He was startled to see three guys standing behind him and wondered where they came from.

'Wish it would rain,' said Rafael.

'Yes we need it,' replied the driver.

Rafael offered his hand in a greeting, then introduced Joseph and Bastienne.

'My name is Hazan Uzan, and I have been instructed to drive you guys to Esiroglu which is about five miles from here.' 'A plane will pick you up there and fly you to the Incirlik Air Base, so let's get going.'

Thirty minutes later Hazan stopped on the outskirts of the town. A short while later a US Bell Boeing V22 Osprey with both vertical and conventional landing and take-off capabilities that was sent from the Air Base in Adana, hovered above the extraction point.

Incirlik Air Base is within an urban area consisting of one point seven million people, some seven miles east of the city, and twenty miles from the Mediterranean Sea. It hovered momentarily before landing in a cloud of dust.

Hazan bid the three farewell and drove off before the Osprey had taken off. An hour later as the plane taxied to a holding position at Incirlik Air Base, Rafael noticed Barnaby Heathcott, Chaviv Yudin, Director of Mossad and Étienne Beaulieu, the Direction générale de la Sécurité extérieure, (DGSE) France standing alongside a passenger stairway waiting for the plane to come to a halt.

Barnaby was horrified when Rafael and Joseph disembarked and made their way gingerly down the stairs.

'Sweet Lord in Heaven, what have they done to you two guys?' 'We need to get you to the hospital immediately.'

He summoned a waiting Captain and ordered him to get them to the Thirty-Ninth Medical Group Military Medical Facility which is the only facility in Turkey offering integrated medical care to NATO forces in the region.

The following day, Barnaby, Chaviv, and Étienne conducted a debriefing for Rafael and Joseph. They concluded that the two were extremely lucky to have survived the beatings and the escape.

'For what it's worth, you may not know that the two choppers were in fact American Apache's which from what we understand, had been acquired by Iran from the Taliban after we left Afghanistan, so our agents did America a small favour, by shooting them down.' 'Two less choppers able to inflict pain on western forces, thanks to our President walking away from billions of dollars of military hardware left in Afghanistan,' said Barnaby.

'Yes boss, we realized that,' said Rafael.

'Thankyou boss, for saving our lives,' said Rafael through swollen lips.

Chapter 12

Norfolk Naval Base

Virginia USA

As the taxi turned into the driveway, Yonti's eyes worked the paddock and he could not see any of his cows grazing in the meadow. That's most unusual he thought, as he exited the cab. He paid the driver, then picked up his bag and made his way gingerly up the stairs and onto the deck.

My body aches like hell, he thought.

Everything seemed so quiet and the house looked deserted, so his senses suddenly were on high alert. Hope I am just imagining. Maybe Claire and the boys saw the cab entering the property, and are hiding to give me a fright when I enter. He stopped, looked around, and convinced himself that he let his imagination get the better of him.

He tried the door handle and discovered that it was locked. Most unusual, he thought.

A strange eerie feeling overcame him as he suddenly feared that something may be wrong. His gut told him something was out of place, so he knocked on the door, and there was no response. He made his way to the barbeque, opened the storage door situated below the grill, and felt for the spare key that he had hidden on the inside lip of the grill.

A feeling of concern overcame him as he unlocked the door.

'Hello, I'm home,' he said.

No answer.

Maybe Claire and the boys had seen the cab driving into the property and had hidden somewhere and were about to give him a surprise as he entered. His eyes scanned the room ensuring that nothing was out of place. He breathed a sigh of relief and relaxed a little as everything appeared to be in place, however, he remained on high alert just in case there was a problem and he had misjudged the situation.

He removed his Glock from the rear of his pants, in case he encountered a problem. Always need to be ready, he reminded himself.

He checked all the rooms and everything appeared normal. As he passed a mirror, he suddenly stopped and looked at the image staring back at him. He was horrified to see himself. The first time he had seen himself since the beating.

Geez, I'm going to frighten the shit out of Claire and the boys, he thought.

He made his way into the kitchen and his eyes focused on a note lying on the island bench. He picked it up and read it.

My Darling Yonti,

I can no longer live with the fact, that one day I will lose you.

I admire your courage, strength, and conviction in your determination to make the world a better place, and in some small way, you have succeeded.

Your pursuance of justice is admirable, albeit some may argue that you push the boundaries too far.

I am truly grateful for the life we have had together, and for all that you have done for me and the boys.

I fear the worst and do not want the boys to grow up without a father.

Over time, I, however, have come to the conclusion that you and the CIA are inextricably linked, and I know that you miss the cut, thrust, and chase, of the job, so I am setting you free to continue doing the thing you love most. Catching those who have committed serious heinous crimes and punish them.

You have long ago used up all your nine lives Yonti, and then some. Each time you go off on a mission, I am on edge and know that someday there will be a knock on the door, and a person will be the bearer of bad news.

That's something I do not want to go through as the twins grow up. I am positive that they too, would not want that.

You have come close to death on a few occasions, and have been lucky enough to survive many serious situations.

You have done more than your fair share for America, France, and the rest of the world.

My undying love for you is eternal, which is why I can no longer stand in your way any longer.

I want you to always know that I pray for your safe return each time, as you depart on yet another mission, and will, continue to do so, albeit that I will not know when you are off on another crusade.

May the ray of light shine on you always, Yonti Barr.

All my love,

Claire. xxxxxx

He stood motionless for some time, the tears rolling down his cheeks as he tried to understand what he had just read. Only once before did he ever shed a tear in his life, which was when he heard that his parents had died in a plane crash. This time was different and the tears rolled down his cheeks. He realized that he had lost the people that he loved dearly. He walked into the lounge, sat in his favorite chair, for what seemed hours, and stared motionless at the waterfall cascading in the distance as he had done so many times in the past.

He shook his head, as he tried to clear his vision and focus his thinking on what he had just read, then dialed Claire's mobile phone. No answer, so he left a message. He wiped the tears from his cheeks and felt the need for a drink, so he tossed some ice cubes into a tumbler and poured a three-finger tot of his favorite drop, Johnny Walker Blue Scotch Whisky, then made his way to the walk-in robe in the ensuite and noticed that all of Claire's clothing was missing.

He checked the twin's bedroom and noticed that all their clothing were also missing.

That's when the reality of what had happened dawned on him.

An hour later he shook himself out of the stupor he was in and called Claire again. Still no answer. She is avoiding me, he considered.

Right, so what do I do?

First things first he decided, so he unpacked his gear.

He looked at the image staring back at him in the mirror for a second time and was again horrified at what he saw. His eye sockets were still badly swollen and his face was scarred in various places. Just as well my family were not here to see me, because I would most definitely have frightened the twins.

An hour later he called Claire again, and still no reply. Maybe she has gone to her parent's home or possibly to a friend. Who knows? Can't call her parents because I am not well-liked, so I will avoid that one. He wondered why Claire had done what she did.

'I always come home after a mission,' he said loudly.

'What did she expect me to do?'

'Nothing?'

'Surely she knew that I had to hunt down the people responsible for killing my parents and all those on board,' he said to himself.

All sorts of reasons raced through his head. Buggered if I know, he thought.

A week went by and having called Claire's mobile numerous times, she still did not answer nor return any of his calls. He checked his bank account and there had been no withdrawals and no transactions on the credit card either. She had accumulated a reasonable sum of her own money during the time that she worked in the Navy, however, those funds would quickly dissipate over time.

He called his neighbor Herr Torkel Kaufmann and asked whether he had seen Claire.

'Nein, not seen her, however, she asked me to move your cows to my paddock, until you return, so you can herd them back to your property whenever you choose my friend.'

'Danke Torkel.' 'If you don't mind, I would like to leave them there for a while, until I find Claire and the twins.'

He logged into Claire's account and accessed her credit card. She hadn't changed her password, so he was able to see all the transactions on the card. He scrolled down and noticed various transactions made recently in Sewells Point, the home base of the Norfolk Naval Station, in Virginia, USA, which is also the home base of the CIA.

A person may think that you know everything about your wife, however, as it turns out, you don't, he thought.

Right, so that's where she is, and thank goodness, she and the twins are in no danger, or that some terrorist group may have discovered where we live and kidnapped her and the boys.

He stared at several transactions made at a supermarket, liquor store, and the charge from the Young Guns Pre-School, noting that all were made in Sewells Point in Norfolk Virginia.

Yonti had always been fiercely independent, focused, and a person who was in charge of his destiny.

Right, so if that is what Claire wants, then so be it, he thought, considering his next move.

From memory, she knew no one in Norfolk, so he wondered whether she had re-enlisted in the Navy.

Norfolk Naval Station is located in the southeastern corner of the Sewells Point area of the Commonwealth of Virginia, collectively known as "Hamptons Roads" commonly referred to by the residents in the area. The naval station supports the operational readiness of the US Atlantic Fleet, providing facilities and services to enable mission accomplishment. If she did re-enlist in the Navy, she could be assigned to the Naval Station (NAVSTA) and would most likely be housed in accommodation provided by the Navy on the base.

Two days later, he donned dark sunglasses to hide his swollen face and boarded a Swiss Air flight to Washington Dulles International Airport. He needed to be sure that his family was safe. Having cleared customs, he hired a Jeep Renegade SUV and took a leisurely drive past the Norfolk Naval Station, before making his way to the Island Beach Hotel and booked in. He unpacked his gear and wandered downstairs and found a seat in the lounge, sat there staring at nothing in particular for a few hours. He had a hollow feeling in his gut.

Later that day, he drove back to the Naval Base to familiarise himself with the surroundings, however, was unable to enter to base. Early the next morning he drove to the Young Guns Pre-School, parked in an area with a view to the front entrance, and waited. Claire would most likely start work at around zero-nine hundred hours if she had re-enlisted in the Navy, so she would most likely take the boys to school at around zero-eight hundred hours. He waited patiently and watched as parents dropped off their children, and glanced at his watch, noting that it was zero eight-thirty, and wondered whether he had misjudged the possibility that Claire had re-enlisted in the navy. Moments later he realized that his assumption was correct when he saw a Toyota RAV 4 pull up at the entrance. Smartly dressed in her white navy uniform, Claire got out of the vehicle and shepherded the boys into the school.

It brought back memories of the first time I laid eyes on her at the USA Embassy in Paris.

His heart skipped a beat and he had to restrain himself from jumping out of the vehicle and running to her. He felt the need to embrace her so badly, however, he realized that she may not want to see him at all.

Tears welled up in his eyes again.

I only got back into the action because of the need to hunt and kill those responsible for killing my parents, as well as all the other people on the flight. I would then have gone back home, just as I did, and continue with my retirement life. He felt a tinge of resentment toward Claire for leaving the way she did. That feeling turned to annoyance.

What does she expect me to do? Simply forget about what had happened and carry on with life in the normal way, he thought.

He watched as Claire jumped into the Rav and as she made a U-Turn, he ducked to avoid being seen.

An hour later, he peeped over the fence and watched for a few minutes as the twins played with the other children.

Need to go, because this is killing me, he thought, so he made his way back to the vehicle and pointed it in the direction of the CIA's Headquarters in Langley.

He called Director Heathcott on a secure line.

'Hello Director, I'm in town, and just wondering whether I can pop in and see you, Sir.'

'Hello Yonti, yes I know that you are in town, so that would be great.' 'See you soon.'

How the fuck does he know that I'm in town, and what else does he know about me. This made him rather uncomfortable.

Miss Marple, greeted him as he made his way through the security check.

'Hello Yonti, long time no see.' 'How's retirement?' she said, using his family name rather than the undercover name of Rafael that he was accustomed to whilst working for the Firm.

'Boring, and to be honest, it took some time to adjust to that way of life to be truthful.'

Miss Marple tapped lightly on the door and announced his arrival.

'Hello young man, I was expecting you to pop in.'

'Hello Director, good to see you, Sir.' 'For what it's worth, how did you know that I'm in town?'

'I know everything Yonti.' 'As you know, this is the nature of the business I'm in.' 'I see that the swelling on your face seems to have gone down, which is good.' 'So you have a problem, and if there is anything I can do to help, just ask,' he said pointing to a chair.

Sweet Lord in Heaven, this old codger seems to know everything about me. Wonder if he knows when I take a shit, thought Yonti.

'Well Sir, you seem to know everything about my private life, and as you know my parents died on the Air France flight, along with many others.' 'Joseph Diamond and I nearly lost our lives when we hunted down those responsible, and killed them, with help from you.' 'Thank you, boss, for what you did and for saving our lives.'

'So again, I feel that it's appropriate to thank you for what you did to save Joseph Diamond and myself, from being killed by Major Farukh Zoheri, from the Iranian Revolutionary Guard Corps.' 'I do not doubt that he suspected that we killed his comrades in arms, and was going to put us on trial in Tehran, then execute us in a public square.' 'I'm most grateful to you for saving my skin, Director.'

'No problem Yonti.' 'From what we have found out, the Major survived the crash and sustained some serious burns to his face and parts of his body.' 'He has just been released from hospital.' 'So the reason that I am monitoring your every move, is that I believe that he will seek revenge for his helicopter having been shot down, and intends to hunt you down, and kill you as soon as he has recovered.'

'We have that from a reliable informant in Iran.'

Yonti sat back and listened intently to what Barnaby had just told him. Need to be on high alert, he thought.

'I suspect that we may have a mole in the Firm, albeit that I am not one hundred percent sure.' 'We are investigating the matter at this time, which is highly confidential, so if any information regarding yourself somehow finds its way to the Major, you and the CIA need to be fully aware and be prepared.'

'So, in the meantime, what brings you to pay me a visit?'

'Well Director, as you know Claire left me and took the boys with her.' 'I had a hunch that she may well have re-enlisted in the navy, and if I am not mistaken, she has found residence on the naval base.' 'I don't understand why she did that, however, she left me a note, and stated that she no longer wants to be faced with the possibility of someone knocking on our door bearing bad news.'

'I'm a realist, and to be truthful, if that is what Claire wants, then so be it, said Yonti.'

'I have to admit that I miss the cut, thrust, and chase, of the job.' 'Having hunted down the people responsible for the downing of the Air France plane that killed my parents and all those on board, it rekindled my desire to be involved again.'

Barnaby sat back and reflected on what he had just been told.

'Well, I for one, will be happy to welcome you back into the fold.' 'For what it's worth, my good friend Captain David De Santos, the commander of the Norfolk Naval Base called me a week ago, and asked my opinion on Claire, and whether he should reinstate her to full naval duty.' 'He knew that she was based at the US embassy in Paris and that she worked closely with the CIA, hence his call to me.'

'I learned that she had left you, so I gave him my full blessing to reinstate her because I felt that she and the boys would be safe here on the naval base here in Virginia.'

'So, if you want to re-join the CIA, I think it best, that we revert to the undercover name of Rafael Dujon.' 'You can start whenever you are ready.'

'I'm ready now Sir.'

'Good.' 'Right then, let's get straight to work Rafael.'

'First things first.' 'We suspect that someone working for General Aeronautical Aviation, the company that developed the latest Stealth Drone, called "Invisible," which the navy has adopted as their strike weapon, has been passing on secrets to the Russians, and the CIA needs to take care of this as matter of urgency.' 'The company is based in Prince William County here in Virginia and has a very sophisticated security system, so it is of concern that their system has been compromised, and highly classified secrets are possibly being passed onto Ivan.'

'They were recently awarded a billion dollar contract by Congress to develop the Invisible Stealth Drone for the navy.' 'The top naval brass are deeply concerned that secrets have been passed onto the Reds.' 'So, it's timely and ideal having you getting back into the game, because your expertise in computer engineering is highly valued.'

'We own an apartment in Dale City in Prince William County.' 'It is an ideal place to live, and close to town with excellent restaurants, café's, bars, and entertainment, so this is where I suggest you live until we have sorted out this problem Rafael.'

'Prince William is located in Northern Virginia on the Potomac River and has a population of close to half a million people, approximately thirty miles southwest of Washington D.C. encompassing an area of three hundred and forty-eight square miles in Metropolitan Washington D.C.' 'It's rich in American history, with sites significant to pivotal moments in the American Revolution, the Civil War, and the Civil Rights Movement that profoundly shaped the United States.' 'That's a shortened version of the place.'

Barnaby handed Rafael a new Glock, silencer, and ten clips of ammunition.

'Not your beloved Glock, however, this is his cousin, so I am sure it will do whatever job you require it to do.'

Rafael drove to the address given to him. Rather nice place he thought, as he unpacked his meagre belongings.

He called Torkel, his neighbor, and confirmed that he would be away for some time and asked him to allow his cattle to graze on his land so that the grass could remain at a reasonable level, and to kindly keep a watchful eye on his home.

The following morning, he drove to Langley and Miss Marple accompanied him to a secure soundproof basement conference room. He was surprised to see several of the Navy's top brass and a civilian seated around the conference table as he entered.

'Hello Rafael, let me introduce you to everyone,' said Barnaby.

'Gentlemen, this is Rafael Dujon, the very best agent I have ever had at the CIA, and the person we have been talking about.'

'Rafael, meet Admiral Aquinto, Commander Indo-Pacific, Admiral Usoro, Commander of the Expeditionary Aviation Strike Group Five and Task Forces Fifty-One and Fifty-Nine, Vice Admiral Steward O'Malley Naval Intelligence, Captain David De Santos, Commander of the Norfolk Naval Base, Peter Occhialini, Owner, CEO and lead engineer of General Aeronautical Aviation that developed the Invisible Stealth Drone.'

Rafael assumed his seat at the table and four hours later, he had an understanding of the problem. Not going to be easy to identify the person suspected of disclosing the family secrets, thought Rafael. He focused on Peter Occhialini. Peter met his gaze and seemed rather uncomfortable as he shifted in his seat. He appeared a little nervous, a possible sign that something was amiss, thought Rafael.

If that is not what has happened here, then the possibility exists that some Russian hacker has managed to infiltrate their system and download the company's secrets. Have to keep an open mind, he considered.

As the meeting concluded, Barnaby asked Admiral Aquinto, Peter Occhialini, and Rafael for a few minutes of their time.

'Gentlemen, just so that we are all clear.' 'Rafael is the best agent I have ever had under my command.' 'I trust him one hundred percent, so he will need your full cooperation.'

'You all know me well enough to know that I am a man of my word.' 'I do business with a shake of the hand.' 'That's my bond and my contract.' 'I look you in the eye, and don't need a written document to cover myself, you, or anybody else when I give you my word.'

'Trust is the way I do business, so I fully trust Rafael, and I am asking that you give Rafael full access to anything he wants gentlemen, and be sure, he will delete all information after he is done with it, and will never disclose, or speak of any of this to anyone, once he has completed his assignment.'

Barnaby stood indicating that he had concluded the meeting, and asked Rafael to remain.

'It appears, albeit, none of us can be sure, that we have a possible serious breach of security, so I need you to ferret out whether that is the case, Rafael.' 'The CIA has picked up snippets of conversation on the wire, hence our meeting with Admiral Aquinto which has resulted in us meeting today.' 'Everything discussed here today is classified, and can only be discussed between the two of us.'

'From what I understand, Peter Occhialini had amassed personal wealth of around one hundred million dollars, and spent almost all of it on Research and Development for the Invisible Stealth Drone Project, so he had almost depleted all of his wealth.' 'A brave move to lay it all on the table for one project, to say the least, however, I admire his conviction, and have no doubt that he was confident in what he was developing.' 'I truly admire that in someone,' said Barnaby.

'I have known Peter for several years, so I am hoping that you can shed some light on whether there is a leak within his company, and he has agreed to give you full access to their company secrets and IT.' 'Luckily the Navy liked what they saw and awarded him a multi-million dollar contract, which was verified by the Senate.' 'Between us, I think congratulations are appropriate for Mr. Occhialini.'

Barnaby noted that Peter sat back in the meeting indicating that he was astounded to hear how much the CIA knew, and must have wondered what else Barnaby knew about him. Barnaby watched Peter's reaction during the conversation and saw a glimmer of concern hoping that the CIA had not discovered his lover, because if his wife ever found out, she most certainly would take him to the cleaners.

'So from what Peter told us, all the Research and Development was documented on a separate laptop which was always securely locked up in a safe within a vault.' 'So this makes it rather challenging, to say the least.'

'He also said that the laptop used for development was never out of his sight, and each time they either recessed or at the end of each day, it was locked away in the safe within the vault.' 'He also said that the vault was on a time-delay sequence to lock it and that the entire complex is secured that way.' 'According to Peter, the complex has more CCTV cameras than the White House, and every inch of the place is covered.'

'From what we understand, all Internet access was done on a separate system, and there was no interface with the laptop.' 'They downloaded any information to a separate system, saved it, then copied it to the laptop each time they needed to use the Internet to gather, check, or copy data.'

'So Rafael, I think that you should check all the footage of the meetings, and the surrounding areas because you should leave no stone unturned.' 'He has agreed to you having full access to all their records, including personal information on his team of engineers, as well as their salaries, bonuses, perks, etc. etc.'

'I suggest that you start with viewing footage of the meetings and all other coverage of the facility, and yes, I know that could be hundreds of hours of arduous time spent viewing the footage, but it needs to be done to determine if anything spikes your interest.' 'Also suggest that you put your skill in computer engineering to good use, and hack into each engineer's Internet account, and see if anything jumps out.'

'For your knowledge, Peter is having an affair with a twenty-four-year-old lady who goes by the name of Geneviève Protish and is keeping her in an apartment near to where you are living.' 'God only knows what secrets he may be telling her, so we have planted a bug in her bedroom, however, to date it appears that he has not disclosed any secrets.'

'One never knows what people think when it comes to the power of the pussy.'

'He bought her a new red BMW M2, pays the rent and all expenses such as food, electricity, rates, and water.' 'She lives alone and works as a real estate agent for a company called County Realtors based in their regional office in town.' 'She has blond hair and is rather sexy, so one can understand why she caught his eye.' 'He tends to meet her after work every other day when he supposedly goes to the gym, or that is what his wife believes.'

'Cleary that's how he gets a workout, bobbing up and down.'

Rafael smiled at Barnaby's sense of humor.

'His wife's name is Candice, and they have two children, an eight-year-old girl called Harlow, and a six-year-old boy that goes by the name of Dale.' 'Both are in primary school and Candice is a typical doting mother, focused on the kid's wellbeing, and she has no idea that her husband is having extramarital activities at all,' said Barnaby.

'My understanding is that he intends to leave his wife, and is moving money around, so his wife has no idea of what he is doing.' 'I have uncovered that he put a million dollars into an account in Geneviève's name, and is likely to move a large amount into that account shortly,' continued Barnaby.

'Albeit that Peter and I have been friends for a long time, when it comes to infidelity, I draw the line.' 'That's where we part ways,' added Barnaby.

'As I understand it, his team consists of ten engineers including himself and each of the nine engineers has a two and a half percent share in the business, thus each would have cashed out at around twenty-five million.'

'Handsome sum of money indeed, so that would have left Mr. Occhialini with around three-quarters of a billion.' 'A huge amount of money in anyone's language,' said Barnaby.

Rafael wondered why Peter would have an affair and put a huge part of his wealth at risk, because if his wife ever found out she would undoubtedly take him to the cleaners. Rather, sail off into the sunset and enjoy the fruits of his labor. Doesn't make any sense. He must have a horny cock, he thought.

He immediately got to work and accessed the company's CCTV footage of the outer façade of the complex, and trolled through dozens of hours of footage by fast-tracking the tape and stopping it whenever a person came into view, checking the time, date, and what the person was doing. Nothing appeared out of the ordinary, and there was no footage of anybody entering the complex after hours, except the owner. This took several days to complete. He then viewed all the footage of the meetings and noted that Peter always sat at the head of the table at the far end away from a whiteboard that they used regularly.

He noticed that a couple of times when the footage was relayed onto a screen on the wall from a laptop computer,the team was focused on the images being displayed and Peter seemed to insert something into the laptop which he believed could be a USB stick. It appeared that he had briefly recorded something without the knowledge of the other engineers seated at the table.

Rather strange, thought Rafael.

This happened several times and each time, Peter seemed to insert a USB stick, it appeared that he had recorded something for a couple of minutes.

So why on earth would the owner of the business do that? After all, it's his business, and surely he could access or copy anything he wanted to at any time, considered Rafael.

Twice a week, Rafael would park outside the Young Guns Pre-School front entrance and wait for Claire to drop the boys off, and each time he ducked as she made a U-Turn and headed back to the Base, ensuring that he was not seen. Amazing how she never suspected something could be amiss. After all, she should surely have noticed the same vehicle parked in the same place twice weekly. Amazing that people are not vigilant, and simply go about their day-to-day activities without noticing. His training at Camp Perry under the guidance of his handler fondly known as The Hulk, ensured that his senses were on high alert at all times.

An hour later he peeped over the fence to get a glance of his beloved twins. As much as it affected him, he always wanted to see his two young guns playing and interacting with other children in the playground. He wondered what Claire had said to the twins when they relocated to the Naval Base.

Each time he left, it broke his heart.

Chapter 13

National Intelligence Centre

Maryland USA

Barnaby arranged for the Navy to create a profile of Rafael, making it seem like he had joined ten years previously. He appeared to have risen through the ranks to Captain and was seconded to the Office of Naval Intelligence (ONI), a Naval Investigative Service (NCIS) that determines, who within the Department of the Navy is eligible to hold security clearance and have access to Sensitive Compartmented Information (SCI) or assigned to Sensitive duties. Its headquarters are based at Sicard Street in Washington, and they arranged to have an office for him at the National Maritime Intelligence Center in Suitland, Maryland as well.

Barnaby called Peter Occhialini, CEO of General Aeronautical Aviation to ensure that Rafael had full access to their system with total security clearance, allowing him access to the company's highly classified information including all secret new developments.

Peter had been friends with Barnaby for years and agreed without hesitation to every request he made.

The top Navy Brass agreed to allow Rafael full access to all their sensitive information. Commander Fred Skalbeck agreed that he could have an office at the Navy's Central Adjudication Facility (DON CAF). It is a command responsibility to ensure that appropriate security clearances are obtained from the Department of the Navy Central Adjudication Facility (DON CAF) for members before their transfer to attend courses of instruction requiring access to classified information.

Students normally must be cleared for such access at the beginning of their training period, however, they waived that requirement in Rafael's case. It is administratively inappropriate to place the responsibility for initiating personnel security investigations and obtaining personnel security clearances upon the command conducting the instruction.

Barnaby allowed him to have an office based at the CIA's headquarters in Langley, thus he had multiple offices, making it extremely difficult for anyone trying to get a fix on him. Nobody, except the Top Navy Brass, would ever know that he existed, or that he worked for the Navy, nor where he was at any given time. He would report directly to Admiral Aquinto.

Claire was based at the Office of Naval Intelligence (ONI) at the Norfolk Naval Base in Virginia, close to where Rafael had an office, and he had to take care not to accidentally bump into her. He hardly ever used that office and chose to steer well clear of the area, preferring to use the office allocated to him at CIA headquarters instead.

He found out where she lived on the base and familiarised himself with the neighborhood as a precautionary measure.

Rafael admired the image of himself in his crisp new white naval uniform staring back at him in the mirror. Smart, real smart, he thought as he leaned forward and glared at the Captain's insignia on the lapels. Reminded him of Claire's dress code when he first met her. Wonder what her reaction would be if she saw me now. He saluted himself, then took a selfie, just in case they ever rekindled their relationship, which would undoubtedly surprise her no end.

He reported for duty to Commander Skalbeck at the Navy's Central Adjudication Facility (DON CAF) and was shown to an office allocated to him, and was pleasantly surprised to discover that the office was fully set up and functional. As he entered the office, he noticed the plaque on the wall which read, "Non sibi sed patriae" – Latin for "Not self, but country." Very good, he considered.

Commander Skalbeck talked him through the login procedure and the system protocol. He watched as Rafael did his analysis of the cyber security of the system and was impressed at his computer expertise and how he quickly grasped the inner workings of their system. He introduced Rafael to various members of the team and spent time briefing him on the Navy's concern regarding a possible spy passing on the secrets of the Stealth Drone to the Russians.

Rafael immediately got to work, logged into the General Aeronautical Aviation's computer system and set himself up as a sleeper cell using the simple method of Wake-on-Lan which allows a computer to be turned on remotely. He set up the motherboard by configuring WoL through BIOS, then logged into the OS and made the necessary changes, so that the Wake-on-Lan can turn any computer on when it receives a magic packet. He enabled WoL and set up BIOS correctly so that the software could listen for incoming wake-up requests.

He entered BIOS instead of booting the operating system and searched for the section that pertained to Power Management in the Advanced Section, then accessed the login section and altered the setup protocol with an algorithm to ensure complete covertness.

After he had set it all up, he accessed all the users in the system, downloaded their passwords, and copied them to a USB Stick.

He suspected that whoever was copying and downloading secret documents may be doing it in stages, hoping that it would not draw any attention to what he or she was doing.

Possible that the person had set up an algorithm procedure, hoping to remain anonymous.

Peter Occhialini, CEO of General Aeronautical Aviation, assured him that all people working on the development of the prototype, were compartmentalized and no one had total access to the entire project other than himself.

He requested a full list of names of the people who were involved in the design and development of the prototype and scrolled through the list taking note of the names listed. A total of ten Engineers including Mr. Occhialini were involved. The Assistant Engineer was Otis Wilke.

He checked the company's HR records and focused on Otis' CV, noting that he had graduated with honors with an Aerospace Engineering Degree and majored in Aeronautical Engineering at the University of Washington.

Impressive, thought Rafael.

I need to infiltrate this close-knit group of geeks and try to ferret out if there is a mole and who that might be, so he identified the pub frequented by the group and noted that they appeared to have drinks every Friday evening after work. He made a habit of ensuring that he found a corner seat in the pub every Friday evening and watched as the group interacted with each other. He noted that they tended to be rather loud and boisterous as the evening wore on. The more alcohol they consumed, the louder they got. Not a good sign, thought Rafael.

Could be a good time to make their acquaintance, he thought, so he sauntered over to where they were standing at the bar and summoned the barman.

'Bonjour Monsieur, another Heineken beer please.'

One of the geeks, leaned over and said, 'Oh, so you are French?'

'Oui, I am French Monsieur.'

'Well howdy, I'm Elijah Calascione.' 'So what is a Frenchman doing in Prince William County?'

'I'm investigating propulsion systems for the French navy, and have an upcoming meeting with the Commander of the Naval Base here in Norfolk soon.'

'Well, you have come to the right place my friend.' 'This is the home of aeronautics, and all these guys work for General Aeronautical Aviation, which is a leader in innovation.' 'In fact, we have developed world-leading edge technology that will change the way wars will be fought in the future.'

He was rather inebriated and loose with his tongue, so Rafael offered to buy him another drink.

'Thanks, that's kind of you my friend,' said Elijah.

The barman poured his usual double tot of Bulleit Bourbon Whisky and topped it up with ice cubes and a dash of Coca-Cola.

Clinking glasses, Elijah said, 'down the hatch.'

Seems, he had forgotten about his friends as he struck up a conversation with Rafael.

'So what do you do for a crumb Elijah?'

'I am an Aeronautical Engineer and part of a team that has developed some innovative stuff, designed to keep America safe.'

'Sounds interesting.'

'Sure is, and we have another project under development right now.'

'Well, I've got to get going, so, Au revoir as they say in France,' he said, as he downed the Bourbon, rose, bid Rafael and his fellow workers farewell, then staggered toward the exit.

Will need to look him up when I get the chance, thought Rafael.

Rafael, busied himself each day, accessing all of the nine Engineers' emails, and patiently trolled through all the correspondence on file, however, nothing appeared to be out of the ordinary or of any concern. So he shifted his focus to the threat that Artificial Intelligence posed to companies.

Need to keep an open mind.

He was aware that Researchers at Cornwell University located in Ithaca, New York, had discovered a new way for Artificial Intelligence to steal data keystrokes. This new technology worried him greatly.

AI-driven attacks can steal passwords with an accuracy of ninety-five percent by listening to what is typed on a keyboard. Researchers trained an AI model on the sound of keystrokes and deployed it onto a nearby phone. The integrated microphone listened for keystrokes on a Mac Book Pro and was able to reproduce the keystrokes with an accuracy of up to ninety-five percent.

Test results during a Zoom call were recorded with a laptop's microphone during a meeting with a ninety-three percent accuracy in reproducing keystrokes. In Skype, the model was ninety-one point seven percent accurate. Only a matter of time until technology achieves a one hundred percent accuracy, thought Rafael.

It's a frightening problem facing corporations, governments, the military, and the world at large, he considered.

Companies fiercely guard trade secrets, and the confidential information within software is vehemently guarded, and legally enforceable patent monopoly over an AI system or AI-created invention.

It would be expensive with a potentially uncertain patent application in the future. As AI becomes an increasingly important business asset, companies may protect their AI by treating them as trade secrets, rather than applying for patent protection and facing expensive application processes.

Criminals, hackers, and mole handlers have figured out how valuable Artificial Intelligence is for breaching cybersecurity and exploiting loopholes. Cybersecurity software and programs often remain one step behind, fixing bugs as they appear in their systems. It has been estimated that cyber-crimes cost an estimated six trillion US dollars globally each year.

Attackers use artificial intelligence to do considerable damage, by manipulating machine learning in bots to make mistakes and cracking passwords or bypassing system protocols with Generative Adversarial Networks and data poisoning techniques.

Back in 2018, Defense Advanced Research Projects Agency (DARPA) announced a two billion US dollar investment in human-AI collaborative systems. Anyone familiar with DARPA knows its secretive nature means that AI research goes back to 2018.

US defense technology is contracted to private contractors for manufacturing and many computer networking systems that the general public use as consumers comes from DARPA. The Pentagon has doubled down on artificial intelligence and is figuring out how to fold ChatGPT into their workflows without risking their corporate secrets and intellectual property.

What was troubling Rafael, was that there was a possibility that Ivan was using this technology to access General Aeronautical Aviation's most guarded secrets.

He had to keep an open mind and consider that no one may have been disclosing company secrets, rather that Ivan had found a way through AI to infiltrate the company's closely guarded patents.

A technique used by criminals called "brute forcing" could also benefit from AI, where many combinations of characters and symbols are tried in turn to see if they match passwords. Long, complex passwords are safer; as they are harder to guess by this method. Brute forcing is resource-intensive, but it's easier if you know something about the person. For example, this allows lists of potential passwords to be ordered according to priority–increasing the efficiency of the process. For instance, they could start with combinations that relate to the names of family members or pets. Algorithms trained on data could be used to help build these prioritized lists more accurately and target many people at once–so fewer resources are needed. Specific AI tools could be developed to harvest a person or company's online data and then used it to analyze it all to build a profile of the person or company.

He needed to explore every possible avenue to assess whether there was a mole inside the company, and if any secrets had been passed onto the Russians. Having trolled through a few hundred hours of footage, nothing seemed out of place, so he replayed footage of the meetings that involved all the engineers. Again nothing untoward caught his attention.

From what he had been told, and from what he had observed in the hours of footage that he reviewed, was that the meeting room used by the engineers was in some sort of a vault that had a time delay locking sequence on it, meaning that meetings could only last a certain number of hours before everyone had to leave the room. The room would automatically lock at a certain set time, ensuring maximum security, and the room did not have a conventional ceiling, rather a concrete structure and no doors other than the vault door, nor did it have any windows. The entire structure was encased in concrete with a small air vent that was apparent on the side of the room near the vault door.

The company was extremely sensitive about the need to safeguard its integral property and placed a huge emphasis on security.

So if there is some sort of a leak, how is it happening, wondered Rafael.

The Navy had paid handsomely for exclusive rights of the drone and wanted the patent well-guarded and kept secret. They had been warned by the CIA that there could be a possible breach of data being sold to Ivan, because they had picked up a snippet of electronic chatter, from what appeared to be a handler based at the Russian Embassy in Washington.

Rafael once again replayed the footage of the meetings, and could not find anything of concern, so he accessed the company's security system and trolled through the data. He discovered that only one person had access to it, which was Peter Occhialini, the owner and CEO of the business.

OK, so I need to shine a light on this guy, to see if anything catches my attention, thought Rafael.

Highly unlikely that he is involved, however, I cannot discount him either. He may be selling his secrets. Certainly not likely, but you never know, what people would do when it comes to money.

The question is, if it turns out to be Mr. Occhialini, why on God's Earth would he do that? Wondered Rafael.

He turned his attention to Mr. Occhialini's private life.

He recalled the conversation that he had with Barnaby some time ago, in which Barnaby stated that Mr. Occhialini was having an affair and intended leaving his wife. He was also secretly moving money around. His wife had no idea of what he was doing either. Barnaby had uncovered that he had put a million dollars into an account in Geneviève's name, and intended moving a large amount into that account shortly.

He was going to leave his wife and divorce her at some point shortly. Amazing what a piece of fluff can do to a man, thought Rafael.

He yearned for the opportunity to hug his wife and twins again and had to shake his head to bring himself back to reality and concentrate on the task at hand.

Rafael decided to follow Mr. Occhialini discreetly and see where it led him, so he parked in a secluded spot outside

Geneviève's apartment with a view of the front entrance. On cue, Mr. Occhialini arrived at seventeen-thirty hundred hours, parked his car, and then made his way up the stairs to his lover's apartment. He paused at the entrance and looked around to ensure that he had not been followed. Two hours later he made his way back to his car and drove home. This continued every second day, so Rafael assumed that he serviced his wife every other day.

Randy bastard, thought Rafael.

Rafael placed a Spytec GPS GL300 tracker on the undercarriage of Occhialini's car alongside the exhaust toward the rear fender. Need to track this bloke and see what he is up to. He understood Mr. Occhialini's reason for the high level of security at the company to safeguard its secrets, however, he was troubled by what he had discovered. It appeared that the time sequence security system that had been installed, could only be overridden by Mr. Occhialini himself, and albeit that he had gone to great measures to safeguard the company's secrets, his gut told him something strange was happening.

He checked the number of times that the system had been overridden and discovered that Mr. Occhialini had done this on a few occasions, meaning that he had overridden the time delay lock sequence system and entered the vault.Not sure why he would do that at all and whatever he did, only took five and a half minutes before he exited the vault, which troubled Rafael.

Why would he continue to do this, thought Rafael?

I can understand that you may need to get in once or twice maybe, but not the number of times that he had entered, so something does not add up, considered Rafael.

He discovered that if ever the system was overridden, it would only allow a six-minute window before it resets itself.

If he is doing something untoward, it would take a minute to fire up the computer, and if he was downloading company secrets, he would only have a couple of minutes before he had to shut the system down and get out, so he wondered whether he was downloading design secrets in small segments.

Why would he do that, especially after he had been paid a billion US dollars for the development of the drone? Does not make any sense at all. This troubled Rafael greatly.

The time delay sequence must have been a security measure installed to satisfy the Navy, ensuring that the company secrets were secure.

He called Barnaby on a secure line.

'Hello Boss, if I find out that someone is disclosing secrets to Ivan, what do you want me to do?'

There was silence for a minute before Barnaby replied. 'Well, I know that you cannot use your usual technique on this mission, rather, arrest the person responsible, get the FBI to charge him or her, and let the Navy deal with it.'

'I see, well, I have my suspicion that Mr. Occhialini may be involved.'

'Yes, that's a possibility, because he loaned money from a Russian loan shark known as "Big Red", to complete the project at a forty percent interest rate, and that may well be the reason for whatever he is doing.' 'The loan shark's name is Anatoly Antonov and he is a well-know, ruthless thug, who ensures that he uses violent methods to get paid, so an extremely dangerous person.'

'He resides in Au-Tenleytown one of the most influential residential areas in Washington, and if you are going to investigate him, be very careful.'

Rafael wondered why Barnaby had not told him that before. This old codger keeps all the cards close to his chest, and will only tell a person on a need-to-know basis, thought Rafael.

Chapter 14

Pike Place Market

Seattle Washington USA

Rafael used his expertise in computer engineering to infiltrate Anatoly's emails and discovered several emails from Mr. Occhialini.

One of the emails from Antonov caught his attention.

It read, 'I want it all within the next four weeks.' 'As agreed, you do not have to pay the fifty million back, just give me the blueprints.' 'If you do not comply, you know what the consequences will be.'

It confirmed what Barnaby had told him that Mr. Occhialini had run out of money developing the prototype, and needed to borrow some quick cash to get the project over the line. Now this prick was holding him to account, and wanted the blueprints which one must assume, he would sell to his Russian masters for a fortune, thought Rafael as he sat back in his chair.

He discreetly followed Mr. Occhialini at a distance each day and watched as he continued his normal routine of visiting his lover every second day, before making his way home. This continued for the next couple of weeks until he suddenly deviated from this routine one day and drove toward a pub called, "The Purple Door," situated in Post Alley at Pike Place Market.

Rafael tracked Mr. Occhialini's car, ensuring that he remained some distance behind him, eventually turning into the parking lot at The Purple Door Pub. As he made his way into the complex, his eyes worked the pub, eventually noticing Mr. Occhialini sitting at a corner table with a bald, tubby-looking man.

Rafael took note of the two heavies seated at a table next to where Occhialini and the tubby guy were seated, so he casually made his way to the corner of the bar and ordered a beer. He sauntered over to a vacant table close to where the two were seated and dropped his newspaper on the table. Luckily a pillar blocked most of the view to their table, which was ideal because it allowed him to be able hide behind if needed. The newspaper would come in handy when the two decided to leave because he could open it, pretend to be reading it, and hide behind it.

Could not let Occhialini see him because he would recognize him and the game would be up, so he needed to be extremely careful.

He took great care not to look in their direction, so he opened his mobile phone and activated the record app.

The phone had an inbuilt recording device on it, allowing him to video and record everything that was being said, albeit that he would need to get the CIA technicians to enhance the sound as it was hardly audible. He kept his eyes on the phone, pretending to be texting someone, however, he was recording the conversation and watched the pair interacted with each other. He did not look in their direction, smiling at the iPhone, pretending to have found something humorous in a text.

He watched the image being recorded on his phone, noting that the two spoke in hushed tones. Anatoly appeared annoyed at something that was said and lightly banged his fist on the table to emphasize something that he had said. From what Barnaby had told him, Anatoly reportedly had his hands in extortion, drug trafficking, prostitution, and weapons trading.

He had connections to the Russian State intelligence organizations and their crime partners that operated in both Russia and the United States. Well-connected in those circles, he was known as "Big Red" in the underworld. The name "Big Red" reflected his image, which is that of a short fat guy from Russia. A very dangerous man.

Rafael noticed one of his henchmen stand in his peripheral vision, so he quickly ended the recording, then logged into one of his SMS text messages and continued to respond to a message on the screen. The henchman made his way towards the bar, stopped behind him, and took a look at his mobile phone over his shoulder. Satisfied that he was interacting with an SMS message and was not recording anything, he returned to his seat.

You have to be extremely careful because this huge bastard is most likely carrying some heavy armor and won't hesitate to use it. I hope that I have recorded enough of the conversation to establish what Mr. Occhialini is up to, considered Rafael.

Time to get the hell out of here, he thought.

He finished his beer and made his way out of the pub before the two had finished their conversation. Too dangerous to stick around, and too bad if he missed something important that had been said, he decided.

Later that day he replayed the video recording several times and listened intently to the conversation. He was able to pick up snippets of what had been said. "Big Red" seemed to have reiterated his threat, that he wanted the blueprints in his hands within four weeks or Mr. Occhialini would never see his kids again. Big Red tilted his head toward the Hulk sitting at the table behind him as a warning.

Need to get the technicians to confirm what I think I heard, thought Rafael.

He recalled that Barnaby said that Mr. Antanov lived in Au-Tenleytown, an influential residential area in Washington.

The following day, he donned a peak cap and sunglasses and drove into town. He hailed a cab and instructed the driver to drive him around the area, pretending to want to buy a property, and as they approached Mr. Antanov's residence, he asked the driver to slow down. He noticed the CCTV surveillance cameras scattered around the property.

Right, so this is where the Russian mafia boss lives, thought Rafael as they drove past the residence.

The Russian mafia, referred to as Solntsevskaya Bratva, is a collective of various crime elements, making them one of the most feared criminal groups in the world. No chance of visiting him there, because the joint is heavily guarded, alarmed, and fortified, so best to seek an alternative avenue into his world, considered Rafael.

Rafael again, wondered why on earth Mr. Occhialini loaned money from the gangster, rather than finding funding elsewhere. Did not make any sense at all, so he called his boss to try and shed some light on the issue.

'Hello Boss, me again.'

'Thought you might call Rafael.'

'I have been wondering why Mr. Occhialini did not borrow the money he needed from a bank, rather than borrow it from Anatoly Antonov?' Asked Rafael.

'Well, he did approach several banks, however, none were prepared to risk fifty-million dollars on a project that may never eventuate, so it appears that he had no other choice, but to borrow the money from the Russian mafia.' 'To complicate matters, Mr. Occhialini is porking Geneviève Protish, who just happens to be Anatoly's sister-in-law,' said Barnaby.

'That's where the connection comes into play, and how he ended up borrowing money from the Russian mafia.' 'Gives a whole new meaning to cooking your goose.' 'Clearly, he is in that deep, there is no escape for him now, so we need to catch him red-handed and have him arrested along with "Big Red" and his cronies in the Russian mafia.' 'You need to tread wearily Rafael.' 'These people are killers.'

'So that is how Mr. Antonov got involved,' said Rafael.

'From what I have managed to find out so far, is that he is using his sister-in-law's affair with Mr. Occhialini to his advantage, and maybe, just maybe, he is disclosing company secrets to her in bed.' 'Who knows?' 'So again Rafael, be extremely careful, this bastard is very dangerous,' continued Barnaby.

Each morning Rafael parked the Jeep at the park overlooking the street that Anatoly lived in and waited. At precisely ten hundred hours, each day, he noted that the Russian mafia boss, left his home accompanied by his two thugs and was driven to the Naslazhdeniye Turkish Baths Resort situated in Prince George's County in northeast Washington DC. He noted the sign above the entrance that read-Delight, Enjoyment, Gratification, and Relish and wondered what else they specialized in.

Two hours later Mr. Antonov made his way out of the complex and headed toward a brothel situated in the Logan Circle neighborhood. This seemed to be his daily routine and Rafael made sure that he followed at a discreet distance. He discovered that Mr. Antonov owned the brothel, so this must be where he conducts his criminal activities from.

Rafael had grown a beard over several weeks, and he purposely let his hair grow longer, giving him a somewhat sophisticated regal look when he combed it in a different style, making him somewhat unrecognizable from the time that he sat at a table near where Mr. Occhialini and Mr. Antonov met at the Purple Door Pub.

Need to visit the Naslazhdeniye Turkish Baths Resort and check the lie of the land, so he called ahead and booked an appointment for thirteen hundred hours. He arrived on time and made his way into the complex, taking note of the level of security as he approached the reception desk. The receptionist handed him a couple of towels and pointed him toward the changing rooms. As he made his way down the passage he noticed the two heavies positioned outside a door which he believed could be Mr. Antonov's office. Must be where "Tubby," the mafia boss conducts his business, thought Rafael.

He visited the facility three times a week and appeared to have been accepted as one of the regulars. Each time he visited the complex, he took the opportunity to case the place and seek a possible way of eliminating this mafia bastard. Nobody had bothered to frisk him or check the contents of the sling bag that he carried each time he visited the complex. He was amazed at how lackadaisical and comfortable the mafia boss was in his environment. He must believe that he is bulletproof.

Possibly an opportunity to smuggle my beloved Glock into the joint and take the mafia boss as well as his two heavies out in one hit. He reminded himself that his boss wanted Mr. Occhialini to be arrested and to have the Navy take care of him as well as Mr. Antonov. Pity, real pity because the world needs to be rid of scum like this, thought Rafael.

Rafael trolled through Mr. Antonov's emails looking for other activities he may be involved in. Amazing what a person can find by searching through people's private emails and how much they tend to disclose online. He noticed several emails written in Russian to various unknown people, which he assumed would be fellow Russian mafia bosses, so he accessed a report written by James O. Finckenauer Ph.D. at the International Center-International Institute of Justice to get a better understanding of what he was dealing with.

Russian mafia or the Russian mob groups, Organizatsya, Bor, Bratva, as they are known have adopted names that refer to geographical locations in Russia - Izmailovskaya, Dagestantsy, Kazanskaya, and Solntsenskaya.

The latter is indicative of the local geographically defined roots of some Russian crime groups. It is estimated that approximately fifteen of these loosely categorized criminal groups are operating in the United States and that eight or nine of them maintain links to Russia.

The estimated membership of these groups is between five to six thousand members. It was estimated in a report published by the Global Organized Crime Project of Washington's Center for Strategic and International Studies, ("Russian Organized Crime: Putin's Challenge") that two hundred large ROC groups were currently operating in fifty-eight countries worldwide, including the United States. The threat and use of violence is a defining characteristic of Russian organized crime.

Violence is used to gain and maintain control of criminal markets, and retributive violence is used within and between criminal groups. The common use of violence is not surprising since extortion and protection rackets are such a staple of Russian criminal activity. ROC had engaged extensively in contract murders, kidnapping, and arson against businesses whose owners refused to pay extortion money. Six members of the Gufield-Kutsenko Brigade pleaded guilty in New York to federal racketeering charges involving terrorizing business owners to extort money.

The Tri-State Joint Soviet-Émigré Organized Crime Project looked specifically at violent crimes in the New York, New Jersey, and Pennsylvania regions. According to their report, Russian criminals have been implicated in numerous murders, attempted murders, assaults, and extortion.

Need to be extremely careful, because these are very dangerous people, Rafael reminded himself.

Later that day, Rafael again accessed Mr. Antonov's emails and took note of the message sent to Mr. Occhialini arranging a meeting at the Naslazhdeniye Turkish Baths Resort for the following day at fourteen hundred hours so he contacted Barnaby.

'Hello Boss, as I understand it, Antonov and Occhialini have scheduled a meeting for tomorrow at fourteen hundred hours, so I think this is when he intends to hand over the blueprints of the drone.' 'I can take them both out and retrieve the blueprints if you so desire?'

'Think about it boss, if the FBI arrests them, they are likely to wriggle their way out of this because they will most certainly threaten the judge, or pay him off, so we can end it once and for all and be rid of both in one hit.'

Barnaby thought about it for a minute.

'Well, I tend to agree with you Rafael.' 'It's very risky to take them out, however, what you have said, is very true.' 'This mafia boss has been arrested previously on racketeering charges, but, somehow managed to wriggle his way out of it.' 'So if the opportunity presents itself, then you need to make a judgment call.' 'I'm not agreeing with it, nor am I dismissing it.'

'If you do that, you need to be sure that you can retrieve the blueprints, sanitize the area, and remove any CCTV footage because we don't want to be implicated in any way whatsoever.' 'We have never been there Rafael.'

The next day Rafael arrived at thirteen hundred hours and parked a couple of miles away from the complex. He hailed a cab and instructed the driver to take him to the Naslazhdeniye Turkish Baths Resort and asked the driver to drop him off a few blocks from the complex. He walked the rest of the way and donned a pair of skin-colored plastic gloves before entering and making his way to the reception desk.

'I'm booked for a steam bath and massage,' he said to the attractive receptionist.

Instinctively, he gripped the heavy bag tightly, which gave him comfort that his Glock was hidden where he had put it. The receptionist handed him two towels and he made his way toward the changing rooms, passing the two heavies standing guard outside the door which he assumed would lead to the mafia boss' office.

He did not bother to change and stood on the inside of the door leading to the change room and kept it slightly ajar preventing it from closing. This allowed him to peep through opening and monitor what was happening in the passage. His eyes worked the changing room and he was pleased to see that he was the only person in the room. The two heavies were engaged in conversation and did not notice that the door had not closed. Right on cue, he noticed Mr. Occhialini arrive carrying a large art portfolio bag with shoulder sling straps which he assumed held the blueprints for the drone. One of the heavies tapped on the door and let him in.

Luckily no one was taking a steam bath at the time, so Rafael waited for five minutes before removing the Glock from the bag and attaching the silencer. He activated the safety switch, checked to ensure that there was a round in the chamber ready to be fired, and then placed it in the back of his pants. He ran his hand over it to be sure that he was ready for action. A moment later he entered the passage and walked toward the exit, then in an instant, retrieved the Glock from the back of his pants and shot both heavies between the eyes. All done in a flash.

The two heavies slid gently down the wall and onto the floor. The only sound audible was a faint popping noise as he fired the Glock and a light thump as they hit the floor. He slowly turned the door handle, and as he opened the door he noticed Mr. Antonov bent over what appeared to be a trap door with an opening leading to a basement. He was staring into the abyss.

The muffled sound of a person trying to scream became evident as he tiptoed toward the mafia boss. He kicked him in the small of his back and watched as he tumbled into the pool of water below and was horrified to see several large crocodiles devouring Mr. Occhialini.

Sweet Lord in heaven, this monstrous bastard had a trap door installed under the visitor's chair and must have pulled a lever that opened the trap door resulting in his guest falling into the pool below. He watched as Mr. Antonov suffered the same horrible death as Mr. Occhialini minutes before as the crocodiles started devouring him as well.

Good Lord, how gruesome. Good riddance, thought Rafael.

His eyes worked the office and he quickly identified the CCTV recording device, disconnected it, and searched the drawers for any USB sticks. He found them in a box in the second drawer, gathered them up, picked up the art portfolio, Antonov's mobile phone and a laptop, and collected his bag in the change room, before making his way down the passage to a door he believed would be an exit.

He tried the handle and was pleased to discover that it opened from the inside, so he quickly made his way around the complex and hailed another cab, instructing the driver to take him to the station. He found a café near the station and ordered a coffee. An hour later he made his way out of the station and walked the five miles back to his vehicle.

He called Barnaby on a secure line.

'Hello boss, I'm on my way to see you, sir.'

'Good, see you soon Rafael.'

An hour later Gizelle tapped lightly on the door.

'Rafael, to see you, sir.'

'Thanks Gizelle.'

'Hello Rafa, so what is so urgent that you need to come and see me right away?'

'Here are the blueprints that I retrieved from Mr. Antonov's office, as well as his mobile phone, CCTV recorder, laptop and a bevy of USB sticks,' said Rafael, as he laid the art portfolio bag and items on the desk.

'For what it's worth, no need to worry about him or his two henchmen again.' 'Taken care of all three.' 'This sinister bastard had a trap door positioned under the visitors chair in his office and activated a lever that opened it once he had the prints in his possession, so sadly Mr. Occhialini met a horrible death having been devoured by several crocodiles housed in a pool some forty feet below his office.'

'To be honest, Mr. Antonov, experienced the same fate, so the country is rid of this murderous bastard as well,' said Rafael.

'Oh yes, I almost forgot, his henchmen are no longer a problem either,' added Rafael.

'I think that you will need to get one of your trusted agents to troll through this lot and try to identify who his handler is at the Russian Embassy.'

'Thank you, Rafa, job well done.' 'To be candid, I want you to troll through these USB sticks and see what you can find.' 'You are the only person I trust,' said Barnaby pointing to the bundle on his desk.

'I think that the local police chief and the FBI will have a field day investigating this horrific scene.' 'We will stay out of it and let it play itself out.'

Chapter 15

Colville

USA

Barnaby met with Admiral Rocco Aquinto, Commander Indo-Pacific, in the soundproof command center at CIA headquarters in Virginia.

'Hello Rocco, good to see you,' said Barnaby waving him to a chair at the table.

'Well my friend, I'm pleased to tell you, that we have solved your problem.' 'The agent you met several weeks ago, has managed to retrieve the blueprints,' said Barnaby pointing to the art portfolio on the desk.

'So, as the saying goes, the problem has been solved,' added Barnaby.

'We have been friends for many years Rocco, and you know that I am not at liberty to tell you how he did it, suffice to say, the local police and the FBI are currently investigating what has occurred at Naslazhdeniye Turkish Baths Resort situated in Prince George's County.'

'Thank you Barnaby that solves a huge problem for us.' 'When we awarded General Aeronautical Aviation the contract to develop the drone, we acquired the blueprints and were unaware that a copy of them had been made, let alone have to face the possibility that it could be sold to the Russians.' 'That was until you drew our attention to the possibility that this could happen.'

'A job well done, my friend, and yes, I know that I cannot, nor will I, ask how you managed to get a hold of the blueprints.' 'I assure you that this will not be discussed outside of this room,' said Rocco.

'Clearly, Mr. Occhialini retained a copy of the prints on the company laptop without anybody's knowledge, and as you are aware, the vault they used as an office, had a time-lapse security system, and everyone had to vacate the room before seventeen hundred hours because that is the time that the vault door automatically locks.' 'Anybody left in the vault overnight would die, because not only does it lock, but all the oxygen is sucked out of the room, which was an added security measure,' said Barnaby.

'From what we have discovered, Mr. Occhialini loaned fifty million dollars from Mr. Antonov, the Russian mafia boss to finish the project, because several banks that he approached were not willing to risk that amount of money on something that may never materialize, so it seems he had no alternative, but to borrow the money from this thug,' continued Barnaby.

'He was porking a lady by the name of Geneviève Protish, who just happened to be Mr. Antonov's sister-in-law, so this is how the Russian mafia boss got involved.' 'Clearly, Mr. Antonov wanted the blueprints, which he was going to sell to his Russian masters for a few billion Rubles, so fifty million is a pittance in comparison to the huge payout he would have received.'

'The Good Lord alone knows, what secrets he may have told his lover in bed.'

'From what I understand, Mr. Antonov is no longer a worry to society either.' 'So Rocco, I think you should obtain a warrant to search the premises of General Aeronautical Aviation and secure any other documents relating to the drone.' 'Ensure that you take possession of any other laptops, which will guarantee that you have total control over anything that may be on them.'

'To be sure, to be sure, my friend.' 'Nothing that I have told you can ever be repeated to anyone,' added Barnaby.

Later that day, Barnaby met with Rafael.

'Hello young man,' he offered as Rafael entered the soundproof basement conference room, pointing to a chair opposite him.

'Certainly seems like their deaths were rather gruesome, to say the least Rafa.'

'Yes sir, the only consolation is that we are rid of Mr. Antonov, and his two henchmen as well.' 'Sad ending for Mr. Occhialini though.' 'Having said that, one can in some way, sympathize with him, because he hit a "brick wall" with the banks.' 'Clearly, he was confident in what he and his team had developed, so he was desperate to get the project over the line.'

'True Rafa.' 'What is of concern, is whether he was telling company secrets in bed.' 'Right, so we need to concentrate on finding his handler at the Russian Embassy.' 'I only trust you, so can you please troll through Mr. Antonov's emails and view all the footage you have on the USB sticks and see if anything pops up.'

'It will take some time to go through all the material, so the sooner you get started, the better.'

Rafael believed that the mobile phone may offer a clue to who his handler was at the Russian Embassy. He spent the day trolling through all the emails, however, nothing jumped out at him, so he checked all the addresses in the system and printed a copy of all the contacts in his database. One name appeared in two emails, which caught his attention.

The two emails were sent two minutes apart to a person by the name of Segei Snetkov on the same day, which is what made him sit up and pay attention. There was no further email contact with the person after that, so he sat back in his chair and wondered whether Mr. Antonov had somehow forgotten to delete the two emails.

He accessed the mobile phone and discovered the login code, which was the date of the Russian Revolution notably, nineteen seventeen. How predictable these Russians are, thought Rafael.

The first email seemed to contain some sort of coded message, so he wondered what that could mean.

The message in Russian read, ".Моя сестра хочет с тобой встретиться."

The message was sent a day before his death, so it appeared that he was arranging a meeting to hand over the blueprints of the drone.

Rafael checked the addresses on the mobile phone and discovered that Sergei's name appeared in the usual alphabetical sequence.

The next day, Rafael contacted the agent that he had used previously at CIA headquarters when he had him decode a conversation between the Russian President and the General Secretary of China.

The translation of the email that Antonov sent to the agent, translated to, "My sister wants to meet you."

Seemed like the meeting was arranged to take place a day after Antonov's death.

Seemed that Mr. Antonov was using this meeting to hand over the blueprints of the drone to his contact at the Russian Embassy. He asked Barnaby to check whether this person worked at the embassy.

Thirty minutes later, he received an SMS message on a secure line confirming that Sergei worked at the Russian Embassy and that he was an assistant to the Deputy Chief of Mission.

Right, let the games begin, thought Rafa.

He met with Barnaby the following day and was told that Sergei frequented a gay club called Red Door at Sixty Nine in Colville, the gayest place in Washington every Friday evening, and booked a room. Barnaby mentioned that he always booked the same room 202, and liked smoking a cigar after having had oral sex with a regular partner, so he reached into his desk drawer and extracted a classy gift-wrapped, yellow and black cedar wood 3CT cigar case humidor holder.

Rafael wondered what else the old man knew, and was not telling. He seemed to know everything about everyone, like Edgar Hoover, the late Director of the Bureau of Investigation (BOI) in the seventies. Barnaby was as smart as he was, hedging his bets, in a business that could come back and bite one in the arse. He has a dossier on almost everyone. Smart, real smart, thought Rafa.

Need to learn from this old codger, and cover my tracks, just like I was taught at Camp Perry, he reminded himself.

'What's this boss?' said Rafael looking at the package on the table.

'It's a gift-wrapped cigar humidor holder with a cigar in it, the type that Sergei likes to smoke after sex.' 'Suggest that you find a way to hang it on the room door handle with this note, making it seem like it is a gift, with the compliments of the management, then high tail it out of there before he opens the door,' said Barnaby winking.

'There are no fingerprints on the case or the cigar, so you will need to wear skin-colored gloves, and ensure that you do not leave any DNA on it whatsoever, Rafa.'

'I understand boss.' 'So what is so special about the cigar?'

'The tobacco was sourced from Seco Primings, which has an oily aroma without being too thick, veiny, or bland.' 'His preferred brand is Colorado Maduro which has a medium brown wrapper, made from Havana Seed Tobacco grown in Honduras.'

'Our technicians in the lab soaked the cigar leaves in strychnine poison for several days, dried it, and finally rolled it into a Cuban-like cigar, then wrapped it exactly the way the Cubans do, so he will not be able to detect that it was not made in Cuba,' continued Barnaby.

'The lab technicians believe that the dried leaves will be fatal when inhaled and that the flame will not neutralize the poisoning effect of the smoke whatsoever, and will result in a toxic reaction.' 'It is expected that an hour after having smoked the cigar, his body muscles will begin to spasm starting with the head and neck in the form of Trismus and Risus Sardonicus.' 'Thereafter, it will spread to every muscle in the body with continuous convulsions.'

'Death will come from asphyxiation, caused by paralysis of the neutral pathways controlling breathing, or by exhaustion from the convulsions, and he will die within two to three hours of having smoked the cigar.'

'He is a creature of habit and from what we have observed, he always books the same room, and lights up a cigar as he exits the club, almost as if he is rewarding himself in a celebration of his achievement.' 'His preference is room 202 on the second floor.'

Barnaby reached across the desk, picked up the box using a tissue, and handed it to Rafa.

'Use the hyperreal flesh latex mask inside to conceal your real identity,' he said handing him a plastic bag containing the mask, then took the cigar case humidor holder and placed it into the bag.

'I don't want the police or FBI sniffing around trying to identify the person responsible, so you need to be extremely careful because his death is going to create a diplomatic stoush.' 'In simple terms, don't get caught Rafael.'

'The problem is how you get in and out of the place without drawing any attention to yourself, so using the mask will protect your identity, however, you can only remove the mask when you are well away from the place, and ensure that you do it in a secure location, out of sight of everyone.' 'As you know CCTV cameras are everywhere, so you need to be extremely cautious.'

Rafa fitted the mask on when he got home later that evening and looked at the grey-haired mature-looking man staring back at him in the mirror. This looks like a real person and will work, he thought.

The following Friday, he took the time to don the latex mask, ensuring that it fitted perfectly, and was pleased to see how he had aged in the past couple of minutes. Handsome as he considered, blowing himself a kiss.

This will be a dry run he decided.

He made his way into the club and headed for the bar. Noting that it was almost seventeen hundred hours and ordered a beer. Moments later a gay guy tried to befriend him, so he politely informed him that he was meeting a friend. He caught a glimpse of himself in the mirror behind the bar, gently lifted his glass, and toasted himself.

Bloody handsome bastard, he thought.

He ordered a second beer and caught sight of Sergei as he entered the club, and watched as made his way to a person sitting at the far end of the bar. He kissed and hugged the person that must have been his regular date. They made their way near to where he was sitting and Sergei ordered a bottle of Dom Pérignon Champagne. The pair held hands and appeared to be deep in conversation. Thirty minutes later they appeared to be finishing their drinks, so Rafael made his way out of the bar and headed toward the staircase. He watched as they headed his way toward the elevator, so he took the stairs two at a time to the second floor and waited with the staircase door slightly ajar, just wide enough to check which room they had entered. They were oblivious that they were being watched as they made their way down the passage, hand in hand.

Rafael needed to be sure that they would use their usual room. Need to be back here next Friday and deliver the gift, he thought.

He made his way down the stairs and out of the club, then walked toward the fringe of the town where he had chained his bicycle to a lamp post. He jumped onto the bike and rode back to where he had parked his SUV in a park, then loaded the bike into the cargo compartment and headed home.

The following Friday, he donned the latex mask then retraced his steps from the previous week, and made his way back to the Red Door Club at Sixty-Nine in Colville. He waited patiently at the bar for Sergei to appear and once again the same gay guy tried to befriend him.

'Hello handsome, I see you are back.' 'Your friend did not show up last week so I will gladly be your date for the evening and give you a good time.'

Rafael leaned over and whispered, 'fuck off, I have a partner.'

Seems the only language these people understand.

Right on cue, Sergei walked into the club and kissed his date, then they made their way toward the bar and ordered their usual bottle of Dom Pérignon Champagne

Same old creature of habit, however, this evening I have a surprise for you, thought Rafael.

Almost thirty minutes since he entered the bar and being a person who is a creature of habit, he will finish his drink, then make his way toward the elevator. Rafael gulped down the last of his beer, then headed to the stairwell and waited at the stairwell door until the dinging sound of the lift announced its arrival on the second floor.

He waited patiently for twenty minutes then made his way toward room 202, and ensured that he did not place his feet directly in front of the door, because the shadow would have altered Sergei to the fact that someone was lingering in the passage. He laid the gift on the floor in front of the door, in a position that whoever exited the door could not miss it, then made his way back to the stairwell and exited the building.

He seated himself in a bus shelter over the road and waited for an hour, eventually catching a glimpse of Sergei leaving the club and watched as he paused to light a cigar. Hope it's the one in the gift wrap I left for him, thought Rafael.

Sergei walked to his car parked a block away, puffing on his cigar along the way. Good boy, keep puffing, thought Rafael.

Rafael unchained his bike and rode to where he had parked his SUV in the park. He loaded it into the cargo compartment and made his way home.

He called Barnaby the following morning on a secure line.

'All done boss.' 'I'm sure Dad enjoyed his gift.'

'Yes, I know.' 'Not sure whether you have listened to the news on CNN.' 'They have reported that the Deputy Chief of Mission at the Russian Embassy has been found dead in his apartment.' 'Police and officials at the Russian Embassy are investigating and the reporter stated that they suspect foul play.'

'Nevertheless, who would know what happened Rafael.' 'I need you to take a few days off then meet with me a week from today in my office at twelve-hundred hours.'

Chapter 16

Douglas Park

Arlington Virginia USA

As often as he could, Rafael parked outside the Young Guns Pre-School and waited for Claire to drop the twins off. He was amazed that she did not suspect anything suspicious about the SUV that was often parked in the same spot on numerous occasions. His training always ensured that he was on heightened alert for anything untoward.

He ducked as Claire made a U-Turn and headed back to the naval base. An hour later he peeped over the fence and watched, as his sons played and interacted with friends. Just have to do this as often as I can to see my boys, he thought.

Gizelle ushered him into Barnaby's office shortly after noon.

'Hello Rafa, take a seat.' 'As mentioned we have a mole in the firm and I need your help to identify the person or persons.' 'I suspect that this person or these people may be exposing various agents, and disclosing secrets to an organization called "EyeGlass" which is similar to WikiLeaks.'

'We have already had two of our agents based in London identified by this mole, and both have been eliminated, so we urgently need to ferret out who this person is, and identify him or her.'

'Do you have any idea who this person could be, because you have around twenty-one-and-a-half thousand employees, boss?'

'True, and yes it would be impossible to check every employee, however, I suspect that this person may well be seconded to our Directorate of

Intelligence division.' 'The reason I am saying that, is because this is the only section that had access to a clandestine operation in which the two deceased agents captured a militant Muslim jihadist by the name of Wahid Harroun, and handed him to the Metropolitan Police in Blackburn Town, located in Lancashire England.' 'This jihadist was involved in the planning of a bomb attack at London's Kings Cross Station.' 'Blackburn Town is situated north of the West Pennine Moors on the southern edge of the Ribble Valley, which is eight-miles east of Preston and twenty-one miles from Manchester, and is a haven for militant jihadists.'

'So I recommend that you start your investigation in that department Rafa.' 'As you know, the CIA is responsible to the American people, and operates with oversight from US elected representatives.' 'The Executive Branch and the National Security Council known as NSC includes the President, Vice President, Secretary of State and the Secretary of Defence that provide direction for national foreign intelligence and counterintelligence activities,' said Barnaby.

'The Senate Select Committee on Intelligence, known as the SSCI, closely monitors the CIA, and our budget is scrutinized by the Office of Management and Budget, and they are demanding that we identify the mole or moles responsible for exposing our two agents.' 'So the pressure is on to bring this person or these people to justice,' continued Barnaby.

Barnaby handed Rafael a folder containing a dossier on all the people in the Intelligence division.

Later that day, Rafael read the company profile of each of the ten employees in the Directorate of Intelligence division. All are based at Langley, CIA's headquarters in Richmond. He read the profiles carefully, focusing on each person's personal life, their marital status, hobbies, sporting activities, and interests. Nothing jumped out at him immediately, so he searched social media platforms and tried to discover whether they interacted regularly on any of them.

Everything seemed pretty normal, so he turned his attention to which agents were monitoring the activities of the two agents who had lost their lives and discovered that a team of two people were involved. He noted that both were female, so he re-read their profiles again and discovered that they lived together. Both have a clean record and he discovered that these two were best friends sharing an apartment at Douglas Park called Village Apartments.

Right, these two ladies are Cora Grigoras and Dinah Stolley, so he focused his attention on them and re-read their profiles for the umpteenth time. Both are third-generation Americans with no siblings and all parents have passed, so it seems that these two have something in common. He Googled the apartment and discovered that it was situated on Roosevelt Road, close to Douglass Park. According to their profiles, both visited a gym regularly and loved running. Down my alley, considered Rafael.

Being an athlete who used to compete in triathlons several years previously, however, he could no longer compete due to the injuries sustained in numerous CIA operations. He decided to stake out their apartment and try to discover which gym they attended and assumed that they would most likely go for an early morning run in the park, and most likely go to a gym close to home after work. He felt it would be best if he parked near their apartment, and watched, because the park would be the most likely place that they would choose for their morning run.

He discovered that they drove a Honda Civic, so the following day he identified their car in the parking lot at Langley and followed at a discreet distance as they left work. They eventually pulled up at The Keep Fit, Fitness Center located a few miles from their apartment, and watched as they made their way up the stairs. Dressed in a pair of running shorts and he noticed both girls ogling him, so he paid the fees for a month, then made his way to the male change room and locked his bag in a locker.

A few minutes later, as he started his training routine, one of the girls introduced herself.

'Hello, you must be new here?' 'I'm Dinah.'

'Bonjour Dinah, I'm François,' he said using a made-up alias and turning on the French charm.

'So you are French?'

'Oui, I am.'

'So are you here on holiday François?'

'Oui, I'm an IT Consultant and looking at any possible opportunities available in my field in Virginia.'

'And what do you do Dinah?'

'Oh, how rude of me, let me introduce you to my friend.' 'Cora, meet François.'

'Pleased to meet you handsome,' she replied.

'Well, Cora and I are analysists.'

'I see, must be an interesting job?' Said François.

'Can be at times,' said Cora butting into the conversation.

Rafael admired their curvy bodies. Nice tits he thought.

'Well I have to compliment you both, you are very attractive and very sexy ladies.'

'Oh thank you, François.' 'We could say the same about you too,' said Dinah blushing a little.

'So where are you staying François?' Asked Dinah.

'Well, I have just booked a two-bedroom mobile home for rent at Seven Oaks for a few nights until I find something suitable.'

'Sounds good, so good luck.' 'Hope to bump into you again,' said Cora admiring his physique.

That went well, he thought, as he bid them farewell and made his way out of the gym.

Two days later, he bumped into Dinah and Cora at the gym again.

'Bonjour ladies.' 'Good to see you two sexy ladies again.'

'Hello handsome,' 'Yes, good to see you too,' said Dinah flirtingly.

The girls joined him as he made his way out of the gym later.

'Doing anything tonight François?' Asked Dinah.

'No not really, just going to pick up something to eat and head back to my rental.'

'Well we are going to do the same, so why not join us, and we will toss something into the pan for dinner?'

'That's kind of you, but only if you allow me to buy a couple of bottles of wine.'

'Awesome, follow us to the supermarket François,' said Cora.

They stopped at the Mega Food Mart, and François picked up three bottles of chardonnay and a six-pack of beer, then followed them to their apartment. An hour later, and two bottles of wine later, it was evident that the girls were getting a little tipsy and had become somewhat flirty.

Seems to be going well, thought François, then Dinah changed the subject and asked his view on world affairs. Right, this is where I need to be careful and meander my way into their world, he thought.

'Well ladies, I hate inequality, and I am somewhat of an activist when it comes to matters of dominance.'

'What do you mean?' asked Cora.

'Well, I don't like it when one group or faction dominates the other.' 'To be truthful, there is so much hatred in the world.' 'I would like to see all people irrespective of race, color, creed or religion, live in harmony with each other.' 'I do believe that those that commit or are about to commit a serious crime should be exposed, so I admire Julian Assange, the WikiLeaks founder for having the courage to speak up.'

Both girls nodded in agreement.

'Yes we both agree, and that's our philosophy as well,' said Cora.

'To be truthful, western governments continue to treat all Muslims as terrorists, when the truth is that the greater majority are just like us, wanting to hold down a steady job and provide food and shelter for their families.' 'I know numerous peace-loving Muslims, and do not like the way our French government is treating them back home,' said François.

Dinah stroked his forearm in a flirty manner, signaling that she agreed, and seemingly wanting to make her intention clear. Rafael reminded himself that he was still married, and did want to remain faithful to Claire until it was clear that their marriage was over, so he looked at his watch.

'Wow it's getting late ladies, and I still have some work to do this evening.' 'I'm afraid that I have to get going and head home because I promised to complete a download for a company this evening.'

As he stood, it was apparent that both girls were very disappointed.

'Let's continue this conversation shortly,' he said rising.

'Au Revoir mon beautés,' he said hugging both at the door.

'Yes, let's do this again, say Friday evening, when we don't have to work the next day, François,' said Cora in a seductive voice.

'Sounds terrific.' 'Let's do dinner first, my shout, say around seven o'clock at Fat Albert's Place in Elm Street, if that is suitable?' Said François.

'Terrific François, we will see you there, only if you promise to have a few drinks at our place afterward,' said Dinah seductively, as she leaned forward and kissed him on the lips.

Not to be outdone, Cora hugged and kissed him as well. Wonder if these two are into a threesome, he thought as he made his way down the stairs.

That went well, so I need to alert Barnaby to have the police and FBI on standby and I will need to wear a wire on Friday evening so that I can get everything these two say on tape.

The next day, he met with Barnaby and updated him on developments.

'Awesome, well done Rafa.' 'I will notify the police and the FBI to position themselves near the apartment and be on standby. 'I will get a wire for you to wear, and as you know, you will need to be careful and not let them discover the wire.' 'Hopefully, you will be able to get them to confess to their involvement in the matter relating to the death of our two agents.'

'No need to worry Boss, I will get it done.'

'When you hear me ask the question, what perfume are you wearing, it will be the sign for the police and FBI to break into the apartment,' added Rafael.

Friday arrived and Rafa made his way into Fat Albert's Place and seated himself against the wall with a view of the entire restaurant. He noticed the girls entering right on time. They made their way to the table and greeted him with a hug and a kiss.

'Hello handsome,' offered both ladies, looking radiantly attractive with strapless necklines, cleavage showing their firm breasts, and tightfitting dresses with slits most of the way up the leg.

'Oh wow, you two look gorgeous.'

'And you too handsome,' said Dinah, touching his arm.

They made small talk over dinner, and two hours later with both ladies seemingly well intoxicated, they made their way back to their apartment.

Dinah seemed a little unsteady as she topped up their glasses.

'Cheers,' she said, clinking glasses.

'So where did we leave off a few days ago.' 'Oh yes, we were discussing human rights.' 'I'm interested in your point of view François.'

'Well, as I said, I hate inequality, and believe that one needs to take a stand against it.'

'So, if for instance, you thought that something that the government or one of their agencies did was not right, would you air your opinion, and do something about it?' Asked Cora.

'Oui, I would.' 'In fact, I found myself in a pickle during a demonstration in Paris years ago and I was detained, then released without any charges being filed.' 'The police released me an hour later, so I made my way back to the demonstration.'

'What was the demonstration about François?' Asked Dinah.

'The police are heavy-handed when it comes to Muslims in France.' 'They don't tolerate demonstrations, and don't allow them to air their point of view, and seem to suppress them at every turn.' 'I was at the demonstration, to support a Muslim friend of mine, who was arrested and is still in jail awaiting his day in court,' said François.

'So what do you want to know about me ladies?'

'Are you romantic François?' Asked Dinah, posing a question out of the blue.

'Oui, yes I am.' 'Let's not talk about me.' 'I'd rather focus on you two beautiful ladies,' said François in his best French accent.

'Tell me more about yourselves ladies?'

The girls were both well inebriated and looked at each other. Dinah answered.

'Well, we share your concern regarding Muslims, because we too have Muslim friends who have been badly treated by our government.' 'We exposed two American operatives that we discovered had illegally arrested a Muslim activist in England who the authorities labeled a jihadist. The person's name is Wahid Harroun, and the two operatives handed him to the Metropolitan Police in Blackburn Town, in Lancashire England.'

'He is rotting in jail and no trial date has been set yet,' continued Dinah.

'Oh wow, how do you know that?' Asked François.

'Get on the same page François.' 'We are analysts working for the CIA, and hate the way that the organization sticks its nose in every country's business.' 'They move in the shadows, eliminating people at will, when and wherever they please and are not accountable to anybody,' said Dinah.

'Our boss, the CIA director has blood on his hands as well.' 'He should be jailed and the whole fucking organization shut down,' continued Dinah.

'We recently discovered the name of another CIA agent, namely Rafael Dujon, who from the snippets of information we have to hand is a ruthless killer.' 'We have never seen or met him.' 'Only heard snippets of his escapades, and when we eventually find him in the woodwork, we will expose him as well.'

It was evident that both ladies were well intoxicated. Despite having been sworn to secrecy and an allegiance to the CIA when they joined, they were speaking openly about the organization. They needed no encouragement and were forthcoming in what they thought of the CIA in no uncertain terms.

Rafael afforded himself a slight smile and listened intently.

'What happened to your Muslim friend ladies?'

'Well, he is still in jail, just like your friend, awaiting trial.'

'And what happened to the two operatives that you exposed?'

'They both died in a skirmish that followed.' 'No fucking loss really, because these CIA bastards were acting illegally.' 'Neither Cora nor I feel any sorrow for those two pricks,' said Dinah.

'Who did you expose them to?'

'The Muslim Brotherhood of Allah,' said Cora proudly.

'And that resulted in the two American operatives having been killed?' Asked Rafael seeking confirmation.

'Bloody right it did, thanks to us.' 'We are glad it happened,' added Dinah.

'So by you exposing them, how did you know that the two that had died worked for the CIA?'

'We were tasked with monitoring their every move at the CIA.'

'So you did not warn them?'

'No fucking way François.' 'We were glad that these two pricks died.' 'Hate the way the CIA works, so fuck them too,' said Cora.

'But you said earlier that you both work for the CIA?'

'Yes we do, and we don't agree with what they do, so if we can expose what they do, or save someone from their clandestine activities, we will do that,' said Dinah proudly.

'Should you not be loyal to the CIA ladies, after all, they pay your wages.'

Now well and truly intoxicated with loose lips about to sink ships, François reminded himself not to step over the line, and to be cautious not to be seen to be leading these two into a trap. He sat quietly and observed their behavior, as they both excused themselves and headed for the toilet.

A few minutes later both made their way back to the couch, dressed in see-through negligees. Their voluptuous curvy naked bodies were apparent in the dim light streaming from the side table lamp.

'Oh my goodness, don't you two look sexy.' 'Unfortunately, I am engaged to be married soon,' said François.

'Who gives a fuck, your fiancé will never know,' said Cora as she dropped her negligee revealing her naked body.

'By the way, what perfume are you wearing?' Asked François.

The mention of perfume was the signal for the police and FBI to raid the apartment. A few minutes later the door burst open, and numerous police officers dressed in riot gear bearing shields and guns at the ready entered, followed by three baton wielding officers.

'On the floor, all of you shouted the officer in charge.'

One of the officers manhandled François, dropping him to the ground and placing a knee on his neck.

'What the fuck is going on shouted François?'

'You are all under arrest for being an accessory before the fact for the killing of two CIA officers, and you will be held liable to the same extent as the perpetrators of the killing,' said the commanding officer as he looked at the ladies.

'We have been keeping a close eye on an activist like you Frenchie, so you will most likely be deported once our investigation has been completed,' said the commanding officer as he turned his attention to François.

Barnaby stood in the doorway and stared at the three of them lying on the floor for some time, before finally addressing them.

'We put trust in people like you two ladies, and now we find out that you are traitors.' 'So, you will face prosecution for the death of my two agents in England, and be jailed for life.' 'I will ask the judge to send both of you to Rikers Island and I will ask the Head Warden, Jessop De La Deico, to be particularly harsh in his treatment, ensuring that your stay is a memorable one.'

'And you Frenchie, will be charged with aiding and abetting, a crime that carries a ten-year sentence.' 'After you have served your sentence, you will be deported back to France.'

Barnaby turned and left without saying another word.

Chapter 17

Joint Base Pearl Harbor-Hickam

Oahu, Hawaii, USA

❛That was a successful operation, Rafa.' 'Thanks for getting it all on tape.' 'It's a small win for the families of the two agents that lost their lives, and hopefully that can bring them closure.'

'No one ever knows who could turn out to be a traitor, and we can only hope that a judge will hand down severe sentences for these two,' added Barnaby.

'I would love to have told them that I am Rafael Dujon, boss.' 'Just to see the look on their faces.'

'We have uncovered another pressing problem, and I need you to help me solve it, Rafa.' 'Having said that, first things first.' 'Have you contacted Claire yet?'

'No sir, I have not, and I am unsure whether I want to do that.' 'I am extremely unhappy that she left, and rather annoyed at the way she did it.' 'She should rather have sat me down, and explained her reasoning to my face.'

'For what it's worth Rafa, according to her commanding officer, Captain David De Santos, the commander of the Norfolk Naval Base, Claire is doing a sterling job, and she has uncovered an issue with our latest Nuclear Submarine, namely, Tranquillity.' 'She discovered, that during the build of the Submarine, someone must have installed a GPS tracker somewhere in it.' 'The tracker works on a specific low frequency, and whilst GPS trackers don't work underwater, it appears that Ivan has developed one that does.'

'The USA has named all its Submarines after a state, however, in this instant, they have broken protocol and named the latest one that they launched a year ago Tranquillity.' 'Possibly because it means, calmness or composure, something that will be needed in the heat of battle.' 'Tranquillity is the latest Nuclear Class Submarine to be commissioned into the US Navy.' 'She is a large ship with a slimline profile, and is supposed to be stealthy, making her harder to be detected.'

'Ivan has developed some type of sophisticated technology that allows them to detect a Stealth Submarine, and follow it without being discovered,' said Barnaby.

'This is creating far-reaching problems for our Navy because the Reds will be able to detect exactly where Tranquillity is at any given time, and be able to destroy it.' 'Ivan views Tranquillity as a new age major threat.'

'Ranging codes travel from satellite to the receiver and must be modulated onto a carrier wave.' 'Original GPS designs use one of two MHz signals, however, it appears that Ivan has somehow managed to develop a roving MHz signal, making it extremely difficult to detect.' 'Apparently, they only transmit at a specific time each day and only for a few seconds, making it almost impossible to detect,' continued Barnaby.

'Satellites circumnavigate the earth every ninety minutes, and Claire discovered that they seem to transmit a three-second signal, every ninety minutes, so clearly sixteen times a day, which is each time that the specific satellite is overhead, updating Tranquillity's position.' 'GPS signals include ranging signals, used to measure the distance to the satellite and navigation messages.' 'The navigation messages include ephemeris data, used in trilateration to calculate the position of each satellite in orbit, and information about the time and status of the entire satellite constellation, called the almanac.'

'From what Claire had discovered, Ivan not only had developed this roving low-frequency MHz signal but also has linked it to a specific satellite that is capable of receiving these messages.' 'She has also identified the satellite that Ivan is using to receive these transmissions at these specific times, and only when the satellite is in a certain position.'

'Clever, very clever indeed,' added Barnaby.

'Claire has been tracking Ivan's Submarines and noticed that Tranquillity was being tracked by one of their stealth nuclear subs and our crew was unaware that they were being followed.' 'The navy brass is now aware of this and has recalled Tranquillity.' 'So, we need to try and identify the person or persons responsible for placing the GPS tracker in the sub and find the device.'

'This of course is a wakeup call for the Navy, who now need to up their surveillance during the construction of all new subs, and they need to try and identify where the person or persons may have hidden the device.' 'No easy task.'

'The revival of the multibillion-dollar effort, known as the Integrated Undersea Surveillance System (IUSS), next-generation sonar technology, woven into all our subs, is engineered to work in tandem with "Fly-by-Wire" technology to better identify threats operating at various depths and speed.'

'With "Fly-by-Wire" technology, a human operator will order depth and speed, allowing software to direct the movement of the planes and rudder to maintain course and depth, Navy program managers have told Warrior Maven,' said Barnaby.

'The ship can be driven primarily through software codes and electronics, thus freeing up time and energy for an operator who does not need to manually control each small maneuver.'

'Previous Los Angeles-Class Submarines relied upon manual, hydraulic controls.' 'This technology, using upgradable software and fast-growing AI applications, widens the mission envelope for the attack submarines by vastly expanding their ISR potential.' 'Using real-time analytics and an instant ability to draw upon an organized vast database of information and sensor input, computer algorithms can now perform a range of procedural functions historically performed by humans,' continued Barnaby.

'This can increase the speed of maneuverability and an attack submarine's ability to quickly shift course, change speed, or alter depth positioning when faced with an attack.' 'A closer-in or littoral undersea advantage, Navy strategy documents explain, that this can increase "ashore attack" mission potential along with ISR-empowered Anti-Submarine and anti-surface warfare operations,' said Barnaby.

'The US Navy's published "Commander's Intent for the United States Submarine Force," which was published earlier this year, and wrote - "We are uniquely capable of, and often best employed in stealthy, clandestine and independent operations." 'We exploit the advantages of undersea concealment which allow us to, conduct undetected operations such as strategic deterrent patrols, intelligence collection, Special Operations Forces support, non-provocative transits, and repositioning, the Navy strategy document explained,' added Barnaby.

'The Columbia-Class Submarines also have what's called a Large Aperture Bow, conformal array of sonar systems designed to send out an acoustic ping, analyze the return signal, and provide the location and possible contours of enemy ships, submarines, and other threats.' 'Clearly it's not working to identify Ivan's stealth sub, because they have not detected it so far.'

'That's the long-winded version of what we are dealing with Rafa.'

Rafael sat back in his chair considering what he had just heard. If that is correct, then one could assume that whoever installed a GPS tracker, would position it in the conning tower, because it's closest to the surface.

'Captain Ziggy Bombardo hails from the same office that Claire is assigned to.' 'He has been briefed on your marital status with Claire, and sworn to secrecy regarding the two of you, so I am confident that he will honor that confidence.' 'I want you to assume the alias of Alain Toussaint for this mission Rafa,' said Barnaby as he handed him all the relevant identification documents.

'It is imperative that we keep your identity hidden, for obvious reasons.'

Barnaby arranged for Rafael to have clearance to visit Unique Boats, the company that designs and constructs all Nuclear Submarines for the USA, situated in Williamsburg Virginia. His clearance included being able to view the blueprints of the design. This would be done in conjunction, with, and in the presence of two senior executives of the company, under the strictest security conditions. He would be accompanied by Captain Ziggy Bombardo from the office of USA Naval Intelligence.

As they parted ways, Barnaby said, 'You don't want Claire to know that you are involved, so I have devised a plan to keep your identity secret.'

Two days later Rafael met Captain Bombardo and the pair made their way into the lobby of Unique Boats. They were put through a rigorous security check and then headed for reception, where they were met by a host and ushered into a conference room.

A short while later, the conference door swung open.

'Hello, my name is Carl Banasiewicz and this is Luigi Caporossi,' he said as they swapped the customary introductions.

'I am the chief engineer, and Luigi is my assistant,' he continued, pointing to chairs on the opposite side of the table.

Captain Bombardo insisted that Carl and Luigi, sign a classified confidentiality agreement before they discussed any issues.

'So, as we understand it, the navy suspects that someone has planted a GPS tracker somewhere in Tranquillity, and has involved the CIA,' said Carl.

'Affirmative, because the ship is being tracked by one of Ivan's stealth subs without the crew's knowledge, which has far-reaching consequences for the navy, so we need to establish who has installed this tracker, and where he or she has hidden it' said Captain Bombardo.

'This is classified, and only the four of us can know about this, therefore it needs to be closely held, and only discussed with the people in this room,' continued Captain Bombardo.

'We know that it could be hidden anywhere on the ship, so let's start with blueprints and work our way through that,' suggested Captain Bombardo.

Eight hours later, and with no clear indication of where it could be hidden, they called it a day.

'Let's reconvene at zero-eight hundred hours gentlemen,' instructed Captain Bombardo.

The following morning, they reconvened and picked up where they left off the previous day.

'Carl sat back in his chair and said, 'If someone has planted a GPS tracker in the boat, it could be anywhere, and from what I understand, it won't work underwater.'

His demeanor indicated that he was cock sure of himself, and appeared to be overconfident that their security was not compromised in any way.

Arrogant prick thought Alain. I'm sick of these fucking aliases as well, so maybe I should go back to retirement and tend the few cows I have.

'To the best of our knowledge that is true, however, it seems that Ivan has somehow managed to develop a system that does work underwater because one of our intelligence officers has been monitoring a Russian stealth sub, that is following Tranquillity without the crew being aware of their presence,' said Captain Bombardo emphatically.

Alain asked to see the blueprints of the raised portion above the deck that is called the Fairwater or Sail that serves as a Bridge and Lookout Station during surfaced operations.

'Was this section of the Submarine made here at Unique Boats, or was this outsourced to another engineering company?'Asked Alain.

'Everything is done in-house.' 'The naval contract insisted that we keep all construction at home.'

'So who worked on the Fairwater or Sail as you guys call it?' asked Alain.

'There is a team of six that constructs all the Bridges for every Submarine we construct, consisting of two specialist welders and four fabricators,' responded Carl.

'Are these guys on site at the moment?' Continued Alain.

'Yes they are,' said Carl, as he stood and made his way to a large window overlooking the covered dry dock submarine construction facility.

He pointed to a section of a bridge being constructed to the side of the facility.

'See those guys working over there,' he said pointing in their direction.

'They are the crew I spoke about, and you can see that they are currently manufacturing a Bridge for a new submarine under construction,' continued Carl.

'I take it that you have had all staff thoroughly checked with security clearances, before being employed?' Asked Alain.

'Of course, we have Monsieur,' brazenly replied Carl.

'Can you confirm that the entire complex, inside and outside has roving CCTV cameras that are monitored twenty-four seven, Carl?' pressed Alain.

'Affirmative Monsieur,' Carl responded with a snotty attitude.

'Thanks, Carl, that's all for today, I think that we can wrap it up.' 'We will be back in a few days, so you will be notified of the date and time of our arrival,' said Alain.

'Just a friendly reminder, all conversation between us is classified, as outlined in the confidentiality agreement that you signed,' added Captain Bombardo.

A week later Tranquillity berthed at its homeport at Joint Base Pearl Harbor-Hickam, Oahu in Hawaii, and was quickly transferred to the enclosed high-security Intermediate Maintenance Facility Dry Dock and Waterfront Production Facility at the base.

Two days later Alain and Captain Bombardo were transported by helicopter to the base, and as the chopper hovered for landing, they noticed Commander Tripp O'Sullivan waiting to receive them.

He saluted Captain Bombardo as they exited the helicopter.

'Good morning Captain.'

'Good morning Commander.' 'Meet Alain Toussaint, from the CIA.'

Commander O'Sullivan wondered why the CIA was involved. They exchanged the usual handshake, then followed the Commander to an office inside the dry dock facility.

'Captain David De Santos, the commander of the Norfolk Naval Base, called me and informed me that one of his intelligence officers has uncovered an issue with Tranquillity, and from what I have been told, they suspect that a GPS tracker could have been installed in the ship without anybody's knowledge.' 'I have been instructed to fully cooperate with you and allow you access to every part of the boat,' said Commander O'Sullivan.

'Follow me,' said Commander O'Sullivan as he led the way to the balcony erected outside the office allowing for an outdoor view of the dry dock.

Alain marveled at the size of Tranquillity, as the last of the water was being drained out of the dry dock.

'Impressive boat,' said Alain.

'Yes she is,' replied Commander O'Sullivan.

'Right, shall we get down to business then,' offered Commander O'Sullivan.

Captain Bombaro laid a confidentiality agreement on the table, and ordered Commander O'Sullivan to read it, then sign it.

'As you can see, our meeting is classified Commander, and any discussion that we may have needs to be closely held between the three of us in this room.'

'Do you understand Commander?'

'Aye aye, Captain, fully understood.'

'What exactly are you wanting to do Captain?' he questioned

'Let's start with viewing the blueprints of the boat, and in particular the Fairwater or Sail and the Bridge,' instructed Alain.

Twenty minutes later Commander O'Sullivan laid them out on the conference table.

If there was a GPS tracker on board the ship, Alain was convinced that it could have somehow been hidden somewhere in the Fairwater or Sail on the Bridge. His gut told him that this would be the most logical place as it would be closest to the surface, so he focused his attention on the plans of the Bridge. He studied the blueprints carefully looking at the design and layout.

'So the periscope, which is an optical instrument used to enable the Captain or an observer to see his surroundings is used whilst submerged.' 'From what I have read about a periscope, is that it contains two mirrors or reflecting prisms to change the direction of the light coming from the scene being observed.' 'The first deflects it down from the vertical tube and the second diverts it horizontally so that the scene can be viewed conveniently,' said Alain.

Continuing he said, 'a telescopic optical system provides magnification, that gives as much of wide arc of vision as possible, including crossline or reticle pattern to establish the line of sight or the object under observation.'

'Impressive,' said Commander O'Sullivan.

'Right, enough of that Commander.' 'Can we go on board?' Asked Alain.

'We certainly can.' 'Follow me.'

The three of them donned helmets, and safety vests and were escorted onto the boat by one of the sailors standing guard duty at the gangway. They made their way through the belly of the ship and up the Escape Trunk to the Bridge. Alain was impressed by the sheer size of the ship and realized that the cylindrical shape of the Bridge was around eight feet in diameter and some fourteen feet long, situated directly above the control room.

He focused on the narrow tube-like device that housed the periscope and wondered whether a small GPS tracker could be hidden somewhere in its housing, then noticed a small brass plaque that was around three inches wide by roughly an inch and a half wide.

The plaque was preserved using a non-corrosive sealant cover, and positioned on the edge of the rim that ran around the Bridge. Despite having been installed a year previously when the Submarine was commissioned, it looked as good as new.

The inscription read-"God Bless All That Sail in This Ship," –President Trent January 2020.

He noticed that it was secured by four brass-coloured rust-resistant screws.

'Do you have a Phillips Head screwdriver?' Alain asked the sailor.

'No sir, I don't.'

'Can you please find a drill with a Phillips Head attachment?'

Twenty minutes later the sailor arrived with the drill and the attachment. Alain dismissed the sailor, then put his weight onto the drill, and gently unscrewed the four screws, He removed the plaque as well as the watertight rubber seal, noticing what appeared to be a GPS tracker lying in the housing compartment.

He pointed it out to Captain Bombardo, who then dismissed Commander O'Sullivan, because this was classified and needed to be closely held, on a need-to-know basis.

Alain extracted a pair of plastic gloves and donned them, then carefully removed what he believed was a small GPS tracker.

'And there you have it, Captain.' 'Right where I thought it might be,' he said.

Alain called Barnaby on a secure line.

'Hello Boss, I found it, sir.'

'Excellent Monsieur Alain.' 'I will arrange for you and Captain Bombardo to hitch a ride on a military flight leaving Oahu in Hawaii heading to Chambers Field Naval Base, leaving in three hours from now.' 'You will be met at the base by agent d'Avray and Van Der Jong and driven directly to Langley.'

'See you soon, Monsieur Alain, job well done.'

Each time he flew home after a mission, he was able to relax, allowing himself a few drinks from the flight attendant's trolley, which was the stimulus for relaxation, allowing him to switch off. He always found himself in a relaxed frame of mind when flying on a commercial flight, albeit, that his sensors remained on high alert. Highly unlikely that another commercial flight would be shot down or sabotaged by Ivan, like the Malaysia Flight Seventeen, which was shot down by Russian-controlled forces over Eastern Ukraine. World reaction and sanctions imposed on Russia took care of that scenario.

Unfortunately, this military flight did not cater for free drinks on board, so he settled in for a long flight.

All the more reason to use aliases, so no one knows who I am on any flight, even on a military mission here in the USA, he considered.

This allowed him the opportunity to unwind because his fellow passengers had no idea of who he was, what he did, or what he had accomplished.

His mind wandered back to the love of his life Claire and his twin sons. He suddenly became annoyed at what she had done as he recalled the letter she had written and how she left. Does she ever consider what I have done to save the planet? Does she not know how many times I have put my life on the line, to keep her, my boys and the world safe? Does she even love me? He thought.

The flight time was ten hours, so Alain and Captain Bombardo took the time to catch up on some much-needed sleep. The screeching tires woke Alain from a deep sleep. Six out of ten for that landing thought Alain.

'Right, back home at last,' he thought.

'I can't wait to get rid of this alias.' 'Sick and tired of changing names on every mission.'

A week later Tranquillity slipped out of the dry dock to resume patrols in the Sea of Okhotsk, in the western Pacific between Russia's Kamchatka Peninsula and the Kuril Islands, southeast of Japan's island of Hokkaido.

Chapter 18

Richmond

USA

Agent d'Avray and Van Der Jong waited patiently for the pair to deplane.

'Well, well, if it's not our dear friend,' 'Bonjour Monsieur, long time no see,' said agent d'Avray.

'Bonjour, true, long time no see.' 'So you two still have the cushiest job in the firm,' replied Rafael.

'Meet Captain Bombardo.'

'Right the Boss is waiting, so let's get going,' said agent d'Avray.

Forty minutes later, Gizelle tapped lightly on Barnaby's door announcing their arrival.

Barnaby rounded the table, offering his hand to both.

Captain Bombardo saluted Admiral Rocco Aquinto.

'Take a seat gentlemen,' said Barnaby pointing to chairs on the opposite side of the table.

'So, from what you told me, Rafael, you managed to find the GPS tracker.' 'Brilliant job young man.'

Rafael placed a zip lock bag containing the tracker on the table.

Captain Bombardo looked somewhat confused.

'By the way and with respect sir, who is Alain Toussaint?'

'Well Captain, the name of Alain Toussaint that he used, was merely an alias for this mission.' 'As you know, his real name is Rafael Dujon.'

'Well Rafael, on behalf of the navy, I would like to thank you for finding the GPS tracker.' 'Clearly, this has serious consequences for us, because we now need to find out who placed it there.' 'There has been a breach of trust here, so I am hoping that you can try to fathom out who is responsible and bring him or her to justice,' said Admiral Aquinto emphatically.

'There is a crew of six that work on all the Bridges that Unique Boats build Admiral, and I believe that one of them is possibly responsible.' 'Question is, which one.' 'We now need to identify who that person is,' replied Rafael.

'I think it best that you lie low at this time Rocco, and give Rafa the time to investigate it properly.' 'Don't want to give whoever is responsible a heads up at all.' 'Once Rafa has identified the person, the navy can take it from there my friend,' added Barnaby.

Rafael had a gut feeling that it could be one or more of the people who worked on the Bridge, so he trolled through the names of the six workers who worked on the Bridge at Unique Boats and turned his attention to where they lived. He spent hours identifying their financial status and family connections. Nothing jumped out at him and no alarm bells were ringing. The two specialist welders and four fabricators appeared to be solid, good family people, so he turned his attention to the two welders. Both were Hispanic and lived in the low to middle-income area of Hopewell. Their annual incomes were in the seventy-thousand dollar range, and both were up to their ears in debt, having bought units valued at around three-hundred and thirty-thousand dollars.

Barnaby confidentially arranged for Rafael to have full access to all the employees' names working for Unique Boats.

Rafael Googled The City Council of Hopewell and checked the statistics of the suburb of Hopewell, focusing on the demographics of the area, noting that it ranked within the bottom fifty percent of all schools in Virginia.

Hopewell has a population of twenty-three thousand four hundred people, of which forty-seven percent are white, forty-four percent are African American and seven percent are Hispanic.

He accessed the employment agreements of Enzo Batista and Ignacio Delgado and noted that both had been employees for over ten years with excellent records and had been commended for their work ethic.

Both had received high praise from their foreman and received an award confirming their achievement. Nice, but no financial gain for excellence, so I still can't discount these two as possible suspects, thought Rafael.

Eight percent of Richmond City's population was born outside of the USA. Rafael wondered whether one or both of these two people could have hidden the GPS in the ship, because they may be desperate for the money. After having run a thorough background check on both, he concluded that the two were honest hard-working men, trying to build a life for themselves and their families.

He knew that possibly, one or both could have planted the tracker, so he decided to follow them after work.

Traditionally, people from the same ethnic background tend to stick together, so he assumed that these two would be friends and hang out with each other. Both shared a ride to and from work to save money, so he hacked into their banking accounts and noticed that they both had minimal balances at the end of each month. He discovered that Enzo had four boys ranging in age from two to ten, and Ignacio had two children, a pigeon pair. Good Roman Catholic family men.

They both worked a second job on Saturdays and Sundays as dishwashers in a restaurant close to their homes, so he was convinced that he could discount them as possibly being the person or persons responsible.

Right, need to shift my focus to Carl Banasiewicz and his underling, Luigi Caporossi.

Both were family men, married with children, living in middle-income suburbs. First things first, thought Rafa.

He turned his focus to Carl and discovered that he earned one hundred and sixty-five thousand dollars per annum and lived in Oilville. His underling, Luigi earned one hundred and twenty-five thousand dollars per annum and lived in Sandy Hook. Both lived in middle-income suburbs eleven miles apart, and both appeared to be solid, however, something troubled him about Carl's overconfident smirky attitude, that suggested a smug, cocky, and condescending type of person.

I need to take a drive and see where these two live, then investigate each person's bank account. He made a note of their addresses and took a leisurely afternoon drive, driving slowly past each person's home. Looks pretty normal, he thought. So he decided to take a closer look at their activities after work each day and discreetly followed them after work. He noticed that both stopped at The Money Pit, on Lafayette Street, a local pub for a few beers after work on Fridays, so he made his way into the bar and watched as both made their way to the slot machines.

He positioned himself at the bar, careful to ensure that he could not be seen by the two of them and that he had a clear view of the casino. He watched as Carl appeared to be feeding a large sum of money into the machine, occasionally winning big, only to see him keep on feeding the one-arm bandit as if he was hoping to strike it rich.

Dumb prick, does he not know that casinos pay out small amounts regularly and a couple of larger amounts to keep you playing? Seemed as if he was spending a couple of hundred dollars, so he knew that it was time to leave before they spotted him, so he made his way out of the casino and headed home.

Later that evening, he hacked into Carl's account and noted that he had a healthy bank balance and that he withdrew two hundred dollars every Friday, clearly gambling money so he was addicted. Right, this guy has a problem, considered Rafael.

Maybe, just maybe, the prick is in over his head and is trying to hit it big.

Rafa wondered how he could have three hundred thousand dollars in his account. Impossible to have saved that amount of money on his salary. He discovered that he no longer had a mortgage on his home, even so, it would be almost impossible to have accumulated that sum of money on his salary. The house would be valued at around the seven hundred thousand dollar mark, and the upkeep of this semi-luxurious home complete with a swimming pool and gymnasium would be expensive. So, did this prick win a jackpot or could he have possibly taken payment for installing the tracker into the Submarine?

Not sure, however, I need to investigate this further, considered Rafa.

He learned that Unique Boats were due to complete the construction of another Nuclear Class Submarine within the next twelve months, so if he was taking a bribe from the Russians, he would need to keep an eye on this bastard.

The following day, Barnaby called Rafael.

'Hello Rafa, well the FBI managed to get a partial fingerprint off the tracker and have matched it to Carl Banasiewicz, the Chief Engineer at Unique Boats.' 'It took some time because the print was very feint, however, the new technology that they had developed, helped them to get a clear picture, which they then matched, confirming that it belonged to Mr. Banasiewicz.'

'From what they have managed to uncover so far, is that he has a gambling addiction, and it seems that he agreed to install the GPS tracker for a large sum of money.' 'Clearly, he did that to finance his addiction.'

'Mr. Banasiewicz was arrested and confessed to having planted the tracker on the boat.' 'Nobody knows that he was arrested because the FBI pulled him over at a roadblock as he was making his way home, so as of now, he has simply disappeared.''His family are distraught, and have reported him missing, so unbeknown to them, he will face charges of treason.' 'Watch this space,' said Barnaby.

'Well Rafa, we can only hope that some judge sends him to jail for a long time and that the sentence is commensurate with the crime he committed.'

'Boss, you know my philosophy when it comes to treason.' 'In my view, people like him should not enjoy a long-term holiday at taxpayer's expense.' 'We should simply have gotten rid of him because what he did is treason, boss.'

'Unfortunately, the navy and the FBI see it differently,' said Barnaby.

The FBI notified Barnaby that Luigi Caporossi was Carl's brother-in-law, and Rafa wondered whether he knew what Carl was doing, so he decided to follow him and see where it led.

He recalled that Luigi also seemed to gamble a bit on the slot machines, and recalled seeing Carl hand him a wad of notes. At the time, he did not take much notice of it, because he considered that he may have borrowed the money from his brother-in-law. Now that the FBI had arrested and charged Carl with treason, he felt that he had to follow the trail to see where it led.

Rafael hacked into Luigi's mobile phone and checked all the calls that he had made and received since Carl had been arrested. He discovered that he had called a person by the name of Danya Gorgal several times. Wonder who he could be, so he traced his mobile number to an address in Great Falls, located in Fairfax County, the richest suburb in Virginia.

Right so what does Mr. Gorgal do for a living, wondered Rafael.

He spent several days investigating him and discovered that he was a fifty-five-year-old retired man who was well-known to the police and other law enforcement agencies. He had a record of racketeering, albeit he had been arrested and charged on two occasions, he was released, due to a lack of evidence.

Interesting person. Best check him out, thought Rafael.

Barnaby managed to get hold of a photograph of Mr. Gorgal and sent it to Rafael.

Rafael drove slowly past his home the following day. Very posh home, he thought.

He hacked into Luigi's mobile phone again and noticed that he had just made a call to Danya minutes earlier, so it seemed like he was setting up a meeting with Mr. Gorgal.

The following day, he pulled up at sixteen hundred hours and parked his SUV a block away from the entrance to the car park at Unique Boats, facing in the direction of the city, and waited. He glanced at his wristwatch and noted that it was seventeen hundred hours, the time that workers normally clock off after a day's work. Still no sign of Luigi's red Chevrolet Trailblazer SUV, so he reminded himself to be patient.

He noticed the red SUV making its way out of the carpark an hour later in his rearview mirror, so he fired up the motor and followed at a discreet distance. Thirty minutes later Luigi turned into the car park at the Money Pit, and Rafael watched as Luigi shook hands with a man at the entrance, who he identified as Danya Gorgal by the photograph that Barnaby had sent to him. He followed the two into the bar without being noticed and found a seat at the far side of the bar, with an obscured view of the table that the two were seated at, then activated the recording device on his mobile phone, pointed it in their direction and turned up the volume.

Not ideal, because I am way too far away, however, it would have to do. He would need the CIA to filter out all the noise and enhance the sound to be able to decipher what was being said. Thirty minutes later, it became apparent that the two were about to leave and as they stood, Rafael bent down pretending to pick something up off the floor, ensuring that Luigi would not get a glimpse of him. He watched as they headed out of the bar.

Later, he replayed the recording, albeit that it was very faint, he thought he heard Danya say that they should meet a week from today back at the bar.

He sent the recording to a technician at CIA headquarters and waited in anticipation for a response.

The CIA used various methods such as iZotope and RX Dialogue to isolate surrounding noise and amplify sounds to get a clear voice imprint of what was being said. They also used AI technology to remove ambient background noise in the environment, prioritizing the primary voices in the conversation. The voice isolation software technology differentiated the conversation between the two and the babble in the background in the noisy environment.

The next day, Rafael received a clear copy of the conversation between Danya and Luigi from a technician at the CIA.

Amazing technology, thought Rafael.

He listened intently to the conversation, and it became apparent that Luigi seemed to have taken over where Carl had left off, and was seeking to jump on the bandwagon and enrich himself. He could make out that the two had discussed compensation of half a million dollars, which would be paid if Luigi successfully installed another GPS tracker in the submarine currently under construction. Payment would be made after the ship was commissioned and launched in twelve months and the GPS tracker had been tested.

Three days later Rafael met with Barnaby, Admiral Aquinto, and two FBI agents in the conference room at CIA headquarters.

He played the recording that the technician had made of the conversation between Danya Gorgal and Luigi Caporossi, confirming that Luigi would place a GPS tracker into the new submarine due to be commissioned.

The FBI agents confirmed that they had enough evidence to act and arrest Danya Gorgal and Luigi Caporossi.

Chapter 19

Kentucky

USA

The Central Intelligence Agency (CIA) had secretly been collecting information on Americans' private lives for decades. Their surveillance program had been exposed by two Democrats in the Senate Intelligence Committee, namely Senator Raul Montoya and Senator Emilio Nunez. According to the allegations made by the two Democrat Senators, this had been concealed from the public and Congress for years.

The two Senators argued that the CIA operated outside of the statutory framework that Congress, and what the public believe, governs the firm. These two Senators had frequently criticized the CIA over time, stating that the organization should not be allowed to reveal or use data collected on the American people.

The CIA and the National Security Agency (NSA) are barred from investigating Americans or US businesses, however, foreign communications, often snare American messages and data, which is viewed by the agency as incidental. The Senators were worried about the type of information that these agencies were vacuuming up in bulk, and how they use the information to spy on Americans.

Rafael, poured himself a three-finger tot of his favorite drop, Johnny Walker Blue Scotch Whisky, dropped some ice cubes into the tumbler, then turned on the television, and made himself comfortable on the couch.

He caught the end part of an interview on television in which his boss, Barnaby Heathcott, Director of the CIA was being grilled by these two Senators.

They claimed that the CIA and NSA posed a more serious threat to liberty in America, than the enemies they claim to protect the USA from.

Barnaby meandered his way carefully through the interview without disclosing anything that the CIA does, is involved in, or was involved in, other than to make a lasting closing argument that resonated with the American public.

'You two Senators, have the privilege of sitting in your cozy chairs, and throwing barbs in every direction at the CIA and NSA, and hope that something sticks.' 'Neither of you were born in America, and neither of you has served this country in the military, nor in any way contributed to the country's security in any shape or form, yet you deem it your right to criticize law enforcement agents and officers, who put their lives on the line day in and day out, to safeguard this beautiful land.'

'I would be ashamed to publically air the views, that you two hold so dearly.'

Albeit, that the interview was not over, Barnaby stood indicating that he had had enough of the rhetoric peddled by these two. Protocol determines that an interview is over when the chairman declares that it is, however, it was clear that Barnaby had had enough, and did not fear the consequences of abruptly ending the hearing.

Rafael nodded in agreement and poured himself another stiff drink.

Deep down, he was troubled by these accusations and decided to "take their number," and started investigating the pair of them. Seems that they are trying to divert attention away from something, he thought.

The CIA intercepted a communication on the wire between a person by the name of Jabulani Kagiso and Senator Nunez. Very Interesting, I wonder who this Jabulani is, thought Barnaby.

Let's see where this takes us.

I will view this as the opening salvo, so you two had better duck, because the main artillery is about to be unleashed, thought Barnaby.

Senator Nunez and Jabulani had openly discussed the transportation of gold bullion from South Africa into the USA for safekeeping in the telephone conversation. South Africa is a country riddled with theft and corruption, where many government officials have been found to have broken the law, however, none have ever been brought to justice.

The ruling ANC President in South Africa needed to find an alternative place to keep the gold safe from looters, and turned to the United States Bullion Depository, often referred to as Fort Knox for assistance.

Barnaby reached out to a retired police officer, Hendrik Van Der Bijl, the Brigadier who was in charge of the disbanded Scorpions, an arm of the South African Police (SAPS) in South Africa, that was replaced with the Hawks, by the then President Zuma.He met Hendrik years previously at a conference on law enforcement, and this highly trained collective of police officers in South Africa, often called The Directorate for Priority Crime Investigation (DPCI), had a specific mandate to address cases where great technical expertise is required for cessation of crime.

The decision to replace the Scorpions with a new organization, namely The Hawks, came from a resolution taken by the ruling African National Congress (ANC) at their fifty-second National Conference in two-thousand and seven in Polokwane province, in Limpopo, South Africa.

The ANC argued that government oversight was needed in such a body, to avoid the agency being used as a political tool to investigate politicians, following a power struggle between sitting President Thabo Mbeki and Jacob Zuma, which resulted in an investigation into Zuma's involvement in an arms deal.

Hendrik was forced into early retirement by the ruling ANC Government, however maintained an interest in the agency for years following his retirement. He updated Barnaby on the corruption and theft by ANC government officials and went to great lengths to discuss Jabulani Kagiso's involvement in numerous crimes in South Africa.

Jabulani held the prestigious position of Secretary General of the ANC and had been the focus of many corruption and fraud allegations in South Africa, however, due to supposed lack of evidence, he has not been charged to date. The ANC executive turns a blind eye to corruption by one of its own cadres.

The conversation between Senator Nunez and Jabulani troubled Barnaby.

Why on earth would these two be discussing the transportation of gold from South Africa? Considered Barnaby.

Fort Knox is a fortified vault building situated next to a United States Army post of Fort Knox, in Kentucky. It is operated by the United States Department of the Treasury and is used to store a large portion of the United States gold reserves, as well as other precious items belonging to the federal government. Fort Knox currently holds 147,341 billion fine troy ounces of gold valued at over seven trillion US dollars, and West Point holds 54,067 billion fine troy ounces of gold bringing the total value of gold held for the Federal Government of the USA to a staggering 11,041 trillion US dollars.

West Point is the oldest continuously occupied military post in the United States.

The ruling ANC (African National Congress) party in South Africa, announced that their gold reserves totaled 125,41 tonnes and had asked the United States to house half of it for safekeeping at Fort Knox. They had been slowly moving the precious metal to the United States over a few months, and the last shipment landed in Kentucky the previous day.

The South Africans dreamed up an innovative way of transporting the gold, which was to encase the gold bullion within cases of fine wine from the Stellenbosch wine-growing region of South Africa. Each pallet of gold bullion stored at Fort Knox and West Point contained eighty gold bars weighing a total of one tonne, so the South Africans halved the number of gold bars to forty per pallet, enclosing them within an outer layer of cased fine wine. Each layer of outer-cased wine totaled sixteen, four on each side of the pallet, leaving a gap in the middle where the forty gold bars were hidden. They then added a layer of cased wine on the top to conceal the gold bars.

The President of South Africa had somehow got wind of a plot to hijack some of the gold bullion, rumored to have come from Hendrik Van Der Bijl, which prompted him to take action to safeguard the bullion and reach out to America for assistance.

What Barnaby had learned from Hendrik, was that corruption and theft within the government in South Africa is rife, and to date, none of the government officials had been charged, and that they continue stealing from government coffers. He learned that Jabulani was suspected of being instrumental in the disappearance of hundreds of millions of Rand's, from government coffers, and the sitting President had little power to remove him from office, due to him controlling a large faction of the ANC national executive.

This is what prompted the President to relocate half of South Africa's gold bullion reserves to the United States because he feared that this corrupt politician would most likely have devised a plan to raid the stash of gold and enrich himself and his cronies in the ANC.

Barnaby summoned Rafael to a meeting at CIA headquarters.

'Hello Rafa, we have yet another problem.' 'This time it involves two US Senators and a South African ANC government official.' 'The two Senators are Raul Montoya and Emilio Nunez, and a South African government official who is a person of interest. 'He goes by the name of Jabulani Kagiso.'

'Weren't those the two Senators that grilled you at the Senate Committee hearing, boss?'

'Yes, that's them.'

'Well, I must say, you took them to task boss.' 'I watched the end part of the hearing and you embarrassed the two of them, no end.'

'I don't suffer fools lightly,' Rafa.

'I suppose you have heard of the disappearance of the consignment of gold bullion from South Africa Rafa, so I need your help to try and establish where it is, and help the South African Government, FBI and police recover it.' 'I suspect that the two senators could be involved, however, I cannot prove that.' 'I believe that the Senate hearing was orchestrated as a cover, for what they were about to do, so I need to get to the bottom of this without the South Africans, FBI, or police knowing that we are involved.'

'From what I have been told by a retired white police officer in South Africa, is that he uncovered that the address on the manifest transporting gold from South Africa to Fort Knox had been altered.' 'All the other consignments of gold sent from South Africa were sent directly to Fort Knox, however not on this occasion.' 'The South African President reached out to us to store half of their gold reserves, because he believed that a corrupt official in his government was planning a gold heist, which as it turns out, was correct.'

'From what we have been told, the cargo landed in Kentucky yesterday eveing, so time is not on our side,' added Barnaby.

'We have hacked into the two Senators' mobile phones using the malware we created, and picked up snippets of a conversation between Senator Nunez, and a South African government official, namely Jabulani Kagiso, discussing the transportation of gold bullion from South Africa.' 'This alerted me to the fact that something may be underfoot and I believe that they concocted a plan to steal the last consignment of gold being transported from South Africa, which is what has happened,' said Barnaby emphatically.

'There are 400 troy ounces of gold in a bar, valued at, US$1,997 per ounce at today's value.' 'Now multiply 400 troy ounces by today's price of US$1,997 and you get a value of US$798,800 per gold bar.' 'Now multiply that by 40 gold bars on each pallet and it comes to US31,952 million.' 'They sent 10 pallets, so now multiply that by 10 and you get the staggering amount of US319,520 million for the entire consignment,' said Barnaby.

'A handsome payday for anybody stealing the gold,' continued Barnaby.

'We are in the wrong business, boss.'

'I suggest that you start by visiting the address detailed on the manifest and see what you can find, Rafael,' said Barnaby.

Rafael immediately visited the address detailed on the manifest and discovered that it was a warehouse rented in a new industrial estate, called Park Five Three Six in the City of Independence in Kentucky, a sprawling one-hundred-and-eight-acre industrial site, off the new four lane KY536 highway.

He decided to visit the Realtor who leased the property, so he made his way to the office of Dynamic Realtors.

As he entered the office, he noticed a very attractive young lady seated at the reception desk and decided to turn on the charm.

'Oh wow, you are drop-dead gorgeous, Belle Femme,' he said in his husky French accent.

'What's your name beautiful lady?

'My name is Davina Romano.'

'That's a sexy name and it compliments your beautiful looks.'

The receptionist blushed openly and smiled broadly at the compliment made by this handsome man standing in front of her. He continued to shower her with compliments and asked for her mobile number.

'My name is Monsieur Gilles Toussaint, and I am a sign writer who erected a business sign on the outer façade of a warehouse that your company leased and manages, called Innovate Solutions.' 'I have been trying to contact the person responsible for payment, and have tried calling the number I was given numerous times, however, it appears that it is not connected, so I am hoping that you can help me?'

'I think it's only fair that the person who rented the warehouse pays me for erecting the business sign on the outer facade, so I hope that you can help to get paid,' said Gilles.

He charmed his way, using his husky French accent, eventually convincing her to disclose the name and contact details of the company they had on file of the person who leased the property. She was happy to impart all the information on file including the person's name that signed the lease, the bank that he used for the periodic payments, as well as his registered home address.

She confirmed that the lease was signed by a person by the name of Douglas Moore.

Armed with Douglas Moore's address, he took a leisurely drive to Glenview, rated as the richest city in Kentucky, which boasts an average income of four-hundred and eighty-seven thousand dollars per person per annum. The median home prices in the area are around one million three-hundred and twenty-five thousand dollars, and it's a sixth-class city, situated along the southern bank of the Ohio River in northeastern Jefferson County in Kentucky.

Certainly, an affluent suburb, thought Rafael as he drove slowly, meandering his way through the residential area.

He drove past the address that he was given, stopped a couple of doors down the road, then took a leisurely stroll past the home, and pulled a couple of letters out of the mailbox, noting that the name on the envelopes did not match the name given to him by the pretty lady at the Realtor's office.

Just as I suspected, thought Gilles.

He called Barnaby and asked him to investigate whether a person by the name of Douglas Moore existed.

Later that day Barnaby called Gilles and informed him that nobody by that name lives in Kentucky.

Right, so whoever leased the warehouse must have set up a bank account some time ago using an alias, or lives somewhere else in the USA. If so, why would he give that particular address and who would that person be? Possibly a family member thought Gilles.

He took a drive to the industrial estate noting that it was gated and that there were CCTV cameras scattered around the complex. He discovered that there was a camera positioned at the entrance to the complex, and called the Realtor's office to establish the name of the company that owned the industrial estate.

'Bonjour Belle Femme, it's Gilles Toussaint again.' 'I'm at Park Five Three Six in Independence, and wondering if you can give me the name of the company that owns or has developed this industrial estate.' 'The reason that I am calling is that Monsieur Moore does not live at the address you gave me, so I need to contact the developer or owner of the estate and try to get some more information.'

Ten minutes later she gave him the company's contact details.

'Merci Beaucoup Davina.'

Barnaby reached out to the owner of the estate and cleared the way for Gilles to view all the CCTV footage they had of the estate, so he made his way up the stairs leading to the company's head office, announcing himself at reception.

'Bonjour Madam, my name is Monsieur Toussaint, and I have an appointment with Monsieur Thomas Stolly.'

An hour later, armed with a USB he made his way home. Right, let's see what we have, thought Gilles as he inserted the USB stick into his laptop.

He fast-forwarded it, and trolled through a few hours of footage, eventually noticing a Volvo VNL long haul truck and trailer making its way into the estate. The white truck and trailer had no signwriting on it, so he jotted down its number plate and watched as it stopped in front of the Innovative Solutions warehouse.

He counted the pallets that the forklift driver unloaded, confirming that there were ten pallets, as detailed on the manifest. Unloading the pallets took around thirty minutes to complete, and noticed three vehicles parked in front of the warehouse and wondered whether they belonged to the people who had arranged the heist.

The truck driver hopped into his cab and made his way out of the complex thirty minutes later, having completed his delivery. Ten minutes later, the forklift driver, jumped into his car and drove out of the complex, so he took note of his number plate. Need to interview this guy, he thought.

Later that day he interviewed the forklift driver, who confirmed that he was hired to unload a consignment of wine and was specifically instructed to take great care not to damage or drop any of the pallets. He confirmed that pallets seemed rather heavy for cases of wine and it seemed that the forklift had been hired. He was paid in cash.

It appeared that he was not part of the heist, concluded Gilles.

Normally Fort Knox would use their regular logistics company to move gold bullion around the country, however, on this occasion, it appeared that whoever tampered with the manifest, managed to engage an alternative carrier to deliver the consignment to the warehouse at the Park Five Three Six industrial estate. Gilles wondered if Fort Knox was even aware that another consignment of gold had been flown to the USA.

He continued watching the recording and an hour later, he caught a glimpse of two males making their way to the two GMC Sierra 1500ATX V8 SUVs parked in front of the warehouse, and he watched as they backed into the warehouse. One red and the other black. It appeared from an obscure angle that they had closed the roller door, making it impossible to observe any movement close to the inside of the warehouse door. He fast forwarded the CCTV footage until he saw the two SUVs, making their way out of the warehouse. The rear cargo areas of both vehicles were covered with tarps, hiding the pallets from the prying eyes, and he noticed that both SUVs' rear suspensions were close to the ground, indicating that they were carrying heavy loads.

They must have broken down the pallets, removed the wine, and repacked the gold bars onto separate pallets to relocate the bullion. Yep, gold is heavy, thought Gilles.

Wonder if that's what they did and if so, would they return for the wine? I think so, he convinced himself.

Don't think that they will simply let good wine go to waste, thought Gilles.

Gilles wondered whether the truck driver had any knowledge of the consignment he was delivering, or whether he was under the impression that he was delivering pallets of wine. He was sure that this was what would have been detailed on the manifest, so he rewound the disk, replaying the earlier footage of vehicles entering the complex, that had parked in the allocated parking area in front of the warehouse, and noted each vehicle license plate number as it entered.

Will need to check the license plates and try to identify the owners of each vehicle, he thought.

Later that day, he met with Barnaby at CIA's headquarters.

'This is the footage I was given by the Realtor who manages the estate on behalf of the owner,' he said handing him the USB stick.

'I will need you to get your technicians to identify the faces of the people on it.' 'Hopefully, you can identify the owners of the vehicles by their number plate, so that we can trace them, boss.'

Barnaby forwarded photographs of the three people who had parked the vehicles in front of the warehouse to his technicians and asked them to match the number plates to a name, to identify them as a matter of urgency. The technicians discovered that all the number plates had been reported stolen and none matched the vehicles. After hours of tedious investigation, the technicians eventually discovered that the vehicles had been hired from Kentucky Car Hire based in Frankfort Kentucky, under the company name of Big Haulage and paid by bank transfer directly into their account.

Appropriately named. At least these people seem to have a sense of humor, thought Barnaby.

He checked the US Small Business Administration register, and searched for a company by the name of Big Haulage Winners and discovered that no such company existed. Just as he thought.

Gilles visited the offices of the car hire company just as they were about to close for the day, and was notified that the person who hired the vehicles, did so online, and arranged for them to be delivered to a warehouse in an industrial estate at Independence, so there was no CCTV footage of people collecting them. Payment was made using a bank transfer directly into the company's account, from a person by the name of Douglas Moore. Clearly whoever had arranged that payment, was using the same alias that he used when renting the warehouse, and was being extremely cautious to conceal his real identity.

Another dead end. Gilles decided to start with the logistics company that delivered the pallets to the warehouse. It was late afternoon and almost closing time, so he drove to the offices of Kentucky Express, based in Louisville as the sun was setting. Luckily Barnaby had cleared the way for Gilles to view all footage of the CCTV cameras scattered around the estate, so Beau Salotto, the CEO was expecting him.

Gilles was ushered into a conference room and Beau confirmed that his company was contracted to pick up ten pallets of wine at the airport, at around lunch time which had been flown in from South Africa, and deliver them to a warehouse owned by a company called Innovative Solutions at the Park Five Three Six industrial estate, based in the City of Independence. He checked his computer and told Gilles that the logistics driver was due back at the warehouse within ten minutes and that he was free to interview him on his return.

Gilles waited at the entrance to Kentucky Express, and eventually watched as the truck made its way into the company's premises just as darkness was about to set in. He approached the driver as he got out of the cab.

'Bonjour Monsieur.' 'I have just spoken with your CEO, Monsieur Salotto, and he has agreed to allow me to speak with you about a recent delivery that you made to Innovative Solution at Park Five Three Six industrial estate in Independence.'

'When you delivered the pallets of wine, did you notice anybody else in the warehouse, other than the forklift driver?'

'The only person that I had close contact with, was the forklift driver, however, I did see three men gathered in a group toward the back of the warehouse, that seemed to be having some sort of a discussion.' 'Two guys were white, and the other was an African American.' 'I could not hear what was being said because the forklift was rather noisy.'

'Was there anything in the warehouse?'

'No, it was empty.'

'Thanks, you have been most helpful,' said Gilles as he made his way back to the SUV.

Barnaby called him.

'Hello Gilles, our technicians have managed to get an identification of one of the three people who entered the warehouse before the logistics company dropped off the ten pallets.'

'They used a new face recognition software program that we developed to identify people not wanting to be identified.'

'Our team developed a machine to learn algorithms to locate fourteen key facial points on a person's face,' 'The system only needs to see a fraction of facial points around the eyes and mouth region of the face, to be able to guess where the other points are likely to be.'

'Despite anyone wearing a mask or sunglasses, the system can see through the disguise and identify a person's features, even if they are wearing a rigid plastic mask, similar to the Vendetta masks that protesters use,' continued Barnaby.

'So, the good news is that we have a one hundred percent match to the South African diplomat that goes by the name of Jabulani Kagiso.' 'The South African President confirmed that Mr. Kagiso had recently traveled to the US, supposedly on a fact-finding mission, and two of our agents secretly detained him at Cincinnati/Northern International Airport, before he boarded a flight to Dubai a short while ago.'

'Albeit, that he had diplomatic immunity, the South African Government has waived it, due to the serious nature of his involvement in this crime, which is not related to his diplomatic role.' 'This has allowed the South African President an opportunity to get rid of one of his fiercest opponents, so he will be charged under USA law and will face a long-term prison sentence here,' said Barnaby.

'From what I have been told, he has confessed to his involvement in the theft of the gold bars and implicated both Senators Montoya and Nunez.' 'He also told us where the gold bars were being held, and how they intended to transport them to Dubai.'

Continuing Barnaby added, 'the South African President has asked the FBI, not to return him to South Africa to face charges of theft and corruption rather that he be charged in the USA.' 'So Gilles, I think it is time to pay these two guys a visit and recover the gold, and no, you can't keep a couple of bars as a reward for a job well done.' 'I will SMS their addresses to you shortly, and no, you cannot simply eliminate them either, because this story is about to become headline news, so we will have to hand them over to the police and FBI to arrest and charge them.'

As Gilles drove past Senator Nunez's home, he noticed that the garage door was not properly closed and remained slightly raised, and noticed that the light in garage was on. He parked a few doors down, and then quickly made his way down the neighbor's driveway. He jumped the fence, ensuring that he remained hidden toward the side of the garage door behind the brickwork, and was careful not to stand directly in front of the door, which would have alerted whoever was inside the garage, to a stranger loitering outside.

He could hear two men having a hushed conversation, so he set his mobile phone to record and crawled on his stomach under the door, enabling him to see the legs of the two guys seated behind the two heavily laden SUVs. He checked the number plates on the two SUVs, confirming that they were the same vehicles he had seen at the warehouse. Both vehicles were heavily laden with their cargo storage areas close to the ground, confirming that these guys had not unloaded the gold. The gold bars were still in the SUVs.

Right, these are the two SUVs I saw at the warehouse, so I'm right on point, thought Gilles.

Neither saw Gilles crouched behind the rear wheel of the red SUV and he listened intently to what appeared to be a disagreement between the two, ensuring that he was recording their conversation.

'Raul, we agreed to what we were going to do with the gold before the fucking stuff landed, now you want to change everything.' 'No fucking ways Amigo.' 'We stick to the plan and move it to Dubai as planned.' 'We already have the boat waiting to be loaded tomorrow so don't try and opt out now Camarada.' 'It's way too late.'

The conversation appeared to have gotten a little heated, so he continued listening to what was being said. The two changed to Spanish, which he was not able to follow, however, he was confident that he had recorded the conversation. A moment later one of them offered to pour another drink for his mate, and he heard both glasses clinking, as they appeared to have resolved their dispute.

Seems like these two were confident that they had pulled this off, so he reduced the sound on his iPhone and sent Barnaby an SMS.

Gilles stood and made his way toward where the two were seated. He pointed his beloved Glock, fitted with a silencer at the two as he rounded the front of the red SUV, catching both totally by surprise. Both were unaware that someone had entered the garage and were stunned.

'Gentlemen, this is your lucky day.' 'Both of you, lie face down with your hands behind your head, and don't fucking move, or even breath, instructed Gilles.'

Five minutes later several heavily armed police and FBI agents arrived. Gilles watched as they cuffed the two, and read them their rights. Barnaby stood rigidly and watched the proceedings. He lifted the tarp of one of the SUVs and stared at the pallets of gold for a few minutes.

'Always wanted to see what gold bars looked like,' he said stroking one of the bars.

He turned to face the two Senators and addressed them.

'Hello gentlemen, hope you still remember me?' 'Funny how things come back and bite you in the arse.' 'For what it's worth, I will be at your trial sitting in the front row, so look out for me.'

'I will insist that the two of you enjoy an extended tour at Rikers Island and are never released.' 'Take the time you have to reflect on what you have done and never forget about karma, because it works.'

'And yes, we at the CIA ensure that the bad people like you two, are brought to justice.' 'I hope that the Warden at Rikers Island makes your stay a very welcome one.'

'I'm sure that both of you are wondering how I knew about the heist.'

'Well I am the Director of the CIA, and I know everything, so enjoy your stay gentlemen.' 'I only spy on the bad guys.'

Thank the good lord I can now get rid of the alias of Gilles and revert to my CIA name of Rafael, he thought as he and Barnaby turned and made their way out of the garage.

Whilst I understand why Barnaby keeps giving me a different alias each time I go on a mission and his reason for doing that, it does make me sick, having to change names on every mission, thought Rafael.

I should go back home and tend my cows. The cows know me as Yonti Barr, he thought.

Chapter 20

Tenerife

Canary Islands

'Excellent outcome Rafael.' 'The South African President asked me to pass on his sincere thanks.' 'From him and me, thank you for a job well done, Rafael.'

'I have identified the boat that they were going to use to move the gold to Dubai.' 'The South African diplomat, Mr. Kagiso, has voluntarily surrendered the name of the boat and the captain's name 'He is using that as a plea bargain to try and wriggle his way out of being charged,' said Barnaby.

'The captain is a person of interest, who has been involved in people smuggling, money laundering, and prostitution.' 'I can confirm that his name is Carlos Campos and he is the captain of the sloop that the two Senators hired to move the bullion to Dubai.' 'He had been charged several times in the past, however, thanks to an extremely clever and well-versed lawyer, he has managed to avoid any jail time.'

'His lawyer's name is César Lopez, and he has represented many bad guys in the past.' 'He has not lost a case to date.' 'So a very competent lawyer that has exploited every loophole in our law,' continued Barnaby.

'Both these gentlemen are Mexican, and have been in the USA for over two decades.' 'Mr. Kagiso disclosed the name of the yacht that the two Senators were going to use to transport the gold bullion to Dubai, and we have been led to believe that it is a large ocean-going super sloop, with an LOA of one hundred and fourteen feet, so a large vessel.' 'I would imagine that a ship of that size would have a crew of three or four.'

Barnaby used one of the CIA's spy satellites to hone in on the vessel as it set sail from Rubaiyat Boat harbor, where the sun-kissed shores of Harrods Creek meet the sparkling waters of the Ohio River. The harbor is a hidden gem like no other for those seeking a thrilling adventure on the water, or a peaceful retreat surrounded by the beauty of nature.He zoomed in on the yacht and checked its name, ensuring that he was following the correct vessel, as it headed in an easterly direction toward the top of Africa.

The sloop was christened "Hidden Treasure," an appropriate name for a vessel hired to transport a heist of gold bullion, thought Barnaby.

He reached out to the commodore of the yacht club, commonly known as the President, and asked him to confirm that Carlos Campos was the registered captain of the Hidden Treasure. The commodore confirmed that Mr. Campos had registered Mina Rashid Port in Dubai, as his destination with stops at the Canary Islands, Morocco, and Malta.

'I wonder why he would sail to Dubai if he does not have the gold on board.' 'Something seems dodgy,' said Rafael.

Barnaby sat back and reflected on what Rafael had just said.

'Wonder whether there is a connection to the huge diamond theft that took place at Christie's a week ago.' 'The investigation is ongoing and the police and FBI have not solved that case yet,' said Barnaby.

'Christie's had scheduled an auction, and a day before the auction, jewelry valued at fifty million US dollars went missing, and no one knows how the thieves pulled it off.' 'Fancy colored diamonds and Kashmir sapphires in one hundred and fifty lots were to be auctioned. Amongst the jewels were a highly sought after, rare pair of fancy vivid orange-yellow diamond earrings valued at around fifteen million dollars and a flawless blue diamond expected to fetch around ten million dollars.'

'My gut tells me that this may be the reason that Hidden Treasure had sailed.' 'Clearly, they have somehow got wind that the two Senators had been arrested, and decided to set sail, so clearly, they must have something of value on board.' 'Let's put a toe in the water and see what pops up,' Rafa.

'I think I should send you and two other agents to the Canary Islands to check the boat when it arrives'. 'The two other agents, I have in mind are qualified seamen that sail regularly over weekends, and you three may find that the boat has the stolen jewelry on board,' said Barnaby.

Barnaby requested all the information that the FBI and local police had on the theft and passed it on to Rafael to investigate. Rafael read through the police report and concluded that the jewelry must have been stolen by some trusted employee at Christie's. The person must have had access to the vault where the jewelry was being kept, and the police report stated that they had thoroughly investigated all staff and had not discounted anyone at this stage yet. The investigation was ongoing.

Rafael started by viewing the internal CCTV footage at Christie's auction house situated at the Rockefeller Center in New York and spent dozens of hours trolling through the footage.

He replayed the tape numerous times and watched as the steward pushed the trolley of jewelry past the night guard and down the passage toward the vault at eighteen hundred hours. The camera's view of the passage was obstructed as the steward rounded a corner and it appeared that there was no footage looking back to that part of the passage from another camera angle.

All appeared to be normal, so he picked up the action from a camera situated around the corner. This camera had a view of the door to the vault, so he switched the camera to slow motion, selecting twenty-four fps, and replayed the footage several times. Slowing down the movement, allowed him to see more detail that he may have missed at normal speed.

At first, he did not notice any issues, however, having replayed it repeatedly numerous times, he detected a faint flicker on the screen, so he noted the exact footage on the tape and the time that it had occurred, and replayed it repeatedly at that exact time. He noticed that the flicker appeared each time.

He continued to pay close attention, as he continued to watch the footage and detected another slight flicker later in the footage, so he rewound the tape and replayed it again several times. The second flicker remained constant at the exact time and at the exact footage on the tape.

It appeared that someone had stopped the footage when the first flicker occurred, then inserted a static recording, making it seem like nothing was happening in the passage, and when the second flicker occurred, the recording must have ended at that point. Whoever tampered with the tape, must have reverted it to the original tape and continued recording. Someone had tampered with the tape, cut, spliced, and inserted the static footage hoping that no one would notice, making it seem like nothing had happened in the passage. Using this method would have resulted in them being able to delete any footage of the jewels having been stolen. Very clever indeed, considered Rafael.

The flickers were so faint, that the FBI and police had not detected it, so it appeared that the steward and someone else were involved. They must have stolen the jewels during the time that they stopped the footage, and restarted it, having substituted the static footage, depicting that everything was normal, before restarting the recording. Smart, real smart, so whoever did this, must have intricate knowledge of using recording equipment, thought Rafael.

They had selected a time, just as the steward was about to place the jewels into the vault, before locking it up for the night. No one had accompanied the steward, nor was anyone monitoring what he was doing, because he was one of their most trusted long-term employees. He had been tasked with locking up valuable jewelry for years after they had been on display and Christie's had never had a problem. Nobody suspected him of being involved. Strange that a company's security is so lackadaisical, especially when there is a consignment of high-valued jewelry in their possession, considered Rafael.

The exact time of the first flicker was eighteen hundred hours, which was clearly when the person stopped the footage and inserted the footage, displaying a static screen without any movement in the passage, and the second flicker happened exactly thirty minutes later, at eighteen hundred and thirty hours. The vault is set on a time delay system, so the thief could not get into the vault to remove the jewels after he had stored the jewels for the evening, therefore it must have been stolen before it was put into the vault and during the period that they had altered the footage.

Let's start by interviewing the night guard and then the steward, thought Rafael.

The following afternoon, he was joined by another agent. They set up a camera and recording device in a conference room at Christie's head office, before interviewing the night guard. Rafael decided to take an aggressive approach.

The guard's name was Leon Walker.

'Hello, Mr. Walker, my name is Monsieur Gilles Toussaint, and this is agent Ship Arnold,' he said.

'As you have been informed, we are here to interview you, regarding the theft of the jewels,' he said reverting to the same alias that he used previously, to safeguard his real identity.

Leon appeared rather nervous and fidgety, shifting regularly in his chair, a clear sign that he was hiding something. His response to questions seemed rather vague, so Gilles changed his strategy to one of rapid-fire questioning and did not give him the time to answer. This unsettled Leon and he started sweating, another indication of guilt.

'So Monsieur Walker, you and the steward, Mr. Hugo Young, were in cahoots with each other.' 'From what we have learned, is that you two have somehow stopped the recording of the CCTV cameras and inserted static recording footage, making it seem as if things were normal, then you stole the jewellery.' 'Hugo placed the jewelry into a bag which he gave to you for safe keeping until your shift ended at zero six-hundred hours the next morning,' said Gilles.

'When morning arrived, you simply picked up the bag, clocked out, and left.' 'Nobody bothered to check your bag, after all, you are head of security at Christie's,' continued Gilles.

'How am I doing so far Mr. Walker?' Asked Gilles forcefully.

Without waiting for an answer, he continued, 'So I will give you one chance to come clean, because your friend is currently in another interview room, possibly spilling the beans, so you will both shortly be on your way to Rikers Island.'

'This is your only chance to confess, and tell me where the jewels are, and maybe, just maybe, I will put in a word with the DA for you, and he may offer you a reduced sentence.' 'If you refuse to cooperate, the deal is off the table.' 'The FBI are waiting outside to arrest you and take you to jail,' continued Gilles.'

'You know, Rikers Island is a wonderful place.' 'A place where the guards turn a blind eye to what happens in jail.' 'I'm sure that some gang boss will no doubt take you for his bitch.' 'So this is your one chance to come clean,' said Gilles.

'You have no proof.' 'I want a lawyer,' demanded Leon.

'Good choice Mr. Walker, however, before I call a lawyer, you had best tell me where the jewels are right now, or the deal with the DA is off the table.' 'One last chance.'

'Oh yes, let me update you.' 'You stopped the CCTV recording at exactly eighteen hundred hours, then inserted your pre-recorded tape for thirty minutes ending it exactly at eighteen-thirty hundred hours, and the static footage that you inserted, showed no movement in the passage at all.' 'Smart, real smart, Mr. Walker.'

'As you can see, we have worked out exactly what you did,' continued Gilles.

'Your shift ended at zero six hundred hours, so well before the staff arrived for work, and plenty of time to casually pick up the bag and leave after you handed over to the next security guard.' 'Jewels in hand, you headed home,' pressed Gilles forcefully.

Gilles could see that Leon was petrified and shaking openly, so he stood as if he was about to leave. The guard would know that the game was up.

'You won't tell me what happened, so the deal is off the table,' said Gilles as he headed for the door.

'Wait.' 'Wait, if I tell you, will you confirm that the DA will look upon what I tell you favorably?'

'I can't promise that, however, my boss wields a lot of influence, so I will ask him to negotiate some sort of a deal for you.'

Like hell, I will do that. People like you should rot in jail, thought Gilles.

He handed him a pen, and paper, and instructed him to write down everything that they had done.

A while later, he read the confession aloud.

'So, everything I said earlier was true.' 'You two spliced the tape and inserted a tape with static footage on it, depicting that all was normal in the passage leading to the vault.' 'Which one of you had that bright idea?'

'That was me, he confessed in a somewhat boastful manner.' 'I studied Information Technology when I was younger, and I am an amateur filmmaker in my spare time,' said Leon confidently.

'Zip-a-dee-do-dah, for you.' 'What did you do with the jewels Leon?' Demanded Gilles forcefully.

'A man called Campos approached me some time ago.' 'He knew that valuable jewelry were going to be auctioned and offered me two million dollars in cash to steal the jewels, so I involved my good friend Hugo, because we toll day in and day out here, without any recognition for a measly salary, so this was an opportunity to make some serious money for ourselves.'

'So when did you hand over the jewelry to Mr. Campos?'

'I called Mr. Campos as soon as my shift ended, and we arranged to meet immediately at Top of the Rock at the Rockefeller Plaza.' 'I needed to get rid of the jewels immediately and get paid because I knew that the police would suspect both of us as having been involved, and would most likely search our homes, so we needed to dispose of it ASAP.'

'Where have you hidden the cash, Leon?' 'Best tell me or the deal with the DA is off.'

'I hid the money in a locker at Frankfort Union Station because Hugo and I agreed that we needed to lie low for several months until the dust settled.'

'So where is the key to the locker Leon?'

'On my keyring.'

'I see, so give me the key ring and I will notify the DA that you have been most cooperative.'

He sent Barnaby an SMS, notifying him that the night guard had confessed. A few minutes later the FBI and police arrived and arrested the steward and night guard. Thank goodness I can now get rid of the alias, thought Rafa.

Sick of having to change my name every time I am on a mission.

Barnaby continued to monitor the progress of Hidden Treasure and estimated that it would arrive in the Canary Islands within the next four days, so he booked flights for Rafael and the two agents to fly there the following day.

The Canary Islands, also known as the Canaries, a Spanish autonomous community and archipelago in Macaronesia,situated in the Atlantic Ocean, sixty-two miles west of Morocco. He expected the vessel to berth at Tenerife for supplies.

As Rafael, agents Ozias Freling, and Ivo Tartal deplaned in Santa Cruz de Tenerife, the capital of the island, they felt the warm breeze blowing into their faces.

'Rather pleasant boys,' commented Rafael.

'Right guys, let's book into the hotel, and check the lie of the land.'

They rented a yacht, at the Yacht Charter Santa Cruz de Tenerife, an excellent starting point for cruising the Canary Islands, and berthed it, in anticipation for the arrival of Hidden Treasure.

Two days later they were sitting in the Enigma Bar overlooking the harbor, enjoying a couple of beers when they noticed a large sloop sailing slowly into the harbor. Rafael, watched it approach through his binoculars and confirmed that it was Hidden Treasure. He watched as it made its way toward the jetty, and as she turned toward its port side, he checked the name again, confirming that it was the correct boat.

'Drink up boys, let the games begin.'

Barnaby had sent the agency's Gulf Stream to the islands in preparation for a quick exit.

They made their way back to their hired yacht and busied themselves with menial tasks around the boat, making it seem that they were getting ready to sail the following day.

Hidden Treasure berthed at the end of the pier on the opposite side, and having tied the sloop to the jetty, one of the crew made his way toward the Harbormaster's office. Rafael followed at a discreet distance.

He wondered whether the person could be Carlos, and followed him into the office. He overheard the crew member introduce himself as Carlos Campos, the captain of the Hidden Treasure, so Rafael busied himself by pretending to be looking at various charts and overheard him tell the Harbormaster, that they would be in port for two days to replenish supplies before sailing to Malta.

The two CIA agents watched as two crew members made their way toward the Superyacht Supplies Shop to replenish supplies, leaving one crew member on board Hidden Treasure.

They befriended the remaining crew member that had remained on board, and struck up a conversation, pretending to be in awe of the magnificent sloop. The agents continued to heap praise on the condition of the sloop and asked if they could take a peak below. The crew member was hesitant at first, so Ozias turned on the charm.

'Just want to take a quick peek at what it looks like below, my friend, and we will be on our way.' 'Your boat is luxurious compared to our dingy over there,' he said pointing to their hired yacht.

The crewman agreed, however, stated that his boss would be pissed off if he saw them, so they would need to be quick because they have to be off the boat before he got back from the Harbormasters office.

'Promise that we will be quick, just want to take a peek at the inside my friend,' reiterated agent Ivo.

They followed the crewman down the stairs into the cabin. Ozias removed his weapon and placed it on the nape of the crewman's neck. Ivo frisked him and instructed him to take a seat. He bound his feet and hands with Flexi Cuffs.

'Make yourself comfortable my friend and let's wait for your shipmates to arrive.' 'Where have you hidden the jewels?' He asked forcefully.

'I don't know what you are talking about.' 'We are sailing around the world and we don't have any valuables on board.'

'We will see about that,' said Ivo as he covered his mouth with duct tape.

Ivo searched all the lockers eventually making his way to the main cabin and tried the door handle. It was locked as anticipated, so he kicked the door in and made his way to the cupboard which was also locked.

Rafael sent Barnaby an SMS on a secure line, confirming that they had sighted the boat and that he had confirmation that the captain is Carlos Campos. He notified Barnaby that he should keep the Gulf Stream on standby for departure later that evening.

Ozias noticed the captain and the two crew members pushing a trolley full of supplies heading back to the boat and warned Ivo. They watched them through a porthole window and noticed Rafael following close behind, so they positioned themselves near the cabin door and waited. They felt the boat tip to one side as the three got on board.

Rafael extracted his beloved Glock fitted with a silencer from the rear of his pants and followed them on board.

'Down you go gentlemen,' he said pointing the gun in their direction.

'I have a nice surprise for you lot.'

As they entered the cabin, they were confronted by two agents pointing their weapons in their direction and noticed that their compatriot had been handcuffed with duct tape around his mouth.

'Take a seat Mr. Campos, and you two as well,' he said looking at the crew members.

'Make yourselves comfortable gentlemen,' instructed Rafael.

'What is this about shouted?' shouted Carlos.

'You are trespassing, and I will report you to the authorities.'

'Is that right.' 'Well go ahead.' 'In case you have not noticed, we hold all the cards here,' said Rafael, as the agents frisked each of them, handcuffed and duct taped their mouths.'

'So Mr. Campos, we understand that you were going to transport the gold that Senators Raul Montoya and Emilio Nunez had stolen to Dubai, however, you got wind of the fact that they had been arrested, so you set sail immediately,' said Rafael.

'Oh yes, I almost forgot, you had the jewelry that was to be auctioned at Christie's which had been stolen on board.' 'I also know that you paid Leon Walker, the security guard a handsome fee of two million dollars for the jewelry.'

'So, you set sail knowing that at least you had part of the bounty on board.' continued Rafael.

'How am I doing so far, Carlos?'

Carlos shook his head from side to side indicating that he disagreed and mumbled something inaudible through the duct tape.

'Let's see if I can find the jewelry,' said Rafael.

Ivo mentioned that he had searched all the lockers and did not find anything, however, was about to kick in the locked cupboard door in the main cabin, when they saw the three crew members heading back to the boat, so he decided to wait until they were all on board.

'Thanks, Ivo, I will do the honors,' said Rafael.

He made his way into the kitchen and found a large knife which he used to pry the door open with.

'Ah, here it is,' he said as he removed a large duffle bag.

He tipped some of the jewelry out of the bag confirming that he had found the treasure

'You are going to join Senators Raul Montoya, Emilio Nunez, the steward Hugo Young, and the guard, Leon Walker, for an extended stay at Rikers, compliments of the USA government, then you will be deported back to Mexico.' 'That's if you survive the long-term jail sentence.' 'By that time, you will be an old man with your balls hanging on your knees, that's if you still have them intact.'

'By the way, your smartarse lawyer won't be able to wriggle you out of this one,' said Rafael.

'This is your lucky day because you will get to see the sun rise tomorrow.'

'My boss knows the warden at Rikers Island very well, and I am sure that he will put a word in for you, ensuring that your time there will be memorable,' said Rafael.

They waited until zero two hundred hours, then made their way onto the jetty and headed toward the hired Combi. They bundled the four crew members into the vehicle. Rafael fired up the engine and pointed the Combi in the direction of Tenerife airport. They skipped immigration and left the hired combi on the tarmac, with the key in the ignition. Minutes later, The Gulf Stream taxied onto the runway, and the pilot engaged full throttle. Rafael looked at the cloudy night sky as they climbed to cruising altitude.

Barnaby placed his backside on the door of the black GMC SUV and watched as the Gulf Stream was on its final approach into Biglers Mill, the CIA's private airstrip.

Barnaby turned to the six FBI agents and said, 'Well gentlemen, a good outcome for all.' 'You guys have wanted to catch Mr. Carlos red-handed for years, and each time you arrested him, his lawyer managed to get him off.' 'Not this time though.'

'We now have Carlos Campos in custody, so this time his smart-arse lawyer will not be able to wriggle him out of it.' 'I will speak with the judge, and ask him to sentence Mr. Campos to a very long stay at Rikers Island.'

Rafael and the agents deplaned and led the crew of Hidden Treasure toward the FBI agents.

'All yours boss,' said Rafael as he handed Barnaby the bag of jewels.

Barnaby handed the duffle bag to an FBI agent, turned to face Carlos, and said, 'Pleased to meet you.' 'Have a pleasant stay at Rikers Mr. Campos.'

Chapter 21

JFK Airport

New York USA

Rafael met Barnaby at a local coffee shop and dropped a bag on the table.

'All yours, boss.'

'What's this Rafael?'

'It's the last piece of evidence for the upcoming trial against Carlos Campos. 'It's the two million dollar payment he paid to Leon Walker the security guard at Christie's for the jewelry.'

'Thank you Rafael I will forward it to the FBI.'

The next morning Rafael parked the SUV in the usual spot and waited for Claire to drop the twins off at the Young Guns Pre-School. He watched as she led them into the building, his chest pounding. It had been weeks since he last came to see them due to the various missions he had been on. They seemed to have grown an inch, he thought.

A short time later, he ducked as Claire made a U-Turn and headed past him on her way to work.

He had mixed feelings about her and was still annoyed at what she had done. Thirty minutes later he made his way to the fence, peeped over it, and watched as his boys interacted with a few of their friends.

This is killing me, he thought as he made his way back to the SUV.

Moments later his mobile phone lit up with an incoming call from Barnaby.

'Hello Rafa, please come directly to the office, I need to see you right away.'

Gizelle tapped lightly on Barnaby's door announcing his arrival.

'Hello Rafa, good to see you,' he said waving him to a chair at the table.

'I know that I have said it before, but I feel that I need to say it again.' 'Great outcome for Christie's, and a great outcome for the police and FBI.' 'They finally have their man.' 'Thank you for retrieving the jewelry, and the bag of cash,' Rafael.

'The management of Christie's asked me to hand this letter to you,' said Barnaby.

Rafael opened the envelope and read the letter. It was a heartfelt thank you from the management expressing their appreciation for what he had done. They enclosed a gift voucher to the value of two hundred thousand dollars that could be spent at any future Christie's auction.

'Oh wow, that's a nice surprise.' 'The only time I have received a reward for doing what is right,' said Rafa.

'Well deserved Rafa.'

'Right, let's get down to business.' 'We have another pressing issue to deal with, Rafa.'

'Our intelligence has picked up some chatter on the wire, from Major Farukh Zoheri, of the Iranian Revolutionary Guard Corps.' 'You know him well and as you are aware, he survived the helicopter crash with severe burns to his face and body.' 'You also know, that he has vowed to hunt you down and kill you,' said Barnaby.

'This is serious, so you need to take precautions to protect yourself and your family because this bloke is hell-bent on taking revenge.' 'From what we have learned, the Supreme Leader of Iran has allowed him to join their team at the United Nations.' 'Clearly, this is a ploy to get him into the USA and to be near to where we are based, so it appears that they may suspect that you work for the CIA,' continued Barnaby

'These bastards tend to go for one's family first, to inflict as much pain as possible, then he will turn his attention to you for the final coup grâce.'

'This is a photograph of him clearing customs at JFK yesterday.' 'You can see that he has been badly scarred from the helicopter crash, so there is no doubt that he wants revenge.' 'I have placed a tail on him and he made his way directly to the Iranian Consulate at Twenty-Third Street, here in Washington.' 'I imagine that he may well be staying there,' added

Barnaby.

'Remember, he knows his way around New York, because he lived here for four years before returning to Iran and joining the Revolutionary Guard,' Said Barnaby.

'So Rafael, I think it's time for you to contact Claire and warn her.'

Rafael sat back and thought about what Barnaby had just said.

'Well boss, I'm not sure that I want to do that.' 'Frankly, I have mixed feelings about what she did.' 'To be honest, I am annoyed that she up and left without even taking the time to speak to me.'

'I think it best that you meet with her and warn her boss.' 'I don't want her to know that I'm here.'

Rafael stared at the photograph for a few minutes.

'Pity the bastard did not die in the crash,' boss.

He decided to take a drive on Saturday afternoon and see where Claire lived on the naval base, so he got dressed into his crisp white naval uniform and pulled up at the security gate. The guard inspected his identity card, stood to attention, and saluted him, then opened the gate, allowing him entry onto the base. As he drove slowly past the address, he saw his twin sons playing football on the lawn out of the corner of his eye and noticed Claire sitting on the porch, reading a book. He had to stop himself from jumping out of the SUV and running to hug his boys.

She glanced at the passing SUV, however, did not recognize him with his bushy beard and dark sunglasses. He purposely stared directly ahead as he passed.

Right, so this is where she lives. Best keep an eye on the place, because this Iranian bastard may somehow find out where she lives.

Barnaby called and instructed him to come directly to the office.

'Something important has cropped up Rafael.'

'We picked up a communication from someone in Iran, who contacted Major Zoheri, and from what we overheard, he was given Claire's name, so things are hotting up.' 'I have no idea who the person is that called Zoheri, nor do I know how he found out about Claire.' 'Having said that, I think that you should speak with her, because I believe that she and the kids are in imminent danger.'

Rafael, waited a few minutes, then answered.

'Respectfully sir, as mentioned, I think it best that you speak with her and leave me out of it.' 'I don't want her to know I'm here, boss.'

'As you wish Rafael.'

He decided to follow Claire and see where it led, so he parked on the opposite side of the park overlooking her home on the naval base and waited. A car eventually pulled up at nineteen hundred hours and he saw a young lady make her way to the front door and watched as Claire welcomed her. He wondered whether the young lady could be a child carer employed to take care of the boys while she went out.

Thirty minutes later, another car stopped in front of her home, and a smartly dressed man got out and knocked on the door. Right, so what do we have here, thought Rafael.

Must be her date for the evening. He had to stop himself from jumping out of the vehicle and confronting the visitor.

Claire looked radiant in a pair of jeans, and a loose-fitting white shirt. The man held her by the elbow as he guided her toward his parked car, opened the passenger door to let her in, then rounded the car and jumped into the driver's seat. They headed toward the exit, so Rafael fired up the SUV and followed at a discreet distance as they headed toward Uncle Joe's Café, a popular steakhouse in downtown Norfolk.

Rafael felt pangs of anger and had to contain himself. Having calmed himself down somewhat, and reminded himself that the man may be a fellow naval officer, possibly a friend or even a relative.

Calm down my boy, he reminded himself. Let's not prejudge Claire, and mister suave. Wait to see where this ends, he thought.He managed to find parking with a view of the table that they were seated at, waited, and watched. Two hours later, they made their way out of the restaurant and headed back to the base, so he again followed them at a distance. As he drove past her home, he noticed the man shake her hand.

Lucky prick, because if he had kissed her, I would have broken his bones, thought Rafael.

The following day, he left home at zero two hundred hours and took a leisurely eight hour drive to New York. He arrived at zero six hundred hours, parked near the Iranian Consulate and waited. He sat there for the entire day and on three occasions a police officer asked him why he was parked there, so he flashed his naval identity card each time which seemed to satisfy the officer. He called it a day at eighteen hundred hours after a long day and headed home. He arrived back in Norfolk shortly after midnight feeling rather fatigued and went directly to bed.

Barnaby called the following morning and mentioned that they had picked up a conversation between a person and Major Zoheri and confirmed that the call was made from the CIA's offices. He traced the call to a person in the Directorate of Support Division, however, there were ten people seconded to that division, so he was trying and identify the person that made the call.

Rafael started with the names of those working in the department, and having viewed the list of names, he narrowed his search to two people. The first person was Amal Dawisha, and the second person's name was George Matar.

Both were Arabic and had been recruited into the Directorate of Support Division years previously. They were employed as analysts specifically to monitor Hezbollah in Lebanon.

So why would they be disclosing Claire's name to an Iranian Military officer, is a mystery, thought Rafael.

He checked the two people's family ties and trolled through each person's personnel file in search of a clue. Nothing in the records gave him any indication, so he turned his attention to their ancestry, eventually discovering that Dawisha was a distant cousin to Ali Darwish, a known terrorist in the Jihad Council of Hezbollah based in Lebanon.

He and his friend, Joseph Diamond, a Mossad agent had eliminated him in a daring raid a few years previously. That mission nearly cost them their lives as they made their getaway in a hail of bullets. They had fast-roped down the façade of the building that Darwish lived in and killed him while he was eating his evening meal.

Baffled how this person found out that he was involved in the execution of Darwish, he called his friend at Mossad on a secure line.

'Hello Joe, hope you still remember me.' 'Long time no speak old friend.' 'How's life in sunny London old boy?'

'Hey you old bastard, how the hell are you, Rafael?'

'By the way, I'm back in Jerusalem, so thanks, and yes it's sunny here.' 'Got sick of London's shitty weather.'

'What a coincidence, I was going to call you later today because we have been tracking our friend Major Zoheri.' 'You may not know, that he is alive and kicking and has been seconded to a post at the Iranian Consulate in New York and he is determined to take revenge on both of us, starting with you, then he will turn his attention to me,' said Joseph.

'Clearly, we are both in danger, which by the way, includes Claire and your boys.' 'I believe that you are back at the CIA, so I was going to pay you a surprise visit and come and see you.' 'I will be in New York in two days, so, now that you know, let's catch up then.'

'We need to ensure that does not happen, my friend,' continued Joseph.

Rafael waited for Joseph to clear customs and caught sight of him as he meandered his way through the hoard of people in his direction.

'Shalom, old friend,' he said offering his hand in a greeting.

'Hell Chaver, you haven't changed a bit, my friend.' 'Really good to see you, old boy.'

An hour later, Rafael tossed some ice cubes into two tumblers, poured two three-finger tots of his favorite drop, Johnny Walker Blue Scotch Whisky, and handed one to Joseph.

'L'Chayim, my friend,' said Joseph.

'À votre santé.' 'To your health,' replied Rafael as they clinked glasses.

'We have been monitoring this bastard Zoheri ever since he nearly killed us, and we have discovered that someone in the CIA had sent him information about Claire.' 'The communication came from someone within the CIA, specifically from a person working in the Directorate of Support Division.' 'From what we have managed to find out, this person's name is Amal Darwisha and we believe that he is a distant cousin to Ali Darwish, the terrorist that we eliminated in Lebanon a few years ago,' said Joseph.

As Rafael sipped his scotch, he was astounded to hear how much Mossad knew about the CIA. These buggers have a finger in every pie, even in one of their allies. They monitor everyone and everything at the agency. Amazing, he thought.

'How the hell do you know that Joe?'

'We in Mossad know everything, my friend.'

'Yep, seems that way.'

'Spot on Joe, and yes, we have the same information, so we concur.' 'I think we should pay this person a visit because he has also exposed you as well, so we have a mutual interest in the matter.'

'By the way, have you spoken to Claire since she left, because she and the twins are in real danger?'

Rafael sat back on the sofa and wondered how on earth he knew that Claire had left him. Wonder if these guys know when I take a shit, he thought.

'I have scheduled a meeting with your boss tomorrow at zero ten hundred hours, and I'm sure that he will want you to be present,' said Joseph.

The next morning they met with Barnaby in his office.

'Good to see you again Joseph.' 'So boys, we have a situation here and we need to fix it ASAP,' said Barnaby.

Rafael, you have the dossier and personnel records for Amal Darwisha, so you know what to do and for what it's worth, do not get caught.'

He meant to take care of it in the usual way, without actually saying it. That would solve the problem for all parties.

Rafael and Joseph decided to follow Amal and noticed that he went to the Turkish American Club situated on Alan Street in the Borough of Manhattan every evening after work. From what they learned, he was part of a band and played a musical instrument called a Baglama, also known as a Saz, a type of Middle Eastern guitar.

They followed him at a distance and watched as he parked his car. He unloaded his instrument from the trunk of his car and made his way into the club oblivious that he was being watched.

Joseph jumped out of the SUV and scouted the area looking for any sign of CCTV cameras. Luckily none were visible in the darkened rear parking lot.

'Right, so this is where Mr. Darwisha hangs out,' said Rafael.

'I can't go in because he may recognize me, so let's wait until he leaves then do what we need to do Joseph.'

'I think it best that I park somewhere else and we both catch a bus back here and wait for our boy to exit the club, then we can take care of business,' said Rafael.

They exited the parking lot and headed out of town. Rafael dropped Joseph off a few stops before he eventually turned into a designated parking lot reserved for bus commuters a few miles further down the road. He did that to ensure that no one saw them together. An hour later, they got off at a bus stop close to the club and hung around the darkened parking lot. They found a couple of milk crates to sit on and waited patiently for Amal to make his way toward his car. The music had stopped, so Rafael glanced at his wristwatch, noting that it was just past twenty-two hundred hours, so he was most likely to make his way home soon.

An hour later, they saw Amal carrying his musical instrument and making his way toward his car, so both quickly donned plastic gloves.

'Right, time to take care of things Joe.' 'You need to distract him and I will do the rest.'

Joseph suddenly appeared behind him and asked if he had a light. Amal was taken completely by surprise and seemed frightened by the sudden appearance of this stranger. Rafael quietly made his way around the vehicle and was behind Amal a moment later. He extracted the Emerson's Specwar Custom Knife from its sheath and placed the blade of it on his throat.

'I believe you know me, Amal.' 'Not only do you know me, but you contacted Major Zoheri of the Revolutionary Guard Corps and disclosed my wife's name to him.' 'Oh yes, I forgot, meet my friend from Mossad,' said Rafael holding the blade tightly against his throat.

'Despite what you think, we in the CIA and Mossad have been monitoring you for some time, and you know that we killed a distant cousin of yours.' 'And yes, we viewed your cousin, Ali Darwish as a dangerous terrorist, so we killed him.' 'Now it seems that you want revenge for what we did, so you contacted Zoheri, who is now holed up at the Iranian Consulate here in New York.'

'How am I doing so far Amal?' Pressed Rafael.

Amal merely stared at him.

'Question is, you work for the firm, so why did you do that?' Said Rafael forcefully.

'You are employed in the Directorate of Support Division and your job is to support what we do, not hinder us, you piece of shit,' said Rafael aggressively.

'I merely wanted to flush Major Zoheri out,' said Amal trying to wiggle his way out of a tricky situation.

'Like hell, you were doing that,' whispered Rafael.

Joseph removed Amal's wallet making it look like a robbery gone wrong, stood back, and watched.

Rafael slid the knife across his throat and wiped the blood onto Amal's shirt.

'Like your work Rafael.' 'Bit messy though,' said Joseph.

'Right let's split up.' 'You make your way out of the parking and jump on the next bus and make sure you get off the bus, five stops from here and wait for me.'

'See you at the bus stop Joe,' said Rafael as he turned and made his way down the alley.

Joseph removed the credit cards and remaining cash from the wallet, then dropped them into a bin as he made his way toward the bus stop.

Two hours later, Rafael debussed and found Joseph seated in the bus shelter.

'Right follow me,' said Rafael as he headed toward the parked SUV.

'What took you so long Rafael?'

'Had to wait for the last bus my friend.'

Chapter 22

Norfolk Naval Base

Virginia USA

'Right gentlemen, you solved a problem for the CIA, so thank you.' 'You guys are still in grave danger, so you both need to be on guard because Zoheri is an extremely dangerous person,' said Barnaby.

'I met with Claire yesterday and updated her on the threat to herself, as well as the boys Rafael, and kept you out of the loop.' 'For what it's worth, she did say that she loves you deeply and is missing you terribly.' 'She said that she has wanted to call you many times, however, refrained from doing that, because she believes that you and the CIA are inextricably linked.'

'She may well be right,' said Barnaby.

'She knows that you are no longer at home because she has spoken to your neighbor Herr Torkel several times, and he said that he has no idea where you are.' 'In fact, she asked me if you were back at the firm, and I had to dance around that question.'

Barnaby knew that he could not ask an American CIA agent to kill a fellow American, because it was against the law, so using Rafael and Joseph solved the problem. After all, Rafael or Yonti Barr, which is his real family name, is French and Joseph Diamond is an Israeli.

'Zoheri used his influence with the Supreme Leader of Iran, and got himself seconded to a job at the Iranian Consulate in New York.' 'We all know that this was merely a ploy to get him into the USA, and to be near to where we are based, in the hope that he can track you and your family down Rafael,' said Barnaby'

'We have been monitoring Zoheri, and from what we have managed to find out so far, is that this bastard likes to frequent the "Pussy Cat Strip Club" every so often.' 'This is him staring at pussy at the club which was taken last evening,' said Barnaby handing a photograph to Rafael.

Rafael looked at the badly scarred image in the photograph staring back at him for several minutes.

'Pity this bastard survived the crash,' 'He put Joseph and me through a lot of pain.' 'Time to even the score,' said Rafael emphatically.

'Yes, it's time for you boys to get even, and negate the threat.' 'You need to do it with great care, and do it without being caught because that would be a massive embarrassment for the CIA, let alone the consequences of an argument with Iran as well as a messy trial,' continued Barnaby.

'It would be extremely difficult for him to get onto the base, and I have alerted Captain David De Santos, the Commander of the Naval Base of the situation.' 'He has discreetly placed two armed guards around Claire's house without her knowing, and hasdoubled the guards on the gate, as well as roving patrols driving around the area twenty-four seven, checking all cars and people walking anywhere near where Claire lives.'

'I believe that this bastard may try to follow her when she leaves the base to take the boys to pre-school, and when she picks them up late in the afternoon,' added Barnaby.

'That would be my guess as well boss,' said Rafael.

'From what we have seen, it appears that he has a companion that accompanies him everywhere.' 'Zoheri often catches a cab, however, he has also been seen driving a dark grey Toyota Camry on the odd occasion,' said Barnaby.

'A man who we believe is Zoheri's mate entered the US yesterday, through JFK, and we have identified him as Iraj Zarei.' 'He was the chief of security to the Iranian Major General Qassem Soleimani, the person that we killed in an airstrike months ago.' 'We identified him through facial recognition, and I can confirm that he too, is an extremely dangerous person,' added Barnaby.

Barnaby reached out to the chairman of the Joint Chiefs of Staff, General Randy McGuire, and asked him to confirm the identity of the man in the picture. The CIA knew that he was Iraj Zarei, however, Barnaby kept that information close to his chest. An hour later General McGuire called Barnaby, confirming that the person in the photograph was in fact that of Iraj Zarei.

'That's interesting Barnaby, because we have been hunting this person for months.' 'He was head of security for Major General Qassem Soleimani, the Iranian that you eliminated in an airstrike months ago.' 'As you know, he was not traveling in the same vehicle as Soleimani, when you guys in the CIA hit the vehicle with a laser-guided missile fired from your MQ9 Reaper Drone that killed his boss, so he must have had a premonition that something was going to happen.' 'We have been hunting him for ages because he is responsible for killing multiple US soldiers,' added the General.

'How did you manage to get this photograph of him Barnaby?'

'It was taken at JFK airport yesterday as he entered on a false Iranian diplomat passport.'

'Right, so you can grab this bastard and pass him over to us Barnaby.'

'Not really General, because he is here on a diplomatic passport, and unless we can definitively prove that it's false, we cannot touch him.' 'Remember that the passport gives him Diplomatic Immunity, which is safe passage and freedom of travel in the USA and total protection from local lawsuit and prosecution.' 'In other words, a get out of free jail card.' Having said that, leave it up to us, we will take care of things.'

Later that evening, Rafael parked his SUV in the car park with a view to the front entrance of the club and they waited. Zoheri was a no-show, so they decided to call it a night and head home.

'Right, this prick loves to watch strippers doing their thing, so we should keep an eye on the strip club Joe.' 'Amazing when they are away from the Mullah, they drink alcohol like us westerners, and chase pussy around like they were trying to catch a goat to slaughter for dinner,' added Rafael.

'We need to urgently find where Zoheri and his mate Zarei are.' 'These two are very dangerous people, Joe'

'Yes, I know, because we in Mossad are also wanting to find this prick.'

The next morning Barnaby called Rafael.

'I just want to touch base with you and Joseph.' 'As said, Zarei is an extremely dangerous person, so you guys will need to take great care when going after him.' 'The combination of Zoheri and Zarei is deadly, so take extreme care.'

'Thanks for the leg up boss.' 'For what it's worth Joe and I, are also a deadly combination, so be assured, we will be cautious,' said Rafael.

'The airstrike ordered by President Trent, left the two countries on the brink of war with the Iranian Government vowing a forceful revenge against the USA.' 'Zarei is hell-bent on revenge and may be planning something big,' added Barnaby.

'I know that I keep saying this, however, I need to say it again.' 'Zarei is extremely dangerous, so you guys will need to take great care when dealing with both of these killers, Rafael.'

'Claire will never forgive me if she finds out that you are back at the CIA, and happened to get yourself killed.' 'She loves you Rafael and wants you back, young man.' 'It's just a matter of time.'

The following morning, Rafael and Joseph drove back to New York and parked opposite the entrance to the basement car park of the Iranian Consulate situated on Third Avenue, trying to get a fix on Zoheri. The office is situated on the twenty-eighth floor, so they assumed that Zoheri would commute there by car and park in a designated spot in the basement. He would most likely reside elsewhere. Two hours later, it was evident that Zoheri was not going to visit the Consulate, so they left and drove back to Norfolk.

A long drive to and from New York, however, it needed to be done, thought Rafael.

Most office workers start work at zero nine hundred hours, however, this bastard is not a normal office worker. He comes and goes at various hours. They had no idea where he was living either, so they had to start at the beginning. Joseph called a friend of his at Mossad and asked for assistance in trying to identify Zoheri's address.

Rafael and Joseph's mobile phones lit up within a minute of each other. Barnaby called Rafael and Joseph's friend from Mossad called him, both notifying them of an address that Zoheri was living at.

'Right, got the address Joe,' said Rafael, as he turned to face Joseph.

'So have I,' said Joseph.

They compared addresses and concurred that both were the same.

'What a coincidence.' 'That's amazing.' 'Hope this is a good omen, my friend,' said Rafael.

The address was in Great Neck, a region on Long Island, consisting of nine villages, and a community consisting mainly of Jewish Persians, who have managed to recreate a corner of ancient Persia there. It is a mere thirty-five-minute drive from the center of Manhattan and an easy commute.

'Let's take a drive and see where this prick lives.' 'Amazing that he would want to live in a mainly Jewish community.' 'Iranians hate Jews more than they hate Imperialist Americans,' 'Maybe, he is using that to hide his real identity, Joe.'

'Remember that this prick lived here for four years, so he would know his way around town,' said Rafaael.

Thirty minutes later, Rafael's mobile phone lit up again with another incoming call from Barnaby.

'Hello Rafael, we have discovered that there is a third person in the picture.' 'A person that goes by the name of, Iraj Jahan.' 'He was Zarei's second in command and was also traveling in the same car that Zarei was traveling in when we hit Soleimani's car and killed him.' 'It seems that Zarei has brought reinforcements with him, so tread warily,' added Barnaby.

'That missile strike left the two countries on the brink of war, with the Iranian Government vowing a forceful revenge against the USA.' 'Clearly, the games have begun.'

'Thanks for the update boss,' said Rafael as he ended the call.

They drove slowly past the address, which was a modest home in Saddle Rock Estates.

'You know Joe, tomorrow is Sunday, and it is the annual Persian Parade day, which was founded in two-thousand and four, by a group of Iranian Americans wanting to keep the Persian culture and traditions of their homeland alive.' 'It takes place on Madison Avenue every year in midtown Manhattan,' said Rafael.

'Apparently, it features costume dancers, musicians, and marching units highlighting the cultural history of the Metro area's Persian-speaking communities from Iran.' 'Despite increasing tensions between the two nations, there are Iranian-American communities scattered across the country,' continued Rafael.

Nowruz, the Iranian Persian New Year, translates to a "new day" and starts the Spring Equinox. It is a joyous celebration of the renewal and rebirth that blossoms at the start of spring, when flowers awaken, and trees come to life with the Nowruz Festival, culminating in the Persian Parade in New York.

'If I was Zoheri, I would want to go to that.' 'Wouldn't you?' Said Rafael.

'Yes, I think you are right Rafa.' 'Away from home, you would want to see how your community is living in Imperialist America, so let's go and see if we can find out if our two friends will be there.'

The following day, they arrived early and split up. Rafael made his way toward Twenty Third Street and Joseph headed toward Twenty Sixth Street between Fifth and Madison Avenues. Both donned peak caps and dark sunglasses disguising their features. They walked amongst the crowd seeking to identify Zoheri.

The crowd swelled as more and more ex-Persians arrived. The road was blocked, and a band was belting out the popular song Behet Ghol Midam, by Mohsen Yegan, a true Persian classical musical piece. Rafael mingled amongst the crowd in search of the two Iranians, eventually deciding to loiter around the food stalls. He believed that these two would want to taste their own countries' cuisine.

That would be my calculated guess, thought Rafael.

He ran his hand down the back of his jacket, feeling the slight bulge of his beloved Glock fitted with a silencer. Hoping that the bulge was not that evident, he positioned himself with his back to the window of one of the shops. His eyes worked the surroundings seeking to find the two Iranians.

He called Joseph, 'Any luck my friend?'

'Nothing at the moment Rafa.' 'I hope these two pricks show up my friend, and have not decided to go to Claire's home today.'

'Yes let's hope that is not the case.'

An hour later, Rafael caught a glance of the two as they made their way toward a food stall specializing in a traditional Persian dish called Khoresht-e Ghormeh Sabzi. The dish is a famous stew normally served on official occasions, rich with five kinds of herbs, red kidney beans, and rice, with an unforgettable taste.

He called Joseph and told him that he had sighted the two. Ten minutes later Joseph made his way toward the Sabzi Food Stall and noticed Rafael standing against a shop window, so he slowly meandered his way toward him, pausing to get a fix on the two from Rafael, then continued down the road for a few yards. He stopped and scanned the terraced seating, noticing the two perched on the top row of seats, enjoying their meal.

Rafael glanced at his watch, noticing that it was already sixteen hundred hours.

Been here for most of the day, so I need to keep a close eye on them, he thought.

Can't afford to lose them now, so I need to work out how to take these two out without anyone noticing. Best to follow these pricks when they go and take a leak, or when they leave, thought Rafael.

The place was busy and noisy, so I best keep an eye on these two. His eyes worked the surroundings, eventually finding Joseph perched on a chair on top of one of the parked floats that were used in the parade. Lazy bastard thought Rafael.

He noticed that the two got up and started making their way down the stairs, so he called Joseph.

'Right, they are on the move, my friend.'

'Yep, I see them.' 'I will be right behind you, Rafa.'

Rafael pulled his peak cap down and stayed thirty feet behind them, mingling amongst the crowd, and watched as they appeared to be making their way toward the Portaloos positioned on the side of the road. They stopped along the way to speak to a few people.

Rafael watched as they made their way into the toilet, however, there were way too many people lingering around the place so, he could not follow them. He decided to wait for them to exit and continue following them. A few minutes later they made their way out of the toilet and headed toward the car park, so he called Joseph.

'Joe, it seems like they are headed toward the car parking garage at Two Twenty West Street, so I am going to hop into the car because we cannot afford to lose them.' 'I will call you back in a few minutes.'

'Yes I know because I am following them at a distance, and I agree.'

'It does seem like they are heading toward the car parking garage.' 'I will see where they are headed, so hurry up Rafael.'

Rafael inserted his parking ticket into the ticket machine and waited for the receipt to be printed and the gate to be opened. The ticket machine took ages to print his exit ticket and seemed to have jammed.

'For fucks sake, hurry up,' he shouted at the machine in frustration.

Eventually, an attendant appeared and started fixing the machine. Way too late now, thought Rafael.

At that point, Rafael knew that he had lost the two Iranians, so he called Joseph.

'You won't believe it, the fucking parking ticket machine is jammed, and I'm waiting for the attendant to fix it.'

'Well these two drove out of the parking garage a few minutes ago, and have disappeared around the coroner, so only the Good Lord knows where they are now.' 'I thought you would be here shortly, otherwise, I would have hailed a cab and followed them.'

'OK, I'll be there as soon as I get out of here.' 'Just wait for me.'

Ten minutes later, he rounded the corner and stopped to pick Joseph up.

'Murphy's law Joe.' 'When you need to do something important, something seems to get in the way.' 'I suspect that these two may well take a drive past the base, so let's head that way.'

They drove down the Five Sixty-Four highway heading towards the Norfolk Naval Base arriving four hours later and parked further down the highway with a view to the main gate. Two hours later they called it a day and headed home.

Rafael wondered what Jahan was doing in the USA. This bastard also wants revenge for what the CIA did to his boss Major General Soleimani, so he is likely wanting to make a huge statement, similar to what Bin Laden did to the World Trade Centres. He called Barnaby to try and get a fix on Jahan and the two Iranians.

'Hello boss, me again.' 'We lost these two Iranian bastards thanks to the parking ticket machine not working, so I am wondering whether you can try and find the grey Toyota Camry that they are using.'

'I'll get back to you Rafa.'

'I know it's late, however, let's take a drive to the Pussy Cat Strip Club and see if they are there Joe.'

They checked the surrounding parking lot and these two were nowhere to be found, so they headed home.

The next day Barnaby called.

'Hello Rafael, we found the Toyota Camry.' 'It's parked outside the Deep Sea Adventures Dive Shop, situated at Thirty-Five Hundred West Mercury Boulevard in Hampton.

'Thanks, boss,'

'Right Joe, let's head there and see if we can find these two.'

'The car's no longer here, said Rafael as he drove around the parking lot.

'Let's have a chat with the manager and see what these guys were doing here,' said Rafael.

They made their way into the shop and walked amongst the shelves pretending to be browsing. Eventually, a shop assistant approached them.

'Hello gentlemen, it's almost closing time, so can I be of assistance?'

'Yes, thank you,' said Rafael.

'A while ago, two gentlemen of Middle Eastern appearance came into the shop.' 'Just wondering if they bought anything?'

'Oh yes, they bought a complete set of diving gear, consisting of a wet suit, flippers, regulator, goggles, four twenty-seven pint twin diving tanks complete with manifold and bands.' 'They asked me to fill the tanks which I did.' 'Took me a while though.' 'They also bought a duel speed electric underwater scooter, with four extra batteries, capable of propelling a person at around four miles per hour.'

'They said that they intend doing some serious underwater traveling.' 'Whatever that meant.' 'The total cost was around twenty-eight thousand dollars and they paid in cash.' 'That's the biggest sale I have ever made,' said the assistant boastfully.

'Why are you asking?' inquired the assistant.

'It's to do with national security,' replied Rafael producing his naval identification card.

Continuing he asked, 'When did they leave?'

'About thirty minutes ago.' 'I noticed one of them jumped into a cab and the other followed in a light grey Toyota.'

'Thank you, you have been most helpful,' said Rafael.

They made their way back to the SUV.

'My gut tells me that Zarei is planning something big, that's why he bought the scuba gear Joe.' 'I think he may be planning to blow up one of the Aircraft Carriers berthed at Norfolk.' 'There are two Aircraft Carriers berthed at Norfolk currently.' 'The USS Gerald R. Ford and the USS Enterprise are both in port, so they could be likely targets.'

'Question is, how will they get anywhere near these two carriers?' 'The only way would be to use the electric underwater scooter I assume,' said Rafael.

'Surely, the navy has sensors installed in or near to where all their ships are berthed as well as divers in the water at all times?'

'If I were him, I would try to swim underwater using the underwater scooter that they bought and head straight for the carriers and plant some sort of explosive devices on the hull of the ships.' 'He would need to make several trips, hence the need to have the underwater scooter to speed things up, and would need assistance in doing that, so that is where his cadres, Zoheri and Jahan come into the picture.'

Wonder what part Jahan will play in all of this, thought Rafael.

'The shop assistant at the dive shop told us that they only bought four twin sets of scuba tanks, so that would mean that Zoheri and Jahan would be minding the explosives hidden somewhere on shore, and Zarei would need to make several trips underwater to place the explosive charges on the bottom of the carriers.'

'That's what I would do if I was one of them, Joe.' 'We need to think like these bastards.'

'Imagine the impact and mileage that this bastard would get out of it, if they were to succeed and were able to sink one or both Carriers in the US's back yard Joe.'

'Agree, however, it would take one hell of a lot of explosives to sink an Aircraft Carrier though.' 'We can never discount what these people are capable of,' Rafael.

'So, if what we are thinking is going to happen, where would these two hide the explosives and where would they start their mission from, Joe?'

Rafael used Google Maps and searched the areas surrounding the base.

He thought that the area of Little Theatre in Gentrified Hipster Land near the Children's Hospital of Kings Daughters would be an ideal place for them to launch their operation.

Chapter 23

Norfolk International Terminals

Norfolk Virginia USA

Rafael called Barnaby and asked him to conduct surveillance of the docking area in and around the two Aircraft Carriers.

'My gut tells me that these two bastards may be planning to attack the two Aircraft Carriers that are in port at the moment, boss.' 'The reason, I'm saying that, is that we discovered that they bought a complete set of scuba diving gear including four twin sets of scuba tanks and all the diving accessories needed for deep sea diving including a duel speed electric underwater scooter, with four extra batteries, capable of propelling a person at around four miles per hour.'

'One can only conclude that they are preparing to do something daring.' 'Something huge to make a statement, something similar to what Bin Laden did to the Twin Towers.' 'The Gerald R Ford and the Enterprise are the two US Aircraft Carriers in port right now, so one can only imagine the mileage they would get out of sinking one or both whilst they are in port, which is supposed to be a safe haven for US warships,' added Rafael

'Good thinking Rafael.' 'I will give Captain David De Santos, the Commander of the Naval Base a call and alert him to that possibility.' 'I will also increase our satellite surveillance of the area,' he said ending the call.

Barnaby called Captain De Santos and gave him a heads-up.

Captain De Santos immediately summoned the Chief Master-At-Arms and his assistant to his office and updated them on the threat. They quadrupled the detail on all the gates, increased security patrols along the fence line, as well as roving patrols within the base, with instructions to stop any suspicious person or any suspect activity on the base. He quadrupled the number of divers in the water with strict instructions to eliminate any person seen anywhere near any of the ships berthed in the harbor and advised the personnel monitoring the sensors to be on high alert.

He arranged to have the Air Force fly helicopter loops over the base at regular intervals, and put the base on a heightened security level, instructing patrols to stop and search vehicles, frisk anyone walking around the base, and check all security identification cards.

Claire was sitting on her porch watching the twins playing in the garden and noticed the increased security patrols driving around and a helicopter flying regularly overhead. She wondered what was happening, and decided to call her boss.

'Hello Jake, sorry to worry you on a Sunday, but have you noticed the increased security around the base?'

'Yes, I have.' 'I was stopped twice on my morning run, frisked, and instructed to produce my identification card.' 'Most unusual, so something is going down, because my second in command has just called me and informed me that the base has been put on high alert, so yes I concur, something is happening.' 'I will let you know as soon as I manage to find out Claire.' 'In the meantime, stay home,' he said ending the call.

Claire instructed the twins to come indoors and she locked the doors. Wonder what on earth is going on, she thought.

Need to check all the residential areas around the base, to make sure that these two do not launch their operation from there. Most people wouldn't even give them a second glance and would not realize the threat, thought Rafael.

He pointed the SUV in the direction of Edgewater, a residential area close to the naval base, and drove around the area in search of the grey Toyota Camry.

'No sign of them here Joe, so let's head to Larchmont and Lochaven and see what gives over there.'

They drove around the suburb, searching for areas where a scuba diver could slip into the water without being seen, however, to no avail, so he turned the vehicle around and headed toward Colonial Place.

Still no sign of the two Iranians, so they drove through the Midtown Tunnel toward Gentrifield Hipster Land eventually passing the Little Theatre of Norfolk.

'None of the places we have visited offer an ideal place to park and hide a car where it will not be seen.' 'Certainly not ideal for a scuba diver to enter the water either, then swim to where the two aircraft carriers are berthed, even with a propelled device, because it is way too far.' 'We need to keep looking Joe,' said Rafael.

'If these bastards are going to attempt to blow up one or both of these Aircraft Carriers and somehow manage to achieve that, can you imagine the consequences resulting from that?'

They made their way past Oro Azteca Mexican Restaurant on Hampton Boulevard, turned into Baker Street, and made their way toward the water's edge.

'No place to hide here either Joe, so let's keep moving,' said Rafael.

'We need to find where these two intend to launch their mission from ASAP,' continued Rafael.

They drove past the Children's Hospital of Kings Daughters. Way too many people milling around here for anyone to hide a car and attempt to carry out an operation from here as well concluded Rafael.

They headed down the North Military Highway, past the Wawa Restaurant toward the Norfolk International Terminals, a semi-automated container terminal situated on the fringe of the Norfolk Naval Base.

'Ah Ha, this could be an ideal place to hide their scuba gear and even possibly hide the car inside one of the containers Joe,' 'So let's visit the office and check out if anybody has hired a shipping container or two in the last few days,' said Rafael.

They made their way into the reception area and asked the receptionist if they could see the manager. A while later a lady approached them.

'Hello, my name is Genevieve Porter.' 'I am the operations manager.' 'How can I help you, gentlemen?'

'Hello Genevieve, my name is Rafael Dujon.' 'Thank you for seeing us, we were wondering if someone or some company may have hired, or booked a container in the last couple of days.' 'This is a matter of naval security,' said Rafael flashing his naval identification card.

'Follow me, gentlemen,' said Genevieve as she made her way to her office.

She fired up her laptop computer.

'Let's see.' 'Yes, in fact, a company registered in Pakistan shipped a container to us and asked us to house it in our loading bay area so that it could be unloaded.' 'It was unloaded yesterday and is currently lying in the loading bay, then it has been booked to sail back to Pakistan a week later after it has been loaded.' 'The company is called Pakistan International Forward Freighters, in Gwadar.' 'I hope that this will help you.'

'Thank you most sincerely Genevieve, you have been most helpful,' 'Could you point us to where it is located and kindly give us the container number?' said Rafael.

Later that evening, they had an emergency locksmith meet them at the terminal to unlock the container. He cut a spare key and as soon as he left, they opened the container. They noticed the scuba diving gear neatly stacked to one side and took note of the two wooden crates located near the door. Rafael looked at what appeared to be some type of inflatable air mattress and concluded that the Iranians most likely intended to use it to put the underwater explosive ordnance on and pull it along behind the scuba diver.

'Wonder what's in these crates, Joe' 'I bet it's filled with underwater explosive ordnance.' 'We best lock this container, find a place to hide, and wait for them, because I'm positive they will return soon,' said Rafael.

The local police department had been notified of the threat by Barnaby and were conducting random searches including roadblocks, so it was unlikely that these two would commute there by car. Rafael and Joe found an ideal hiding place between two containers with a view of the container, sat down on the concrete floor, and waited.

The evening dragged on, and eventually, the darkness faded, signaling the coming dawn.

'Been a long night Rafael. 'My backside is sore from sitting on this concrete,' 'I'm hungry my friend, so give me the car keys and I will get us some breakfast,' said Joseph.

Rafael watched as Joseph drove out of the complex and stood to stretch his body. These two are likely to launch their mission in darkness, so it's unlikely that they will do it during daylight. We best stay here for another night, thought Rafael.

Joseph returned with a bagel and salon for himself and a bacon and egg roll for Rafael.

'Hope the coffee tastes OK,' he said as they sat down on the concrete floor.

'Would be nice to have a table and chairs with some cushions Rafael.' 'My backside is hurting like hell,' said Joseph.

'Right Joe, you go and take a nap in the SUV and I will stay on post and keep an eye out for our friends, then when you eventually decide to get up, I'll take a nap.' 'We need to stay on point and keep an eye out for these two.'

The afternoon dragged on into the night, with a half-moon revealing itself through the cloudy sky. They sat patiently waiting for the two Iranians to show themselves.

'This is the part of the job I hate Joe.' 'Fucking boring my friend.'

'True.' 'So Rafael, let's be honest with each other shall we.'

'Your real name is Yonti Barr, and the name of Rafael Dujon is merely an alias that you use when you are at the CIA.' 'Your real identity remains a secret at the CIA.' 'Barnaby gives you a different under-cover name for each mission.' 'How am I doing so far my friend?'

'Really.' 'And how do you know that Joe?'

'We in Mossad know everything, old boy.' 'And yes, I have known for some time that Claire walked out on you with the twins, re-joined the Navy, and is living a stone's throw away from here on the base.'

'I also believe that she has regrets for what she did, and has wanted to call you many times, however, she believes that she cannot break the connection you have with the CIA, and fears that someday, someone will be the bearer of bad news.' 'She could not live with that fear any longer, Rafael.'

Somewhat astounded that his friend knew so much about him, Rafael merely stared at Joseph for several minutes before responding.

'Yes, it's time to be honest with you.' 'Director Heathcott insisted that I adopt the name of Rafael Dujon when I joined the CIA, to hide my true identity.' 'This is for your knowledge only.' 'He wanted to protect any future family I may have, and hide my identity from the American Authorities.' 'As you know, the CIA operates clandestinely in the shadows.'

'To be honest, I am sick and tired of trying to remember the various aliases I have to use on every mission and would love to be able to go back home and revert to my real family name,' 'That's the name my cows in the paddock know me by,' said Rafael smiling broadly.

'I need to go to the toilet my friend, so stay awake until I return old boy,' said Joseph as he stood and made his way toward the portable ablution block used by stevedores, crane operators, and truck drivers.

Rafael watched him disappear around the corner as he headed toward the toilet situated a short distance away from the main company office area. He rested his head against the container and wondered whether Barnaby had revealed his real name to Joseph, however, dismissed that, because he is a person who never reveals anything, other than on a need-to-know basis, so he concluded that Mossad was as highly competent, efficient and secretive as the CIA.

A short while later, he noticed the shadows of three cyclists making their way through a side gate in the dark, heading in the direction of the container in the loading bay. He slowly got to his feet avoiding any sudden movement that could alert them, and ran his hand over the back of his jacket, feeling for his beloved Glock. He extracted it from the back of his pants and watched as the three stopped at the container that they had identified.

He covered the ground between them quickly, and one of the cyclists noticed his shadow moving in their direction and shouted something in what appeared to be Arabic, then took off, leaving his compatriots standing next to the container. Rafael was convinced that they were the Iranians, however, knew that he could not take a shot at the person fleeing, because he may well be an innocent person reporting for his early morning shift. Lucky bastard, he thought.

Rafael was alongside both of them in an instant and as one stooped to unlock the container, he pointed his beloved Glock directly at him. He motioned for both to lie on the ground and glanced at the cyclist as he disappeared in the darkness.

What a pity, thought Rafael, then turned his attention to both lying at his feet and took half a step back, to ensure that they were not able to try and grab his legs and wrestle him to the ground.

Ten minutes later Joseph appeared out of the darkness.

'Well, well, what do we have here Rafael?'

'While you were away on a sabbatical Joe, I managed to capture these two intruders.' 'Unfortunately, their mate must have seen me and took off on his bike, so we have two of them.' 'As the saying goes, two is better than one or even none.'

Joe frisked them, removed his belt, and bound Zarei's feet. He asked Rafael for his belt and did the same to the other person.

'Well, we have confirmation that the key fits the lock.' 'This guy looks like Zarei, he said shining the light from his mobile phone on his face and this other guy looks like Jahan.' 'The guy that managed to get away, was most likely their mate Zoheri.' 'Not sure because he rode off into the darkness, before I could get a look at him.' 'Pity I could not collar him as well, because that bastard is the one intent on getting even with us,' said Rafael.

'So Mr. Zarei and Mr. Jahan, welcome to the Land of Liberty,' said Rafael, as he punched Zarei on the nose. Blood splattered all Zarei's clothing.

He grabbed him by the balls and squeezed as hard as he could. Zarei cried with pain, tears streaming down his cheeks.

'What the fuck are you and your cadres doing in America, you bastard?' Shouted Rafael.

'We know that you sneaked into America on a false passport and that you were Major General Soleimani's chief of security,' said Rafael staring at Zarei.

'You and Jahan were traveling in the car following your boss, survived the missile that hit his car and killed him.' 'We also know that you were planning to blow up one or both of the Aircraft Carriers in port and were about to launch your daring mission this evening, Mr. Zarei.'

He did not respond, merely glared at Rafael through teary eyes. Clearly, he did not understand English very well.

Jahan lay quietly on the concrete floor, so Rafael kicked him in the head. He lay there half unconscious.

'What do we do with these two pricks, Joe?' 'Let's take them to a remote site, kill the mother fuckers and be rid of them.'

'No, we at Mossad want these two alive.'

They locked the container and bundled Zarei and Jahan into the SUV, placing one on top of the other on the floor in front of the rear seats. Joe sat on top of them, then dialed someone on his mobile phone as they drove out of the container terminal.

'Shalom Chaver.' 'I have two in custody, so you had best meet me at the designated area.' 'Cool, we will be there in forty minutes.' 'Affirmative, we will meet you at the arranged place in forty minutes,' said Joe as he ended the call.

Joseph asked Rafael to drive to Cumberland Airport, an unused airstrip with an unpaved runway that had not been used since nineteen fifty-two and used Google Maps to navigate the way. The area alongside the runway was overgrown with grass and two derelict hangers had somehow stood the test of time.

As they turned into the airfield, the headlights shone momentarily on a helicopter parked next to one of the hangers.

'So what are you going to do with these two bastards Joe?'

'We are going to take them back to Israel and interrogate him, then we will kill them.' 'You, Barnaby, and the person that escaped, which was most likely Zoheri, are the only people who know that we have taken these two into custody, so they will simply disappear.' 'After we have had our bit of fun with them, they will wish that they never met us.'

'Like the way you guys work, Joe.'

'I'm going home Yonti Barr,' said Joe, using his family name. He took Rafael's hand in a farewell gesture.

The two hugged and slapped each other on the back.

'Two Mossad agents jumped out of the helicopter, cuffed Zarei and Jahan, bound their feet with rope, and used duct tape to cover their mouths. They dragged them toward the helicopter.

'See you some other time,' said Rafael as Joe turned and jumped into the helicopter.

Rafael waved as the chopper pilot revered the motor. Moments later they were airborne heading out to sea, possibly to a freighter sailing somewhere in international waters off the Norfolk coast.

As Rafael got into the SUV, he realized that Joseph had kept his belt.

Bloody thief, he thought as he headed home.

Best focus on hunting down this other prick before he tries to kill Claire and the twins thought Rafael.

He called Barnaby and updated him on what they had found.

The police and FBI were quickly on the scene and secured the container.

Pity, real pity, thought Rafael as he headed back to the naval base.

Have to find Zoheri ASAP, he reminded himself.

Chapter 24

Virginia Beach

Virginia USA

Barnaby summoned Rafael to a meeting in his office.

Gizelle tapped lightly on his door announcing his arrival.

'Hello Rafael,' said Barnaby, pointing him to a chair at the table.

'Job well done again young man.' 'I have just spoken to the director of Mossad, and he has asked me to pass on his sincere thanks.' 'The Israelis have been hunting Zarei and Jahan for years and intend dealing with them in the same way that they dealt with a number of their people in the past.'

'Nobody, except you, Joseph, and I, know that we have captured Jahan and Zarei.' 'Zoheri does not know that the Israelis have them in custody, so we need to take care of him for more reasons than one.' 'This is a secret that you need to take to the grave, Rafael.'

'Yes, boss, I understand.'

'The police opened the two crates, and just as you guessed, it was full of underwater explosive ordnance, so clearly they intended to attack the two Aircraft Carriers.' 'Captain De Santos asked me to pass on his sincere thanks.'

'Right, so we now need to find Zoheri Rafael, and take care of him before he tries to get even with you, and possibly kill Claire and the twins.'

'As mentioned a couple of days ago, Captain De Santos, the Commander of the Naval Base, has increased patrols around Claire's home without her even knowing, however, you and I believe that Zoheri will try to take them hostage when Claire drops the boys off, or picks them up from pre-school.' 'He may try something if ever she is off the base.' 'I do think it would be appropriate for you to meet with Claire and warn her about the threat, Rafael'

Rafael sat motionless staring at Barnaby for some time before answering.

'Boss, I don't want her to know that I'm here in Norfolk, so I think it best that you kindly meet with her and warn her.' 'It's best that I keep moving in the shadows as always, sir.'

The following day, Barnaby met with Claire over a cup of coffee at Bellisimo Café. The Café is the newest business situated next to the Q80 Waterfront Gym on the base. A ribbon-cutting ceremony was held the previous day, with Captain De Santos and other naval dignitaries in attendance.

'Hello, Claire.' 'Well this is rather nice,' said Barnaby looking over the place.

'Hello Director, yes the décor is outstanding.' 'Hope the coffee is as good as the décor.'

'You asked to see me urgently Director, so what's happening?'

'Has this something to do with the heightened level of security we have seen around the base?' 'I have seen several patrol cars driving up and down our street, at all hours of the day and night, so are we expecting some sort of an attack Director?'

'Not to my knowledge Claire.' 'It may well be that Captain De Santos is merely conducting a security exercise.'

'Sir, you have never been a good liar, so something is going down, isn't it?'

'Well yes, but nothing to do with the base itself.' 'It concerns you and the twins Claire.'

Claire sat back with a worried look on her face and listened intently to what Barnaby was saying. The look of concern on her face said it all.

'About three months ago an Iranian Major was flying in a helicopter searching for Yonti and Joseph Diamond in Iran.' 'Both had escaped capture from this Major.' 'The helicopter he was flying in was shot down by another operative of ours.' 'He survived the crash and sustained horrific facial scaring.' 'The information I have to hand is that he is hell-bent on revenge, which is where you and the boys come into the picture.'

'He entered the US via JFK International on the pretense of being an Iranian diplomat recently.' 'I believe that he is seeking to equal the score and may intend to harm you and the boys, Claire.' 'I believe that this is how he intends to get to Yonti.' 'You therefore need to be on guard twenty-four-seven, and be vigilant at all times.'

Tears welled up in Claire's eyes and she placed the palm of her hand over her mouth.

'Why me?'

'So what you are saying, is that Yonti shot him down, and he knows that, and he is now coming after me and the boys?'

'Tell me the truth, Director.' 'Was Yonti the one that shot him down?' Demanded Claire.

'No, he did not shoot him down.' 'One of our operatives did.' 'He and Joseph Diamond were in Iran and had been captured after they concluded the mission to avenge his parents' death, in the Air France Flight AF145 disaster that killed one hundred and twenty passengers and six crew.' 'For what it's worth, they eliminated the two people responsible for the downing of the Air France flight that killed Yonti's parents, and were intercepted at the Turkish border by this Iranian Major.'

'If you recall, he told you that he was going to hunt down those responsible for killing his parents and kill them, which he did.' 'Yonti and Joseph Diamond were detained as they were about to exit Iran at the Kapikoy Checkpoint border crossing post into Turkey by a Major in the Iranian army, that goes by the name of Zoheri.' 'He is the person that suffered horrific face scarring and the person that entered the US through JFK on a diplomat passport.' 'He is the one, intent on getting even.'

'Oh my God, I need to call Yonti and ask him to come and see us,' said Claire. 'He will never forgive me if something happens to the boys.'

'Do you know where he is right now Director?'

'I have no idea where he is right now Claire, however, I can assure you that the Navy is well aware of the threat and has increased their security level around the base and has doubled down on patrols around the base, so I believe that the threat won't come from within the base, rather externally,' said Barnaby.

He wriggled his way out of being honest because, in answer to her question, the truth was that he did not know exactly where Rafael was right now.

'I suggest that you stay on the base until we get a fix on him Claire,' added Barnaby.

'The boys have karate grading tomorrow which is Saturday and I simply have to be there.' 'I cannot miss that, because this is their grading to a yellow belt, which they have been training hard for, and have been looking forward to for a couple of months.''Yonti would be very proud of them if he knew,' she said.

She stood, bid Barnaby farewell, and left the café without drinking her coffee. She headed back to her office.

Should I call him, she thought?

I know that I have not answered his calls, but surely he will answer my call, she considered.

As soon as she got back to the office, she called him. No answer as anticipated.

'Damn it Yonti, answer the call,' she whispered and tried again.

She called their neighbor, Herr Torkel Kaufmann.

'Hello Torkel, its Claire.' 'Have you seen Yonti lately?'

'Nien Claire, he has not been here for months.'

'Thanks Torkel.'

Where the hell is he? She thought.

Right, I will need to be very careful when I take the boys to school and pick them up later each day. Luckily I can do my grocery shopping right here on the base, thought Claire.

She called Yonti several times when she got home, however, to no avail. He simply ignored the calls.

Yonti's mobile screen lit up several times with incoming calls from Claire and each time he simply let the call ring out.

Later that day, he drove past the address that Zoheri was supposed to be living at several times. Each time he noticed that the grey Toyota Camry was not parked in the driveway. Where did this bastard go? He wondered.

Maybe, he was holed up at the Iranian Consulate, so he drove to Twenty-Third Street in Washington and parked his car down the street. The one hundred and ninety-five-mile drive took him a little over four hours. He made his way toward the underground parking on foot and waited until the rolling security garage door had been activated by someone, then calmly walked down the ramp into the underground parking. He walked up and down the rows of cars on every level seeking the grey Toyota Camry. Not there, so he made his way back to his SUV and headed back to the base.

Been a long day. He felt a little fatigued from the long drive to Washington and back. This bastard has gone to ground, so I wonder where he is right now, he considered.

Back home, he poured himself a three-finger tot of his favorite drop, tossed some ice cubes into the tumbler, and sat on the couch. Need to think like him. If I were him, I would be holed up at a friend's place, somewhere out of sight for a few days. He has certainly been spooked by what had happened at the container terminal and would know that we are onto him, thought Rafael.

The next day he drove around the outer perimeter of the base in search of the grey Toyota Camry.

The screen on his mobile phone lit up with an incoming call from Barnaby.

'Hello Rafa, just to give you a heads up.'

'One of the surveillance cameras at the entrance to the Seattle Highway Ninety Nine Tunnel picked up the Grey Toyota Camry making its way toward Washington.'

'Seattle is in King County and is eleven miles from Washington.' 'We are searching the area for any known Iranian residents in the area.'

'We will monitor him and as soon as we find him, I will let you know where he is.'

'Thanks, boss, I need to get to him before he gets to Claire and the boys.' 'I drove to Washington and back yesterday so I will make my way back there right away.'

Four hours later Barnaby called him again.

'Where are you, Rafael?'

'I'm heading into the Washington DC city as we speak boss.'

'Well Zoheri has disappeared, and we have desperately been trying to find him.' 'Having said that, we have located the car,' said Barnaby.

'It's parked down the road in Forty-Ninth Street, between Webb University Centre and the Kate and John R. Broderick Dining Commons, however, he is not inside the vehicle.' 'He parked the car in a metered parking area and I think that he could have abandoned the vehicle.'

'He may have caught a bus to Norfolk because he parked near the bus station.' 'The bus ride to Norfolk takes four and three-quarter hours.' 'I'm not sure, just a hunch Rafael.' 'This means that he most likely caught the bus from Union Station Bus Terminal Slip Fourteen, located in front of the Diehn Center for Performing Arts.'

'The distance is one hundred and ninety-five miles, and the duration is almost five hours, so you best head back to Norfolk.' 'The bus left an hour and a half ago Rafael.'

'You must be kidding boss.' 'I just got here and now I must go back.'

'I'm afraid so Rafael.' 'And, to be truthful, I'm not even sure that he is on the bus.' 'A calculated guess.'

'OK, thanks boss, I'll turn around and make my way back.'

Four hours later Barnaby called him again.

'Hi Rafael, the bus arrived in Norfolk a while ago, and he is nowhere to be seen.' 'He did not get off the bus, so I am wondering whether he hid between the seats on the bus and has taken the return trip to Washington, intending to jump off along the way, then somehow make his way back to Norfolk.' 'I can only assume that he could have done that when the drivers changed and the new driver possibly did not check the coach for items left behind.'

'I'm an hour away boss.' 'He is a slippery person for sure.' 'He is trying to avoid being seen, so I am convinced that he will head back to Norfolk and that he intends to capture Claire and the boys and hold them to ransom to get to me.'

An hour later he called Barnaby on a secure line.

'Hi boss, I'm almost back, so any sign of Zoheri yet?'

'Nothing at the moment, however, we are following two people who got off the bus at different stops on its return journey to Washington.' 'Both were female, so clearly not him.' 'He has simply vanished into thin air Rafael.' 'It's now twenty-two hundred hours, so hard to track someone in darkness, albeit that we have the technology to do that.'

The following morning being a Saturday, Claire left the base on her way to the twin's Martial Arts Grading Class. Both boys were grading, and she simply could not miss it. She was on heightened alert as she drove out of the base, constantly checking her rear view mirror to ensure that they were not being followed. Nothing happened along the way, so she let out a sigh of relief when they eventually got back home.

Barnaby was tracking her all day and nothing happened, so he wondered where Zoheri was and when he was likely to make a move.

He called Rafael.

'We are missing something here Rafa.' 'This guy cannot simply disappear into thin air.' 'He is like Houdini and seems able to vanish at will.' 'I wonder whether he actually caught the bus or somehow managed to avoid detection and possibly caught the train to Norfolk.'

'We are reviewing all the footage at Norfolk Railway Station at present, which is the terminus of the Amtrak Northeast Region.' 'The all-stops train journey normally takes six and a half hours, so we are also checking CCTV footage at Washington DC Railway Station.' 'That train left around the time that we saw his Toyota parked near the station, so if he caught that train he would have arrived in Norfolk yesterday.'

The following day later Rafael met with Barnaby in his office at CIA's headquarters.

'We have been unable to locate him.' 'No sign of him at all.' 'He has not popped up on any of the ten CCTV cameras that our team has been viewing, so I'm buggered if I know where he is right now, or even how he has managed to avoid detection.' 'Clearly, he must have an accomplice,' said Barnaby.

Rafael believed that he would try to take Claire and the boy's hostage and use them to flush him out.

Zoheri would be aware of the heightened security measures, making it impossible for him to access the base, so his focus was to keep a watchful eye out for whenever Claire left the base. Her routine saw her leave the base each morning and late afternoon when she took the boys to pre-school, then picked them up in the afternoon. She also had to take the boys to karate training three times a week.

Wonder whether he would try to take them at karate training. That would be the most logical place to carry out his mission, concluded Rafael.

Rafael had not cut his hair or his beard for months and both had grown long, giving him the look of wild caveman.

Good camouflage. Doubt whether Claire or the boys would recognize me at first glance, thought Rafael.

He took note of the route that Claire drove each day when she left the base to take the kids to school and pick them up later in the day, as well as when she took the boys to karate three times a week. She was a creature of habit, and always drove along the same road at the same time. Very predictable, considered Rafael.

Easy for someone wanting to get a fix on her, thought Rafael.

His handler, known as "The Hulk," due to his huge physique at Camp Perry, the CIA's secret clandestine training facility, located in York County, Williamsburg, Virginia, fondly referred to as "The Farm" by those that underwent basic training there, had drummed into him, to always be aware of danger and never be predictable. He suffered through six grueling months of basic training hell under the guidance of "The Hulk," which stood him in good stead during his time as a CIA agent.

Claire was oblivious to the fact that she never changed her routine, despite him telling her to be careful over the years. Women just don't think, he considered.

She had chosen to register the twins at the Nakajima School of Martial Arts under the guidance of Sensei Diachi Nakajima, a fifth Dan Karate Instructor, based on a recommendation from a colleague at work. Albeit that the Dojo was eighteen miles from the naval base, she was happy to drive them to training three times a week, because she was very pleased with the way that the Sensei treated the boys. Strict discipline and respect were expected in the Dojo, which Claire felt was necessary in the absence of their father.

The route to the Dojo winds its way through Hampton, taking around 20 minutes. Claire normally pulled into MaccaBurger's for the weekly treat for the boys, the only time she allowed them to eat junk food, was after martial arts training.

The following Saturday morning, Claire drove the boys back from karate training. Rafael followed some distance behind ensuring that she did not suspect that she was being followed and watched as she turned into the car park in front of the store. He parked the SUV close to where she had parked and waited. Claire and the boys made their way into the complex and ordered their meals. His eyes worked the parking lot scanning every corner of it, however, he did not notice the person crouching and making his way around the rear of Claire's car.

A few minutes later, Claire and the twins made their way back to her car, when the man suddenly appeared in front of them. She froze, realizing that it could be the Major that Barnaby was talking about and instantly recognized him by the scarring on his face.

Rafael had to stop himself from jumping out of the SUV and confronting him because he realized that the man held a knife to Claire's throat. Be calm boy, he reminded himself. At a distance, the man appeared to have facial scarring, so he was convinced that it was Zoheri.

'Get into the car instructed the assailant,' and he jumped into the rear seat alongside the twins.

He placed a knife at Claire's throat. 'You don't know me, however, I know you and I am looking for your husband.'

'I have no idea where he is.' 'We have not seen him for almost a year.'

Rafael watched as Claire drove out of the parking lot and headed in the direction of Hampton. He followed at a distance and immediately called Barnaby, updating him on what had happened.

'No need to worry Rafael, I have been monitoring her all day and have her on screen right now.' 'She seems to be headed toward Hampton and I can see that you tailing them about two miles behind.'

'Please don't lose them, boss.' 'I need to sort this guy out once and for all.'

A few minutes later Barnaby notified Rafael that they had turned toward Hampton, so he assumed that Zoheri would try to find a remote location and make Claire stop there.

'Yes, I know Rafael, I'm following them on the satellite feed.' 'Stay on the line because it looks like they are headed toward the Long Island Rail Road.'

'Thanks, boss, I am about two miles behind them, so I don't think he would suspect that he is being followed.'

'Claire turned onto a dirt road leading to the Long Island Rail Road, so I think that this is where he is going to make her stop and wait for you,' said Barnaby.

'I asked Admiral Starwarski, the commander of Seal Team Six to mobilize his team and fly them to a location close by to support you.' 'They are already in the air and should be there within the next fifteen minutes.'

'Thanks, boss.'

Rafael used Google Maps to check the area and followed down the same road. His car was hardly visible in the dust churned up by Claire's car. He parked close to the turnoff, jumped out of the SUV, and ran in the same direction that Claire had driven. He followed the dust lingering in the air and ran as fast as he could along the dirt road. He stopped when he saw Claire's SUV parked alongside the railway line in the distance. As he made his way toward the tree line alongside the railway track, he heard the distinct whoop-whooping sound of helicopter blades, pulsating, oscillating, and slapping in the distance.

Reinforcement are on the way, he thought as he edged closer to where Claire had parked, somewhat out of breath.

He took great care to remain hidden in the undergrowth, edging forward, ensuring that he controlled his breathing, and watched as the two choppers circled overhead. Each chopper landed on either side of where Zoheri was holding Claire and the twins.

Zoheri was focused on the two choppers and did not notice Rafael making his way toward them in the thicket.

The choppers hovered close to the ground and the seals peeled out of the choppers, forming a V-shaped formation on either side of where Zoheri was holding Claire and the twin's captive.

Barnaby was patched into the communication between Admiral Starwarski, the Seal Team Six's commander, and their team leader, Cree Cosay on the ground. He was able to communicate directly with Cree on the ground. The entire team overheard Barnaby communicating with their leader and waited for further instructions.

Zoheri held the knife tightly at Claire's throat and pulled her toward a tree, positioning his back against it, and waited. He positioned the twins in front of Claire, as he tried to cover himself from one of the seals taking a shot at him.

The team leader's earphones crackled to life.

'Stand by for a call from CIA Director, Barnaby Heathcott.'

Moments later, he spoke directly to the team.

'Hi Cree, the people being held hostage are Claire Barr, and her twin sons. She happens to be the wife and her twin sons, who are family of the best agent I have ever had under my command.' 'You may remember him from two missions that you conducted with him years ago when he was involved with your team to rescue my family that had been taken hostage in Wood Village, as well as the time when you guys assisted him in neutralizing the threat from the Russian President Pushkin, when he tried to sail a container ship called Sea Thunder, laden with high explosives into Baltimore harbor,' said Barnaby.

'The person that has taken Claire and the twins hostage is an Iranian Revolutionary Guard Corps Major, namely Farukh Zoheri, and he is here to seek revenge for having sustained horrific facial injuries when the helicopter he was traveling in, was shot down by one of our operatives in Iran.' 'He was perusing Rafael and a Mossad agent who had escaped capture in Iran as they attempted to cross into Turkey some six months ago.'

'Don't look around now, because my agent is making his way through the bushes toward Claire.'

'Yes Director, I have him in my peripheral vision,' answered Cree.

'You know what to do, so please ensure their safety,' added Barnaby as he ended the feed.

'Bring her husband to me,' shouted Zoheri.

Rafael removed the Glock from the back of his pants as he closed the gap. A short while later, he was within shooting range of Zoheri. Neither Zoheri, Claire nor the twins had seen Rafael hidden behind a tree twenty feet alongside them.

The Seal Six Team Leader shouted something inaudible at Zoheri forcing him to look in the other direction which gave Rafael the time to reposition himself to take the shot. He noticed that Zoheri had moved the blade of the knife slightly to the side of Claire's throat as he looked in the Team Leader's direction, so Rafael took a deep breath aimed, and gently squeezed the trigger. The only sound audible was a faint popping noise. Claire was most surprised to see Zoheri fall to the ground and jumped away, noticing the blood stain against the tree.

At first, she thought that one of the Navy Seals had taken the shot and did not notice Rafael standing twenty feet from her.

As the Seals got to their feet, she pulled the twins closer to her body shielding them from seeing the dead man lying against the tree, and rushed toward the Seals to thank them.

'Don't thank me, madam,' 'You need to thank that man over there,' said Cree, the Team Leader pointing to Rafael standing next to a tree.

Claire turned to look at the man noticing the gun in his hand pointing toward the ground. She did not immediately recognize him due to his long hair and beard.

'Sweet Jesus in Heaven, is that you Yonti Barr?'

He merely stood motionless as the twins ran toward him and into his arms.

'Daddy, daddy,' they shouted.

Claire ran toward him and threw her arms around him in a warm embrace. Tears streamed down her cheeks as she hugged him tightly and kissed him passionately. She pushed his body away from her and stared at him for a minute.

He stood motionless for some time, arms at his side without embracing her because he had mixed feelings about what she had done and was not sure how to react. In that instant, he was unsure whether he wanted them to get back together because she had hurt him by what she had done. He gathered himself, and he realized that he still loved her and was happy to have her back in his life.

He came to terms with the reason she left him and understood that she did not want him to be involved with the CIA any longer, fearing that someday a person bearing bad news would knock on the door.

'I knew that you would be here Yonti.' 'I just knew it.' 'I just knew it.'

'Please forgive me for leaving Yonti.' 'I now know that you had to avenge your parents' death as well as all those that perished on the Air France Flight,' she said tears streaming down her cheeks.

Take me home my handsome man,' she said looking him in the eye, with her mascara smudged cheeks.

Rafael turned and saluted the members of Seal Team Six, gave them a wave, and turned to leave.

Later that evening, back at Claire's home on the base, Yonti poured Claire a glass of Chardonnay and poured himself his usual three-finger tot of his favorite drop, Johnny Walker Blue Scotch Whisky, and tossed some ice cubs into the tumbler.

'À Votre santé Mon Pétale,' he said to Claire sitting at his feet. They clinked glasses.

The twins changed into their karate outfits and proudly paraded in front of him.

'You should be proud of them Yonti,' said Claire.

'Yes, I am.' 'I was very proud when I saw Sensei Nakajima grade the boys to yellow belt.'

Claire looked at him in disbelief.

'You were there?' 'How did I not see you?'

'I have always been near you without you even realizing Claire.' 'I was never going to allow any harm to come to you and the boys.'

The doorbell rang and Claire answered the door.

'Oh my goodness, Barnaby.' 'What a pleasant surprise.'

Barnaby handed her a bottle of Dom Perignon Champagne, as he headed into the lounge.

'Well Claire, no need to resign.' 'I did that for you and Captain De Santos sends his best wishes. He asked me to pass on his sincere thanks to you for your service to the Navy, and wishes you both a happy life together.'

He turned to face Rafael.

'Well Yonti Barr, you can now finally get rid of all the aliases you have used over the years.' 'I have retired the name of Rafael Dujon, and I have also resigned you from the Navy, Captain Dujon.'

'This is a letter from Captain De Santos,' said Barnaby as he handed him the letter.

He handed Claire a picture of Yonti in his crisp white naval officer's uniform for her to keep. Claire was astounded to learn that Yonti was a captain in the Navy.

'How did that happen Barnaby?' Questioned Claire.

'That's a long story.' 'I'm sure that Yonti will tell you some day.'

Yonti merely shrugged and tilted his head.

'I have arranged for our Gulf Stream to fly you to Switzerland leaving in two days, so you best start packing,' he said as he rose to leave.

'Au Revoir Yonti Barr, and thank you for all you have done for the CIA, the USA, France, and the rest of the world,' said Barnaby taking his hand for one last time.

He turned to face Claire.

'You should be extremely proud of Yonti Barr.' 'You have no idea how he has saved the world from total annihilation nor what he has done time and time again.' 'He is one in a trillion.'

Chapter 25

Biglers Mill

Virginia USA

As the family made their way up the stairs and into the belly of the Gulf Stream, they were greeted by the Co-Pilot.

'Bonjour Monsieur Dujon' 'Bonjour Madam Dujon.' 'Good to see you again.' 'You know where everything is, sir, so make yourselves comfortable.'

'I thought that Barnaby had retired the name of Rafael Dujon?' Said Claire.

Yonti merely shrugged his shoulders.

'Oh wow, this is luxurious Yonti.' 'Talk about traveling in style.' 'Sounds like you are a regular on board.'

'You may say so.' 'Company perks, Claire.'

'And, you have never mentioned it,' said Claire, realizing how little she knew of what he did.

Yonti merely smiled. Thank the Good Lord, that it's the last time I will hear the name Rafael Dujon, he thought.

He made his way to his usual seat on the port-side, and Claire sat opposite him.

The twins were excited to be flying in a private jet and could hardly contain themselves.

Barnaby waved as the Gulf Stream turned onto the runway. He knew that it was most likely the last time that he would see Yonti Barr.

The pilot engaged full throttle and they were amongst the clouds minutes later.

Claire leaned forward in her seat and held his two hands.

'I am deeply sorry for writing that letter to you, Yonti Barr.'

'I am deeply sorry for leaving the way I did, Yonti Barr.'

'I have regretted doing that every day, Yonti Barr.'

'The biggest mistake of my life, Yonti Barr.'

'I have wanted to call you a hundred times, and apologize for having done that, Yonti Barr.'

'I could not bear the thought of someone knocking on the door one day, bearing bad news, Yonti Barr.'

'That's why I left, Yonti Barr.'

'I did not want to have to tell the boys that their father had been killed, Yonti Barr.'

'It would have killed me as well, Yonti Barr.'

'You and the CIA have been inextricably linked, Yonti Barr.'

'I understand that the pursuance of justice is what drives you, Yonti Barr.'

'I want to turn the page, and start again, Yonti Barr.'

'I am very proud of you, and everything you have done to make the world a better place, Yonti Barr.'

'Thank you for saving my life as well as the boys lives, Yonti Barr.'

'I love you, and have always loved you, Yonti Barr.'

She knelt at his feet, passionately kissed and hugged him, tears streaming down her cheeks.

Yonti merely smiled. He too had tears in his eyes.

Exhausted, he was sound asleep minutes later.

Claire stared at him for what seemed like an eternity. She realized how little she knew of what he had done to save the world in all the years she had known him.

About the Author

Sid De Beer was born in Johannesburg South Africa and immigrated to Australia in 1993. He has been married to his wife Nadine for 47 years and has 3 daughters, Odette, Shi-Anne and Kim and 7 grandchildren, Blake, Kegan, Shayna, Logan, Hunter, Ryder and Sienna. He is happily retired and lives in Cranbourne East, Victoria, Australia.

'I live every day like it's my last.'